Holy Terror

Also by Josephine Boyle

A Spectre in the Hall (Piatkus)
Summer Music (Love Stories)
Maiden's End (Piatkus)
Knock, Knock, Who's There? (Chivers)

Holy Terror

Josephine Boyle

PIATKUS

For Gladys Watson

First published in Great Britain in 1993 by
Judy Piatkus (Publishers) Ltd of
5 Windmill Street, London W1

**The moral right of the author
has been asserted**

*A catalogue record for this book is available
from the British Library*

ISBN 0 7499 0211 6

Phototypeset in 11/12pt Compugraphic Times by
Action Typesetting Limited, Gloucester
Printed and bound in Great Britain by
Mackays of Chatham PLC, Chatham, Kent

Chapter One

The angel smiled against the low ceiling. The garland of stars hung on the back of a chair, the Santas lay on the table. Deposed balls, bows and bells huddled together in a plastic bag, and all silver frosting and golden tinsel had been stripped away to reveal what happens to living things forced into an artificial environment.

Dead needles rattled on to the carpet as Emily removed the string of fairy lights. She pushed her hand gingerly under the lower boughs and stuck her forefinger into the damp earth. She'd been as kind to the poor tree as she possibly could, but the sooner it was back in its natural element the better.

She climbed up on to the kitchen stool and lifted the angel. It smiled in her hands, holding up its tiny china fingers, arching its feathered wings over the shoulders of the lurex robes which had been glued into an illusion of perpetual flight. Unmarked by its first Christmas, it was put into a box to wait the eleven months till its second. Time to put away the pretty accretions and save the living thing they had clung to.

Emily went out of the glass door into the garden, fetched the spade from the shed and looked around for a suitable place. Tussocky winter grass sloped uphill to the rough hedge. The buddleia near the kitchen door had clusters of new grey shoots all over it and the flowerbed beneath the living-room window still bore a few marigolds. There hadn't been any serious winters lately. Plants slowed down, found things weren't as bad as they'd expected and started shooting again almost immediately. It was resurrection without the uncomfortable death bit first.

1

She took the tree from the table by the front window and carried it up to the end of the garden, where she spent half an hour struggling to break up the compacted soil.

By the time she'd finished the winter sunset was painting the cottage's walls. The kitchen and the room above it thrust out on the left and gathered sparkling red light into their casements, as if there was a fire within. The previous owners had gone in for modernisation and conversion but not quite architectural vandalism, which meant it was just civilised enough for John to live in while still just romantic enough for Emily; it was their first compromise.

Its period was doubtful; people had been 'doing it up' regularly ever since it was built, but the rooftiles were mossy, the fireplace was venerably broad, the narrow stair looked Victorian, the front door had creditworthy claims to be at least late Georgian and the room above the kitchen had beams. The estate agent had gone on a lot about the beams, though their antiquity was debatable – they might well have been no older than the front door. It was, after all, a fairly humble abode, and only the fashion and energy of the last thirty years had lifted it into the des-res category.

Emily had previously tended a small, dank enclosure which was the excuse for calling her home a garden flat, but this was the real thing at last. The red brick wall on the kitchen side had climbers and shrubs all along it, and Christmas roses bloomed profusely at its foot. An ornamental tree leant over the top from next door and brushed a big shrub rose with its branches, and she looked forward to seeing in a few months whether it would break out in pink or white or deep red.

Her gaze moved above the six feet of worn red bricks and remained fixed until the high purr of the telephone sounded through the open glass door. She ran down the garden and dropped her muddy shoes on the scraper.

'Hello, John?'

'How are you, darling? Had a good day?'

'Yes, I really got stuck in. Then I suddenly realised that yesterday was Twelfth Night, and that if the decorations didn't come down quick we'd be landed with seven years' bad luck.'

'That's mirrors, isn't it?'

'Yes, course it is. I can't remember what happens to you if you leave a bit of mistletoe up on the seventh.'

'You get kissed to death,' said John.

'Oh, good. Where are you?'

'Still at the office, but apparently the Braintree branch is up the creek due to signal failure. Can you pick me up at Witham?'

'Yes,' she said, 'are you getting a train soon?'

'I intend to have a damn' good try. My briefcase and elbows are ready spiked.'

'O.K. See you at Witham. Love you.'

'Love you.'

There was plenty of time to go back to her studio, up among the beams above the kitchen. The room was about fourteen by twenty, with narrow bare boards which the last owners had probably put in, one or two lumps of worm-perforated wood sticking out of the plaster, a wooden wall-plate all round at a height of seven feet and bare rafters which Emily and John had revealed by stripping out the ceiling. The window at the gable end was tall and modern, to give plenty of light.

This was the moment when she made sure that the work of her hands was up to standard and that the day hadn't been wasted. She leant over the table, stroked the tawny velvet pomegranate and explored the spilling, golden seeds with her fingertips. Tomorrow she would stitch it into place on the frame, couch gold thread around its luscious form and scatter a few more seeds over the tablecloth behind which the saint sat and pointed morals with her scarred hands. When it was in place she would start on the goblet, at the moment just a piece of silver organza.

It was dark now. She peered through the window and could no longer see the tree against the hedge. She imagined its needles in the form of stitches and pictured its bark represented by brown folkweave. Ornaments would be fun to do — a chance to use up all those metallic cuttings.

She changed her jeans and sweater for a loose jacket and a long skirt, put the dinner in the oven, left the living-room light on and closed the front door. There was a stiff breeze

3

getting up and light rain started to patter on to the windscreen as she backed out into the road. Drops glittered in oncoming headlights and were swept across the glass in silver bars. Crystal beads and silver threads on black velvet. Something behind the head of a madonna, perhaps? No, Mothers' Unions liked things all bright and beautiful, not dark and mysterious. Just a picture, then, and call it Windscreen or Rainy Night.

Even with the extra miles, she beat the train. The car park was crammed with wives, many summoned to rescue husbands cut off from their own transport by the distance from Witham to Braintree. It was three trains before John came round the corner, ducking his head down into his upturned collar as the rain hit him. Some women peeped their horns or flashed their lights, a few even got out of their cars and waved. John didn't need that sort of help; there was only one custom-painted striped Volkswagen there. He slid in beside her, scenting the car with the smell of wet raincoat and filling the front seat with the happy reality of his existence.

'I'm sure it's bad for my image, travelling in a thing like this. You'll have to change it soon, it's on borrowed time.'

'When the next cheque comes in. We'll go via Braintree, so you can pick up yours.'

He got home before her, by virtue of a nearly new BMW. She parked her car and saw him within the window, lit by the flickering log fire. He had taken off his jacket and stood in striped shirt and blue tie, head bent to watch the television in the corner. We've been married three months and we're still happy. It's going to be all right.

She walked up the path, glanced to the right at the red brick wall which continued into the front garden, and stepped into the home made complete by his presence.

'Dinner smells good,' he said, eyes fixed on the box. His hair was dark and neatly cut, his build slim but not skinny. He gave the impression of being much taller than her, but there was really only two inches in it. Emily was a cheerful, vigorous girl of five foot eight with a rosy complexion and masses of curly brown hair, and looked,

4

with every justification, as if she'd been brought up on a farm.

'It's moussaka. Do you think they're really going to do it?' she added, standing beside him and watching solemn-faced big names marching in and out of important places.

'Yes, I'm rather afraid they are.'

'Well, he might still back off at the last minute, and anyway, there's nothing you or I can do to stop it,' she said comfortingly. 'Even if we write to our M.P. or go and parade with banners, it will either happen or not happen as if we'd never been born.'

'The Stock Market doesn't like it,' he said gloomily. 'It's going to affect everything in the world.'

'Even embroidery? I'd better hurry up, or I'll have a nine-foot wall-hanging left on my hands.' She put the avocado vinaigrette on the table. 'Come on John, turn it off.'

The previous people, or P.P.s, as they had taken to calling them, had gone in for the full fitted kitchen, but to John's surprise, Emily had ripped it out with her own hands, sold it to someone who was converting another cottage and dragged a dismantled dresser off a skip. John thought she was mad, but he also thought she was remarkably clever. He wasn't sure about the drying herbs which hit his head, or some of the interior decoration she brought with her, either, but what did you expect when you married someone arty?

One kitchen window looked down the garden, and at the sink by the side door you could look out at the brick wall. Emily ran hot water and looked up over the promising tangle of dormant climbers to where a dim light burned. John brought in more dishes.

'I saw her again today,' said Emily. 'She was prowling round the garden in a headscarf and Burberry.'

'Did she say hello?'

'She had her back to me.'

'Do you think she's alone there?'

'I don't know. I'll have to listen to the gossip around the shops.'

He went back into the living room and presently she heard the music for the nine o'clock news. There he goes again.

5

What's the point of worrying about it, it won't change anything. We're not alike at all — it's opposites attracting. I wonder if it really is going to work?

He was still watching when she'd finished the dishes, sitting in deep concentration on the edge of the settee and leaning forward with elbows on knees. He obviously wasn't going to talk so she went up to her studio, pulled out a gleaming length of blue damask and attacked it with her shears. When he came up later he looked tired and ruffled, as if he'd been pushing his hands through his hair.

'Nearly finished?' he asked.

'Yes, this is the border. There'll be gold braid twisted like this, and this fringe at the bottom. Then the lining and it's done.'

'Aren't you clever?' he said, examining the fine stitching which delineated the saint's features on her pale silk face. Twinkling red glass gems spangled the golden aureole round her head as if they were drops of blood. It had seemed appropriate for one so absorbed in suffering that the wounds of Christ broke out on her body like a rash.

'I can't juggle money, like you can.'

'What a name. We ought to adopt her as our patron saint,' he said, stroking the pomegranate. There was certainly something miraculously unpredictable about the event that brought John and Emily together. A sudden storm of rain in an otherwise blazing summer had caught him halfway between the wine bar and the office, and drawn him for a few minutes into the porch of St. Cyneberga's, Nunnery Court, just as Emily emerged from an interview with the vicar.

'I doubt if she'd be pleased to think she'd set up an occasion of sin,' said Emily, 'and as a matter of fact there are several Saint Cynebergas.'

'Was this one depressingly virtuous, then?'

'Used to go in for the mortification of the flesh.'

'Ah, kinky.'

'No, she was trying to achieve purity and get closer to God.'

'I can't see the logic of that,' said John impatiently. 'Presumably God made her the way she was, and if celibacy didn't come naturally He must have intended her to marry and have

6

kids. I distrust extreme ascetics, they're just voluptuaries in disguise. They're neurotics.'

'Well, neurotic or not, she worked miracles; look at those stigmata.'

'They're self-inflicted. Look, those wounds were in the palms of her hands, weren't they? Where all the holy pictures put them and where she'd imagined them when she was indulging in sado-masochistic meditation. But the real wounds of Christ weren't there at all. They've found out now that the nails would have gone through the wrists, and if it had been a genuine miracle that's where they'd have been on our Saint Cyneberga, and on all those other stigmatised hysterics.'

'The Danes killed her,' said Emily, putting in a last word for her. 'She sang all the way to the place where they hacked her to death.'

'I like her less and less,' said John.

'Well, as long as the vicar likes her that's all that matters. I'll have to bring it up to town in the car, so we'll be able to meet for lunch. Can I park in your basement?'

'I'll die of shame.'

He went down to switch on the ten o'clock news.

Emily stitched the silver goblet on to the damask table cloth and thought again about saints, martyrs and asceticism. Persecution and martyrdom involved the horror of helplessness, but with self-inflicted pain a dreadful, involuntary experience became self-indulgence. And if you hated the world and longed for death, then martyrdom could be seen as self-indulgence, too. Surely it was only a genuine sacrifice if you wanted more than anything else to go on living. She sighed.

She didn't understand it, but then it wasn't her job to understand it. She'd done her duty by St. Cyneberga's church by making something as beautiful as she could, and now it was up to the people who saw it. Like saints and religious teachers, the artist set forth his personal vision and the rest of mankind either swallowed it whole or sugared it into palatability. Or even perverted it so that 'no man ever yet hated his own flesh' became the deliberate scarring of that same flesh with hair and metal and leather.

7

Yuk, what a mental state to get into.

'You need a nice cup of tea, Emily,' she told herself in her mother's bracing, plummy tones. It now seemed inevitable that the wait for the kettle to boil should be employed in standing at the sink and staring upwards.

The house next door was quite close to its garden wall, and it was remarkably tall and remarkably deep, so that the cottage appeared to be cowering down like a small boy in the vicinity of the school bully.

At the front, Holly House and Holly Cottage sat side by side, ignoring each other and looking across the road to the church, the windmill and a small settlement of cottages which seemed as if they had quarrelled with the rest of Little Hocking and taken themselves off in a huff.

But at the side, the cottage kitchen window eyed its giant neighbour apprehensively and Holly House kept steady watch on the cottage, having a great many windows with which to do it.

Its front was a dignified, red-brick block, surmounted by a clock which stood always at eleven-fifteen and a turret in which the bell hadn't rung within living memory, not even in a high wind. The windows were high stone mullions, some glazed, some blocked up and painted black. It seemed likely that Holly House had first stared out at the standoffish church when the Tudors ruled and religion was a matter of life and death.

Built against its back was a timber-framed block with separate roof and high end gables. Its metal-framed windows followed no particular plan, and its plastered white wall was interrupted by patches of left-over pargetting and a carved head, stuck about halfway up in absolutely no relationship at all with the fenestration or any other feature of the architecture. Thus the seventeenth century had made its mark.

Next, a narrow brick slice, with Georgian sash windows through which could be seen a wooden stair, then after that the bricks slid down into a broad single-storey block with a high chimney and tall windows, probably Victorian.

Finally, at least a hundred feet back from the façade and hanging on like the dung cart after the Lord Mayor's Show, the twentiety century contributed a glass lean-to just visible

8

above the garden wall; from the sublime to the ridiculous in four hundred years.

Emily very much wanted to get a look inside.

Apart from the frustrations of commuting, about which he was reasonably philosophical, the only thing that John disliked about living in the middle of Essex was that he had to leave home before the post came. He had been known to ring up when he reached the office to find out what had arrived, and if anything important came by the second post Emily usually rang him. His anxiety amused her, being so different from her own approach to life, but she sometimes wondered if it was going to increase with age to the point when it would become a real problem. She supposed it was the job — although being a freelance embroideress was hardly a secure existence. The difference probably lay in the fact that she didn't expect to be secure, and he did.

Therefore, when the post fell through the probably-Georgian front door and hit the five-week-old carpet on Wednesday the sixteenth of January, she rang him with an inventory and found him well into a professional worry about how the market was going vis-à-vis the Middle East.

'But thanks anyway, darling, and have a good day. Stick a needle in St. Cyneberga for me — she'll love it.'

A blue envelope addressed in grimly determined black ink had been forwarded from her previous address. MISS EMILY DERBY it shouted at her, then, having got her attention, mumbled through Garden Flat, 16, Harborough Street, N.1 before the rest of the post code, under renewed vehemence, transmogrified into a row of exclamation marks. Emily had not lived in Harborough Street and occupied number seventy-six in the one where she had. One way and another, the missive had obviously caused the sorting office some problems, as the stamp had been franked more than once.

Mrs. Patrick Roberts, who did not even use her Christian name for her signature, had just returned from a visit to Tinthurst, near Maidstone, Kent, where she had noticed a certain pulpit fall and bible marker. She had been told by the vicar that these were the work of Miss Derby (though

9

she seemed to suspect that he was probably lying.) Should Miss Derby be able to confirm that this was so, she might like to submit designs for a piece of work for Mrs Roberts' own parish church. A quick response would be advisable, as other artists were being considered.

Emily could picture her, the driving secular power of her parish, the terror of the more timid W.I. members and the bane of the vicar's life. Probably not a good idea, that one. The next letter was from her agent.

'Dear Emily, I've had quite an interesting inquiry from Halfyard and Poole, in Basildon. They want a hanging for the entrance hall and seem to be open-minded about the design, apart from its having a local reference. I suggest you give them a ring and make an appointment to go and talk it over. They sound as if they're prepared to be generous, by the way. Love, Sophie.'

Well, there went Windscreen or Rainy Night for quite a long time. Hurray, that'll help with the car — hello, why have we got four gas bills?

This morning, the Royal Mail had delegated the postal deliveries of four houses into Emily's hands. Perhaps the postman was distracted by the Middle East as well.

She did a quick sort on the dining table, put her coat on and went out — letters were important and Emily was naturally considerate and habitually obliging, as long as she didn't feel she was being taken advantage of. Turning right out of their collapsing gate (which the energetic P.P.s hadn't quite got round to before their marriage started to fall apart) she walked through the laurel hedge of Peepers and posted Mr G.B. Mort's gas bill and Mrs Christine Mort's holiday brochures through the polished brass letterbox in the glossy black front door. On the other side, what sounded like a Rottweiler pounced and probably tore them asunder.

Through the white wicket gate of Mill View Cottage, she struggled up a path which was such a mess of mud and broken paving that she began to have sympathy for the negligent postman. The letterbox snapped up Miss Felicity McCarthy's gas bill, chewed her needlework catalogue and bit Emily's fingertips. Within, something small and snappy hurled itself at the door.

10

She took a quick look at her own home as she walked past it, trying to see it from the ankle-turning, finger-trapping angle, and was reassured to see that it seemed, on the whole, postman-friendly. It hadn't even got a dog.

The red brick wall continued along the front of Holly House, then round the bend in the road. Opposite the front door, a superb pair of wrought-iron gates were set beneath a matching overthrow. A lantern hung from it, but its glass was gone and the bulb was missing. Its function was now taken over by a fairly unlovely modern wall light shining on the right-hand corner of the house.

She opened the gate with some effort and stepped into the paved, enclosed courtyard, while the house looked disdainfully over her head towards the church, with its mind on higher things. The big brick porch which stuck out in the middle had a front door which was quite obviously not original and that appeared to be made of brown-painted hardboard, then Emily discovered that there was no letterbox, nor a handle, nor even a keyhole. The doorway was, in fact, boarded up.

She looked around for a clue as to what the postman usually did to compensate for this fairly basic lack of amenity. There was a wooden box beside the porch which might conceivably have done the job once, but it was half-full of rain water. There was no stone to put letters under, nor a polythene carrier bag hanging invitingly on a hook. The windows were all closed and the stone sills above her reach, as the ground floor stood high on the slope which continued down to the church and then rose again to the windmill. She looked round the passably swept courtyard and saw another gate by the light, on the opposite side from her cottage.

The opportunity to pry was irresistible. Armed with her watertight excuse, she pushed the gate open and passed through.

The first thing that struck her was that the garden was very well kept. A smooth stretch of lawn accompanied the house all the way to its back extremity and beyond, and rolled round the corner with the brick wall on to the lane. The herbaceous borders had obviously been cleared and tucked up for the winter by a professional hand, and

11

beyond the grass, the ground disappeared under a plantation of shrubs and trees whose leaves had been removed as soon as they fell and replaced by well-rotted compost of just the right crumbly consistency.

A path ran beside the side wall of the house and she followed it down, holding the post in her hand like a safe conduct and scanning the garden for signs of life, particularly canine. She passed the sixteenth and seventeenth centuries unchallenged, and then the path took a turn inwards to arrive at the narrow piece of eighteenth century, where a door of quite staggering style and beauty suddenly confronted her. It had the lot — fanlight, doorcase, canopy, brass doorknob and knocker, iron doorscraper and lantern.

The letterbox swallowed Mr. Curran's post in a single painless gulp, owing to the fact that the flap had lost its spring, and nothing attacked it but silence.

If she'd been sure there was no one in, she'd have walked on past the Victorian extension and had a quick look at the lower part of the garden before she retreated, but it was not yet eight in the morning and the burning light seemed to prove that the owners were at home. She returned through the empty courtyard, closing both side and front gates carefully in case they were watching from their bedroom window.

Up in her studio, her day's work began. She cut St. Cyneberga from the frame and laid her face down on the ready-padded table for pressing. When it was done to her satisfaction, with not a crease or blemish in the smooth fabrics and with all beads, embroideries and cords standing clear and proud of the surface, she brought the sewing machine over and prepared for the stitching on of the border.

Then more pressing, then the twisting and stitching of the ornamental braid, then the fringe, then, with a spotlight turned on to brighten the dull January afternoon, the hand sewing-in of the fine blue cotton lining. Now the final press of all, the sliding of a rod through the cloth loops at the top, a bit of dangerous footwork on the step ladder, and St. Cyneberga hung complete against the inner wall of the high, raftered room.

Emily sat for some fifteen minutes in the old easy chair

12

by the window, appraising her completed work. There was a place on the skirt beneath the rosary she hadn't been quite satisfied with – did it show as much as she'd feared? The folds of the wimple beneath the chin, did they look natural? Did the bleeding pomegranate and the silver chalice look as if you could pick them up?

Suddenly she was starving. The house was in darkness when she left the room; outside, a whole day had passed from sunrise to sunset and departed for ever, and the only bit of it she'd seen had been her few minutes' postal duty. She went down, made herself a pot of tea and a huge sardine and tomato sandwich, and took the tray upstairs. She sat down in the chair and looked again at the hanging. Yes, it was all right. She'd produced what she'd been aiming at.

This was always a good moment. She wanted to go and bring someone in, to say like child Emily, who had just finished painting a picture or embroidering a traycloth, 'Look what I've made, Mummy.' Well, John would be back in an hour or two and he'd oblige, once she'd fed him.

Out in the winter darkness millions of tired, bored people struggled home on overcrowded trains and buses and would struggle out again in the morning, with no emotion to carry to their work except resignation, and she was enjoying this fulfilling and rewarding moment and already saying, 'What shall I make next?'

I'm so lucky. I have the gift of creativity and the chance to use it, and I am very, very lucky.

She went down to wash up breakfast, cook dinner, and to smile up at the dim light suspended in darkness on the other side of the wall.

John helped her get the hanging down and on to the table for packing.

'When are you going to deliver it?' he asked.

'He says there'll be lunch-hour communion on Friday, and if I come after two-thirty he'll be at my disposal.'

Washing up was watched again by the light next door, and coffee was drunk silently before the T.V. news – all of them, one after the other. It didn't look good.

'What's the attraction of being a martyr at that age?' asked

13

John, watching the frenzied enthusiasm of the dark, moustached young men gesticulating at the Western cameras.

'It's the feel-good factor, they won't have thought it through. And they hate us. They'd cheer for anyone who'd tell the West to stuff its arrogance. He'll back down,' said Emily confidently, 'he must know he can't win.'

'I don't think what he knows has much to do with it – it's what he wants to know and what he wants to appear that matter to him,' said John, looking worried.

'Can't we turn it off now?' she suggested hopefully, 'I don't think we've actually talked to each other for days.'

Just before they fell asleep, he listened in to the news summary. It still didn't look good.

'It's started,' said John, putting the cup of tea on the bedside table.

'What?' said Emily, coming out of the fog and looking at his depressed face.

'They're bombing Baghdad.'

'Oh no!' She sat upright in bed.

He started dressing. 'Well, that's it then, all aboard for Armageddon. The market'll hit rock bottom.'

'How awful,' said Emily, feeling quite miserable. It wouldn't last long, despondency wasn't in her nature, but she felt sorry for everyone concerned right up to the moment John left the house.

The post was of no interest or importance, so she went straight upstairs to pack St. Cyneberga, singing to herself as she handled tissue and brown paper and wielded the parcel tape. Occasionally she remembered about the war and stopped and felt sad, but her natural good spirits kept reasserting themselves. She had made something new and was about to offer it to the world.

She rolled the completed package down to the end of the worktable and felt elation again at the sight of the bare, inviting surface. What should she begin now? Well, she'd ring up Halfyard and Poole for a start and get some idea of what they had in mind, then she could do some sketches.

It was quite sunny this morning. She went to see how the Christmas tree was, then looked up at the house next

14

door, block by block, window by window, studying high chimneys and off-centre gables, scrutinising brick and stone and plaster and brick again, as if she was trying to work out a puzzle.

This was really getting silly. Every time she came out she ended up staring at that place. Every time she stood at the sink her eyes went up to it. Every time she went out of her front door her head swivelled to the left and there she was examining an old brick wall and peeping above holly trees at weathered gables, lichened roofs and a stopped clock.

But it was such a fascinating house; the contrasts between the different ages, the bits and pieces windows, particularly those blocked, black-painted mullions in the front block. It was probably full of alterations from the centuries' perpetual modernise, chop-about and do-up. She hoped the glass lean-to wasn't typical of what her own time had done, it so often considered plastic and formica preferable to oak and marble.

It was her first free day for months and she decided to spend it doing a picture of Holly House.

Two hours later, when the ink and wash picture was nearly finished, she saw a face looking out from the wooden stair behind the eighteenth-century window, and it wasn't long afterwards that she heard a voice, with a high, flat timbre capable of turning the listener to stone. 'I say!'

She looked up and smiled. Emily had a beautiful smile. She'd often been told so, but still had no idea how immediately it warmed the heart of its recipient.

'Hello. How do you do?' She put her pad down and started to walk towards the brick wall. 'I'm Emily Wakelin.'

'No,' disagreed the voice, then elucidated its meaning by the rest of the sentence, 'do bring it with you.'

Emily returned to the easel, picked up the pad and her skirts and fought her way through the bare shrubs to the wall.

The long, sharp face with its aquiline nose was in its seventies, she guessed. The skin was wrinkled, but the eyebrows were pencilled in grey and the mouth was defined in a strong red. The dark brown eyes were not to be trifled with, and the hair beneath the head scarf was grey, but still a dark grey. Of

15

the rest of Mrs. Curran, only one hand could be seen, gripping the top of the wall. The nails were painted but chipped, the fingers were clean but scratched, and there were at least three unmistakably serious rings below the prominent knuckles.

'I hope you don't mind,' said Emily, passing it up.

The expected polite denial didn't materialise, which was disconcerting from someone who seemed unlikely to omit courtesies without intention. The picture was removed to the other side of the wall, and all Emily could see was the top of the bowed head. She wondered what she was standing on.

The head raised itself.

'You are a professional artist.'

'I went to art school, but my main work is embroidery. I was just doing that for my own pleasure.'

'I would like to buy it. Bring it round as soon as it's finished.'

The pad was handed back, and before Emily could speak again the head was gone. Her immediate thought was not, Hurray, a sale, but, I'm going to get a look inside that house.

The strength of her excitement came very near to being unpleasant.

Chapter Two

She went after lunch, as soon as she was sure the picture was properly dry. She put a mount on it and slipped it into a folder, then agonised over the ticklish matter of the bill. She knew what she would charge a stranger, but with a next-door neighbour an unsatisfactory commercial transaction could sour the relationship for years.

The high gate squealed under her hand and the slope of the ground dragged it closed as soon as she was through. Her footsteps echoing, she walked across the courtyard, through the side gate and into the garden. At the glorious Georgian door she wielded the knocker, and after three times, tentatively tried the folder against the letterbox, through which she could see a worn coconut mat. It was too small. Well, if they were out she could at least take a quick look at the back view.

She walked past the Victorian extension and into another courtyard, where the glass lean-to turned out to be every bit as awful as its roof had threatened. It was of the date when no concessions were made to any style of architecture but the shoebox school, and before the proper conservatory swept back into fashion with a swish of nostalgic skirts. It contained carpet, wicker furniture and shelves of sleeping geraniums agaisnt the house wall.

There were two square flowerbeds full of roses in the courtyard paving, all hard-pruned to the point of brutality.

'I did them last week,' said the high, chilly voice right behind her. 'It's been so mild that they were shooting already.'

Emily turned. 'I couldn't get any answer at the side door,' she said defensively.

'I'm working down in the kitchen garden,' said Mrs. Curran. 'If you don't get an answer, always look in the garden.'

Suddenly future intimacy seemed to be offered, indeed assumed, though in a tone so expressionless that it might have been enmity. This voice was going to take some getting used to, it was like a different language. How did you tell when she was annoyed, or even angry, if there was no variation in inflexion or tone?

'Do you do it all yourself?' she asked.

'No, we have a man. That is the picture.'

'Yes,' said Emily, offering it.

Mrs. Curran spread her earthy fingers before her to demonstrate their unfitness for the task of acceptance.

'Come in.'

She opened the door into the lean-to and they passed between the clutter of chairs and tables to a Victorian door. Beyond were lobbies, pantries and lots of things hanging on hooks which did not appear to have been disturbed within living memory; they had the numbed resignation of Dickensian wards in chancery. Finally, a near-ecclesiastical portal admitted them into a huge kitchen.

It was painted entirely white, though chips here and there betrayed the dark brown taste of the past. The dresser, cupboards and range still lined the walls, but they were punctuated in the gaps between by three fridges, two gas stoves of different ages, a central heating boiler, a twin-tub and a Miele automatic, which was humming through its whites programme. Even now, there was still room for more replacements to be introduced without the trouble of removing old equipment. You could tell which items were no longer in use by their silence and their rust. On the table stood a large collection of china ornaments, including some which ought to have been in the bank, and the newly washed table china stacked beside it was far too good for everyday use in any normal household. Mrs. Curran disappeared through yet another door and there was the sound of running water, while Emily examined the room with more concentration than would have been polite in the presence of its owner.

The ceiling was very high and there was a louvre in the centre, though the handle against the wall had been painted into immobility. One big window looked over the lawn to the shrubbery, while the other faced the red brick wall. Holly Cottage ducked down behind it, holding its breath.

Mrs. Curran came back in the process of removing her Burberry, but retained her headscarf as if it were a badge of rank. Beneath she wore a brown woollen sweater, a fleece-lined waistcoat, a tweed skirt, thick brown stockings and brogues.

'What beautiful china!' Emily couldn't help exclaiming.

'I'm just going to wash it. I don't let the woman touch it, of course. Now,' she said, advancing on the picture.

She studied it flat on the table, in her hands, at the window, propped against a pile of plates and finally against a colossal iron-stone jug on the mantelpiece.

'Yes,' she said. 'Yes, very nice. I should prefer a grey mount. You won't need to take it away.' There was no question mark at the end of the sentence.

'I'll cut one and bring it in.'

The woman sought and found her handbag, and the chequebook which came out of it was an immediate guarantee of respectable old money. She opened the envelope, scanned the bill and wrote the cheque without batting an eyelid, so that Emily was torn between regret that she hadn't charged more and apprehension that her lack of expression might be covering up outrage at the price. She thanked her and expressed the wish that she would enjoy the picture. Mrs. Curran said that she intended to, and seemed about to show her back to the lean-to. With her chance of seeing more of the house on the point of being snatched away, Emily said quickly 'That's a most beautiful door you have at the side. I'd like to draw that one day, if you wouldn't object.'

'Oh, would you,' said Mrs. (gosh, no, thought Emily, looking at the cheque, Lady) Curran. 'You particularly like architecture.' Again a statement rather than a question.

'Yes.'

'Oh. Well, come and have a look, then.'

Emily gave a silent whoop of glee in the secrecy of her soul and followed her ladyship out of yet another massive door into yet another lobby, where the breeze whistled gently through the loose flap in the fabulous door. From there she was presently conducted through a glass one so textbookishly Queen Anne that she was at a loss for words, and into the posh part of the house.

It was difficult to grasp the plan, as there were corners and crannies and sudden turns of direction. Impressive linenfold hid nothing more than a broom cupboard, while a low, demure door ushered you into a timbered dining room which was furnished like a stately home, except for a television and a chair piled with rugs and cushions. Another dark lobby opened into a stone-paved hall hung with paintings and armour, from which a carved door led to the blocked porch.

Heavens, what a house to burgle, thought Emily. It's full of treasures and I haven't even seen a burglar alarm.

At the foot of a broad staircase they entered the most astonishing room so far − a perfect, panelled drawing room of about 1750, brought bumpingly down to earth by a pair of twin beds with maple bedheads and an armchair with a very high back, once more overflowing with rugs and cushions.

'George,' said Lady Curran, 'this is Mrs. Wakelin from next door. She's done a frightfully good picture of the house and I bought it.'

The pile of rugs moved and held out its hand. It felt like a scraggy, uncooked chicken. Emily nearly shuddered at its clamminess, but managed to stop herself. This man was very ill, and had probably been so for a long time.

He put on his glasses, took the picture and studied it carefully, then smiled and handed it back to his wife.

'So you like our house,' he stated.

'I think it's wonderful. And you've so many beautiful things inside it.'

'I'm glad you think so,' he said, pleased. 'I like to share it and there aren't many chances nowadays.'

Unlike his wife, his voice was warm and well-modulated, although illness had made it weak and his enunciation slow. He had a lot of yellowish-white hair brushed straight back from his brow, and faded blue eyes in a face which had shrunk tightly on to its bones. The paisley scarf tucked into the neck of his woollen dressing gown was an indication of departed style.

'Could we find Mrs. Wakelin a cup of tea?'

'Yes,' said Lady Curran flatly, with no messing about. 'Indian or China, Mrs. Wakelin.'

'Oh, China, please,' said Emily rather nervously. She was used to being liked and found her hostess's lack of response unnerving. Lady Curran's face was giving nothing away as she left the room.

'Look round if you want to,' said Mr. Curran, noticing her eyes moving from side to side. 'I'm afraid the light's not very good in here. The holly trees have grown far too big, and our daily says the windows are too high to climb up and clean them. She suffers from vertigo. The switches are by the door. Turn them all on.'

The window, which retained its stone mullions within the later panelling, looked out on the courtyard, or rather over it. You could see the church and cottages in the dip on the other side of the road, and the mill perched on the high ground beyond. Beside the door was a large fireplace on the inner wall with a glass-doored cupboard built into the panelling the other side, within which the amount of Bow, Chelsea and Meissen had reached sobering proportions. There were many pictures, the large oils hanging from the rail by gilt chains, the small from minimally puncturing patent hooks in the centre of panels, and there were quite a lot of Holly House in various media and of several dates. Emily realised with gratification that her own work was probably going to join them.

The drawing-room furniture had mostly been stood against the wall to make room for the beds and there was a small dressing table beneath the window. Emily suddenly felt awkward about prowling around someone's bedroom and he seemed to read her thoughts.

'I know, it's a pity to spoil this beautiful room, but we decided to bow to the inevitable two or three years ago. I just couldn't manage the stairs any more, and I didn't want to spend the remainder of my life marooned on the

21

first floor. I stay here until the afternoon, then my wife usually helps me into the dining room for the rest of the day. I like to see the television, especially the news.'

'It's not worth seeing today.'

'No, it isn't,' he said seriously.

'You've been ill for some time, then, Mr. Curran?'

'A very long time,' he said, and didn't enlarge on the statement.

'How long have you lived here?'

'I was born here. It's been in the family for nearly two and a half centuries.'

'So your ancestors put in this room and the beautiful door round the side?'

'And the servants' stairs and the kitchen, though my great-grandfather did them all over again. They also chopped the rest of the house around. In fact some of the things for which my family has been responsible over the years are nothing short of vandalism,' he said with a wry smile. 'This house is a hotch-potch. It's really almost impossible to date all the separate parts and you can't be sure what's been hidden away.'

'It must have been an exciting place to be a child in,' said Emily, imagining endless games of hide and seek.

'Oh, yes. Rather too exciting if you were of a nervous disposition, but fortunately I was a boy of healthy insensitivity, as were my three brothers. My poor sister was not so blessed, I'm afraid; she always seemed glad to go back to school, and left home for London as soon as she could.'

'Does she come back now?'

'She's dead,' he said regretfully.

'What about your own children?'

'Ah, they're a tough breed. It's due to the dominance of my wife's genes, no doubt.' He laughed. 'My sons breeze in here like a breath of fresh air every few weeks and my grandchildren swarm over the house like an occupying army. Children are a great blessing, Mrs. Wakelin, or perhaps you already know that for yourself?'

'Not yet,' said Emily, 'I've only been married three months.'

'Really,' said Lady Curran, entering with a tray, 'that is

a remarkably quaint remark for a girl of your generation, Mrs. Wakelin. I don't suppose you take sugar and milk with China tea.'

'No, thank you.'

She nodded and passed the cup.

I've scored points, Emily realised with amusement.

'I expect you'd like to see upstairs now, wouldn't you?' said Mr. Curran as the teacups were stacked. Emily watched with some alarm as Crown Derby was rattled one piece upon another, little apparent care being exercised by Lady Curran's angular hands. The Woman couldn't possibly have been more of a threat to it.

'It's too dark now,' she said. Full stop. Outside, the twilight was well advanced, and the holly trees framed a dark blue landscape pierced by distant cottage lights.

'My wife is quite right,' said Mr. Curran, 'it is much easier to see by daylight. Would you like to call again?'

'Yes, I would,' said Emily with pleasure.

'And how is Holly Cottage?' he asked as he shook her hand. His still felt like a piece of bony carrion, but she was conscious now that there was a warm soul within.

'Very comfortable,' she said. 'We love it.'

'I'm so pleased. You are the sort of person it needs. I felt that the last couple were not really in tune with it. Au revoir, then.'

Lady Curran marched her straight past the Georgian door. 'It sticks,' she said.

Expelled from the lean-to, Emily walked round the corner and picked her way down the side of the long house. She was just getting concerned about tripping over when a brilliant light shone into her eyes from the level of the first floor. Security was not completely lacking, then. As she walked through the front court, the window to the right of the porch was blacked-out by the drawing of the curtains, and only the lumpy glass-and-wire light on the corner showed that the Currans were at home.

The next morning, the news was full of the first missile attack on Israel. They took their breakfasts on to the settee

23

and watched television in silence until it was time for John to leave.

'I'll see you for lunch, then,' he said, looking as stricken as if he were off to war himself.

She had to take the front seat out to get St. Cyneberga into the car, but after that the day was plain sailing. On the north-bound carriageway of the M11 a jack-knifed lorry had caused a six-mile tailback. She passed by feeling very lucky she wasn't on the other side and even more lucky, she reminded herself, that she wasn't in the Middle East. Emily's disposition was so naturally happy that she occasionally had to give herself reminders that other people's were not, often with very good reason, and endured five-minute penances of sadness on their behalf, although she knew it did absolutely nothing to increase the gaiety of any suffering individual or nation.

She entered the City via Aldgate, reached St. Cyneberga's by half-past twelve and was very relieved to see that the Vicar had kept his promise about parking. Nunnery Court was little more than a rat-run with yellow lines down both sides of its pre-Fire width, but the Wren building had a paved churchyard and a gate large enough to allow a vehicle to enter. It stood open, and she parked the car between the west end of the south aisle and a gentleman in a full-bottomed wig pointing to his C.V. on the plinth beneath his feet.

As she entered the wine bar and waved at John the man with him looked at her long, print skirt and said something. Every other young woman there was showing her knees.

'Hi,' said John, 'you look lovely. Martin here said "Tess of the d'Urbervilles", when he saw you.'

The conversation around them was predictable; the Gulf, and its effect on the finances of the City of London. Emily let John and Martin get on with it while she stared into space and experienced the butterflies of one going in for an exam.

The Vicar had the Vestry table ready covered with dust-sheets. Emily felt a few more butterflies as they unpacked, but knew as soon as the last couple of feet rolled off the wooden rod and revealed St. Cyneberga's pale, ascetic face, that she was home and dry. He was overjoyed.

24

Singing with sheer happiness, she drove out of the City of London before the worst of the rush hour and was home in plenty of time to put the dinner on.

They usually had a lie-in on Saturdays, with breakfast in bed, but today the radio was going non-stop about the Gulf War. The first planes had been lost and the first Iraqi prisoners taken. Everyone was pleading with Israel not to retaliate and peace demonstrations were going on all over the world. John wouldn't turn it off. His face was solemn and strained and he said very little. It must be awful to be such a worrier. She hugged him for a bit, feeling very sorry for him, then went into the studio in her dressing gown and started doing sketches for Halfyard and Poole.

From there, all she could see of the next-door house was the kitchen and lean-to, but as she glanced up she saw a crowd of people besieging its tatty rear and being greeted by Lady Curran. She could hear the chatter even with the window closed, and there were high, excited children's voices, though the wall hid them from sight.

Later, she unpacked more bygones from her single life and wondered how to fit them into her new circumstances, while John pottered round the garage with oil or paint or whichever petro-chemical-derived substance was necessary for the particular job he had set himself that weekend. After lunch she did some gardening and listened to the children rushing about next door.

'I'm going to have a swing!' announced a high voice.

'All right, Vicky, mind you don't fall. We ought to do something about this glass roof, it's leaking. It's so mild at the moment he could sit out here if it wasn't for that.'

'Dad, Granny says we can go up and see the clock, if you come with us.'

'In a minute, Charles, I want to look at this.'

'Well, I'll go ahead, then, I know the way.'

'You are *not* going on your own!'

'Oh, Mum!'

'What do you think about putting in a lift, Simon, it would mean he could have a proper bath once in a while.'

'Well, it's a bit late, now. He's got the downstairs shower

room, and the bedroom's organised. It'll only upset his routine again.'

'*I'm* not coming to see the clock. I'd rather go and have a swing.'

'You're scared!'

'I'm not! It's all dirty.'

'Granny! Granny! Victoria won't come up to see the clock! She's scared!'

'Don't be so silly, Tom, there's no reason why she should have to do anything she doesn't want to,' said Lady Curran's high, flat voice. Emily thought she must be rather a formidable grandmother.

'All right, kids, let's get it over.'

Emily rose from the weeding and straightened her back. Presently, small figures passed upwards before the servants' staircase window with the scurrying haste of animals set at liberty. She imagined them rushing from room to room and bumping into the old furniture, watched by their ancestors' painted eyes.

Lights started to go on in upper windows, and after a few minutes a tiny yellow square suddenly gleamed at the back of the clock turret. Emily pictured the excitement of those most fortunate children, exploring that most ideal grandparents' house, and wanted more than anything to be up there with them.

She was working near the brick wall when a woman's voice said, 'I don't know why they stay here.' She sounded cross and irritable and as if she rather wanted to go home.

'He'd die if he left,' said a man.

'I'd die if I had to stay,' said the woman.

'You won't have to, Simon and Deirdre will take over.'

'Poor them.'

'They like it. So do I. In fact we all love the place except you.'

'Can I look in the cellar, Granny?' piped a voice in the background.

'Yes,' said Lady Curran on a similar note. 'Watch out for the mice.'

'Why on earth doesn't she put down poison, or at least get a couple of cats?' muttered the woman's voice.

'Now then, Isabel, it's not long now.'

Oh, dear. From what Mr. Curran had said, Emily had pictured a big, cheerful, united family, but perhaps this was that occasional interloper into such circles, the daughter-in-law who has never fitted in.

She didn't see them go. Their car must have come in the back lane at the bottom of the garden, hence the entry via shoebox land, and they would have departed the same way. Was that side door never used? If it was her house, she'd get it oiled and planed so that it opened and shut as sweetly as a nut and she would enjoy going in and out of it every day of her life. But then, if it were her house, she'd open up the front porch and receive people in the stone-floored hall which had welcomed visitors for four hundred years.

Emily outlawed the news that evening, apart from a single bulletin, and they had dinner complete with candles, a blissful cuddle by firelight and then an early night. John was just going to turn his portable radio on when she took it out of his hands and lay on it, which shortly proved extremely uncomfortable.

She took the grey mount in on Monday morning. This time she looked round the garden before she started knocking anywhere. She found the kitchen garden, which was today under the boot of the Man, and then went into the back courtyard, where the Woman was hanging out washing. She was not much older than Emily, and quite pretty. She stared at her across the clothes line, with a peg in her mouth.

'Is Lady Curran in?'

The Woman shook her head, fixed a pair of pyjama trousers with the peg and said, 'She's gone up to Safeway's.'

'I'm from next door. Shall I take this in?'

'If you like,' said the Woman, still staring.

Emily had a closer look at the lobby on the way in. One might have thought the Currans' children were still in residence and even at school, from the burdens on the hooks. It seemed unlikely that the regulation raincoat and the brown canvas cricket bag were in present use by either Mr. or Lady Curran, or that they had ever sported a green, red and white striped scarf. A store room door stood ajar,

27

and within were shelves of homemade preserves and a floor
piled with assorted bats and balls and other sports paraphernalia. Really, she thought, I *am* being nosey.

In the kitchen, the washing machine was busy again and
the Crown Derby had been put away, but a few pieces of
Meissen still stood on a retired fridge. She peeped through
the door through which Lady Curran had previously gone to
wash her hands; it led to a big scullery with a shallow, lead-
lined sink, a copper in one corner and a rolled-up badminton
net in the other.

She went back into the kitchen, frowning. *Really*, she
thought, I am behaving *very badly*. I wouldn't dream of
doing this normally. Even as a stately home visitor she'd
never been of the breed that fingers curtains, peeps into
drawers or pushes open doors marked 'Private', but this
house was like an encyclopaedia full of arcane information
and she wanted to look up every single entry.

She was having a disgracefully hard struggle with herself
about the half-open drawer in the table when the Woman
came in with the empty washing basket. She put it on
the table, said 'Phew', sat down and lit up a cigarette.
She didn't look like a daily help, in fact she wasn't even
wearing an apron. She had a black mini skirt, black tights
and shoes, a large loose mauve sweater printed with a
design in gold and big gold earrings. Her face was com-
prehensively made-up and her hair tinted and well-cut. She
looked curiously at Emily's clothes, which today consisted
of a long black cotton dress, a brilliantly patterned cardigan which reached nearly to her knees and silver chains
and earrings.

'Will Lady Curran be long?'

'She might go in somewhere for coffee. She takes her
chance while I'm here, you see, 'cause she's tied in the
afternoons and evenings. He's not supposed to be left.'

'Well, I'd better leave this on the table, then.'

'I'm going to scrub it now – she likes it scrubbed once
a week. Put it out there,' she said, nodding and blowing
out another puff.

Emily didn't need persuading. She pulled open the door
and went into the high, narrow lobby, the door closing

behind her on its rising butts and shutting the silence in around her.

To her left stood the Georgian door, attended by a leather umbrella stand with a full muster of contents and a black iron doorstop in the shape of a rearing horse. To her right the lobby was terminated by two doors, while ahead was the glass door into the rest of the house. There was a long, low marquetry cupboard with a very good gilt mirror above it, and a brass lantern hung from the ceiling. The walls were papered in a gold and white pattern and covered with framed prints. She laid the mount on the cupboard between a monogrammed clothes brush and a lone piece of modern equipment – a telephone, answerphone and fax all in one white plastic casing. Lying in the tray was a sheet covered with figures which she absolutely refused to let herself look at. There were limits.

One of the doors on the right was slightly ajar. Three steps got her near enough to hook it a few more inches with her forefinger, and after that the final invasion was easy.

She found herself in the high, hollow slice of Georgian brick among the tangle of banisters which she had glimpsed through the window. The stair didn't go straight up, as a well-behaved one should, but split in two to twist in opposite directions and enter the main house by separate doors. It was none too clean, slightly rickety beneath the feet and rather depressing in atmosphere, owing to the grubbiness of the walls. Well, that was a surprise, after the beauty of the rest of the house, but then it was the servants' stair, and there weren't any proper servants to use it now.

She only just got back to the kitchen in time to avoid an embarrassing exposure of her curiosity. Lady Curran was advancing on the door from the other side, and the Man was in the act of putting a large box of shopping on the kitchen table.

'Hello!' Lady Curran exclaimed and stared, while Emily waited, quaking.

'I brought the mount, it's in the lobby.'

'Yes,' said Lady Curran. 'Well,' she continued at last, 'I suppose you want to see the rest of the house.'

29

The wide main staircase rose towards a leaded window, accompanied on its left by the ubiquitous landscapes and portraits and on the right by a very handsome handrail. The second half-flight turned back in the opposite direction and deposited them on a square landing carpeted in red and surrounded by doors of various periods. Her hostess ushered her briefly into a bedroom which seemed huddled beneath the weight of the centuries and a bathroom reminiscent of a vintage seaside boarding house.

They went up a step from the landing into a broad corridor with a pair of high glass doors at the end.

'I won't open them,' said Lady Curran, 'they're rusty.'

'No, of course,' said Emily, looking through grubby glass at the stone parapet on top of the porch. From this height, the overgrown hollies partly obscured the view across to the church, cottages and windmill, but it must once have been an enviably amenity.

On each side of the corridor was a huge, lofty bedroom, their grubby eighteenth-century panelling revealing the reason for the blocked side mullions. They had big fireplaces, bathrooms tucked into corner dressing rooms, surprisingly little furniture, apart from yet more prints and paintings, and a distinct chill about them.

The surprise, not to speak of let-down, was immense. They might have been in a different house, with very different owners, the contrast was so great. Everything was unheated, uncleaned and unmaintained, some of the window mullions were crumbling and there was an unmistakable smell of damp in the emptiest bedroom, which had presumably once contained the dressing table and the maple twin beds. Emily was disappointed and intrigued at the same time. She studied the pictures, which were mostly old prints, liked some, disliked others and did a swift double take and experienced strong distaste of another. Heavens, fancy living with that!

Lady Curran now barged through yet another door on the landing which joined the top of one branch of the servants' staircase. They descended to the parting of the ways, then climbed the other side to a door beyond which stairs continued in a much ruder form to the next floor.

30

More rooms, older and more neglected, with strange mixtures of furniture or no furniture at all, with historic features perfectly preserved or atrociously disfigured, with total period atmosphere or modernities of such unsuitability that they achieved the level of comedy.

The decay became more apparent and the dust more pervasive. Cupboards momentarily opened by her apparently bored guide provided glimpses of old toys, piles of mildewed magazines and rusty, disused water tanks. A strip of paper had fallen from the wall and disclosed the crumbling remains of hair plaster. Another partition was made of asbestos, its texture whiskery under green gloss paint.

Although the roofs now began to slope in, rooms were still tucked in odd corners and at odd levels, and there were snippets of stairs to accommodate them in unanticipated places.

'I expect you'd like to see where the clock is.'

'Oh, yes,' agreed Emily.

There was quite a lot going on in the roof, and somehow one didn't feel terribly comfortable about what it was. They stood at the top of a stairlet so rudimentary as to be beyond a joke and surveyed blackened rafters, moss-packed tiles, a boardwalk across chewed joists and the top of blocked mullions peeping above them. Emily looked with some dismay at the outward bound course before her. No wonder Victoria had opted out.

'It's up there,' said Lady Curran, pointing up and to the left where an opening seemed about as far as one could go without joining the pigeons cooing on the ridge-tiles. 'It's quite famous.'

Emily gathered up her skirts and started to pick her way, suspecting that she could probably lose those points again if she followed Victoria's example. She could hear wind sighing through gaps in the tiles, and saw the dust and rubbish between the joists stirring in its draught. At least, she supposed it was the wind; there could be a flourishing community of wild life up here. She reached the other side, climbed a final flight of wooden steps and entered the clock room.

It was very small, and mostly occupied by several cubic

31

feet of mechanism. She looked at the letters and date carved on its wooden frame and learned it was a very old clock indeed.

There was writing on the walls, in the usual fashion of humankind when it has achieved a climb. People inscribed their names on top of towers, within the dome of St Paul's and in books specially provided on Alpine peaks, and this climb was quite arduous enough to draw forth that primitive urge. It was like the impulse to throw coins into water, in that case a race memory of gods to be placated, in this perhaps a triumph over gods beaten.

Only she didn't honestly feel as if she'd beaten the *lares et penares* of Holly House. In that tiny room, with its foot square window looking down on the back roofs and the naked metal clock mechanism standing before her like a sprung steel trap, she felt more as if she was teasing a lion.

'Can you see the names,' Lady Curran called.

'Yes,' she said, making herself look. John Curran 1793. Stobart Smith 1824. Lucy Powell 1896. L/Cpl. W.F. Parkinson 1943 dot dot dot dash. Kilroy was here. You lucky people.

'Did you have soldiers here?' called Emily over her shoulder. There was a scuffling and thudding and Lady Curran's face came up the steps and poked in at the low door.

'Yes at first, then it was requisitioned for bombed-out families. George's parents had to move out for the duration, but luckily they had the cottage then.'

'Where was that?'

'Your cottage,' she said, sounding as if she meant 'Your cottage of course, stupid', although she almost certainly didn't. 'The family owned it until the sixties. We sold it then because it just wasn't worthwhile renting any more with the new laws.'

'Do you happen to know when it was built?'

'No,' said Lady Curran, sounding as if she couldn't care less. 'I expect it was for one of the outside staff – there was a lot more land round the house once.'

They returned across the tumbled wood of the roof space

32

and down the stairlet. They looked into more rooms of different sizes and apparently different ages. There was a 1940s kitchen. There was a practically untouched sixteenth-century room tucked under the roof on the other side of the clock turret, with its mullions still filled by leaded casements. Reached by a stair all its own was a quaint, panelled Georgian linen room which looked down upon Holly Cottage, and a room with a claw-footed bath had a wonderful view over the village behind the house, should one want to enjoy a view whilst nude and wet. By the time Lady Curran returned her through the servants' door on to the first floor landing. Emily was feeling completely confused and disorientated.

'It must be very difficult to keep it all in good repair,' she said, though she meant impossible.

'Oh, we don't bother now,' said Lady Curran, dismissing the problem. 'We might give the first floor some decoration this summer, in case the children come to stay, but for ourselves, as long as the ground floor is comfortable that's all that matters.'

'It must be rather sad for Mr. Curran to see it no longer as he knew it.'

'He doesn't see it,' said Lady Curran, adding a cold stare to her cold voice and making Emily wish she could sink through the floor. 'When he's gone Simon will give the whole place a spruce-up before he takes over.'

Emily thought with some seriousness of the enormous task facing poor Simon, not to speak of whether by the time poor Mr. Curran finally died, the upper floors might not already have collapsed on to the lower. She shuddered.

'You are cold,' said Lady Curran sharply, as if it showed weakness. 'We don't put the heating on up here unless it gets icy. Have another look round, if you like, then come downstairs and have coffee.'

She stalked towards the broad, red-carpeted stairs and started to descend, holding the carved handrail and turning out her knees in the way which betrayed rheumatism.

Emily went back up the step and took another look at the two great, deserted bedrooms. She felt sad at their abandoned and neglected air. They had been beautiful, and could be again if they were cared for. But caring took money, and for the first time she wondered if the Currans' apparent wealth was now merely residual.

She paused and looked again at the print. Really, how could people live with things like that? It was very old and very historic and probably quite valuable, but it had no place hanging on the wall of a family home.

She walked away from it, briskly at first, then more slowly, then with steps dragging as if the chilly air had suddenly thickened to resist the movement of her body and clog up her lungs. She struggled on towards the landing, while the cold hand gripped hers and tried to pull her back.

Chapter Three

She stepped down on to the landing and instantly it was gone. She was shaking all over and so shocked that she could hardly walk, let alone run. Her stomach was hollow with that terrible sensation of fright which draws all strength from the rest of the body and has almost the intensity of orgasm. For a few dreadful seconds she thought her legs were going to give way, so that she would be stranded on the empty first floor of Holly House, ready for the unseen thing to put its cold hands upon again. That is, if it consisted of anything else *but* hands.

She held on to the handrail all the way down, still trembling. Lady Curran was standing at the bottom looking up.

'Are you all right.'

Emily looked at those inquisitorial eyes and tried to work out whether the truth would go down well or not.

'I suddenly felt rather faint,' she said. 'Could I use your cloakroom, please?'

'Of course, there it is. The coffee's brewing. Or would you prefer warm milk.'

Ugh, no, thought Emily and then, Oh dear, she thinks I'm pregnant.

She went through the door indicated at the bottom of the stairs, and sat down between a hand basin full of ivory-handled shaving things and a shower cubicle with a chrome wall handle and a non-slip mat. She stared at the pile of toilet rolls tucked under an inconsequential beam in the corner. I've met a ghost, she told herself. Not seen one, but definitely experienced one. It was only a few seconds, but it was real enough. It was horrible. It was the most frightening thing which has ever happened to me and I never want to feel as frightened as that again. I've met a ghost. I can't stop shaking. Am I going to be sick? If I am, she'll be certain I'm pregnant. I've felt a ghost. I mustn't be sick, so I'll cry instead, I've got to get this shock out of me somehow. Where's my hanky? Oh God, I've been touched by a ghost ...

When she finally cleaned up her face and emerged, she heard the clinking of cups and the murmuring of voices in the bed-drawing room. She entered with some embarrassment and met Lady Curran's full frontal stare. She had at last taken off her head-scarf, and her hair was thick, coarse, chin-length and streaked with white like a badger's.

What did one do in a situation like this? One would never comment on a bad smell in a house, or say that one's tea was not as one liked it, and might even be valiantly reluctant to inform the hostess that her pet had behaved in an antisocial manner on your foot, but was it impolite to ask: 'Have you got a ghost?'

'Black or white, Mrs. Wakelin,' Lady Curran offered.

'White, please, one sugar.' She didn't usually, but sugar was good for shock. She had just about stopped shaking, now.

'I hope you didn't find the climb too exhausting, Mrs. Wakelin,' said Mr. Curran kindly. 'It's a bit of an expedition, isn't it?'

'Yes,' she agreed huskily, and cleared her throat. 'So many rooms,' she added as Lady Curran stared at her again.

'It depends on what you count as a room,' said Lady Curran, dumping the pot back onto the tray and flexing her wrist. 'If you count walk-in cupboards and bathrooms and such like, there must be about thirty.'

'Oh,' said Emily, drinking down the hot, sweet coffee. I've met a ghost. These people live in the same house as a ghost, and they must know about it. Shall I say something?

'They were all in use before the War, as my father had a full staff of servants,' said Mr. Curran, 'but we've needed fewer and fewer over the years. There's still a service lift running up from the front hall to the children's nursery next door to the clock.'

'All on their own?' Emily asked, clearing her throat again. Poor little kids.

They both looked at her sharply.

'Nanny was there,' said Lady Curran.

'You've very subdued today, Mrs. Wakelin,' said Mr. Curran attentively. 'I do hope we're not boring you.'

'No, of course not,' said Emily faintly and thought, How soon can I get out of here?

'John, something horrible happened to me today.' She started to tremble again.

He turned from the television and the war, put his arm round her and pushed her head on to his shoulder.

'What was it, darling?' he asked anxiously. 'Were you attacked?' John saw the world as very largely hostile, and one of his most persistent worries was that Emily might be attacked.

'No, nothing as bad as that. Well, in some ways it was almost worse, because I didn't know how to cope with it. I went in next door again and Lady Curran showed me over the rest of the house; it's never used now and in quite poor condition. At the end, when I was left alone for a moment − I felt a hand take hold of mine.'

He sat very still and she felt him tense. 'Are you sure?' he said at last, sounding very calm, but it was the calmness of a controlled performance rather than nature.

'Yes, absolutely sure. It only lasted for a few seconds while I was walking through the oldest part of the house, and the minute I stepped down into the later block it was gone. I was so frightened that I've been shaking on and off all day.'

'What did the Currans say about it?'

'I didn't tell them. It seemed rude to mention it, like remarking that their curtains were worn, or that you've just got a splinter off one of their chairs.'

'It's all pretty battered in there, is it?'

'Oh, not on the ground floor, that's beautiful, and anyway, that's not what I meant. It was just a matter of

37

manners, I didn't want to make a fuss. I mean, they must know about it, it's the ancestral family home, Mr. Curran was born there. All the Curran children started out living at the top of the house in a sixteenth-century room which now looks ready for either the Hammer film crew or the demolition ball. They must be an insensitive lot.'

'How awful,' said John, looking quite upset. 'You won't be going back, then?'

'I can't *not* go back. I've asked if I can draw the side door.'

'Well, I expect you'll be all right in the garden. And you needn't go upstairs again, need you? Ghosts usually stay in one particular room, I believe. I mean, if the Currans are quite happy living on the ground floor, there can't be anything unpleasant there.'

'I really do hope not,' said Emily fervently.

'It must have been a pretty weird experience. A friend of mine saw a ghost once. He was working late in an oldish office building off Poultry, and this man in black suddenly walked past the door of an inner room. He looked in but there was no one there. He said he felt as if he'd fallen into cold water.'

'That's how I felt,' said Emily in a small voice.

He hugged her harder. 'Do you want a drink?'

'Yes, please.'

Emily devoted the next few days to Halfyard and Poole. She rang up the managing director, with whom she had a few courteous if jargon-ridden words before she was passed on to the man who was in charge of P.R. and Community Projects. Mr Knipe's enthusiasm for this particular project appeared to know no bounds, and his anxiety to meet Emily in the flesh made him positively importunate. As for the date he preferred one sooner than yesterday, which in this case meant tomorrow.

Emily left for Basildon with a folder of rough drawings and colour schemes. It was really a complete waste of time until she had seen the *situ* in which the hanging was going, but would show willing and give a good impression.

Halfyard and Poole were forty years established in a

sprawling white factory on the outskirts of the town, with glass winking at the sky above the business end, and at the winter-bare front garden before the computer-pushing end. The reception area was enclosed in a glass tower and the place designated for their dive into the waters of artistic patronage was on the wall behind the cantilevered staircase, facing due east.

Mr. Knipe, who had greeted her with such cordiality and respect that it was quite painful to have to disappoint him, listened with dismay as she broke the bad news.

'I'm afraid you can't have any sort of textile there – it'll fade within months. It would just be a waste of my time and your money. What you need is a painting, perhaps a mural.'

'Oh, but the board are very keen on an embroidery. They saw the wall hanging you did at Hitchinson's, and wanted something similar.'

Hitchinson's at Harlow was a horticultural firm, and the immense, craning clump of appliqué sunflowers which Emily had installed up the stairwell had certainly been one of her happiest and most light-hearted inspirations.

'Well, I don't think flowers are quite appropriate here, are they? Not if you want something to do with your products. Perhaps you'd better find someone else.'

But there was to be no backing out; she was going to do a wall-hanging for Halfyard and Poole whether she liked it or not. However, Mr. Knipe was very anxious indeed that she should like it, and said so at regular intervals.

'What we could do, if you like, is to rethink the position of the project. The canteen is one possibility, there's a nice long wall at one end. Or, of course, the boardroom, though we did want a site which would be seen by a large number of people, as a public statement if you like. Or a sharing with our workforce of the significance, if you like, you have discovered in their products. No, wait a minute, the recreation hall. That gets used for all kinds of what could be called interfaces, if you like, between workers and management, and even, if you like, between the firm and the community at large, as it's frequently let out for functions. Yes, it would be like Halfyard's reaching out to Basildon as a whole, and inviting it to share in our creativity. If you like,' he finished limply, noticing a grinning group of girls in overalls and mob-caps at the door.

'It's welcome to share mine,' said one, 'if it likes.'

Emily received the impression that Mr. Knipe was considered a bit of a joke.

The space in the recreation hall Mr. Knipe had in mind was about twenty feet long and fifteen feet high, and the discussion of themes for the hanging was followed by a tour round the factory with a white-overalled gentleman introduced as Cormac Steele-Griggs. Struggling to hear through the hum of the machinery, Emily had thought for a moment that that was what the factory made. (We export more than three million cormic steel grigs every year, Miss Derby.) At the end of the tour she still wasn't sure what the end-products were, except that they were bits of recognisable items assembled by other factories.

'Take some samples with you, and see what they say to you,' encouraged Mr. Knipe.

What the bulging cloth bag said to her all the journey home was clank, clink, tinkle. It had better be an abstract.

Her days became filled with planning, from which she came round each evening to greet John, share news of their days and eat together. When she took him upstairs to show him her day's work, he was as impressed as usual.

'*How* big?' he exclaimed. 'And what on earth are those?'

'They did tell me. Something like flywheeels, sprockets and grunge-nurdlers. They're much in demand, apparently.'

'Even in a recession? If I were you, I'd get an advance quickly, Em, before they find they can't afford it after all. Business is not looking good anywhere.'

From then on the evenings tended to deteriorate as he watched news bulletin after bulletin, and filled in the gaps with L.B.C. and an earpiece.

'John,' said Emily pleadingly,' can't you wind down in the evenings? This isn't good for you.'

'The war doesn't stop at five, darling,' he said. 'I've got to keep up with developments if I'm going to cope tomorrow.'

'What about us?' she asked, 'that's just as important.'

'Of course it is,' he exclaimed. 'Look, Emily, this crisis isn't going to go on forever, and when it's all sorted out we'll have lots of time together.'

'I hope so,' she said doubtfully. 'Supposing something that would affect the City did happen in the middle of the night, could you really do anything about it before you went in next morning?'

'Well, no,' he admitted, 'but I'll be prepared, you see – one step ahead.'

'Not if you don't relax, you'll just be a wreck.'

'You're so good for me, Em, I'm very lucky. Shall I wash up tonight?'

'Let's do it together.'

The light watched them from next door.

'You're staring at that house again,' he said, polishing a wineglass with care.

'I'm trying to work out where the light is. It's above the dining room in the seventeenth-century bit, so it's either in a funny little bedroom or in the bathroom, which, by the way, is quite a come-down from oil paintings and Meissen, or then again it might be out on the landing at the top of the main stairs.'

'Which is the room where you met the ghost?' he asked, leaning forward over the sink and looking up into the darkness.

'You can't see it from here. I'll show you tomorrow.'

'Funny sort of next-door neighbour,' he said thoughtfully. 'I hope it doesn't pop in for a cup of sugar.'

As she lay in bed she wondered how far she was from the first floor of Holly House. She calculated its blind mullions were about twenty feet from the roof of the cottage, and its ancient floorboards just below their bedroom ceiling.

She set her face at the appropriate angle, as if to keep an eye on it while she slept.

When she saw John out to the car in the dark morning, he walked down to the front of Holly House and stood outside the gates, looking up. She followed him, a bit concerned that Lady Curran might be on the watch from the

41

drawing room. The curtains had been slightly drawn and the light was on inside.

'Which room?' he asked.

'I don't think we ought to stand and stare like this, it looks so rude,' she said in a low voice, eyeing the window. 'The right-hand one on the first floor. It's absolutely massive, so is the one on the left. The centre window, which is really a folding door on to the top of the porch, is in a corridor. At the other end, there's a step going down into the next range. That's where it stopped.'

'So it was in the corridor as well?'

'Yes, and in the whole first floor front for all I know.'

'Where do they sleep?'

'The room below,' said Emily, glancing at it again and hoping very much she wasn't being observed. 'Come on, John, this is rude of us, and I'm not very happy anyway. I keep thinking something's going to leap out of the front door.'

'I don't know how,' said John, looking at the blank shuttering. 'Don't go in there again, Em,' he said putting his arm round her as they went back to the car, 'I hate to think of you being upset. I want your life to be happy and peaceful.'

'Well, I am happy and peaceful most of the time,' she said, laughing. 'In fact, I'm probably happier than I've any right to be. I wish I could say the same for you.'

'Oh, I'm all right,' he said, smiling and looking devastatingly good-looking. 'I'm much better now I've got you, anyway. You be happy for both of us. Can you manage it, do you think?'

'Probably,' she said, a bit disturbed at having such a responsibility thrust upon her. She hadn't realised before that that was to be the arrangement. 'But don't overdraw your account. You've got to pay some happiness in, too.'

'Haven't I?' he said with sudden concern.

'Up to the last few weeks.'

'Well, I can't help it at the moment,' he said urgently, 'it's the war and the oil crisis. Once that's over it'll all be different. I really will make you happy then, you do believe that, don't you?'

'Yes, John, of course I do.'

No matter how absorbed in work artists may be, and at times they can make City workaholics look like dilettantes, they have to eat, and so after three days which produced a painting of the wall-hanging with which Emily was reasonably pleased, she walked into the village above and stocked up with enough food to enable her to disappear again. The walk was invigorating after days without exercise, and she enjoyed several chats on several subjects, from the advanced state of gardens to the alarming reports of the war.

Little Hocking had a good shopping centre on top of its gentle hill, and had retained its original population despite the influx of yuppiedom, resulting in upgraded shops but the minimum of descent into mere business. There were a few more estate agents and interior designers, but still plenty of really useful things like reasonably-priced butchers, practical ironmongers who knew that buckets didn't have to be made of plastic and a needlework shop where you could buy individual items instead of just kits. This shop, entitled *Art for Art's Sake*, also had a painting department in an erstwhile cartshed at the side and catered not only for retired amateurs, but for a fair number of professionals who came in from country retreats some miles away.

That morning, the shop contained two elderly gentlemen discussing brushes and a thin, anxious, elderly woman in a herringbone tweed coat trying to match a piece of tapestry wool.

'It's not right,' she told Mrs. Hubbard with distress, 'there's a definite difference on tone. It just won't do.'

'Well, it's a different dye-lot, Miss Barton, you should have made sure you had enough to start with.' Mrs. Hubbard was a big, happy, immediately appealing lady who made one feel that needlework was great fun and weren't we all lucky to be having such a lovely time? The hand-written signs in her window offered exciting opportunities for artistic fulfilment through wool, cotton, silk and lurex, and dangled valuable heirlooms before the eyes of her customers' posterity. Every project they embarked upon was blessed by her interest and

43

inquired after during its gestation until the triumphant lady brought the end result in for stretching, framing and admiration, just like Emily and her mother all over again.

She searched busily through a box of range-ends under the counter, shaking her curly blonde head. 'I very much doubt if you'll be able to get hold of the proper match. You could unpick bits of it and shade the new wool in, so the line doesn't show.'

'She'll notice,' said the woman, pushing her glasses up on to her nose with something very near to desperation. 'I'll have to unpick all the background I've done and start again with new wool.'

'What a nuisance,' sympathised Mrs. Hubbard. 'It's another kneeler, is it?'

Miss Barton nodded sadly and Mrs. Hubbard seemed to understand the full seriousness of the situation. 'Is there any way you can alter the design, so it looks as if it was intended to be that way?'

Emily stood waiting patiently to be served, and glanced down at the half worked canvas with the blue background against which the agitated needlewoman was holding a skein of wool, dabbing it here and there among the gold and white crosses as if she would find a bit it matched if she tried long enough. The top of the kneeler was nearly completed and the background also stretched all down one side.

'Excuse me,' Emily said tentatively, 'but if you unpick the top of the side bit until you've got enough to complete the top, then fill in the gap with a border and carry it all round, run a line of border colour down each corner, then finish the other sides with the new wool, it shouldn't show at all.'

There was silence while the two others worked all that out. Then: 'She's right!' exclaimed Mrs. Hubbard. 'It won't notice, Miss Barton, 'specially if you do it all in similar shades of blue. And if you use star stitch for the border it will be even better.'

'She was once very rude about my star stitch,' said Miss Barton stiffly, 'and she doesn't like us to change the design.'

'Well, why not? She does!' said Mrs. Hubbard robustly.

'She put her family crest on that cushion in the chancel, and nobody remembers that being passed by the committee.'

Emily recognised this sort of conversation; it was the very essence of parish politics. Miss Barton turned to her with gratitude.

'How very clever of you! We should get you to join us. We're in the middle of furnishing a chapel, and there's so much to be done. We're having the big pieces professionally made, but the canvas work is never-ending.'

'Well,' said Mrs. Hubbard in a low voice as the woman vanished, 'I hope she gets away with it. Mrs. Witherley-Bashe runs that circle as if they were sewing mailbags. Believe me, it is not a happy ship. I think that's a mixed metaphor, isn't it? Right, dear, sorry to keep you waiting. You got your saint lady finished yet?'

'Finished and delivered. I'm just starting on a huge abstract for a factory. I think I may have been mad to take it on, but it's quite a challenge.'

'That's good,' said Mrs. Hubbard. She nodded her head in the direction of the departed. 'I pity the professional who gets that job – she'll be criticised and frustrated from start to finish. Danger money, that's what she'll need.'

Her fingers sped over the electronic till keys as she totted up Emily's purchases. The pixie which Emily felt sure made the thing work peeped away merrily inside and at last thrust out the long white receipt.

'You'll want an itemised one as well, won't you?' said Mrs. Hubbard, giving her her change. 'My word, it's something when you earn so much for your needlework that you actually have to pay tax on it. It must be lovely to be so successful.'

Emily didn't say that the sort of income needed to reach the personal tax threshold was hardly a fortune, and that handwork of any kind was paid hour for hour at less than a sweated labourer. But there was nothing she would rather be doing, and the figures Sophie was able to negotiate for her were creeping up all the time.

She was just about to leave when Lady Curran walked in, Burberried and head-scarfed. It gave Emily a bit of a start, as if she might have brought the lodger with her.

45

'Good morning.' The stare was as expressionless as usual, and the voice the usual highpitched stream of consciousness, as if she was talking to herself. 'I'm just picking up your picture. It is ready, Mrs. Hubbard.' No question mark.

'It is. Did you say it was a present for this lady?'

'No. Mrs. Wakelin is the artist.'

'Really? Well, I never knew you painted as well.'

'It is signed,' Lady Curran pointed out, turning the neatly packed painting over on the counter and ripping off the brown paper.

'In my maiden name,' Emily pointed out gently.

'Yes, and I didn't even know your married one, did I?' smiled Mrs. Hubbard with a hint of 'so there' in her voice. She might come from a local family, but she certainly wasn't a forelock tugger. 'That's a lovely picture, Mrs. Wakelin, and from such an unusual angle. I've only ever seen Holly House from the front. No, just a minute, I went to a fête in the garden when I was little, but I can't remember much about it.'

'Yes, that was before my husband became ill. We used to open the garden a lot then. There.' Lady Curran held up the picture.

She'd done it proud; a gilt frame of a costliness which made it more than worthy of the drawing room.

'When are you going to come and do the side door,' asked Lady Curran, handing the picture to Mrs. Hubbard to wrap up all over again.

'Well, I'm afraid I've just started a very big project, so I mayn't have time for a bit.'

'But this only took you a couple of hours, I watched you. I would like one of the house from the other side, so that we have the pair. What project.' Again no question mark.

'A wall-hanging for a factory.'

'Oh, yes, you're a needlewoman, aren't you. Won't it get frightfully dirty.'

'Probably, but I always try to use dry-cleanable fabrics and it won't be in the manufacturing part.'

'She's just done a saint for a church in London,' said Mrs. Hubbard with some pride.

'Really,' said Lady Curran, very nearly looking interested.

'They want some things for the chapel in the church, you must have a word with the vicar. It would be nice to have a local artist, and very convenient all round with you living so near. He'd be able to pop in and see how things were coming on, and so would all the committee. Now it's a nice day, Mrs. Wakelin, I think you should come round and do that picture this afternoon. I know you said it was the door you were interested in, but I should like you to enlarge the view to take in the whole house.'

'I'm afraid I can't come today,' said Emily politely but firmly, 'I have to go out.'

'Tomorrow, then. After lunch. Then perhaps you would join us for afternoon tea. Goodbye.' Exit.

The shop suddenly seemed very peaceful.

'Will you go?' asked Mrs. Hubbard casually, peeling a piece of sticky tape off her hand-knitted floral cardigan.

'If it doesn't rain,' said Emily, rather hoping it would.

'Poor Mr Curran, I used to like him,' said Mrs. Hubbard sadly. 'Fancy you knowing them.'

'I live next door.'

'Do you? Oh, Holly Cottage! Well, well, are you quite comfortable there?'

'Yes.'

'Oh, that's good. These things always work themselves out eventually, and it was probably just the fault of that last couple — they weren't right for it, really. Yes, Mr. Kermode, you've decided on that one, have you?'

Emily walked into the butcher's and ran her eyes absently over the lamb cutlets. Why shouldn't they be comfortable in the cottage? What was wrong with the P.P.s? And did she have to do that picture?

47

Chapter Four

Mr. Knipe liked the design, but seemed disappointed that it wasn't more figurative.

'When you said it would depict the progress of our products from raw steel through to assembled machinery, I thought perhaps you would have various members of our staff standing by a conveyor belt – a stylised conveyor belt, if you like, I realise that you must have some artistic licence. Still, the red glow in the top righthand corner and the flowing silver stream turning into the various parts, and then just the suggestion, if you like, of consumer durables in the bottom left-hand corner – yes, a most original vision, and of course it's all entirely in your hands, Miss Derby. The board will be most interested. If you like, I'll let you know the decision in a few days.'

She was a bit cross when she got home. She often had this problem when she'd been told the design was entirely up to her and that the customer wouldn't dream of interfering.

She started getting the dinner together, glancing up at the light in the mysterious centre of Holly House. It was the landing light, she was sure, hanging over that big red-carpeted square at the top of the stairs. She stopped and stared yet again. Just how did the plan go? She really couldn't remember. The latticed window through which it shone was either the bathroom or that little low-ceilinged bedroom which abutted on to – no, was it the main stairs? No, no no, that was the other side, and wasn't there a cupboard somewhere which had a blocked-up door in the back which had once led to – no, can't remember, and as for up there ... She looked up at the parts of Holly House which were now almost entirely lost in the dimness of another night, of which it had seen so many thousands.

I really don't want to go in there again.

'Make an excuse,' said John, appreciating his dinner better once she'd turned off the television and hidden the radio in the linen basket.

'I did that today. I didn't have an excuse for tomorrow.'

'Well, make one up.'

'How can I, when it was me who asked if I could do another picture?'

'Well, don't go in to tea, then. Say you feel ill.'

'Goodness, no! She suspects I'm pregnant already.'

Emily set up her easel before the shrubbery. She hadn't enjoyed opening the gates and crossing the courtyard, and she didn't look up at the first floor windows. Now the other side of Holly House stretched before her, not footless behind a wall, but extending down to where bare flowerbeds and well-swept grass lay prostrate at its feet. Red brick and stone on the left, mullions blank except for the nursery at the top. Gosh, that was a long way up for small children, I hope the window didn't open right out. Above sat the clock turret, with the silent bell under its own little roof.

The seventeenth century block had been re-plastered properly on this side, with no left-over bits of pargetting. Set in behind it was the Georgian slice and its delectable door, with another sash window above and the same tangle of banisters within. Then the huge, lumpy kitchen with its redundant chimney. She couldn't see the lean-to from here, which was a blessing. She would probably have to lose a bit of the kitchen, too, but that was no great loss. Right, let's get it over. Eyes down.

She worked as quickly as she could, aware that winter afternoon light faded quickly. At three-twenty, Lady Curran appeared from the direction of the kitchen garden and piped 'How much longer will you be.'

'Not long, the light's going. I'll finish the pen work at home.'

'Come in as soon as you're finished and I'll make the tea.' She disappeared.

Emily looked up at the tall, blank mullions of the bedroom. I'm going in to that house again. I'm going to sit right under the floor of that room, sip tea and make polite small talk. Panic started to stir in her like pain.

She packed up her things and left them in the lean-to, making sure they were not under the crack in the roof although it hadn't rained properly for ages, in fact the reservoirs were still low from last summer's drought. John was very worried about the reservoirs. Emily saw no point in getting into a stew about it — worrying wasn't a rain dance.

In the kitchen, the long, scrubbed table bore clues to the occupations of Lady Curran's day. A trug basket held garden gloves, secateurs and fragments from the springs of winter-green which stood in a Doulton Hannah Barlow jug beside it. At the other end were used jugs, bowls and spoons, and the scent of hot cakes was in the air.

Emily moved out nervously into the eighteenth century. Deep blue showed beyond the chill breath of the letterbox, and the brass lantern caught the gilt in the wallpaper like weak sunshine shimmering on water. She turned the brass handle of the glass door and passed through into the seventeenth. Dark panelling, the broad stairs on her left, and as yet only heavy darkness above, pressing down onto the lit lower floor. Nasty. She forced herself on past the cloakroom to the sixteenth century and knocked for admittance. Behind her, a door opened and Lady Curran's voice sliced through the centrally heated atmosphere.

'Mrs. Wakelin. In here please.'

With relief she turned back a hundred years and went into the dining room, closing the door behind her.

Mr. Curran was in his usual cocoon of blankets beside the big open hearth. A trio of muscular logs awaited immolation on the iron firedogs, but his draped legs were bathed in the red glow of an electric fire. At the end of the polished table, Lady Curran enthroned herself behind a silver teapot like an Edwardian hostess, her badger-grey head bare.

The room was lit by table lamps, and the gilt frames of

the oil paintings glowed against the walls. The latticed bay window ahead, which was certainly not as old as it pretended, afforded yet another dim glimpse of Holly Cottage crouching behind the red brick wall.

'Good afternoon, Mrs. Wakelin,' Mr. Curran greeted her. 'I hope you didn't get too cold out there? January is hardly the time for landscape painting.'

'It's been mild, as a matter of fact,' said Emily, 'though the wind's getting up a bit now.'

'Is the picture finished?'

'Not quite. I'll let you have it tomorrow.'

He nodded, Lady Curran poured her tea and neither went into the coy, could-I-just-have-a-peep routine. She liked them for that.

'Would you like some seedcake,' stated Lady Curran, wielding the knife. Homemade seedcake! Emily hadn't tasted that since her Great Aunt Joan died, and you couldn't buy it anywhere now. Yet in secret hiding places like this, all over England, elderly ladies were probably still making it for afternoon tea.

'Oh, yes, please.'

She sat in the stillness as they ate and drank, her glance moving round the room and out of the window. It was the situation in reverse, with her sitting in Holly House and looking at the cottage, though the kitchen window couldn't be seen above the wall.

'It's funny,' she said, 'from this side my house looks as if it's hiding, doesn't it?'

'Does it,' said Lady Curran, not turning round.

'What do you think it's hiding from?' asked Mr. Curran. The fire lit him from below like the demon king in a pantomime, so that in contrast his voice seemed weaker than ever.

'Its big brother, I suppose.'

He laughed and Lady Curran stared. 'You have a real artist's imagination,' she said. 'Do you write as well.'

'No.'

'And why should it fear its big brother?' pursued Mr. Curran gently. 'I trust that is not a symbol of how you feel, Mrs. Wakelin, I shouldn't like you to feel threatened by us.'

51

'Oh, I don't,' said Emily, 'in fact I very rarely feel threatened, I'm lucky that way.' Her eyes rose momentarily to the chamfered beams of the ceiling.

The phone rang. Lady Curran left the room and they heard the swish of the glass door closing behind her.

Mr. Curran sat and looked at her, smiling.

'Mrs. Wakelin,' he said at last, 'what was it that happened to you last time you were here?' He watched as her blue eyes widened and the colour moved up over her full cheeks. She swallowed her tea quickly and set down her cup.

'I'm sorry, I was just tired from all the climbing.'

'Healthy young women do not become faint after a climb. My wife says you are probably pregnant.'

'Well, I'm not,' said Emily, feeling as if she was being backed into a corner. She tried to smile but her honesty showed through her eyes and suddenly formed her face into an expression of bewildered, lost misery.

'Was it upstairs?'

She nodded once, then again and repeatedly, and her hands clenched and her eyes filled with tears.

'I'm so sorry,' he said earnestly, 'I wouldn't have had you upset for the world. I felt affection for you at first sight. No,' he said, raising his skeletal hand urgently, 'please don't misunderstand me. I'm not a conceited fool who believes lovely young women are attracted by broken-down old men, and I'm not making a pathetic advance to you, just telling you the truth. You radiate joy and goodness, Mrs. Wakelin. You make the world seem better by just being in it. I hope you have a husband who appreciates you.'

She went hot with confusion and the tears escaped down her cheeks.

'It's quite frequent, is it?' she asked, her voice not quite in control, her throat aching.

'Well, not lately. At least, so I am told.'

'Your bedroom's under there. Don't you ever hear anything?'

'There's never been anything to hear. It's a silent thing, either felt or seen, that's all.'

'But you used to sleep up there, didn't you? How could you stand it?'

52

He looked at her, wrinkling his brow.

'What you must understand is that it's always been there, like a draughty window or a leaking roof. If you live in a house with, say, a broken floorboard, you don't scream every time it creaks or trips you up. You just say, "Bother the thing", and go on your way. Do you see what I mean?'

'Bother the thing!' exclaimed Emily weakly. 'It's hardly a broken floorboard, Mr. Curran.' Her face was now pale and her left hand was wiping the remembered sensation off her right.

'No, not if it is new to you, and unexpected,' he admitted regretfully. 'I am very sorry, Mrs. Wakelin, very sorry indeed. Won't you tell me what happened? It might make you feel better.'

'It took my hand,' said Emily, still rubbing it. 'It was terribly cold and felt as if it was trying to lead me somewhere.' Her eyes went up to the ceiling and he reached towards her in sympathy, although too far away to touch her.

'It's all right, it's never up there, just in the oldest part of the house at the front. I take it that was where it happened?'

'Yes. Does that mean the whole front block is — affected,' she asked, shying away from the right word.

'Some parts, not all. Believe me, Mrs. Wakelin, it won't harm you. It has always been there and we never even think about it, but we should have warned you.'

'I'm not sure it would have made much difference,' said Emily, now shaking slightly. 'I've never had an experience like that before, and I can't see myself taking it as calmly as you, even if I'd been expecting it. How often does it happen?'

'It's difficult to say. I seem to remember incidents occurred in groups, say over a few months, then it would be nothing for a while. We'd sometimes have a troublesome year, and I needn't say that that coincided with servant trouble. Still, that's hardly a problem these days. Mr. Selby and Mrs. Mumford only come during the day.'

'Do they know about it?'

'Probably.'

'And your grandchildren?' Emily asked curiously.

53

'Oh, you saw them, did you?' he said, smiling and obviously proud. 'Splendid little savages, aren't they? Yes, they do, though I don't think they've ever experienced anything.'

'The little girl seemed rather nervous. I couldn't help hearing,' Emily added apologetically, 'I was in the garden when she said she wouldn't go up to see the clock.'

'Well, it's hardly a place for a girl.'

Emily was brought up short by such a chauvinistic remark from this perfect gentleman, but then realised it was merely a case of generation gap courtesy. For Mr. Curran, the polite way to treat a woman was to assume she was fragile, like one referred to an obviously plain woman as a member of the fair sex. But the assumption was not necessarily implicit that she was; after all, his wife was about as fragile as a master of foxhounds.

'How long has it been going on?'

'Well, it was here when the family bought the house.'

'And do you know who or what it is?'

'No, no, not really,' he said, shaking his head. 'There are stories and legends and doubtless whopping great lies, but – ah, there you are. And what is the news today?'

He seemed suddenly more alive, his head raised, his ears pricked like the proverbial warhorse who said 'Ha, ha!' Lady Curran glanced at the notepad in her hand.

'Down, but not too bad.' She handed it to him, plus several fax sheets.

He made a quick study of the pages then stabbed at something with a thin, urgent finger. 'Tell them to sell.'

As soon as his wife had gone, 'I hope this doesn't mean you won't be visiting us again?' he said seriously. 'I should very much regret not having the pleasure of your company in future.'

'How does your wife feel about – ' began the now horribly embarrassed Emily, her hand rubbing away again. He laughed.

'Abigail was brought up on an estate where a medieval gardener used a hayrake on the Grand Avenue, a pink lady played a non-existent spinet in the bathroom and a wild boar charged through the herbaceous border every time a member of the family was about to die. The feeble happenings in this house hardly caused her to raise an eyebrow. Occasionally when they have got particularly tiresome she has put her foot down and taken certain steps, but it was definitely nothing to do with nerves.'

'She seems a remarkable lady,' said Emily.

'Most,' he agreed gravely, but with the suggestion of a smile at the corner of his mouth.

'What steps did she take?'

'Well, for instance, you may have noticed a door on the landing that once led into the bedroom above mine. It kept coming open. Most inconvenient if you were a light sleeper, and also very draughty until we had the central heating put in, so she had it blocked and turned into a cupboard. It didn't stop the man coming through, though.'

Emily felt her scalp prickle. 'What man?'

'I never actually saw him myself, but my mother did quite often and she said he had a pale, bearded face and a long black cloak. He comes through the sealed door but stays at the same level as the bedroom, so wherever he's going, it's in a part of the building which was replaced by the seventeenth-century block. He's supposed to look extremely distressed and disappear about the centre of the landing.'

'Do you think he was a monk?' asked Emily, experiencing a sudden deep, sincere urge to go and put the dinner on next door.

'Why? Oh, the black cloak. No, I don't think so, he hasn't a tonsure. Abigail,' he said as Lady Curran returned with the replenished teapot, 'Old Beaver — he doesn't look like a monk, does he?'

'No,' she said, glancing at Emily as if taking the temperature of her shock factor, 'I think he's Elizabethan. One of those frilly ruffs round his neck.'

'You've seen him?' exclaimed Emily, quite awestruck at the woman's sang-froid.

'Yes, he used to pop up quite often.'

'When was the last time?'

'Oh, I don't know, about three years, wasn't it? You remember, George, it was when we were still sleeping upstairs, because I met him one night when I was on the way to the lavatory.'

'How dreadful! Did he always appear at night?'

'Oh no, it could be any time, but it was only for a few seconds. Nothing to worry about, really. What's the matter, Mrs. Wakelin, feeling peaky again?'

'She had an unfortunate experience last time she was here,' said Mr. Curran. 'I've apologised to her but it's a bit late, I'm afraid. It was the hand-holding business.'

'Oh dear,' said Lady Curran, staring at Emily with a mixture of curiosity and regret. 'So you're not pregnant,' she added with quite breathtaking affrontery.

'No,' said Emily firmly, but blushing. Her kitchen was now calling with the earnest persistence of the far Coolins. She had really had enough of this household for the day, if not for ever. She stood up, announced the absolute inevitability of her immediate departure and thanked them for their hospitality. Mr. Curran held her hand.

'You will come again?' he urged her. 'I should so appreciate it. And there's really nothing to fear, I promise you.'

'I'm afraid he's bored,' Lady Curran said as she marched Emily rapidly through the kitchen. 'He reads and watches television, of course, but he was always an outdoor man and he misses the open air and all that man-talk.'

'Don't his friends come to see him?'

'One or two, but a lot of them are dead now, and his brothers all went out to the colonies when they were young.'

'What about people from the church?' asked Emily, on the point of being expelled from the back door into the lean-to.

'Oh, that's never been his cup of tea. He won't have the vicar in the house.'

'Really?' asked Emily, gathering up her easel and case. 'Is he difficult, then?'

'Of course not,' said Lady Curran coldly, 'he's an absolute poppet. Goodbye.'

The journey through the darkness up the side of the house was eerie, even with the security light for company. Her panic as she crossed the courtyard was such that she very nearly broke a cardinal rule of politeness and consideration and left both gates open, in order to bring her escape from the premises forward by a few seconds. But childhood training prevailed. 'Always shut gates, Emily love,' her mother said, 'else dogs and children get in and out. Animals and children should be kept the right sides of gates, then there's no harm done.'

She drew the side window curtains as soon as she got home, and they remained that way all weekend. Every time John drifted in the direction of any sort of broadcasting receiver, Emily pulled him into the garden, to the local pub, or for a long walk across the fields. The result was that he wound down quite a bit and life began to feel more like a married one.

On Monday morning, she cooked breakfast in a wine-coloured cotton damask wrap which made her look like Guinevere. The early arrival of the newspapers gave John the opportunity to immerse himself in the world's problems from Braintree to Liverpool Street, but he always did a first run through at the breakfast table.

'Em,' he said suddenly, pausing over his wheatflakes, 'who is it you're doing that wall hanging for?'

'Halfyard and Poole at Basildon.'

'Did you get an advance?'

'Not yet. Sophie will ask for it as soon as the Board has approved the design.'

'Oh dear.'

'What do you mean?' She leant on his shoulder and scanned the pink pages, rubbing her cheek over his hair. She read the headline with disbelief, the first paragraph with alarm, and then the rest of the article with growing resignation. 'Oh, well, it wasn't really my sort of thing anyway,' she said with a sigh. 'I thought it was too good to be true.'

'I'm so sorry, darling. I ask you, who'd have thought it? Selling to the Iraqis!'

'Well, I'm sure they were originally encouraged to by the government, and it's not their fault if they've done an about-turn. It's not even arms.'

'Not as such,' said John, 'but who knows what all

57

those bits and pieces could be made up into? Remember The Gun.'

'There's a big difference between nuts and bolts and a gun the size of a tube tunnel.'

'Now that *would* make a bang,' reflected John. 'Anyway, it seems unlikely that Halfyard's will be requiring the luxury of an embroidered hanging for some time.'

The post brought a cheque for St. Cyneburga from Sophie and an ecstatic letter from the vicar which put a smile back on Emily's face and sent her to fill in the consecration date in her diary. At nine-forty-five, she was about to ring Sophie and tell her the bad news when there was a knock at the front door.

On the step stood a thin woman in her sixties who appeared small to Emily, although she was a perfectly respectable five foot four. Her fine hair was halfway between mouse and grey and permed into a style which it seemed reluctant to hold, as its limp droop was braced up by hairslides and kirbigrips. Her face was pink and smooth, its only lines being a single one across the brow and one either side of her thin mouth, etched there by a habitual calm, firm smile which didn't show the teeth.

She wore pearl stud earrings of the minimalist school, a waterproofed jacket, a knee-length tweed skirt and lace-up shoes. Her brown leather organiser bag looked as if it really meant business.

'Good morning. Are you Mrs. Waiting or Waking or – '

'Wakelin.'

'Ah yes, I thought Miss Barton must have got it wrong.' The serene mouth conveyed that much of its smiling time was occupied by Miss Barton. 'She informed me that you were a professional embroideress, is that so?'

'Yes.'

She nodded. 'My name is Margaret Witherley-Bashe, and I'm in charge of the needlework party working on the Tappett chapel at the church. No doubt you will have heard about it. If you cared to submit designs for the altarcloth or any other of the pieces we would be very willing to consider them. I can't promise that your design will be accepted, of course, it would be up to the committee.'

58

She smiled again, a smile as tight as an unopened tin. I am the committee, it conveyed.

'I'm afraid I'm rather busy at the moment,' said Emily hoping her phone call to Sophie would prove it so.

'Oh! Actually, I wrote to every church needlewoman I could find, but I don't recall your name.'

'I work under my maiden name. And you didn't like any of them?'

'They were not quite suitable,' her visitor said, the smile now indicating the absolute nature of her standards of suitability.

'Then it seems rather unlikely that I should be able to please you when so many have failed. I should go right to the top and approach the Royal School of Needlework.'

'Well, I did, of course,' retorted the woman, 'but there were difficulties and we really could not come to a comfortable agreement.'

Ah, you want a cheap job, thought Emily. Absolutely what you want in design, absolute perfection in execution and the absolute minimum in the way of pay. She smiled.

'Well, Mrs. Witherley-Bashe, all the business side is handled by my agent, whose address I'll give you willingly if you'd like it.'

'Oh. But I'm sure that as you're a local we can have a more intimate relationship than that. I mean, the other ladies are all giving their talents and time voluntarily for their church.'

Blackmail now.

'Mrs. Davidson will discuss it all with you. Look, here is her card.'

'Yes,' said Mrs. Witherley-Bashe, taking the piece of pasteboard without looking at it and seeming reluctant to allow it entry into her handbag. The smile was getting harder. 'But you will, of course, want to see the chapel, whether your representative permits you to take the job eventually or not.'

'That would be necessary,' Emily agreed.

'How about this morning? I am going over there now for a committee meeting. May I tell the ladies that you will be coming?'

'You may,' said Emily, adopting without intention her would-be patron's regal turn of phrase. 'I will be most interested to hear your requirements. What time shall I come?'

'The meeting is at ten, but as we shall have private matters to discuss first, it would be best if you didn't arrive until half-past. You understand, of course.'

'Of course.'

She felt like putting her finger to the side of her nose and winking. She started laughing as she closed the door. Should she turn up at ten and eavesdrop on the needlework committee's deepest secrets after all? Whatever could they be?

Emily was used to the immense seriousness expended on the pettiest of things in local affairs, the rage which could be provoked by a misplaced word, the long vendettas started by a moved flower arrangement or an altered running order in the parish concert. This was going to be a walking-on-eggs meeting, but all the more entertaining for that. She certainly didn't intend to take on the job, not after the warning words of Mrs. Hubbard and Miss Barton.

Goodness knows how many people had turned down or been turned down by the St. Mary Magdalen project. it seemed very likely that she was the last resort, a captive prospect who could be personally nagged into taking on a task to be carried out under the perpetual invigilation of Mrs. Witherley-Bashe.

She rang Sophie and gave her an update on her professional situation.

'I should at least give it a try, Emily,' she said. 'Things aren't getting any better.'

Chapter Five

Emily crossed the road and walked down the lane to where church and cottages bridled together in their exclusive hollow. At least, it was a lane once, but had been straightened to allow a free flow of traffic to Great Hocking, three miles away. The church's companions in exile had been bisected, and the removed homes had started up a new schismatic movement on the other side.

The gravelled approach to the church gate was lined by terraced cottages so neatly painted and so drowned in flowers that it comprised one of the Great Views of England. All over the word ex-pats and Anglophiles flicked through their Beautiful Britain books and calendars and said 'Little Hocking Church', as instantly as they said Dunster Market or Corfe Castle or Finchingfield Green. The lychgate into the churchyard was not a Victorian reproduction or a twentieth-century war memorial, nor even a careful, painstaking restoration based on three unrotted beams and a few original tiles; it was absolutely genuine, give or take a few patches. The sill was bowed to ground level by the feet of the centuries and scratches on the coffin shelves marked the measure of their burdens, ranging from very long to sadly and pathetically short.

Emily passed under its lopsided roof and up the paved path to the church door. The ground around had risen a little over the centuries, but not as much as most old churchyards due to the provision of a charnel house beneath the chancel. This had been sealed up in the late-nineteenth century, once the remains had been subjected to final examination by various local doctors and antiquaries. They prodded and measured and scraped the bones, gazed into the eyes of the skulls and eventually published their findings, which were much as might have been expected, i.e. that the people who ended up in the said charnel house had not been very well.

The church was largely Perpendicular, although bits and pieces of previous churches turned up in unexpected places to intrigue architectural historians. It boasted Norman foundations to the tower, twelfth-century sedilia in the chancel and a blocked window behind the organ console which *might* be pre-Conquest − a very distinguished feature indeed.

Within, the nave was lit by clerestory windows reminiscent of Suffolk, and to the left of the crossing a certain amount of noise could be heard going on. It increased in volume as Emily advanced upon it, her flat, rubber-soled shoes nearly silent on the stones, her flowing purple skirt brushing against the poppyhead pews.

'I don't see why he shouldn't carry a trowel,' someone was insisting. 'His father was a brickmaker, and it would be a lot nicer than depicting his own job. I mean to say, what would one use as the symbol for that? One just trembles to think.'

'If it was good enough for him, it should be good enough for us,' said a determined voice. 'He was a humble man, a very humble man.'

'But we really can't have a picture of him standing there rake in hand, or whatever they used −'

'Bucket and spade?' an acid voice suggested.

' − it just wouldn't be decent. By all means have him in working men's garments. I mean, tights and a leather jerkin and one of those rather attractive hoods with capes would look nice and perhaps some sort of rough cap in his hand to show reverence, and he could be looking up as if a message had suddenly come to him − .'

'We are not discussing an Annunciation, Jean,' broke in the voice of Mrs. Witherley-Bashe, 'and *I* feel, Mrs. Gage, that his occupation would be best left out of the scheme altogether, it is not relevant. The only part of Tappett's life we are concerned with is his resistance to Catholicism and his sacrifice for the Protestant Faith. In my opinion, that will best be conveyed by a simple robe and a Bible in his hand.'

'He couldn't read,' said the acid voice.

'And a long robe would be so middle-aged,' carped the first voice. 'I mean, he was only twenty-two. Why *not* tights and a sort of jerkin thing and a hood?'

'You are thinking of Robin Hood,' said Mrs. Witherley-Bashe. 'We are in the sixteenth century, not the twelfth.'

'Fourteenth,' said the acid voice. 'There is no record of Robin Hood before the fourteenth century. All that King Richard stuff was stuck in years later.'

Emily stood by the clustered shafts of a crossing pillar and waited to be noticed and invited into the transept. Mrs. Witherley-Bashe's complexion was becoming pinker, and she was moving her head from side to side as the committee members spoke, in a way that definitely threatened trouble. This was obviously the Tappett Chapel-to-be. There was an old stone altar and a collection of chairs in front of it, but the rest of the objects lying around were of a temporary nature. Builders had left boards, cement bags, ladders and a resolute-looking iron framework, a plumber had abandoned a loose radiator, and one or other of them had made a large hole in the wall. Plastic sheeting sucked in and out of it at the bidding of the breeze.

The committee members were sitting among the chairs with their allegiance apparent from the distances between them. The acid-voiced lady was closely allied to Mrs. Gage, 'Jean' was fairly near to Miss Barton and Mrs. Witherley-Bashe sat alone near the altar, in a chair inscribed 'In memory of Henry Francis Innwell, Vicar of this parish'. Her handbag was hooked over the back. She glanced at her watch.

'Well, the girl will be here in a moment, so we'll have to hear what she suggests. I just hope she doesn't want to do anything too outré. She's a bit of a hippy, I'm afraid. Looks as if she laughs a lot.'

Emily stepped smartly behind the pillar. It was not the first time her cheerfulness had given offence. People sometimes got very uptight about happiness, as if it were immoral.

'Her husband seems conventional enough, he's a high-powered accountant in the City,' said the acid-tongued one. 'Terry spoke to him on the train last week. Very nice, apparently.'

'Really?' asked Mrs. Witherley-Bashe, not sounding convinced. 'Oh, well, perhaps she's all right then. You can't always tell with these artistic types, they seem to feel they have to dress the part.'

'Like pillars of the rural church in tweed,' dug the acid one relentlessly. She was wearing a scarlet woollen coat and high-heeled black shoes, and her hair and make-up were quite ferociously urban. Mrs. Witherley-Bashe pretended she hadn't heard her.

'We'd better get the designs and fabrics laid out in the vestry, so she can see the colour scheme we're working to. It's always advisable to lay down guidelines at the beginning, then people can't go too mad.'

Chairs scraped on the floor like a fanfare of trumpets, and feet and voices gradually faded and were cut off by a slam initiated by a sudden bellying of the plastic. Emily emerged and studied the chapel, looking round for clues to the identity of the eponymous Tappett. It appeared he was not the local worthy she had anticipated, and the wall tablets and the tomb on the end wall were the property of the Lethabys. (Who they?)

She waited long enough for her arrival to seem tactfully separated from the row in the transept, then knocked on the vestry door. The murmur of voices within included the chairwoman's comment: 'She's late.' On opening the door, however, she had the smile in place.

The four other ladies were standing round a table which looked rather like a jumble sale, piled with fabric, skeins of wool and pieces of worked canvas. After introductions, Mrs. Witherley-Bashe elucidated their significance.

'We are, as you can see, having a colour scheme of blue, yellow and white, with silver and gold as well, of course. A few areas of beading and sequins where it is appropriate, but this is not to be excessive. The kneelers are being worked to one design and colour scheme, but the needlewoman is permitted to make her own choice of

64

stitches, which gives a certain amount of freedom for self-expression whilst retaining unity.' She seemed pleased by her democratic gesture.

'Great Hocking have theirs all completely different, and I think it looks lovely,' said Mrs. Gage obstinately. 'Everyone did their own design and signed it with their name. Where it could be seen,' she added with emphasis. She was a small, round, grey-haired woman with red cheeks, a snub nose and eyes which seemed to glow with enthusiasm.

'That was a completely different concept,' stated Mrs. Witherley-Bashe. 'Great Hocking is just an unsophisticated country church, but the Tappett chapel is a solemn celebration of faith. Walter Tappett suffered because he stayed faithful to Protestantism.'

'I thought it was because he wouldn't conform to Catholicism,' said Mrs. Gage argumentatively. 'I've always thought of him as a courageous rebel, doing his own thing and refusing to do as he was told.'

'Who was Walter Tappett?' Emily asked gently, as the atmosphere started to deteriorate again.

'He's our local —'

'A most valiant young man who was burned at the stake in the reign of Mary,' Mrs. Witherley-Bashe interrupted Mrs. Gage. 'He refused to deny his Protestant beliefs and was martyred in the market place at Braintree, together with two others. We've always had a small plaque in the church, but it was high time a proper memorial was made and his story properly told. What we want, Mrs. Wakelin, is a hanging behind the altar showing Tappett in a long, plain robe and holding the Holy Bible. He should have short brown hair, brown eyes and look very sincere but not too saintly. He was quite an ordinary man, you see, so it wouldn't be right to make him look ascetic. A saint, of course, though the Anglican Church doesn't actually "dub" them, so to speak, but a modest saint, one of those ordinary, salt-of-the-earth common people who have so much to teach us.'

Emily's heart leapt with joy at the glorious way Mrs. Witherley-Bashe was giving herself away.

'Do you have a drawing?' she asked.

'Well, no, we presumed you'd do that,' she said, looking

65

as if she was already about to ask for her money back. 'Why?'

'It sounded as if you'd worked out the design and just wanted me to copy it.'

'She does,' said the woman in red, with a smile as tart as her voice. She had been introduced by the name of Bolsover. 'You do what you like, Mrs. Wakelin, I'm sure it will be lovely. A new angle on the project will be most refreshing.'

'I'm sure I'm always ready to listen to anyone's ideas,' said Mrs. Witherley-Bashe, getting pink again but not letting the smile slip.

'Right,' said Mrs. Gage promptly, 'then there's things about Walter Tappett you should know, Mrs. Wakelin.' She was dressed in a particularly down-to-earth raincoat and stained brown suede ankle boots. Emily suspected she was probably involved with Brownies. 'First, he was a very common man inded. He couldn't read or write and his job was clearing out gutters and cesspits.'

'Oh, really, Mrs. Gage, that is just not relevant!'

'Of course it's relevant! If we'd been living then we'd none of us have gone near him, let alone talk to him or revere him, and it wouldn't just have been because he smelt, either. We are furnishing a memorial chapel to a man that none of us would have taken a blind bit of notice of,' she repeated, nodding hard at Emily.

'I would,' said Jean Lake in a hurt, aggrieved voice. 'I'm not a snob.' She was a willowy woman with a soft, kind face, wearing a grey flannel suit, navy blue tights and moccasins.

'Secondly,' said Mrs. Gage, setting her chin, 'I don't believe he was what any of us would call religious. He didn't go in for theological argument or bible quoting, or any of that hairsplitting they indulged in to prove they loved God more than anyone else. At his trial, Mrs. Wakelin, they questioned him about whether he believed in all that stuff, the real presence, Papal authority, justification etcetera, and all he said was, "I'm an ignorant man and don't understand such things, but if the Lord Jesus say I am His, no man can say I am not. I will answer to Him alone."'

'How very honest of him' said Emily.

'He was tortured, of course, but they couldn't move him. They told him he was stupid, whereas they were learned men who'd studied these things all their lives and done the thinking for him. All he had to do was agree to believe what they told him. "I can't," he said, "I can't believe what I don't understand."'

'I don't imagine his Protestant pastors would have cared much for that either,' said Emily, a square, determined, obstinate face growing in her mind's eye, staring out at the observer and saying, 'Here stand I, and I'm not going to say something I don't believe.' A bolshie, one of the awkward squad, a sore thumb just asking to be chopped off, a man who could have turned up in any period, in any part of the world, in a trade union, in a government department, in any religion or none, and who wouldn't tell a lie to another, to himself, and most of all, to God.

For someone right at the bottom of the social pile to resist the religious frenzy of the sixteenth century, when every man was drunk on theology, was astounding. I don't say I'm right, he said, I say I don't understand. God knows I don't understand, and all I can do is live as the Lord has told me to live. But I can't pretend to know when I don't know.

'I can see why you're proud of him,' said Emily.

In a time of taking sides there was no place for the non-joiner. In a time of fanaticism, who could tolerate reason and moderation? He was a thorn in the side of the self-righteous, a reproach which showed them up. Toleration would allow the possibility that he might be right and the fanatics wrong, so he must be badgered and bullied and brought into line, under the precept that he who was not with them was against them. Tappett might have pointed out that another Gospel had it completely the other way round, but it would not have helped his situation at all. Religion had become the same thing as politics, so he was too dangerous to be allowed to live.

'How big do you want it?' asked Emily.

'We thought about five feet or less.'

'No, we didn't,' said Mrs. Bolsover immediately. 'We decided last time that it ought to be seen clearly from

67

the body of the church, so it had to be at least eight or nine feet high.'

'No, that would be far too obtrusive. But perhaps a few words at the bottom in old English script. We thought "Blessed are ye poor" would be appropriate.'

'*You* did,' said Mrs. Gage. 'I think it sounds just plain patronising.'

'Why don't we give Mrs. Wakelin a free hand?' asked Mrs. Lake suddenly in an irritable voice. She had been sulking over the throwing out of the jerkin and tights. 'Who knows? She might come up with something that we *all* like. After all, that's what we're employing her for.'

'If her design is satisfactory,' stated Mrs. Witherley-Bashe firmly.

'Don't be silly, Mrs. W.B., there's no one else left to do it, is there?' said Mrs. Bolsover, her P.H. level no different. 'It's either her or one of us, and frankly we're all up to our necks in tent stitch. You get on with it, Mrs. Wakelin.'

'And don't forget, he mustn't look respectable,' said Mrs. Gage with great emphasis. 'I'd like him to look as if he was trouble. All those in favour of Mrs. Wakelin doing it, regardless.' Three hands went up.

'Mrs. Gage, I am the Chair!' Mrs. W.B.'s face was very pink indeed.

Miss Barton hadn't said a single word.

Mrs. Bolsover came and sat beside Emily in the nave, where she was imagining the effect of the hanging and working out the size which would make the best impact.

'Don't let her bully you,' she said bluntly. 'She's determined this project is all going to be done her way and some of us don't see why it should be. Just because she was born in the vicarage! Her father was a difficult man too, I've been told. Have you got any ideas? Unusual and original ones, preferably.' Seen close to, her face looked like a disappointed doll's, all painted up with nowhere to go. Emily guessed she must be about forty.

'I don't really know enough about him yet. Can you tell me a bit more?'

A hand came over Emily's shoulder bearing a large book

in a polythene cover. The action had the drama and authority of the first appearance of the ten commandments.

'I forgot to give you this, Mrs. Wakelin, it's *Foxe's Book of Martyrs*. Take care of it, please, it was my father's and therefore *rather* precious.' Mrs. Witherley-Bashe smiled violently at Mrs. Bolsover and departed for the south door.

'I can't stand people who wear rubber soles,' said Mrs. Bolsover. Emily drew her feet in under her skirt. 'Well, I can't say that's my idea of light or uplifting reading, but a hundred years ago no one in search of religious inspiration would have been without it.'

'I know. I had to investigate a Catholic martyr once, and they recommended Bishop Challoner. You don't half need a strong stomach for hagiology.'

Mrs. Bolsover looked at her curiously. 'How many of these things have you done? Are you terribly good?'

'I don't know. I know if I've produced what I intended and whether I've done it up to my own standards, but whether anyone else is going to like it I've no idea. It certainly won't be any good if you don't follow your own light.'

'To thine own self be true, just like Walter Tappett. Only it wasn't his beliefs he was being true to, but his ignorance. I think it would be nice if the words on the hanging were: "I don't know." Think how many people who saw it in future years could sympathise with that.'

'Sounds like a saint I could identify with, certainly,' said Emily, opening Foxe. It was a Victorian edition, offering notes, illustrations, additions, and 'an essay on Popery'. 'I suppose this gives all the gory details of what was done to him, poor man. That's what I dislike about the cult of martyrs — their deaths efface their lives. Artists, in particular, only seem interested in wallowing in blood and pain, instead of showing how they lived and what sort of person they were. Nobody did paintings of St Stephen healing, or of Sebastian and Lawrence doing anything but dying horribly.'

'They were trying to hold up a good example.'

'But a lot of sado-masochistic thrills must have been got this way. They put evil into people's minds, not good,' Emily complained unhappily; the illustrations were pretty revolting. 'It was their lives that really mattered.'

69

'Then show how this one lived,' said Mrs. Bolsover.

Emily walked back up the lane, wishing Holly House weren't quite so near to her home. It stared across at the church tower while her cottage, with its head well down, seemed to be begging her to come and hold its hand. She studied the ancient brick front as she climbed the slope. It was held together by pins, the round iron ends marking the floors. She wondered when it was done. Any contemplation of Holly House set her wondering. She crossed the road. Were the Currans looking out of the bed-drawing-room window? Was anything looking out of the first floor windows? She looked away quickly in case it was. She reached her gate.

'Mrs. Wakelin!'

Mrs. Witherley-Bashe stood at the gate of Mill View Cottage. Emily stopped and waited for her to come up, but she didn't move and Emily realised that the cry had been a summons. She walked along to her deliberately, trying not to grin at such arrogance.

'I just want to make sure that you understand me, Mrs. Wakelin. What we do *not* require is a saint in an overall and helmet carrying a torch. Is that clear?'

Emily endeavoured to keep a straight face while assuring her that nothing had been further from her mind. She could see someone who was presumably Miss Felicity McCarthy peeping through the cottage window, and as her visitor started up the broken path the front door opened. A Yorkshire terrier shot out as if its mistress's last word to it had been: 'Kill!'

Mrs. Hubbard had been absolutely right. St. Mary Magdalen's needlework group was not a happy ship.

Chapter Six

Emily rang Sophie and asked her to negotiate the fee and get an immediate deposit. It would, she suggested, be advisable to imply that no design could possibly be forthcoming until this was paid. Meanwhile, she would lie low, read up Foxe, do one or two drawings and not be at home to Mrs. Witherley-Bashe.

Having taken this decision with a clear conscience, she gave no guilty start when the doorbell rang just before her early lunch. She left her coffee, bread and cheese on the kitchen table and slid quietly behind the door which led into the living room, where she squinted at the window through the crack. No more than a few seconds' wait showed her Lady Curran retreating down the path. She crossed the room, opened the front door and called after her.

'You were in the garden,' stated Lady Curran, marching up the path again. She didn't wait for a response, so neither lie nor confession was necessary.

'I'm taking the picture straight up for framing. We have the children coming this weekend, and George wants both pictures hung by then.'

'It'll be finished this afternoon.'

'Oh. I thought you said this morning.'

'No, I don't think I did,' said Emily calmly. 'Do you want the mount the same colour?'

'Yes, and the same size. Look, it really must go to the shop today, so would you mind bringing it round.'

'All right.'

The meal was eaten, the painting was finished and

71

mounted, the brief look at the television proved that things weren't getting any better in the Middle East and the doorbell rang again. Emily peeped out of the bedroom window this time, to find the round, grey-haired caller in the act of looking up. She went down.

'Ah! Hello, Mrs. Wakelin. We met this morning, the name's Gage. Now, I just want a word in your ear about our Walter. I always call him our Walter because I feel so fond of him, and I'm sure he wouldn't mind. The point is, I don't like the idea of him looking saintly, it just isn't appropriate. Please do forget the robe. I've got this book on Tudor costume and there's a very good picture of a working man which would do splendidly. I've marked it here and you're very welcome to keep it for as long as you like. Right, well, I won't keep you any further, I'm sure you're very busy. I'm really looking forward to seeing what you come up with. 'Bye 'bye.'

She bounced off down the path, her ankle boots carrying her away to other enthusiasms.

The weather was rather miserable by now; clouds, slight drizzle and a chill breeze, but still pretty soft going for January. Emily put the costume book with Foxe, draped a bright floral shawl over her head and shoulders, wrapped the painting in a plastic bag and left for Holly House.

She stood with her hand on the ornate ironwork of the gate, gazing through and upwards. Its grubby, pinned-together frontage, its grimy upper windows, the sheer height of it in proportion to its width, seemed less comfortable every time she approached it. The holly trees rattled and sent more bunches of yellow prickles down into the yard, to threaten the feet like caltrops on a battlefield. She looked at the glass doors above the porch. Are you in there? Are you looking down at me?

There was a sudden tattoo of knuckles on glass. She nearly fainted until she saw the movement in the bottom right-hand window and obeyed Lady Curran's beckoning hand.

Through the front gate, through the side gate, along the path, past the Georgian door and the kitchen ...

Lady Curran was already in the lean-to. The plastic bag was removed. 'Oh, yes. Very good. Right, I'll show George, then take it up to Mrs. Hubbard's. You won't mind sitting with him for half an hour.'

Well, yes, to be honest I will, thought Emily, though she smiled sweetly. One, I have got things to do, two, I don't like your house any more, and three, I don't want your husband talking to me like he did last time, especially if we're alone.

She followed her through the time machine of Holly House, from the twentieth to the seventeenth century, where the invalid sat in his dressing gown and his plaid woollen rugs among the oak and the beams. His wife thrust the picture at him and he slowly removed his glasses from his pocket.

'I think it's frightfully successful,' announced Lady Curran.

'So do I,' he said, smiling at Emily.

'Mrs. Wakelin is going to keep you company while I'm gone. Goodbye.'

Emily took a chair on the other side of the broad dining-room hearth, feeling very uneasy and fairly miserable, for her.

'Would you like to take off your shawl?' he asked.

She removed its gaudy folds and fringes and pushed her fingers through her hair. He was looking at her as if she were a painting herself.

'How are you today, Mr. Curran?' she asked, trying to relax. The sixteenth-century block started behind this fireplace. Perhaps the fireplace and chimney stack were part of it. In which case ...

'I've not been too well,' he said. 'I do sometimes have bad nights, but I'm better now. Now tell me about yourself. I hear that you're doing some work for a factory.'

'No, not now. The firm has had to withdraw.'

'Ah! So are you considering the Tappett Chapel project?'

'Well, yes,' she said, taken aback, 'but how did you know?'

'We possess a telephone,' he pointed out gently. 'Do you think you can feel at home with such an unconventional saint? Or do you prefer gold lamé halos and ecstatic expressions?'

'I doubt if I'd have felt at home with him, but I can

73

certainly admire him. Withstanding all that horrible cruelty when he hadn't even got a faith to sustain him.'

'He most certainly did have a faith,' said Curran as strongly as his voice would allow. 'He believed in Truth. What he didn't believe in was the inevitability of receiving any reward for it. That, to my mind, is the highest of all virtues. Virtue as its own reward.'

'It's a remarkably abstract concept for an uneducated man, isn't it?' said Emily, frowning. 'People like him were brought up believing that social status was ordained by God, and that He expected you to do what the upper classes said and swallow everything you were told. So why didn't he? Where did he get the idea from, that an ignorant man of low intelligence had the right to make up his own mind about such enormous and complicated mysteries? Don't you think that it might just have been colossal arrogance? You know how sure of the rightness of their opinions a really stupid person is. Perhaps that's all it was — arrogance and stupidity, like his judges said.'

Curran laughed. 'Well, I agree that complete ignorance of a subject has never dissuaded anyone from expressing an opinion on it, but Tappett wasn't expressing an opinion. He was admitting that he didn't have one and wasn't prepared to take someone else's on board just for convenience's sake. And because he was ignorant it doesn't mean he was unintelligent. In fact, I think his intelligence shines out in everything he did and said.'

'I can't really take to martyrs, they make me feel uncomfortable and inadequate,' admitted Emily, rubbing her long, pale hands together and caressing her silver craft rings. She was unaware of the grace of her actions. Curran watched her with near-fascination. 'I hate pain, and the thought of going through such a hideous experience of it just for an idea — I mean, I could understand if it was to save someone else, like the Catholic priests who wouldn't give away the hiding places of their colleagues, but I could never do it myself. I made a set of vestments once for a church dedicated to St. Edmund Campion, and had to read up the Catholic martyrs. They weren't all one undivided body, like I'd always thought. There was a lot of infighting going on about the way the English Mission should be run, and even about what it was aiming for. In a way they were all dying for slightly different causes. Some priests were rooting for a Spanish Invasion, and others like Campion thought that was atrocious and that their only duty was to bring the sacraments to their flock. They still killed him, though.' She stopped short and laughed. 'Goodness, this is a pretty heavy conversation, isn't it?'

'I find it fascinating,' he said, gazing at her. Emily laughing was a captivating sight. She stopped quickly and looked down, anxious to avoid further compliments.

'You're interested in religion, are you?' she said.

'Oh, yes. There's nothing which shows up the murky corners of human nature better than religious belief and devotion. For instance, is there anything more self-revelatory than a man passionately preaching the unlimited love and forgiveness of God, and accepting with equanimity the doctrine of eternal punishment? How can he praise a God like that?'

'Because he's frightened of Him, I suppose.'

'There's certainly a lot in that, Mrs. Wakelin,' agreed Curran. 'After all, the Greeks called the dreaded Fates "The Kindly Ones", for the same reason; Christians are not the first people to believe God is susceptible to flattery. But I feel the real reason lies in the fact that Man creates God in his own image, then worships him. If a man can accept cruelty and injustice in his God it is because those things are in himself and he needs justification for them.'

'But why did it matter so much to the church that a single humble man, one of the lowest of the low, didn't understand theology and said so?' Emily puzzled. 'What did it matter? Why couldn't they leave him alone?'

'Power, Mrs. Wakelin!' Curran said with sudden vehemence, striking the arm of his chair with a skeletal hand. 'They couldn't afford to let one single person get away from them, or the whole lot might start slinking off. Organised religion isn't about goodness, or truth, or even salvation, it's about keeping people in order! In the case of the medieval Catholic Church, which, you must remember, was the *only* church, it was about total control over *all* people *all* over

75

the Christian world, not just for the whole of their lives, but for *ever*. Think of it! The feudal system extended to all eternity. Always a serf or a bondsman or a vassal, with no hope of liberation. You don't think those churchmen saw the life to come as an escape from the world, do you? No, no, they saw it as this world all over again, with the bishops and the cardinals still in charge and at the right hand of God, the obedient laity still following them like sheep, and the disobedient laity being imprisoned and tortured just as they were on earth. Has it ever occurred to you, Mrs. Wakelin, that even to this day the churches' liturgies use the language of feudalism? The Lord. *My* Lord. The modern world doesn't understand the significance of that word.'

Emily, wide-eyed, stared at his flushed cheeks, the brightness of his eyes and the triumphant smile upon his face. A man riding his hobby-horse can be boring, but when it is a compulsive Valkyrie ride it is a disturbing spectacle. He seemed to be on the point of physical collapse from the sheer power of his passion.

'You obviously care a lot about it,' she said nervously, wondering what on earth she should do if something dreadful suddenly happened to him before her eyes.

'I care about the terrible harm it has done,' he said, his voice trembling with anger.

'What is your religion?'

'I have none. I reject it. It's for those who are afraid of life and who need the comfort of magic rituals and good luck charms, and a reward for being good or a consolation prize for being unlucky. It's for people who can't take on the responsibility of growing up and running their own lives. Listen, Mrs. Wakelin — I really can't go on calling you Mrs. Wakelin. May I call you Emily?'

'Please do,' she said faintly.

He didn't invite her to call him George. He leant forward urgently in his chair.

'Well, listen, Emily. There have always been men who climb higher than their fellows, up out of the human valley and on to the mountain tops so they can see over into the country beyond. I hope you'll excuse my hackneyed and sentimental metaphor, but it's the clearest way I have of expressing my meaning. So, the climber stands on this mountain and looks at the view. It's very beautiful and rather strange, but so large and so distant that he can't see it very clearly, and as he comes down from the mountain he is already forgetting much of it. So he paints a picture of all he remembers in order to show others what he has seen. But his skill is limited and somehow once it's down on canvas it doesn't look quite as it should. The sky isn't the right colour and the strange, beautiful flowers only look like the ones in his own valley and the colours aren't brilliant enough and the proportions of the city are not quite right and in one or two places he has smudged the paint or left a hair from his brush. But it's the best he can do and he says to other people, look, this is what I saw and it was wonderful. This is what is at the other side of the mountain.'

Emily heard a door slam in the distance. She stared at him as he continued his sermon, which gave the impression of having been rehearsed, mentally and verbally, many times in order to reach its present form.

'So all the people who aren't able to climb up to see the view for themselves study the picture closely. They make copies of it and give them to other people and these people study it in turn. "This is the wonderful land on the other side of the mountains," they tell still more people. "You will observe that its sky is a rather strange shade of blue and that the walls are slightly askew and the towers lean, and that a lot of it is smudged." They point to places where the artist has made mistakes and say, "The great city has a blob on its wall just there, and you will see that the inhabitants have cross-eyes and always wear red clothes." The people say, "Goodness, fancy that," then they make further copies of the picture, but perhaps this time the printing is not very good, and the next lot of people who get these copies say, "My goodness, the city on the other side of the mountain has yellow sky and the colour from the flowers spills on to the grass, and that blob on the wall must have a very special purpose if we could only know it."

'Now just occasionally someone who looks at the picture for the first time says, "I think perhaps there isn't really a blob on the city wall, and that sometimes the inhabitants are dressed in other colours beside red", but by now the picture is regarded as if it were the city itself, and anyone who doubts it is perceived to be doubting the very existence of the city, and this make people afraid and angry and they attack the doubters . . .'

The door opened and Lady Curran entered. Emily's relief was immense. Mr. Curran's face now looked so ghastly that she had been surreptitiously looking around for a telephone. His wife looked at him, poured him a glass of water and opened a bottle of pills on the sideboard. He swallowed them down, closed his eyes, and leant back in his chair.

'What was he talking about,' she said.

'Religion,' said Emily anxiously, on her feet in case she was about to be ordered out of the house. 'I'm so sorry.'

'Not your fault,' she said. 'Did he bore you.'

'I wasn't a bit bored,' said Emily, 'but I was afraid he was going to be ill.'

'Put the lamp on, please.' She was rubbing his hands and smoothing his brow, her face as sharp and expressionless as ever, but her movements betraying tenderness and concern. It was as if her face didn't belong to the rest of her body, like that child's game where one marries up head, body and legs from three different figures.

Emily suddenly realised that the light had faded, and that the last few minutes of impassioned monologue had been conducted only by the light of the electric fire, which must have added greatly to her unease without her being aware of it. She went to the bay window and switched on the brass lamp which stood on a walnut table. The light hit the red brick wall outside and etched itself into the pitting on the bricks, threw ivy leaves into deep contrast and shimmered off the white wall of the cottage. As she stepped back from the lozenged glass, the reflection of the room behind her came together like a jigsaw and she saw Lady Curran bend and kiss the top of her husband's head. When she turned round, she was looking as hard and cold as one of the fireirons in the hearth.

'Is he better?' Emily asked.

'Yes. The pills don't take long. There's no need to worry, Mrs. Wakelin,' she added as she saw Emily's anxious face,

78

'he'll be right as ninepence in a minute. Did he frighten you.'

'Yes.'

'Oh dear. Look, fetch me the fax sheets from the telephone out in the lobby, would you. The stock market prices always bring him round.'

Emily stepped out of the dining room into the stillness of the house and, the moment the door closed, was hit by irrational terror.

The stairs confronted her, rising into darkness with the blue outline of the staircase window hanging above its shadows. To the right she could see the doors to the stone hall and the bed-drawing room, the barriers which shut off the haunted sixteenth-century block of Holly House. Even the cloakroom door at the foot of the stairs looked sinister. She rushed for the glass door to the service quarters and pressed its handle down with a phobic near-certainty that it would prove to be locked, but it squeaked and allowed her into the lobby, where Lady Curran had switched on the brass lantern. It was very quiet there, but the whisper of the closing door and the puff of the wind through the letterbox were more company than she wanted. She caught up the faxed sheets and forced herself to return. It was going back past the stairs which was the worst. The darkness at the top had the solidity of power about it. It could have hidden anything. It might have been on the point of bringing forth monsters from its invisible womb.

Lady Curran took the fax from her shaking hand.

'You're out of breath,' she observed. 'Did you run.'

'I hurried,' said Emily, painting despite her effort to appear calm, 'I wanted to bring it as soon as possible.'

Curran opened his eyes and reached feebly for the sheet.

'There, he'll be better now,' said his wife. 'Sit down, you look a bit shaky.'

'I think I ought to go now, if you don't mind. My husband often rings me about this time. If the trains are having problems he lets me know and I meet him.'

'Oh. I see. But don't go for a minute.'

'Why?' asked Emily, dreading being sent on another lonely errand into the nastier corners of Holly House.

Lady Curran picked up her handbag from the table and took out her cheque book.

Mr. Curran's finger rapped upon the paper. He was already looking very much better.

'Just a minute, George,' his wife said, 'debts first.' Once handed over: 'I'm going to make some tea now. Are you sure you won't stay.'

'No, really. No.'

They went along to the kitchen together. Lady Curran picked up the kettle and carried it into the scullery.

'Goodbye,' she said over her shoulder.

'I'm sorry he got so upset,' Emily said, feeling quite wretchedly guilty about it and sure the woman was annoyed with her.

'Don't worry,' the high flat voice came from beyond the open door and above the spurt of a tap which came straight off the mains, 'he cares about things too much. He's even worse after he's read the papers, especially at the moment.'

Emily opened the ecclesiastical back door. 'You must come and see the picture when it's hung,' called Lady Curran as she closed it.

Out in the back yard, with only the light from the back door fanlight for illumination, terror struck Emily again. She was down the furthest end of the house from the haunted part – yes, say it, Emily, the haunted part. You're living next door to a haunted house and you're going to have to go into it fairly regularly unless you can hide under the furniture every time Lady Curran calls. But how did she know the trouble was only at the front?

Gardens have been haunted at times, haven't they? And I've got to walk up the path beside the house and cross the courtyard in front of the rooms where – and I'm going to have to walk under that awful frontage, and I'm sure it's going to break apart and come crashing down upon me, because it's just too old to stay up much longer, and the wind is getting stronger ... It's no good, I can't do it.

She stood rigidly in the darkness, seeing the bulk of the back of the house before her and hearing the insistent whisper of the wind moving the creepers on the garden wall, rustling the herb bushes around her feet and hooking her skirt onto the bare bones of the butchered roses. She pulled it sharply and heard the tear as it came free.

Seconds later she was scrambling over the top of the brick wall and falling into bare, bristly bushes on the other side. She was halfway across her lawn before she realised with a groan of regret that the fleshy crunch beneath her as she landed had been the Christmas Roses.

Chapter Seven

'I think he's a bit unbalanced,' said Emily, staring out of the windscreen. Today the train had run but John's car had not. 'He seemed a real old-fashioned gentleman, but then he started staring at me and paying compliments, and now he's treating me to tirades about the iniquities of organised religion. Honestly, John, it was so embarrassing.'

'Oh dear.' In the light of the oncoming headlights, John's face became that of a man whose duty it is to look after the little woman. 'Want me to have a word with him?' he said, his voice acquiring a slight edge.

'Oh no, of course not,' she said, instantly on the point of dissolving into giggles. 'He's no threat at all, really, he can't even get out of his chair on his own. Poor old thing, I do feel sorry for him, stuck in there with only books and newspapers and the television for stimulation. No wonder he gets het up about them. He used to be very active, once, his wife says.'

'What's wrong with him?' asked John.

'I don't know. I assumed it must be cancer, but it seems to have been going on for years and years. He's terribly thin.'

John went rigid as full headlights came round a corner, accompanied by a horn angry at anyone using the lane which was its property.

'Prat,' he said. 'Another of those people the world would be better off without. You heard the latest about Saddam?'

'No.'

'He's threatening to use nuclear weapons.'

'Oh God,' she said. 'What did the man say about your car?'

'Be ready tomorrow morning. What I thought was, you could run me into the station, then go and pay him and pick it up, then park it at the station for me to pick up at night –'

'They won't be open that early and I won't have time to hang about,' said Emily firmly. 'It'll be much more sensible for you to ring him from work and make the arrangements.'

They had dinner in front of the fire and the television, sober and silent before the miseries of the Middle East. Even Emily was beginning to wonder whether St. John the Divine was right after all.

It was dark when they left for the station next morning and Emily kept her eyes away from Holly House, but when she returned past the church an hour later it challenged her in the morning light, a red winter sunrise bathing it in flames.

There was someone standing on her doorstep.

'Good morning,' she said as she slammed the car door.

The little white-haired woman turned and looked at her, pressing her lips together as if in anticipation of a difficult task, or perhaps in an attempt to keep in words which were bursting to come out before the right moment. She was wearing a long brown coat that Emily's professional eye recognised as very expensive cloth which had worn well for many years and which might possibly wear well into the next century, should its owner be able to do likewise.

Emily joined her on the step, her glance flicking across the red brick wall and the bulging hollies intruding over the top. Oh, for goodness' sake, stop doing that, will you?

'Are you the embroidery lady?' Her voice was thin, with a slight crack and wobble as if she was nervous. 'I'm Felicity McCarthy from Mill View Cottage. I would like a few words with you if you can spare the time?'

'Of course! Please come in,' said Emily warmly, anxious to reassure her. 'Excuse the mess, I had to take my husband to the station this morning, his car's blown something.'

She drew the curtains, removed objects left over from last night from the settee and invited Miss McCarthy to sit down. She sat on the edge of the cushion, watching the stowing of books, sewing, newspapers, *Radio Times* etc, into other places, and the brushing off of scattered nut-shells on to the rug.

'Aren't you afraid they'll jam the vacuum cleaner?' she asked tremulously.

'We've got one of those orange things which swallow anything.'

'Goodness, they're quite a price, aren't they?'

'I believe they are. It was a wedding present,' said Emily, feeling like a bloated capitalist in the presence of faded gentility. 'Would you like some coffee?' she offered.

'No, thank you, I can't stay.' The voice still sounded quavery, but it was apparent by now that Miss McCarthy was not at all nervous, merely suffering from old age. Emily thought it must be dreadful to have your own mouth lying about you. It must drive old people mad with rage and frustration to hear their voices expressing a weakness and apprehension they didn't feel.

'I want to ask what you have been told to do about the wall hanging for the church? I asked Margaret when she called on me yesterday, but she wouldn't say a thing about it. Said it was all confidential until the committee has made the final decision. Is that true?'

'I'm not really in a position to say,' Emily said carefully, beginning to see more and more clearly the great danger of getting herself into the middle of a village row and even being forced to take sides.

'You mean she's told you to keep your mouth shut?' Miss McCarthy wobbled indignantly, like a bagpipe.

'No, of course not,' said Emily quickly. 'What I mean is that I haven't even done my design yet, and I don't know whether they'll accept it when I do.'

'Well, in that case, I should like to give you my opinion first. There's no need to tell anyone else, it'll only cause problems, but I want to show you this.' She took a folded paper from her pocket and undid it slowly before handing it to Emily. It was a page torn from a glossy, coloured

84

magazine, showing a corner in an old church with a poem beneath it. There was grey, carved stone, a small stained glass window, a flower arrangement on a stand and an embroidered banner hanging against a pillar. The poem was about time immemorial, forebears, simple faith, noble toil, final rest, country, Queen and God, in that order.

'Isn't it lovely?' asked Miss McCarthy. 'Not too gaudy and yet colourful, and such a lovely attitude, so dignified. Could you do it like that?

'Well,' said Emily pleasantly, 'it's certainly very nice, but this is a bishop, isn't it? In fact, it looks like Thomas à Becket. I can't really dress Walter Tappett like that.'

'Oh, but I think he should have some sort of vestment on. I mean, the Catholic church in Fairfield Street has a statue of St. Edmund in the most gorgeous robes. We really can't let them outdo us, can we?'

'Well, he was a king, wasn't he?' said Emily gently.

So it was not only a matter of personal animosities; some of the ladies were still battling on with the Reformation. Perhaps the McCarthy bit was more significant than Felicity's accent indicated.

She didn't get rid of her for an hour, although she refused coffee three times, tea twice and repeatedly said she couldn't stay long. Emily obtained a great deal of information from her, some by intention and some shown unaware like a drooping petticoat. She learned who she disliked and why, and how the different social cliques of Little Hocking were made up, and how she came to live there, and how she had come down in the world (death duties badly planned for), and why her front garden was such a mess this year (a long bout of 'flu in December) and about her dog Pom's bout of stomach trouble just after Christmas. He was better now, but easily irritated. (His name might well have afflicted him with a schizoid temperament.) It was the doorbell which finally shifted her, with the panic of one who has been caught in the act.

'Hello, Felicity, on the same errand, are we?'

This time it was the acid voice in the red coat. By the time Miss McCarthy had reached the gate, the new visitor had re-introduced herself as Mandy Bolsover.

85

Her errand was indeed the same. She left with Emily a book of Holbein prints, the place marked by a folded-up begging letter from the Save the Children Fund.

'I know the clothes are wrong, too rich, I mean, but it's the face. It's young and challenging and really very interesting, and I like the hat.'

Emily thanked her and put it with the others.

The phone rang as immediately as if it had been queuing for its turn.

'Ah, Mrs. Wakelin. I have Margaret Witherley-Bashe with me, and we have some things we wish you to see. Could you come round now, please.'

'Is that Lady Curran?'

'Yes.' Who else? seemed to be implied.

'Er, will it take long?'

'You have an appointment.'

'Yes, fairly soon.' The shopping was an appointment, wasn't it?

'Well, come now, while Margaret's here. You can always come back later for another look.'

Emily hurried through the courtyard, wondering whether it was better to shut her eyes or keep them wide open just in case.

Mrs. Mumford was hanging washing again. 'Hello. You're to go straight in.' This morning she was wearing high heels and a gold ankle chain.

They were not in the kitchen. She went into the lobby and through the glass door. Light flooded down the red staircarpet from the latticed window and seemed to mark a flarepath towards the half-open dining-room door. She pushed it tentatively. The room was empty.

Emily looked at the stairs, the door to the bed-drawing room and the heavy oak slab which closed off the entrance hall. All led to parts of the house she would rather not enter. Finally, after much swallowing and deep breathing she called out 'Hello?' and froze into apprehensive expectation that something would now come and get her. From upstairs came the sound of distant footsteps and the creak of floorboards. It walks out of the cupboard on the landing, but makes no noise. It is seen and felt, Mrs. Wakelin, not heard ...

'Is that you, Mrs. Wakelin.'

'Yes.'

'Come up, please.'

Her skirts whispered against the carved banisters and her hand slide silently up the polished handrail. The polish was dark in the grooves at the sides, and light in the centre where the hands of centuries had caressed it. She barely touched it in case she might find one of those hands still there. Her flat, soft-soled shoes pressed the thick carpet and occasionally aroused a creak beneath it, though she stepped lightly to keep such sounds to the minimum. But it is not heard, Mrs. Wakelin, it is felt and seen. As she climbed, the view from the latticed window came up like a lift and showed her first trees, then shrubs, then trim lawn and flowerbeds. She turned her back on the outside world and climbed again.

She stopped at the top because to go any further meant passing the cupboard on the left and the door was open. Then scrabbling sounds behind reassured her that it contained a human being, or at least Lady Curran or Mrs. Witherley-Bashe.

'Come here,' called Lady Curran's voice, and Emily obeyed her and walked round the door.

The cupboard was quite large. There was a wooden step which jutted out on to the landing and the door swung above it, carved and cracked and dulled with age. Within, the cavity was at least five feet deep and furnished with deal shelves covered with lining paper, browned to the colour of parchment. The shelves were full of bags and boxes and the sort of inconsequential driftwood which gets washed into the corners of houses when a family has been in residence for a long time. Lady Curran was pulling out dusty old pictures and handing them to Mrs. Witherley-Bashe who, as Emily arrived, was carting one away round the corner.

Lady Curran tugged at a cardboard box on the middle shelf and gathered it into her arms. She was wearing a green cotton twill fold-over overall such as hadn't been made since the invention of synthetics. Through the gap left on the shelf could be seen the outline of dusty panels and the dim shape of an entombed doorknob.

'Would you mind carrying this.'

87

The box was deposited against Emily's bosom, which was not protected by an overall but fortunately clothed in a loose, voluminous sweater which had soldiered unwounded through housework, gardening, do-it-yourself and both sorts of painting. Lady Curran picked up a dusty leather suitcase and a Safeways carrier bag and turned left up the step into the broad corridor. For a moment Emily stood still, then followed as quickly as possible, because if she had to be back in this horrible place, she wanted to be close to living people. Left again into the high panelled bedroom. Emily's whole body tensed.

The two women were spreading boxes, cases and paintings out on the checked dustsheet which covered the double bed, looking like a couple of very up-market chars. Mrs. Witherley-Bashe indicated where Emily should lay down her burden and smiled tightly at her. She was wearing an apron, a thick cardigan and a scarf around her head.

'We thought this would help you,' she said with great generosity. 'Mr. Curran very kindly said that you could go through the whole collection to see if there was anything of use.'

'What is it?' asked Emily, surveying the pile of objects and wedging herself into the corner between the bed and the wall so that at least it couldn't creep up behind her. Over there was the door behind the cupboard. It didn't look blocked. There was a handle and a keyhole, and the hinges weren't rusted or painted over. A fine crack showed all the way round, top, side and bottom; in fact the bottom crack was wide enough to allow a chink of light through from the landing.

It was cold in the room, although the smell of warm dust indicated that Lady Curran had turned on the first-floor radiators for the occasion.

'The house archives,' said Mrs. Witherley-Bashe, polishing the suitcase with a duster.

Emily took her hands away from the wall and tucked them under her arms, where no one could get at them.

'I don't quite understand,' she said, keeping her eye on the closed door. If it goes through there on to the landing, it must start from somewhere in this room. This was all here

88

when it was. Just at which point on this big, creaking floor does that figure start the walk which stops abruptly where the seventeenth century demolished the rest of the sixteenth? I wish I knew, then I'd make sure I was nowhere near it.

'Well, for the historical background, of course,' said Lady Curran rather sharply. 'Are you used to reading old documents.'

'No, I'm not.'

'Your Latin.'

'Non-existent. My school didn't teach it unless you were going in for medicine.'

'Oh dear.' She looked at Emily blankly. 'Well, I think we'll just have to sort out the things of the right period and then get George to go through them with you. He's pretty good at that sort of thing.'

I could do without that.

'Look, Lady Curran, I don't think this is going to be all that useful, you know. All I need is a simple account of what happened, like in Foxe, and then a rough idea of the sort of man Tappett was and I'm away.'

Lady Curran's face didn't change. Mrs. Witherley-Bashe's did. She smiled so hard that Emily felt sure it must be hurting her jaw. 'Mr. Curran insisted that you should be shown all the relevant papers,' she said. And so you bloody well will be, the smile said.

The air was so chilly that Emily had started to shiver. 'It's very kind of him, but I should be nervous of taking them out of the house when they're so valuable . . .'

'You may study them here,' said Lady Curran.

Emily shook her head, now miserably cold and wretchedly nervous. 'No,' she said firmly, 'it's very kind of you but I really don't need to. I can get any information I need on costume from pictures' (of which I am getting more and more every day, she thought), 'and the actual historical facts are just not necessary to me. I'm not writing a book.'

I wonder where he was going, and why? What was so important that he hurried from this room and out on to the landing and left that action imprinted in time for ever, like dinosaur footprints in a dried-up river bed?

'Not even the first hearing?' asked Mrs. Witherley-Bashe

89

indignantly. 'The very ink and parchment which was present in the room with him? His very words written down verbatim by the clerk, plus the questions and comments of the justice?'

'You've got that?' asked Emily with amazement.

'Of course,' said Lady Curran flatly. 'This is where Sir Jervase Lethaby lived, the man who was Mary's chief justice in this area. Didn't you know.'

'No.'

'Oh. Goodness. I thought everyone knew. It's mentioned in all the local histories,' she said, very nearly expressing displeasure. 'Well, when the Currans bought the house in the eighteenth century they took over the Lethaby papers too, plus those of another family which had lived here in between. We've always added our own things to them, and there used to be a family museum in one of the rooms upstairs, but unfortunately a lot of that disappeared during the war. We put it in the bank vault in the High Street and it got bombed, which was rather annoying. Fortunately the archives were looked after by the County Authorities, so they were all right.'

I wish I wasn't here. I wish I wasn't standing under a high, dusty, damp-stained plaster ceiling and noticing that some of the panelling is coming away because of mould underneath. I would very much like to be back in my studio in my own house, getting on with the work I love doing. How on earth can I get out of this before I start screaming?

'Look,' she said, 'I'm afraid I have to go now, like I told you. Is it possible for me to take the trial papers with me? I'd be extremely careful.'

'I don't know about that,' said Lady Curran, 'I'd have to ask my husband. And anyway, will you be able to read them. Wouldn't it be better if you came back for a whole day and had him read them out to you –'

Emily's head swam. She pushed herself away from the wall. 'I must go. Can I ring you about it?' She made for the door, both hands under her arms.

'Wait! This might help you.' Mrs. Witherley-Bashe was close behind her.

90

Emily was nearly at the door of the room. Mrs. Witherley-Bashe held a Windsor frame before her, the sort which has a cross at each corner and devout ivy crawling all round it on its knees. Latimer and Ridley stood back to back among waterlike flames in the market place at Oxford, their eyes cast up to heaven and the famous last words emerging from their mouths in balloons. 'Be of good cheer, Master Ridley ...'

'Yes, I know,' she said tersely, 'I know what happened to them, but you don't want me to actually embroider a scene like that, do you?'

'Oh no, I don't think that would be at all appropriate, especially with ecumenical relations being so much better these days, but I do think we should have a feeling of the power of the experience he underwent. In his eyes perhaps.'

'I doubt if anyone is artist enough to do that, and to convey the experience of being burned alive by the use of needle and thread is certainly way beyond my powers. You might as well ask me to reproduce that in cross-stitch,' she added with some force, pointing at the picture she'd noticed on her first visit.

The two women looked up at the long gilt frame and the print within. It might have been a Bosch, it was such a lovingly executed picture of hell. Tormentors, victims, gleeful ghouls looking on; ropes, knives and flames.

'It's the execution of the Gunpowder Plot people,' said Lady Curran. 'George bought it.'

'If you'll excuse my asking, whatever for?'

'Oh, because it's about Catholics and Protestants, like the bishops picture.' She made it sound like cowboys and Indians. 'He's always been interested in that.'

'But didn't it frighten the children?' asked Emily, thinking that it would have scared the wits out of her.

'Well, it's hung quite high. I don't suppose they noticed it until they were big enough not to be worried. Now are you going to take any of these things, Mrs. Wakelin, or shall we just sort out the ones you need and leave them here for when you come again.'

'Yes,' said Emily ambiguously, edging toward the door. 'I must go – goodbye.'

As she escaped she heard Mrs. Witherley-Bashe say quite

clearly, 'Well! You'd think she'd be more appreciative than that, wouldn't you? *So* insensitive.'

Emily had never felt more sensitive in her life. As she walked along the corridor she was remembering the last time she'd done it, and feeling what it had been like. Although she tried to turn her mind away from it, she relived with intense vividness the coldness of that grip upon her hand, and its refusal to allow her to proceed in the direction she wished to go. She relived the paralysis of her limbs and the agony of trying to move her feet.

The memory was enough to set her heart racing and her lungs panting. It seemed to take so many long seconds to get to the step, considering it was only about twenty feet from the bedroom door. She couldn't run, because the cupboard door was just round the corner and she didn't want to reach it, so she was caught between two fears, two terrifying places, two terrifyingly possible happenings. By the time she got to the step the tension of her memories had stretched her right hand out behind her and drawn her shoulders forwards as if dragging against it. She was shivering with cold and nerves and found the cold was most intense on her extended hand. She tried to pull the hand down and found it would not obey. She found that the remembered grip was now real and that she was being drawn back the way she had come.

'Let me go!' she screamed.

There was sudden silence in the bedroom, then a rush of sensibly-shot feet.

Lady Curran saw Emily's white face and strange attitude and immediately caught hold of her. With no trouble at all she took her down the step and across the divide between the centuries. Emily's legs buckled as they reached the landing and Lady Curran deposited her on a knobbly Jacobean chair covered in threadbare canvas embroidery and pushed her head down between her knees.

'Get the smelling salts, Margaret. In the bathroom cupboard.'

Smelling salts? thought Emily. There's no such thing nowadays ... and blacked out. She came to with a gasp, a choke and a cough. So that's what they smell like; you learn something new every day. A hand was still firmly pressed on to the back of her neck. She remained staring at the two pairs of feet and the red carpet for some time, then said faintly, 'I'm all right now.' The dominating pressure was released and she raised her head and lay back in the chair. Across the landing, the cupboard door yawned open.

'You must have some coffee,' instructed Lady Curran.

'I have to go.'

'You will have some coffee first.'

Mrs. Witherley-Bashe smiled patronisingly. 'There, you look much better now. Are you expecting a happy event, Mrs. Wakelin?'

'Of course she isn't, Margaret,' said Lady Curran. She pushed the cupboard closed as if it were just any old door in any old house.

Chapter Eight

'Where shall I put these books?' asked Mrs. Witherley-Bashe as they reached the bottom.

'On the dining table. We'll let George sort everything out this afternoon; it'll give him something interesting to do and take his mind off the Gulf.'

Mrs. Witherley-Bashe did as she was bidden and Lady Curran pointed Emily in the direction of the bed-drawing room.

'Oh, not in there,' begged Emily hastily. Lady Curran immediately turned her round and took her off in the opposite direction. At the kitchen door, the Woman met them with the vacuum cleaner.

'Ah, Mrs. Mumford, when you've done that we'll be ready for coffee, please. Come into the kitchen, Mrs. Wakelin. It was the hand again,' she told Emily, as they sat down at the table.

'Yes.'

'Did it frighten you.'

Emily's mouth nearly fell open. 'Yes.' She felt uneasy at such lack of perception, as if she was in the hands of someone not quite human.

'It's not important, you know. If you had just stood and waited a moment it would have gone.'

'Have you ever had it happen to you?' said Emily with a hint of accusation.

'No. It occasionally happened to my daughter and also I believe my sister-in-law, and one or two other people have experienced it when they were visiting. That's the

94

guest bedroom, you see.'

Emily's nervous fingers played with her hair.

'Well, I'm afraid that's the last time I go into the old part of the house.'

'But we've got all the papers out for you,' Lady Curran said, looking offended. 'They really are very interesting, and I should think it would be the quickest way of all to get to know Tappett. The dining room is perfectly all right, there's never been any trouble there at all,' she insisted as Emily sat there woefully unconvinced. She looked like a fayre ladye in distress, with her ruffled hair tumbling over her shoulders, her dark blue eyes wide with alarm and her excellent skin as red-and-white with agitation as any ideal Elizabethan beauty's.

'Did Mrs. Witherley-Bashe realise what was the matter with me?'

'Probably not.'

'But she knows about it, I suppose.'

'Oh, I expect she's heard the stories.'

'Haven't you told her it's true?'

'Why,' asked Lady Curran, looking blank. 'We know it is, so why should we bother to try and convince anyone else.'

What a pity people didn't look at creeds like that, thought Emily, then no one would have been martyred at all and I shouldn't be in this alarming situation.

It is difficult to decide how to spend the rest of a day in which one has been accosted by a ghost, especially if it is for the second time, and even more so if it seems probable that you will be subjected to further importunities in future.

After a certain amount of nervous fiddling around and a very scrappy lunch, Emily shut herself up in her studio among the familiar, much-loved tools and materials of her trade and started a sketch for the Windscreen picture. It came out looking like a dated sixties abstract which had hung in her school's needlework room, and she frowned, flicked over the page and drew the Christmas tree, with tip-tilted branches and a tall, angel-bowed apex.

If I do it in fur fabric I can draw out the pile into needles at the tips. Candles would be better than electric lamps, tall

95

white silk ones with the flames worked in lurex threads.

She had done that once on a pulpit fall and it had looked so realistic that the vicar told her he felt like warming his hands at it in the winter. Here comes a candle to light you to bed, and here comes a chopper to chop off your head. Which was at least better than death by fire. How could they walk out to death by fire with joy and praise on their lips and thanksgiving in their hearts? I could never do that, I love life and I'm afraid of pain. I suppose for them the world was hard and cruel and they were absolutely certain that the next one not only existed but was total everlasting bliss.

But at twenty-two. Any death at twenty-two, but that it should be that death . . .

The page flipped over again, abandoning the pretty-pretty tinsel of the modern winter solstice. Beneath her pencil, Walter Tappett started to materialise; first the whole figure, four-square, take me or leave me, then a close-up study of his face, very dark, very belligerent, very straight, what you see is what you get.

She studied him at arm's length, then turned another page and tried again. He had humour now, a slightly rueful twist of the lip which said: 'The world? Look at it. Religion? See what it's done to this lot. Who needs it?' A third try softened him and pushed him down the slope of conventional patient endurance into sentimentality. A fourth gave him the face of Barry, who emptied their dustbin every Wednesday, the fifth became Trevor Cummings who had taken down the ceiling of the studio. That certainly wasn't right – Trev was far too easy-going for a martyr. His form of courage would have been a smart turn in the direction of the nearest transport and a prompt and permanent disappearance.

She started working out the hands. They would have to be real, manual worker's hands, but how far did you take that? Broken nails? Bruises? Hairs on the backs? They emerged from her pencil half-closed ready to grasp his tools, then open against his jerkin, then clenched upon his hips. No, that was too aggressive, he looked as if he was spoiling for a fight, and he wasn't unless the other chap started it. All he had wanted was to be left alone.

She dropped the sketch-pad on to the table and reached

reluctantly for Foxe. If he could take it, the least she could do was to read about it.

'He was of low stature, with thoughtful features. His strength was great because of the rigours of his occupation, for he was a man of no education, earning his bread by the labour of his hands in the most menial of tasks, namely the cleansing of kennels and the sweetening of privies. It is said that he bore always the odour of his labours, which led to his being shunned by all men, save on the Lord's Day, when he put off his labouring garments and repaired to the church, where he listened earnestly to the teaching of the good Master Watkins, who had been placed in his living by the Lord Protector Somerset himself.'

Emily suspected that a fair gap had still been left around Walter Tappett among the poor at the back of the church. A mere change of clothes wouldn't have made much difference to a man who never took a bath.

'Yet on the death of the saintly and much lamented King Edward the Sixth, when the blasphemous idolatry of the mass was restituted, Tappett shortly after began to absent himself from service. He was several times admonished but still continued his abstinence, saying he could not believe that bread and wine made by the hands of working men such as he could be the Lord who dwelt in heaven. How, he said, could the Lord Jesus' body be in both places at the same time, and how could so much bread and wine be made from the body of one man?'

That was fighting talk. Down-to-earth logic usually caused a certain amount of uncomfortable squirming when applied to mystical belief, but while Mother Church was moderately indulgent about debate among her prelates and scholars, her answer to her lowlier inquiring children was always the same; because I say so.

And even among the inheritors of the Reformation, that tremendous upheaval which had shaken up theology and the interpretation of Scripture from one end of Europe to the other, any eventual winner in the How-to-be-Right stakes, no matter how short their triumph or how small their territory, finished up engaging in the same altercation.

How do you know it is so?

Because the Bible tells me.

How do you know the Bible is right?

Because it is the word of God.

He wrote it with his own hand?

He inspired it into the minds of holy men who wrote it down for him.

Supposing they wrote it down wrong. Supposing whoever copied it afterwards didn't like some of it and changed it. *Supposing the Bible is no longer exactly as God wrote it?*

And no matter that their freedom had been won by open debate and individual thought, in every sect Mother Church's hand came down in sharp, stinging rebuke. Blasphemy! Blasphemy! Away with him! Kill! Burn! Crucify! Anything but think.

She worked on through the afternoon, wrestling with the problem of Walter Tappett's appearance. His features began to fade before her eyes, and her head leaned further and further over the paper. Eventually she remembered the existence of the lamp above her desk and worked on beneath its flood of light. She found a pose which pleased her, squared it up and transferred it to a large sheet of cartridge paper. Now the paints, the broad washes of suggested colour and there he was at last, three feet high and leaning forward from the shoulders, one hand held out palm upwards in an attempt to reason with his questioners, the other resting easily on his belt. His eyes met hers and said 'What a much ado about nothing this all is. I'm not saying they're wrong, am I? All I say is that I can't believe it. What's wrong with that?'

Which was very innocent of him. No, he couldn't have been innocent, not in those times, when those who didn't conform died horribly in public. He was just very, very obstinate and very, very brave.

'I like you,' she told him.

'Suit yourself,' said Walter's expression.

She returned to Foxe and re-read parts of it.

'Then said the bishop with exceeding displeasure, "What think you that you outface these wise and godly men who wish only to save you from perdition? Should you not fall down and kiss their garments for their great goodness in struggling for your miserable soul?"

'"Nay," said Tappett, "I thank them right heartily, but shall courtesy to men absolve me of falsehood to God?"

'"Without repentance, nothing can absolve you of the grievous hurt you do God's church."

'"I hurt no man, but ye imprison, torment and kill. Which of us then obeys God's commandment that we should love one another?"

'"Still you cling to your blindness," cried the priest. "You are damned."

'"Nay," said Walter, "I know my blindness, but because you say you see, therefore are you the more blind."

'So when he was brought to the place where he should suffer, the priest said to him, "Recant and return to God's church, as the sole means of salvation instituted by its Master."

'"By my faith," said he, "with servants such as ye, I doubt if your master is one I could be happy with. I shall go trusting in the merits of the Lord Jesus, and he will entreat God for me. No man can know all Truth until he meet it face to face."

'Thereupon they lit the fire.'

Emily closed the book. She didn't want another read of the gory details Foxe went in for – it wasn't going to make the slightest difference to how she depicted Tappett. Her concern was the living man, not the tortured, half-dead body.

John came home when she had only just started to cook. She had been longing to unburden her second unpleasant experience upon him, but the sight of his face thrust it immediately out of her mind.

'What is it?' she asked, putting her arms about him.

'One of our clients has got into a diabolical mess with the U.S. Government. I've got to go over tomorrow and try to sort it out.'

'What, flying? Suppose there's a terrorist attack?' she said anxiously.

'Yes, I had thought of that,' he said, quite sharply. 'Thanks for the reminder.'

It was so unlike him.

'Sorry. Look, it almost certainly will be all right, there haven't been any of the things people were expecting yet, have there, it's all been in the Middle East itself. If you really have to go, then we'll both have to grin and bear it.'

'I'd have preferred you to leave out the almost.'

'It would have been a lie,' she said.

The firm arranged an executive jet from Stansted the next morning, so John didn't have to fly off to the States in the sinister milieu of a nearly empty 747 which might have a bomb or a hijacker on board.

Emily went into the studio and studied Walter by the early morning light. She still liked him. He looked human, straightforward and as obstinate as a mule.

She gave the house a quick tidy and clean, trying not to dwell on the fact that she would be sleeping there alone for at least two days. When they were still living in her old flat she was able to switch off mentally and return to her single life when John went away, but this cottage she had only known with him in it. His nocturnal absence would be as obvious and disconcerting as the loss of a door or a wall.

She washed up and cleaned the sink with the light on. As she rubbed the china, she raised her head in her habitual gesture and gazed at the pattern of the closed curtains instead of at the house next door. She put out her hand to draw them, then left them alone. The water circled gurgling down the waste pipe, the sink was wiped round and she looked up to find her glance still blocked. She polished the cutlery and put it into its drawer, and dried the china and carried it to the dresser, and when she returned to rub down the draining board her eyes still went up to be stayed on white convolvulus and purple knapweed. She swept the floor and tipped the dust into the bin beneath the sink, and rose up with glance ready to meet the spying windows of Holly House, and to focus on where the light burned.

She sighed, reached out and drew one curtain back.

'Good morning,' she said, 'you're a hulking brute of a building, aren't you? I suspect you've got more nasty secrets than any decent, self-respecting house ought to have.'

The phone rang.

100

'Ah, Mrs. Wakelin, you are not busy.'

'Well yes, actually I am, Lady Curran. I'm cleaning the kitchen.'

'You will be finished by eleven. We have put the papers out for you and George is up specially early. He's very much looking forward to it.'

'I have quite a lot to do today,' said Emily politely, unwilling to give offence. 'Perhaps tomorrow.'

'He has already had his shower and his breakfast. I can't change his routine again. Come round at eleven. Goodbye.'

The morning was still dull by eleven, and Holly House looked even less inviting beneath grey clouds and in a spiteful, pushy wind. The gate snatched itself out of her hand with the clang of a cage door, and the dead holly leaves came at her like a swarm of wasps. She hurried down the path beside the house and waited for nearly a minute in the ugly but blessedly modern lean-to, trying to find the courage to start her journey back through time. Mrs. Mumford answered her knock, today in a pink chenille top, black leggings, high heels and three gold chains.

'Hello, he's all ready for you,' she said, staring curiously as she closed the door behind her. 'You like all this old-fashioned stuff, do you?'

'Sometimes,' said Emily, walking slowly into the nineteenth century.

'I like your skirt,' said Mrs. Mumford, following her and eyeing the brilliant woollen fabric which flowed behind Emily's tall, graceful body like exotic plumage. 'Where did you get it?'

'A friend printed it.'

'Did she? She must be clever. Do you think she'd do one for me?'

Emily wrote down the name and address at the huge kitchen table and gave a helpful description of the sort of fabrics Albie Keith produced, while suggesting the possible cost of individually designed, hand-printed textiles with a note of apology.

'Oh, that's all right,' said Mrs. Mumford dismissively, 'I

spent nearly that much on a suit last week, and it wasn't half as nice as that. I reckon I deserve nice things, the way I work. You better go, then, he's waiting for you in the dining room.'

The lantern was out in the eighteenth-century lobby, and the cloudy, windy day glimmered inadequately through the fanlight and whistled efficiently through the letterbox. The glass door seemed heavier than usual, perhaps because she was pushing it with less enthusiasm.

The staircase awaited a few yards beyond, confronting her, inviting her, willing her to climb it. She knocked at the dining room door. To her alarm there was no answer and she felt the stairs almost seem to draw closer. She knocked more urgently and called 'Hello?' Still no response, and the mere presence of that access to the rest of the house was so oppressive at her back that she opened the door and went in, manners or no.

Mr. Curran was asleep in his dressing gown beside the table, all ready for his treat. He was cushion-propped in his big wing chair as usual, with rug tucked round his foot-stooled legs and his pale hair neatly brushed above his silk stock, but his head lolled back with open mouth and his long, thin hands lay exhausted in his lap. The effort of early rising had caught up with him. Emily closed the door quietly and walked over to the long, oaken table with bulbous legs and stretchers the size of floor joists. On it were several leather-bound books and a dusty pile of documents tied up with tapes and encumbered with seals. As Mr. Curran showed no sign of waking for the moment she sat down at the table and opened one of the books. The red-brown powder of decomposing leather stained her fingers like ancient blood and scattered over the polished wood. She took a tissue out of her bag and cleaned up carefully, then kept it between her fingers as she turned the pages.

To an untrained eye, the writing was pretty well impossible. It was small, cramped, curly, and often rose up towards the right-hand corner of the vellum pages. Notes were written in the margins, some words were in red ink which had faded to beige, and even dates were more like shorthand, with lower case Roman numerals bent and twisted into artistic illegibility. Sometimes there were pages of poetry or quotations in Latin (she could tell it was Latin by occasional words like *et*, *sum* or *hic*.) There was one long passage headed by a title so large that the words even triumphed over the penmanship which crowded in on them, and called 'The History of Saint Edmund'. A few pages on was 'The Story of King Arthur' – not all of it by any means, possibly just the bit about the founding of the Round Table, from the full roster of knights' names which seemed to be present. It was a funny collection altogether, almost like an anthology or a commonplace book.

She closed it and pushed it away from her, trailing rosy dust behind it. She picked up a folded document which resisted her with grim determination. Even when opened it continually tried to leap back into its folds, like a recalcitrant umbrella. She tried again and caught a glimpse of black letters screaming 'THIS INDENTURE . . .' before the vellum snapped out of her hands with a sound like a pistol shot.

Mr. Curran woke with a start and thrust one skinny hand out as if he was trying to stop someone from leaving. He gasped for a couple of seconds, then saw her sitting on the other side of the table in the light from the lamp in the corner, her brown curly hair lit up by an aureole, her eyes wide with embarrassment, her large silver earrings glinting against her cheeks and the soft violet of her shawl setting off her colouring.

'A Pre-Raphaelite,' he said. 'Have you been told you belong with The Brotherhood?'

'Yes,' said Emily, smiling more with amusement than with gratitude for the compliment. She had been told so often that the remark now provoked giggles or even irritation rather than blushes.

'I see you have started without me. What have you been reading?'

'Well, I couldn't actually read any of it properly. What's this book here? It seems to be all bits and pieces.'

His face came alive and he drew the book towards him with some effort, taking no notice at all of the stains on his fingers which he gradually transferred to the pages as he turned them.

'This is the Lethaby Red Book. It's a sort of family scrapbook kept for at least a hundred years and left behind in the house when it was sold in the middle of the seventeenth century. The last Lethaby was killed in the Civil War, fighting for Charles the First. A lot of old families had books like these; stories, anecdotes, accounts, memoranda, genealogy, quotations from literature, anything at all they found interesting.'

'Is there something about Walter Tappett in there, then?'

'There is,' he said, smiling with pleasure and trying to tip the heavy book up so that he could read it. The effort was beyond him. 'Emily, would you please prop this with another book so I can see it? I'm afraid it is a little too heavy for me nowadays.'

She did as he asked her, wiping the leather dust off her fingers again with the tissue, though stains still remained.

'Now you look more like Lady Macbeth,' he said, 'though I really cannot imagine you with real blood on your hands. Now then, the item I want to show you is here, on page fifty-seven. It's a memorandum of the execution of Tappett at Braintree. Several of the Lethabys went and one of them wrote it up afterwards.'

'How disgusting of them,' said Emily, 'I'm not sure I want to hear it. I've already gone into all that in Foxe.'

'Oh, have you? Not a book I would have expected to find on your bookshelves.'

'Mrs. Witherley-Bashe lent it to me.'

'Oh, yes, that I can believe. It's probably her bedside book.'

'Don't you like her?' asked Emily with interest.

'I find her fascinating,' he said, grinning like a mischievous faun. 'Such remarkable self-regard. Such complete confidence in her own worth. How fortunate to be like that. She must never feel real pain, merely irritation. I can see her attending a burning with a comfortable sense of moral duty, can't you?'

'I hope not,' said Emily unhappily, 'I should hate to think that of anyone. I should find it horrible myself, and I can't believe others wouldn't too.'

He nodded sympathetically. 'Yes, I'm sure *you* would, you're such a tender-hearted person.'

'I'm not a saint, you know,' Emily said with a sudden rush of distress. 'You keep on saying how good I am, and I'm not, I've got faults just like everyone else.' It wasn't fair to be persistently labelled as good, beautiful, kind, loving, etcetera, etcetera, all the nice things which people wanted to see incarnated in the world, and which they decided she was suitable to embody and symbolise, like a kind of talisman. It somehow set them free to enjoy their own faults with lessened guilt if there was an Emily to do the goodness for them. In this case, Mr. Curran seemed to think that her unwillingness to think really badly of Mrs. Witherley-Bashe made it all right for him to slag her off with a free conscience.

'I beg your pardon,' he said immediately, the perfect gentleman mode returning, 'I have been most impertinent. Let us return to our task. So you do not wish me to read the whole account?'

'No.'

He nodded. 'Very well, but I think you might be interested in one passage which differs quite significantly from Foxe. You will remember that he describes Walter as holding out his arms in the fire and saying that he denounced the Mass and died firm in the Protestant faith? Well, according to this, it wasn't like that at all. In fact any really rabid Protestants who were there must have been pretty shocked by what he said, that is if they got near enough to hear it. A fire that size must have made a lot of noise.'

'Was Foxe there?'

'No, he was in Basle, but he was given his information by refugees who joined him and from witnesses he sought out when he returned to England after Mary's death. He sometimes gives the names, but in this case he just cites a gentleman who was standing by. Anyway, whoever it was, it wasn't the Lethabys, and this is what they say.' He put on his glasses and leant over the book. Emily steeled herself to hear more unpleasant, ugly, cruel things.

' "Whereupon, the fire being lit, one cried out from the crowd, 'Nay, Walter, thou shalt smell worse soon than thou ever didst in thy life!' " '

105

'Oh God!' said Emily, full of disgust.

' "And he cried back at him, 'If I have offended only thy nose while I lived, it is of no great moment. Yet I cry thee pardon for it.' " I would say that was pretty remarkable, wouldn't you?'

'Yes,' said Emily dully.

' "Then the priest took issue with him for his levity and bade him recant even now. 'No,' said he, 'for there is no salvation in priests or in creeds, or in bells and books, for all these things can be consumed as I shall be consumed. Put not faith in creeds, for what they do to men is of the Devil, not God. Men but catch at the Truth here below, but now I go to grasp it.' And thus saying, the blasphemer was engulfed by the flames and entirely consumed." There,' he said, taking off his glasses, 'not a word about Protestantism, just a thoroughly fed-up common man shouting, "A plague on both your houses", and giving all religion the forked fingers.'

'Well, that certainly reinforces the picture I have of him.'

'Now here's the transcript of the first hearing before Jervase Lethaby, the local justice, held in this very house,' he said, reaching for another book with difficulty. Emily helped him.

'Which room?' she asked, her mouth suddenly dry.

'We don't know exactly, but very probably one of the front bedrooms. It is my opinion and that of one or two architects I have had here, that the whole of the first floor in the sixteenth-century block was one Great Chamber, used for entertaining, business, anything which involved large gatherings of people, and that it was only divided up as it is now in the eighteenth century, when the Currans did a big modernisation. Just think of all the occasions which took place in that room, Emily, doesn't it thrill you? I sometimes try to imagine the people who lived in this house going about their business. And I particularly like to think of Walter Tappett, standing upstairs in front of Lethaby and his private Inquisition, showing them what good sense and human dignity were all about.'

'Do you think that's wise?' asked Emily, looking at the

106

great brick fireplace and being aware of the stone hall behind it, and the erstwhile Great Chamber above that, and remembering with a keen shock the invisible denizen trying to restrain her from leaving the remains of its altered but still existing home.

'Why should I bother about wisdom?' he said strongly. 'I've been like this for years, Emily, and the only excitement I have left is what I can create in my own mind. If I care to people my house with phantoms why shouldn't I?'

'But I thought you'd never seen anything?'

'I haven't, but that doesn't mean I'm not aware that there's something here, and that my awareness probably feeds it.'

'Forgive me for saying so, Mr. Curran, but this is all rather different from what you told me before. I got the impression that you didn't bother about your − happenings − at all, and that none of you took any notice of them, even the children. Now I get the impression that it's very important to you indeed.'

He sat back in his chair and put his head on one side. 'Would you be kind enough to turn on the television?' he said after a few seconds.

Emily did as she was told, walking over to the large set in the corner, her glowing skirts brushing against the stone arch of the fireplace like one of his imaginary phantoms. The picture came up on the screen, of planes and explosions and soaring plumes of black smoke, of a million men waiting to fight what might be Armageddon in the hot sands of the Mesopotamian desert.

'Look at that, Emily,' he said with irony. 'Look at the world and the people in it. What do I want with all that? But in this house, I am the master. Don't be misled by my wife; she is her own woman, but her breeding has taught her that a family house is under the control of men. I believe that the masters of Holly House are still here, and that when I die I shall still be here too. So the happenings here don't concern me at all, if by concern you mean frighten. I accept them, indeed you could say I expect them. This house is a commonplace book in itself, and I am just one of the latest pages. Why should I be afraid of the

others, even if some of them carry stories like this?' He
pointed at the examination of Walter Tappett which now
lay open before him.

'Now,' he said with enthusiasm, 'let us begin.'

Chapter Nine

It was unpleasant. Quite apart from the abuse and the bullying and the self-righteous homilies and the sort of religious attitudes which made Emily want to cry out that they were horribly, damnably wrong, Lethaby's patience was practically nonexistent and his temper on a very short fuse, so that he eventually tried to hurry things along. Curran insisted on reading the lot and she sat with pale, still face and hands clasped in her lap, trying not to let her emotions get too close to the terrible scene.

Tappett gave as good as he got at first, with dour one-liners which came straight to the point, but having had his say he reverted to silence. That Lethaby had a handy pair of thumbscrews in his pocket which he instructed one of the officials present to apply, was not what one expected from a man in his own home, and although it quickly caused Walter to break his silence it elicited no further useful words. It was a nasty, brutish business all through, showing mankind at its most unattractive, not least in the closing words of the clerk.

'He continuing obstinate, despite the earnest appeals of the Justice to open his heart to the Love of Christ, he was borne away to the Bishop's prison, where His Grace may well better prevail with him, by the Mercy of God.'

Emily saw Walter being dragged across the still-extant floor and down long-demolished stairs with the blood running from his broken thumbs and his captors lecturing him about love and mercy.

'They did a more professional job on him later, of course,

109

but he never gave in. He must have been strong, because he still managed to walk up on to the pyre.' Emily looked miserably at her hands, imagining blood spurting from the fingertips.

Afterwards he showed her the documents, not because they were to do with Tappett, but because they illustrated the families which had owned Holly House, especially his own. In turn they bought it, lived in it and sold it, or in the case of the Currans, stayed in it for two hundred years.

Lady Curran appeared in scarf and Burberry at ten to one, back from the shops and coffee with friends.

'Ah! You haven't gone yet. I met Margaret Witherley-Bashe in Safeway's, she's been trying to get you on the telephone. You'd better ring her as soon as you get home.'

Emily did as she was told, and quickly picked up the quivering vibration of offended dignity in Mrs. Witherley-Bashe's voice.

'I have received a letter from your "agent",' she said, making it sound as if she was holding the word in her fingertips and at arm's length. 'She has quoted a figure for the wall-hanging and I must say I find it rather more than I expected.' She paused, waiting for Emily to apologise. Emily did not.

'Yes?' she said.

'Yes. This is not a cathedral, or a large prosperous suburban parish, and our means are limited. I don't suppose you've had a chance to talk to your – er – representative about this properly, and the fact that it is in your own parish, so I thought perhaps we should get together and come to an arrangement between us.' She paused again, waiting for Emily to murmur that well, yes, perhaps that would be an idea.

'I don't handle that side of things at all, that's what an agent is for, but there's nothing to stop you ringing her and discussing it. Her number will be on the letter.'

'But I really don't want to do this at one remove,' said Mrs. Witherley-Bashe, beginning to sound irritable, 'it's not what I have been used to with parish affairs.'

'Well, in that case, you would probably be much happier with parishioners doing the whole project, and if you decide to withdraw your offer to me, I shall quite understand. If you could let me know before I do any more work on it, it will only cost you the price of the drawing I've made.'

'Oh, you've done a drawing?' said Mrs. Witherley-Bashe with sudden interest. 'Bring it round for me to see.'

'When is the next committee meeting?'

'Two o'clock this afternoon, but perhaps I should take a look first.'

'I'll come over to the church at two, then. Goodbye.'

Emily indulged in a laughing, leaping, swirling-skirted dance round the living room, hopping over stools and scuffing rugs until the thought of John in possible danger sobered her. She switched on the television. No bad news from America, thank God, but the Persian Gulf was choked by an oil slick which covered three hundred and fifty square miles, and the million men were ready for the mother of battles to begin.

Miss Barton looked almost frightened. She stared at Mrs. Witherley-Bashe with her lower lip clasped between steadying teeth. Mrs. Lake put her head to the left, pressed her forefinger to her upper lip and changed the angle of her head to the right.

Mrs. Gage drew in her breath with an excited gasp.

'Well, well,' said Mrs. Bolsover with surprise.

Mrs. Witherley-Bashe seemed to be having a sort of seizure, which started with an increased rate of breathing, went on to sniffing, set her hands pulling her cardigan straight and fiddling with the papers on the table, and finally jerked her head back to stare at a skyed, fly-spotted photograph of a former vicar, as one who would say: 'I might have known.' The smile burst out.

'Yes, well, I've no doubt you've done your best, Mrs. Wakelin, but I'm afraid your style is not what we are looking for. As a modernist and a towndweller you cannot help being ignorant of our traditions and standards, and I am sorry to have to disappoint you but – '

'I like it,' said Mrs. Bolsover, her acid voice burning straight through Mrs. Witherley-Bashe's wall of sound and

111

allowing the other members of the committee to force their way unto the breach.

'I think it's wonderful!' breathed Mrs. Gage. 'So alive, so virile!'

'He's the right age, and quite good-looking,' said Mrs. Lake doubtfully, 'but I'm not sure about the clothes.'

'It's totally unsuitable,' said Mrs. Witherley-Bashe firmly, her voice rising. 'He looks as if he's about to grab one by the collar. How can a priest celebrate the sacrament before someone who looks as if he's about to step down and argue with him?'

'The vicar will not be celebrating the sacrament *for* Walter Tappett, or *for* any other human being,' said Mrs. Gage sharply, 'this is not a High Church and it wouldn't be the right place for Walter if it were.'

'I said *before* him, Mrs. Gage.'

'What about the colours?' Mrs. Lake said, stepping back with her eyes half closed. 'Are you really going to have him all in shades of brown and grey? It won't go with the rest of the chapel furnishings, will it?'

'I could introduce some blue,' said Emily helpfully, 'perhaps his undergown showing at the neck and wrists.'

'And where will the gold and sequins go?' asked Miss Barton timidly, wrinkling her brow as if she was really trying to understand.

'I don't think they would be appropriate.'

'But you can't have a church hanging without a bit of glitter, can you? It wouldn't be reverent.'

'He wouldn't have *approved* of that sort of reverence,' Mrs. Gage said excitedly. 'All that glitter and show was what he and his fellow martyrs were against. They wanted the plain, simple truth in a plain, simple church.'

'Yes, well, I think they took that a little far. There's hardly an intact corbel in the place.'

'There's no need to be facetious, Mrs. Bolsover,' said Mrs. Witherley-Bashe firmly, turning her back on Mrs. Gage as if she had completely disappeared. 'No, I'm sorry, the whole concept is wrong. We must have some indication of saintliness and holiness and this just makes him look like anyone brought in off the street.'

112

'But he *was* just brought in off the street,' said Mrs. Gage, tenaciously continuing to address Mrs. Witherley-Bashe's back, 'an enormous number of the Marian martyrs were. That's what's so amazing about them and the way they behaved. Somehow with the priests and bishops you tend to feel that holy heroism was no more than could be expected of them, though that's quite unfair, of course – I mean they felt pain just like everyone else ...'

'I'm sorry, ladies, but as chair of the committee I must insist that either we reject Mrs. Wakelin's design and try elsewhere, or that she agrees to modify it quite radically. I see no reason why his clothing should not be done in a soberly coloured damask, with perhaps a touch of black velvet as trimming and a little gilt lacing on his doublet. And we must ask you to redraw the hands, they look like a prize fighter's.'

'Well how do you expect them to look, when he spent his life shovelling?' demanded Mrs. Gage, getting red in the face and giving the impression that she might shortly come to the boil. 'And when you say we, Mrs. Witherley-Bashe, I presume you don't mean the committee, because at least one of us doesn't agree with you at all.'

'I am well aware, Mrs. Gage, that you disagree with me about most things on principle,' said Mrs. Witherley-Bashe, setting her smile to the sticking place, 'but I don't feel I'm wrong in keeping socialism out of religion.'

'Before this conversation gets just plain silly, I suggest we take a vote,' said Mrs. Bolsover impatiently. 'We can argue the details out later, but let's start by determining whether *on the whole*,' she said forcefully and meaningfully, 'we are in favour of Mrs. Wakelin's concept and are willing to take it as our basis. I presume you don't mind just a few changes, Mrs. Wakelin?'

'Not a bit,' said Emily, 'as long it's what you all want.'

'Very well,' said Mrs. Witherley-Bashe, running her smile up the mast again before having another little fit with her breathing, her hands and her appeal to the dead vicar. 'All those in favour of rejecting Mrs. Wakelin's design completely.'

Her hand went up, followed by that of Miss Barton, and

113

the chairwoman's glance now lighted upon Mrs. Lake.

'If he could just have his shirt neck open – '

'He is not a pin-up, Jean,' snapped Mrs. Witherley-Bashe, 'and his gown is too short already. Do let us have some sense of decency.'

Mrs. Lake's flustered hand rose about ten inches, then as her cheeks grew red she let it down again on to the table and started rotating her rings with a detached, far-away expression.

Mrs. Witherley-Bashe waiting a few seconds then put her hand down with ladylike calm.

'All those in favour of accepting Mrs. Wakelin's design as a start,' she said.

Mesdames Gage, Bolsover and Lake raised their hands in unison.

There were several more arguments before the alterations were decided on, mostly concerned with colour scheme and modification to dress, but when the meeting broke up Emily was feeling puzzled that there had been no mention of the vicar and his wishes on the subject. It had been her experience that the whole flavour of a church and parish was set by the incumbent, his character, his theology, and most particularly the altitude of his liturgy, and it would be a complete waste of time to embark on the actual embroidery before obtaining his approval.

She broached the subject with Mrs. Lake as they crossed the transept, which was today occupied by a plumber filling in last week's hole and a plasterer tidying up after the removal of a charity board, which leant against the Lethaby tomb and shut the recumbent effigies in like an old-fashioned sleeping car. Mrs. Lake looked understanding.

'All in good time, Mrs. Wakelin. We'll let you know when the moment is appropriate.'

Which meant that Emily left the church more than a little mystified. She looked across the churchyard to the extremely charming old vicarage which sat stoically under the tower and endured the clamorous noise of the bells several times a week. The windows were closely shut and there was a thread of smoke rising from one of the chimneys. The winter garden bore only a carpet of early snowdrops on the lawn, but the bare stems tied to the house's walls promised a summer garment of rambling roses.

Emily pinned out a long roll of cartridge paper to receive the full-sized, detailed working drawing, picked up her pencil and went rapidly into the creative artist's semi-hypnosis, in which time and the world disappear from the consciousness and only the work in hand is real.

Now then, the top garment a bit longer, say to the knee. 'More dignified, Mrs. Wakelin; we really don't want quite so much leg showing in sacred surroundings!'

Mrs. Lake had looked as if she wouldn't have minded.

She worked through her cupboards and boxes, sorting out samples of thread, braids and fabrics. She put them together on the table and tried one against the other, searching for contrast and match, for combinations which merged or jarred or set each other off. Occasionally she glanced at the prone drawing and met its eyes.

There, that's the right blue, not ultramarine and Madonna-ish, not lavender and sweetly pretty, a good, no-nonsense Prussian blueish serge, such as a working man might have worn for Holy days, if he possessed best clothes at all. She picked up the bundle of tapestry wool samples Mrs. Witherley-Bashe had given her and held them against it. Not quite right, really. But if she used the colour of the backing blue for the shaded portions of the garment, the underside of his arm, for instance, and the place where his overgown bowed outwards slightly above his belt, that would tie things together.

She held the serge fabric against a piece of russet brown evenweave linen. Not bad, but a bit too tasteful. No, it had to be something really coarse-woven. She was going to forget the whole churchy thing and use hessian and leather, and perhaps stitch his hair in raffia. She met his eyes again.

'It's not you, is it?' she asked, though not really believing it. 'You're too sensible to be a ghost, aren't you? I bet when you got to the other side, you shook hands with your guardian angel, or whoever, and said, "Right, show me where to go," and never looked back again.'

115

His eyes told her nothing. 'What do *you* think?' they said.

By the time the outline was laid down and the details of hands, buttons, lacings, features were emerging from faint pencil into firm, inked lines, the sun was down for hours, the studio lights were on and Emily's stomach had started to complain.

She eased her back, which she hadn't even noticed aching before, and went downstairs, turning on lights as she went. The watchful light of Holly House shone into the dark kitchen until she wiped it out with curtains and her own illumination. She took her meal in front of the television and found nothing much improved.

Upstairs again – all right Walter, you'll do. She made a shopping list of things which would not be obtainable from Mrs. Hubbard and worked out the amount of materials she would require.

John rang just before she went to bed. It was, he said wearily, six o'clock in the evening and he had been rushing round seeing people all day, none of whom were at all pleased with his client or inclined to give him the benefit of any doubt whatsoever. The government agencies were being particularly po-faced and standing on their principles like the authors of the Declaration of Independence. He had had more than enough for one day. 'I wish I was just going to get into bed with you,' he said wistfully.

'So do I. How much longer do you think it'll take?'

'Em, I've really no idea. What are you doing with yourself?'

'I've started that hanging for Little Hocking Church, you know, the local martyr.'

'Oh, that's convenient isn't it? Just across the road.'

'Well, it's not, really – I've got everyone breathing down my neck, and the Currans keep summoning me to their presence in a way I'm beginning to resent. It seems funny to think that only two weeks ago I'd have done anything to set foot inside that house.'

'Any more problems? Ghostly ones, I mean.'

'Everything's fine,' she said, sidestepping and saving him

116

more nail-biting. 'I'm going into London tomorrow to buy things for the hanging.'

'Watch out for bombs!' he warned.

She went into the studio for a final look at Walter Tappett. He lay full-length and full-sized on the table, his eyes upon her, his hand reaching out. For a dreadful moment, he appeared to be on the rack. And she was so cowardly she couldn't even face something as powerless as a creaking floorboard. She wasn't worthy to take on the depiction of this man. Even her imagination wasn't up to understanding his motives, his feelings or his ordeal.

She turned the light out on him and took her inadequacy to bed, immersing herself in a novel she knew from experience would cheer her up. The healthy catharsis of laughter managed to keep her mind from dwelling on her next-door neighbour and gave her a good night.

She awoke at the usual dark, unearthly hour in the morning which was necessary to get John to work and immediately made her first visit to the studio to stand before the drawing of Walter Tappett.

'I'm a reasonable man,' he said patiently, 'and I'm not making waves. Why pick on me?'

She washed, dressed and went down to make breakfast. It was still dark outside and the kitchen bathed luxuriously in warm electric light, though the red of sunrise was just beginning to glow through the window on to the garden. She lifted a curtain and saw the single light burning within the lurking black mass of Holly House. It wasn't those stairs, but in the same space they occupied. That was where he came down sick with agony, across the stone hall and through the front door, off to the bishop's prison and the hell over which his grace presided.

She dropped the curtain and turned on the radio, but once the rosy sun was strong enough to fill the kitchen with cheerfulness, she drew both curtains right back and stared defiantly at the house while she washed up and sang along. The light was off now, and the latticed seventeenth-century windows winked red lights at her. A little craning brought the blocked first-floor mullions into her view, blackpainted as if to stop her spying on the outrage taking place within —

as if she'd have wanted to. On the floor above the smaller mullions were crumbling and one lattice was cracked and patched with cardboard. The piece was shaped remarkably like a head looking down, although she knew perfectly well it was not. Her eyes slid back over the patched pargetting to the head sticking out of the plaster. It could have been anyone, with its blunted features and shoulder-length hair; male or female, malign or benign, holy or secular. It was yet another example of folk memory, like coins in water, that heads should be stuck on walls; from decapitated heads on thatched huts to stone masks outside long houses, from gods' faces on Roman villas to gargoyles on cathedrals, from Coade stone corbels on the porches of Victorian ter-raced villas to Smiley faces chalked on modern walls.

Emily parked her car at Braintree Station and bought an Awayday ticket.

She boarded the waiting train and found Miss Barton and Miss McCarthy farther down the same carriage. They turned and informed each other of her presence, then raised gloved hands and invited her to join them with eager smiles.

'Hello, Mrs. Wakelin, we're having a day's shopping in Oxford Street,' said Miss McCarthy, her voice conveying extreme distress which Emily reminded herself was only apparent. 'Miss Barton has been telling me about your design for the wall hanging. It's quite *modern*, I believe.'

'Well, not really, in fact it's completely naturalistic.'

'But no gilt or beading anywhere!' exclaimed Miss Barton. 'I do think that's daring. Still, I expect you'll put a nice gold fringe on it, and the lettering could be sequined, couldn't it? What has she told you about that?'

No need to ask who 'she' was. 'It hasn't been mentioned. You remember the discussion was all about the figure itself yesterday.'

'She wants "Blessed are ye poor", she told me the other day,' wobbled Miss McCarthy. 'It doesn't seem quite right to me, and I'm not sure the vicar will think so, either. Still,' she shrugged, 'I suppose she ought to know what he'll let her get away with.'

'She'll get her way even if he doesn't like it,' said Miss

118

Barton, looking resigned. 'You'll have to know soon, won't you, Mrs. Wakelin?'

'Well, it can wait a week or two. I shall be busy with the figure for a long time, and won't be laying it on the actual background until it's finished.'

When Emily returned to Liverpool Street in the evening, newspaper posters were announcing the first land battle at Khafzi.

At Braintree, she was putting her packages into the flamboyantly individual Volkswagen when a large, middle-aged man in a pinstripe suit flung his briefcase into the Renault three cars along.

'Did you paint that yourself?' he called, grinning all over his fleshy face.

'No, I bought it from a friend,' she said, smiling back. 'He'd do yours for you, if you wanted.'

He roared with laughter, then looked at her more closely and strolled over.

'Excuse me, you're not Mrs. Emily Wakelin, are you?'

'Yes.'

'Oh, nice to meet you, I'm Terry Bolsover; I sometimes meet your husband on the train home. Not in the morning, he's a much earlier bird than me. Isn't he with you today?'

'He's in America. I've met your wife. I'm doing some work for the Church Embroidery Committee.'

'Yes, I know, I'm a churchwarden, God help me, "And I really mean that sincerely, folks." Still, Mandy and I are well used to the church militant, we were both on the P.C.C. where we lived before.'

'You're new to Little Hocking too, then?'

'Two years. We couldn't move before that because of the children's schools. My wife was very impressed with your design — said it really made you think.'

'I'm glad. Mrs. Witherley-Bashe wasn't.'

'I would say, blow Margaret Witherley-Bashe, but I'm afraid it's not as simple as that. Quite apart from her own preferences she has to handle the vicar. I think you may find that you have quie a *cause célèbre* on your hands sooner or later. People are playing it all a

119

little close to the chest at the moment but when it gets out –'

'Oh, thanks a lot,' said Emily, rather sobered. 'I had realised there were wheels within wheels and decisions behind decisions, and I was wondering why the vicar hadn't put in an appearance yet, but if it matters so much why are they putting off consulting him?'

'Oo-ooh! Mr. Bolsover!'

Miss Barton and Miss McCarthy were hurrying out of the station with trotting, little-old-lady steps, and handbags and Oxford Street carriers gripped in their hands.

'Hello, there! Did you want a lift?'

'Oh, yes, please,' panted Miss Barton, her anxious eyes peering through wispy grey hair, 'the bus is always so full at this time of day. Hello again, Mrs. Wakelin. Goodness, is that your car?'

'Yes, it is, I've seen her coming out of her drive,' said Miss McCarthy, sounding heart-broken and looking at her wrist watch. 'Oh dear, poor Pom will be waiting for me to let him out.'

'Very modern,' said Miss Barton again, looking doubtful. 'Yes, there's certainly going to be a fuss about it.' And she didn't mean the car.

Emily hardly had time to unload the parcels from the car before the phone rang.

'Em! I've been trying for an hour. Are you all right?'

'Of course I am. I told you I was going into London.'

'I know. I thought there'd been an explosion.'

'Oh, John, you'll die of worry one day! No, there's been no explosion. How's things your end?'

'Heavy business lunch just coming up. I'm hoping to sweet-talk a Congressman, so wish me luck.'

'Well, if he's a Congressman the Iraqis particularly dislike, don't accept a lift in his car. There, I can worry too.'

'You never used to,' he said.

Chapter Ten

The first intrusion next morning came at ten past nine.

Emily wasn't feeling her best, having woken several times in the night, once with a feeling that John had called her, and more than once with the impression that she was in a confined place that she had to get out of. John's *Times* had told her that the Iraqi army was massing on the border and that there had been an earthquake in Pakistan. War, famine, plague and now earthquake. She was sitting over her muesli within a tent of barely brushed hair, not at ease with herself. For one of the first times in her artistic life, she hadn't yet been in to see her work.

'Ah! Mrs Wakelin. George would very much like to see your drawing of Walter Tappett. I suggest you come in for coffee at eleven o'clock.'

'Yes, all right, Lady Curran,' said Emily, too tired to argue or take evasive action. After she put the phone down she thought, eleven o'clock coffee. That means the bed-drawing room and being much too close to the sixteenth century.

She drew back the side curtains and watched the house with a certain degree of anguish while she washed up. When all was tidy she went up to the studio.

'Sorry,' she told Tappett, standing beside his apparent bed of pain, 'I'm not really up to you. How on earth did you endure it?'

He looked at her without malice or reproach, and the outheld hand seemed forgiving. She laid her own upon it.

'Stop blaming yourself for nothing,' he said, 'I never saw the point of all that, and being martyred wasn't my idea.'

'You could have avoided it,' she told him.

'No, fair's fair,' he said, his obstinate chin setting, 'a man's got to be able to live with himself.' Or die with himself.

She finished the full-sized drawing and hung the paper up against the inside wall to study.

'So I told them,' Walter said, 'all I'm saying is that I don't understand what you mean, and if I don't understand what you mean, how can I believe it? It stands to reason. I'll have another pint please, love, and one for the young lady there.' Yes, he probably did open his mouth too wide in the ale-house. Was he asking for it?

It was time to go in next door. The weather was turning quite cold now, and she wrapped herself in a warm shawl and sheltered the rolled-up drawing within it like an infant. She carried it into the courtyard, almost making for the blocked front door at first, then round to the back.

'Ah! Mrs. Wakelin!'

She took Walter through the centuries he never saw and arrived at the threshold of his own.

George Curran sat in a chair at the foot of his bed. There was wood burning on the polished, eighteenth-century fire-dogs and the pictures on the walls reflected back many tongues of fire. He greeted her with excitement.

'Over there please, Emily, I've had a picture taken down so there's a nail for it.'

Emily had put plastic poster hangers at either end of the roll of paper and it took only seconds to hang Walter against the pale grey panelling between a painting of Holly House surrounded by large grounds and a portrait of a man dressed so completely in black that he appeared to be trying to hide.

Mr. Curran sat in silence, taking the picture in.

'Oh!' said Lady Curran, which Emily had learnt by now didn't mean quite the same as 'Ah!'

After a moment Curran said, 'That's right, Tappett, you tell them.'

'You like it,' Lady Curran stated.

'Yes,' he said.

'I'll get the coffee, then,' she said, giving the impression

122

that if he had not, Emily would have been offered bread and water.

'Do sit down, Emily,' he said, indicating one of the beautiful chairs against the wall. His eyes stayed on Walter. She fetched a seat and sat by the fire, with her back half-turned to the drawing. From there she could see that her two paintings had been hung in pride of place above the bedheads, and that they looked very nice. Reflected in one of their glasses, Walter stood with his feet in the flickering shadows of the fire. His left hand was out now, and the reversal of his face had given it another expression, less out-going, more strained. She looked away. Presently Curran raised a finger, looked at her with a slow smile and pointed to the ceiling.

'Yes,' she said.

'I'm sure he looked at them just like that,' said Curran with satisfaction.

'Until they started crushing his thumbs,' said Emily, looking back to the reflection in the picture. The fire leapt and cast new shadows over the face. 'How do you sleep beneath that room?' she asked.

'With no difficulty, unless I'm in pain,' he said. 'I regard that as a triumphant scene, and not by any means the worst thing which has taken place within these walls. It's no use worrying about other's troubles when you have your own to deal with. Don't you find that's so?'

'I'm afraid I've rarely experienced real trouble,' said Emily, 'I've always been lucky and healthy.'

'And why shouldn't you be lucky and healthy? It's the way we were all meant to be, and it's not your fault that everyone isn't. Feeling guilty about others' problems doesn't increase the number of happy people, it decreases it by one.'

It was at that particular moment, so that in reliving it afterwards the meaningless phrase, 'decreases it by one' rang repeatedly in her ears and mingled with the shock which set her heart going like a drum-machine and the perspiration prickling her scalp beneath her thick hair, that a small draught of air came from behind her left ear and travelled across her cheek. It didn't stay in existence for more than a second or two, and it didn't recur. It merely pushed against her eardrum then lessened and faded away, and with it came

123

sound which duplicated the changing intensity of the feeling. She sat staring at Mr. Curran, hearing his voice and smiling in response, but blocking out the meaning of his words while she tried to assimilate and understand. It had been for so short a time, and of so little sensation and such small volume, and yet she knew absolutely that it had been there, and that she had felt it, and heard it, and that close behind her in the space occupied by the china cabinet, someone had sighed.

Mr. Curran stopped speaking and looked at her, awaiting a reply.

'Oh, sorry, what did you say?' she asked, the tenor of her voice knocked off balance by the beating of her heart.

'Are you ill?' he asked.

'No.' With its shining brass furniture flashing fire, the heavy, panelled door swung inwards and admitted Lady Curran with the tray.

'Are you sure?' he pursued.

'I heard something.'

'Was it the tray rattling?'

'No, it was like someone sighing.'

They both looked at her intently, not going through all that flannel about 'You don't mean − !' They knew what she meant.

'But one never hears anything, Mrs. Wakelin,' said Lady Curran, preparing to set out the cups. 'It was probably the fire.'

'I'm sure it was a sigh,' Emily repeated, her heart still thudding.

'Then I expect you did hear it,' said Mr. Curran with finality. 'How very remarkable. Do you realise this is the first time there has ever been an auditory manifestation in this house? I knew you were a remarkable person, Emily, and it seems our invisible inhabitant finds you so too.'

'You don't know that, George,' said his wife in her usual flat, high voice as she continued her domestic task. 'Just because no one's ever said they've heard something it doesn't mean it's never happened. Gwendoline would never tell us exactly what she experienced when she was young, and she might well have kept a few sighs to herself.'

124

'Well, whether it's happened before or not, you're honoured, Emily. Tell me, when you were upstairs, did you hear anything then? Was the hand accompanied by words, for instance, which might indicate – '

'No,' she said quickly, 'nothing at all.' Her left hand gripped her right to warm and and protect it.

'A pity,' he said, 'it would be so interesting to have a clue about who or what the presence is, don't you think? Of course, the sigh may not be the same presence as the hand, and the hand may not belong to the figure which comes through the door on the landing – '

Emily was near to going to pieces with nerves. She stood up and pulled her shawl around her, walking restlessly up and down in front of the fire.

'I think I'd like to go now, if you've finished with the drawing. Or I could leave it for you to look at a little longer, if you like,' she added hastily as he seemed about to demur. 'I've got the working drawing finished, so I don't actually need this now.'

'But you haven't had your coffee,' Lady Curran said, challenging her with a cup and saucer. 'Do you find it cold in here?'

'No, I just – look, you may not understand this, living here all the time, but I'm afraid. It's not unreasonable, really it isn't, I'm sure most people would feel the same.'

'But there's nothing to be afraid of,' Lady Curran insisted, 'we've told you that so many times, and I really can't see why you don't believe us. Now just sit down and have your coffee, it will buck you up in no time. Have it black. Very stimulating.'

'It is possible,' said Mr. Curran, watching Emily in a way which seemed sympathetic but which certainly had a hint of experimental interest about it, 'that Emily is more sensitive to these things than we are. We cannot know how such experiences feel to her, or whether they are more unpleasant than we have the right to expect her to put up with. But I hope she will drink her coffee with us, at least.'

Emily sat down on the edge of her chair and drank the buck-me-up. It certainly had a kick to it, and a surge of mental energy quickly followed its consumption. Her hands moved restlessly in the folds of her shawl and she sat on for a few more minutes, hoping to satisfy politeness and save a little more face before making her escape.

Her nerves, however, increased.

Mr. Curran sipped and watched her and talked across the rim of his beautiful cup, telling her how his daughter had always seemed more concerned about the 'bother', as he called it, than her brothers, and how his sister had been rather the same, and it was only to be expected that young women should be more sensitive than young men and boys, and that he hoped she would not let herself be too distressed about it all, she would soon get used to it, and by then Emily's nerves had grown to such an extent that she was in a state of painful agitation that approached terror. And its apogee came when she realised that it was not her own terror she was feeling, but another's. His fear (she knew it was a he) pressed in on her like an electric field and seeped into her brain and emotions and nervous system, and she knew he was so close to her mind and body that he might have been a lover. Her hands pressed forwards as if she was thrusting something away from her.

'I can't, I can't,' she protested, 'please let me go. I'm so sorry but I can't –'

Lady Curran's grip broke the strange union at once and left her merely exhausted and shivering. Mr. Curran was leaning forward.

'I remember!' he exclaimed. 'My sister had a very similar little fit many, many years ago, when she was sickening for scarlet fever. Nanny said she was delirious, but she used the very words you did then, Emily. 'Let me go, I'm sorry but I can't.' It was as if she was answering someone. Is that what you were doing? Did someone speak to you?'

'Not in words,' said Emily, on her feet again, and moving restlessly as if she was trying to escape. 'I just felt there was someone there. It's no use, I can't stay here. Excuse me –'

She pulled open the door and fled the room, straight past the bottom of the stairs, through the glass door and the lobby and into the kitchen. There, she started to cry. The washing machine was chugging away again, and Lady Curran had another little job lined up on the kitchen table. This time it was pounds of Seville oranges and a stainless steel pre-serving pan. She joined Emily within seconds and sat down at the other side of the table.

'Oh dear,' she said, sounding as if she meant 'I've dropped a stitch,' certainly nothing worse. 'I do hope this won't put you off visiting us, Mrs. Wakelin.'

If she hadn't been crying, Emily would have laughed.

'I can't honestly say it will encourage me,' she said, through sniffs.

'No, I can see that, but I *should* appreciate it if you could try and get used to it. You do George so much good. He doesn't often take to people, and he gets lonely.'

If he's that particular it rather serves him right, Emily thought. 'Well, I'm glad of that, but it doesn't do me much good. I tend to leave here on the verge of a nervous breakdown.'

'Oh dear, I do hope not!' She very nearly sounded shocked. 'I wouldn't have thought you were of a nervous disposition.'

'I'm not, I'm usually cheerful enough to ride over the bumpy bits of life like a four-wheel drive. It's just when I come here. Not because of you and Mr. Curran,' Emily explained quickly. 'Perhaps if I only came into the later parts of the house, like here.'

'But I can't expect George to sit in the kitchen!' she pro-tested. 'If only it were summertime, we could all go into the garden and there'd be no problem. Still, the dining room's perfectly all right. Next time, we'll make sure we're in the dining room. It may mean changing his routine, but if that is what you want, we'll have to comply.'

I'd rather not come at all. 'Please say goodbye to him for me and tell him he can keep the drawing for a couple of days if he wants to.'

'He'll like that. In fact I shouldn't be surprised if he talks to it.'

'I've been doing that,' Emily confessed.

'You *are* artistic, aren't you,' she said, staring.

Emily got into her car and drove away from Little Hocking. She found a large, pleasant village cum small town and spent

127

the whole afternoon there, lunching, sightseeing, shopping, immersing herself in unhaunted normality and behaving like the hundreds of other housewives around her preparing for yet another family weekend.

She returned home at ten to six. Holly House was shut in behind its holly trees, and the light on its corner glinted through the wrought iron overthrow.

John rang soon after. 'Where were you today?'

'I took an afternoon off and went out. Did the Congressman succumb to your English charm?'

'Not so as you'd notice, but at least he didn't throw me out. He does *not* like my client and he absolutely hates my client's lawyer, he suspects him of being a closet liberal.'

'Can one suspect worse,' remarked Emily.

'And *he's* like L.A. Law. Moulded out of plastic and a mixture of an offer you can't refuse and have a nice day. Probably about a thousand dollars a minute.'

'They're not trying to blame the firm, are they?'

'No, they couldn't possibly. It's all so silly, because if it hadn't been for the war they wouldn't have made such a thing of it. If only Abdullah wasn't from the Middle East, and moreover not one of *our* Middle Easterners. Any more trouble with the invisible neighbour?'

'Well — well, yes, actually, but —'

'Oh God, Em, I told you not to go in there again!' He sounded panic-stricken. 'Darling, promise me, please, that you won't take any more risks. Whatever would I do if anything happened to you?'

'I don't think it's dangerous, John, they've been living with it for two centuries. Now mind *you* look after yourself. Don't come home on an American or Israeli plane, and be very polite to anyone who looks remotely like an Arab.'

'Promise. I love you, Em.'

'I love you, John.'

A quick look at the news — oh dear — then up to the studio. She had barely glanced at Walter before the phone rang again.

'Ah, Mrs. Wakelin. Where have you been.'

'Out, Lady Curran. Can I help you?' Would you *believe* it?

128

'Would you come in at once, please. George is rather over-excited and would like to speak to you.'

'What, now? Won't tomorrow do?'

'No, he won't sleep if he doesn't tell you now.'

'I won't be able to see my way round there,' protested Emily, feeling not only scared but also extremely hacked off.

'I will meet you in the courtyard with a torch.'

'Where is he sitting?' asked Emily, getting really exasperated that she should be treated with so little consideration. You would really think this morning's events had never happened. How did you get through to these people?

'He is in bed. Please come *now*, Mrs. Wakelin.'

Her steps echoed along the dark, windy road and stopped at the iron gate. Its convolutions gleamed against the porch light beyond, and the house frontage disappeared up into the darkness. She could almost believe she heard it breathe. She waited there until a bouncing light appeared round the corner of the house and Lady Curran's voice called sharply, 'Mrs. Wakelin!'

Emily pressed the latch, leant against the knobbly iron and allowed her weight to push the gate forwards into the courtyard. She couldn't bear to let it close behind her, and pressed the bolt down against the stones with her foot as she passed in. Luckily Lady Curran didn't seem to notice.

'Why don't you use the front door?' asked Emily, starting to pant as soon as she was in the blackness of the garden.

'It was inconvenient.' Lady Curran marched ahead taking the torch with her, and with no attempt to light Emily's feet. She hurried after, hoping not to stub her toe and trying to remember where the steps down into the cellar were.

'Mind the cellar,' Lady Curran called back over her shoulder, 'you nearly fell in.'

Emily felt suddenly furious, which was very unlike her, but under fear the most uncharacteristic emotions surface.

'Is Mr. Curran ill?' she called as the woman strode ahead. The security light flooded out over the lawn.

'Not yet.'

Lady Curran turned for a fraction of a second as they

entered the kitchen courtyard, then the pool of light swung away and up the side of the glass lean-to, leaving Emily to guess wrong about the position of the roses. She had gathered her long skirts in and up, and the thorns made a direct hit on her right calf.

The kitchen light assaulted her eyes and set them blinking until the pupils contracted, then she leant down and looked at the scratch. Blood was running down her torn tights and into her shoe. Lady Curran was already out in the Georgian lobby, but came back on discovering she was alone.

'What's the matter?'

'I've torn my leg on one of your roses.'

'Oh! Is it bleeding? You could put a handkerchief round it.'

'I haven't got one with me,' said Emily, trying to keep her temper and her nerve at the same time. Why on earth do I let myself get into these situations? If this woman is inconsiderate, surely I needn't be considerate to her?

'I'll get something to wrap it. Stay there, in case the blood drips on to the carpets.'

Alone in the big, white, empty kitchen with the dark pressing outside the high skylight and one uncurtained window, and the light from the cottage kitchen through the other pleading with her to return home, Emily held her leg off the floor and watched the glutinous red drops welling out of the wound and dripping on to the lino. It was starting to sting painfully and she sat down with her skirts pulled up over her knees.

At the end of the long scrubbed table, at least a dozen jars of new-made marmalade stood drawn up like a line of sentries, watching her in silence. It was very quiet in there, the quietness which allows you to hear the blood roaring in your ears. It's only nineteenth-century, she told herself, nothing awful happened here in the nineteenth century.

But it was an antechamber to other centuries and other happenings, and somewhere to prepare yourself for what lay beyond. She drew in her breath with little gasps as the pain grew, and thought of Walter's thumbs, and stopped allowing herself to make any sound at all.

Lady Curran bound her up with clean, torn linen – *real*

130

linen, Emily noticed, not just an old cotton pillowcase with a courtesy title. It must be a half a century old. How much hsitoric household textile lay in the drawers, chests, presses and tallboys upstairs?

In the lobby now, and a quick cut from the draught in the letterbox. They were going through the glass door. Oh, that staircase. Broad red-carpeted treads, carved banisters, shining, time-and-Mrs. Mumford-polished handrails, the latticed window above blinded by the night. The door of the bed-drawing room. Excuse me, God, I don't often bother you, but would you mind backing me up this time, please?

Curran's head was turned towards the door, resting on a high pile of pillows. The curtains were drawn and the central heating was on, as well as the wood fire. In fact the room was stuffy and slightly fetid, despite its polished furniture, gleaming gold frames and spotless carpet.

'Here she is, George,' said Lady Curran.

'Oh, Emily,' he started at once, 'I'm afraid I owe you an abject apology. I couldn't rest until I'd told you how sorry I am. Do forgive me.'

She stopped short, unable to believe her ears. This morning he insisted I came into a place which he knows frightens me, where I had yet another experience which he knows I have had before, then he drags me back in here tonight to apologise. These two are on another planet!

'It's all right, Mr. Curran,' she said as steadily and pleasantly as possible. 'Please don't get upset, I'm quite all right now.'

'No, no!' he cried. 'Look! I am so sorry.' His hand pointed across the room. 'I am really mortified,' he repeated, 'when you had been so kind as to entrust it to me.'

Between the two oil paintings, Walter Tappett hung against the panelling, slightly crooked, his face distorted into a travesty, his hand pointing down to the floor, his other hand gripping his belt as if he was consumed in pain. His entire body was ripped from top to bottom.

'What happened?' she asked, after a moment of shock.

'Mrs. Mumford came in here to clean while I was in the cloakroom this morning. When I came back it was like

131

that. She insists it wasn't her, but I'm not sure I can believe her.'

'Well, of course we can't believe her,' said Lady Curran sharply. '*We* didn't do it.'

Emily walked over to the mutilated drawing, feeling quite sick. She had grown used to criticism, as all artists must, but actual, deliberate, spiteful destruction of her work had never come her way before and it was as hurtful as a physical assault. She touched Walter's broken body and thought, Why? How could something which seems so natural and truthful and even inevitable to me produce such outraged hatred in another? Whom have I threatened? Whom have I offended? Why does my honest personal vision offend them so much that they lash out in self defence and cause me pain that I never intended to inflict on them? And why should Mrs. Mumford –

'I suppose we could stick it with something,' suggested Lady Curran. 'Perhaps Sellotape on the back. It could probably be done so that the tear didn't even show.'

But it wouldn't help. The damage had been done, and it had been deliberate damage and done with hate.

'Shall I take it away with me?' asked Emily, smoothing her hands down the paper and trying to join Walter's left side to his right.

'Yes, please do,' said Mr. Curran humbly, 'I have proved completely unworthy of your trust.'

'No, I didn't mean that,' she said quickly, 'you can have it back when I've mended it, if you want.'

'May I? That is so kind of you, Emily, and very forgiving. Still, what else was to be expected of you?'

Emily winced slightly at the unwanted admiration and put up her hand to lift the drawing down. It stopped in the act of releasing the string from the round, iron stud in the woodwork.

'Did you hear that?' she asked, in a a tense voice.

'No,' said Mr. Curran, 'we heard nothing.' His agitation seemed to disappear into thin air and his voice sounded eager. The moan had been a quiet, short sound, like the sigh of the previous visit, as one who would protest, 'Oh, don't touch that, please.' She stayed still with her breath coming fast, waiting. No more sound, but her left side was beginning to

132

feel a sensation of pressure and force and presence. He was addressing her without words, and the message was, Please. If you please. Sweet lady, if you please ...

Lady Curran came towards her, sending the atmosphere scattering like midges before a squirt of insecticide. She grabbed the drawing from the wall and took both it and Emily away into the centre of the room.

'You're far too nervous,' she scolded her on a high, flat note. 'It can't hurt you, whatever you heard. Would you like me to put that in a plastic bag?'

'No, I'll hold it under my shawl.' Emily started to roll up her wounded offspring, with tears behind her eyelids.

'If you wish we will dismiss Mrs. Mumford before you bring the drawing back,' Mr. Curran offered, in an effort to placate her.

'Oh no, of course not,' said Emily, quite shocked that he should think she would demand anything of the sort. 'Not unless you're absolutely sure she did it, I mean, and I can't imagine why she should.'

'It was probably sheer carelessness,' said Lady Curran, 'and to be honest, George, I don't want the bother of getting a new woman used to our ways. There's theft to think of, too, and she's at least honest.'

Please. If you please —

The sensation gathered around her again, pressing and urgent and pleading. The rising of the hairs on her body and scalp was one of the most unpleasant sensations she had ever experienced, as if her very soul was being drawn out through the pores of her skin.

Lady Curran escorted her from the room, and the door into the sixteenth century closed.

'Of course it must have been her,' said Lady Curran, pausing, 'but I really do think it was an accident.' The atmosphere seemed to exude from the room. Emily moved to stand in front of the lobby which led to the entrance hall, but it was still there, like a gas leak. Only when Lady Curran led her away towards the staircase and out of the whole block, did she feel free of it.

'He was so upset I was afraid he'd need the doctor,' said Lady Curran as she marched through the house. The glass door swung closed behind them. She paused and picked up a sheet from the fax tray. 'What do you think of this war business,' she said, studying the nose-diving figures.

'I thing it's absolutely dreadful.' Emily shivered, holding poor wounded Walter in her arms under her shawl.

Into the kitchen.

'Would you like some marmalade.'

'Oh. Yes. Thank you.' The hand she put out to receive it was shaking.

'Do you drink.'

'No!'

'Oh, pity. A brandy might calm your nerves, they're very bad, aren't they.'

'Oh, I *see*. Yes, I think I probably will, when I get home.'

Now they were in the lean-to.

'Goodbye.'

'Please,' Emily said, 'would you light me round to the front?'

'The security light will come on.'

'I know that, but I really would appreciate you coming with me.' The woman looked blank. 'Lady Curran, I am *afraid*. *Please* will you come with me?'

'Oh! Very well.'

Emily hung on to her the length of the windy, hidden garden, and didn't let go until she was actually outside the gate. The bony arm within the woollen cardigan felt tense, as if it wasn't used to being touched.

'Thank you,' said Emily, drawing a deep breath of relief. 'I'll let you have this back as soon as it's mended. I'll phone and you can come and collect it.'

'Oh, but you'll come in for coffee or tea.'

Emily shook her head, all attempts at politeness abandoned.

'No,' she said.

Lady Curran looked at her with near amazement, standing behind the gate with the hollies clashing like teeth and the benighted house hanging over her like Nemesis.

'Have we offended you?' she asked at last, with an audible question mark.

Chapter Eleven

At ten o'clock on Saturday morning, the telephone bell dragged Emily away from the studio, where the traced patterns were pinned to the fabrics ready for cutting. The mended drawing hung beside the working one, almost as good as new except for a faint scar.

She went into the bedroom and picked up the receiver, practising saying no. At the other end of the line it sounded as if a disco was in full swing, and as if the Drug Squad had just pounced.

'Hello, is that Mrs. Wakelin?'

'Yes.'

'It's Mrs. Mumford here. I just want to tell you that − shut up a minute, Cliff! Sorry, I just want to tell you I didn't do nothing to your picture, I never went near it. I've told her I didn't, but she never listens to a word you say and − will you stop pestering her, Cliff? Just leave her alone! You can tell her something over and over and you might as well save your breath. He's all right, I suppose, but − leave her alone! You'll wake your dad and then you'll be for it! Anyway, I didn't want you thinking I'd do something like that and it was perfectly all right when I left the room. It's quite a nice picture, isn't it, but what's it about? It ought to have a bubble coming out of his mouth so as you can tell what he's saying.'

'Well, it will have, in a way, but it hasn't been decided what it'll be yet. Thank you for ringing, Mrs. Mumford, but I didn't really think it was you.'

'Well, tell her that, will you? If she's not careful I'll leave,

135

and then she'll be in trouble. There aren't many as'd put up with her, that's why she has to pay me proper. Who is he, anyway, one of the Currans' ancestors?'

'No, a man who lived in Little Hocking in the sixteenth century.'

'Oh. Well. How do you know what he looked like?'

'I don't. I've had to use my imagination.'

'As if they hadn't got enough pictures already – they give me the creeps, some of them. There's nothing there I could live with at all, really, apart from some of her ornaments, they're quite pretty.' There was a loud crash in the background and a deafening howl of distress. 'You spiteful little bastard! Sorry, Mrs. Wakelin, I got to go. I'm ever so sorry about your picture. See you some time. 'Bye.'

Emily went back to work, the high which accompanied the excitement of creation now well-established and strong enough to carry the work through to completion.

By Sunday there was a coloured plan of Walter pinned together on cambric, like a stained glass window without the punctuation of lead. During the morning a babble of voices drew her to the window, where she saw the heads of the extended Curran family chattering in the kitchen yard. Were those children as unaffected as they appeared to be? If they were true Curran, they probably were, but – She put on Radio Three and let Vivaldi free her mind to concentrate on the permanent creation of Walter's features.

It didn't seem long before there was a knock at the door, but on coming downstairs she saw that the living-room clock stood at twenty to three. She'd forgotten lunch again.

The man on the doorstep was tall, slim, blond and rather good-looking. Emily guessed he was in his late forties and that his jacket didn't know what a chain store was.

'How do you do, Mrs. Wakelin? I'm Simon Curran. I hear you were upset when you went to see my parents on Friday and refuse to go in there again. I do apologise. I'm well aware that they are not exactly a conventional couple and that the house has its disadvantages, but my father's rather agitated about it and it's not good for him, so I wonder if I could discuss things with you?'

'Oh. Yes. Please come in,' said Emily, extremely embarrassed. His précis of the situation made her sound so ungracious.

He sat down on the big, chintz-covered settee, right in the place where John always sat. For a moment she wanted to cry because he was fair instead of dark, and his figure wasn't like John's, and the way he lay back against the cushions was all wrong, and because altogether he just wasn't John and she was missing him so much.

She took her own seat on a low, Victorian chair with worn claret velvet upholstery she was going to replace with tapestry one day when she had time. Her loose green sweater and long black skirt were strewn with threads, and her beads and earrings were caught up in her hair.

'Father said you belonged in the Land of Faerie,' he said. 'I can quite see why he enjoys looking at you.'

'Do you think he'd be satisfied with a large colour photograph?' she said with a touch of weariness. 'Because if so I would pay for it with the greatest pleasure, and I doubt if your ghost would molest that.'

'Ah, so it *was* the ghost. Mother seems quite incapable of understanding that that's a good enough reason for people to avoid the house. She said you were annoyed about the damage to your drawing.'

'Oh dear, I did try to explain it to her,' said Emily, running her fingers through her hair and looking as if she was sighing for her knight's return, which, of course, she was. 'I'm sure it wasn't Mrs. Mumford, I just don't see her as an art critic.' She felt the twinge of pain again.

'I wouldn't rule it out completely, but I had wondered if Father had done it, to have an excuse to call you.'

'Oh no, you don't really think that, do you?' Emily was quite frightened. It made Mr. Curran not just a lonely, eccentric invalid, but a head case.

'Well,' he said, pulling a face, 'he's not the man he was, you know, and prolonged illness does funny things to people. He was very different when we were children. Another possibility's that it was the ghost.'

'Well, yes,' Emily admitted reluctantly. 'What was it like being a child in a haunted house? Your mother seems to

137

think that none of you minded a bit, but surely – small children up at the top of a gloomy old building with only a nanny for company – '

'Only was not a word to be applied to Nanny,' said Simon emphatically, 'she was King Kong with a passionate and frustrated mothering instinct. Well, it wasn't so bad for us boys, because we could enjoy exploring the attics and the roof and Jeremy even had a go at mending the clock when he was ten. Damn, near got it going, too, but Nanny put her foot down about him going out on the tiles to oil the bell. He went just the same, of course, but couldn't work it free.'

'How did he get out there?' asked Emily with alarm at the thought of a ten-year-old balanced on the ridge of the roof above the lethal stones of the courtyard.

'There's a little trap door in the corner of the clock room. Have you ever been up there?'

'Yes, your mother showed me all round the house on my second visit. It's a pity it needs so much work doing to it.'

'I know,' he said, grimacing again. 'Father doesn't realise and Mother isn't bothered, she's not sentimental.'

'I thought she came from a historic house herself?'

'Yes, Firegrave in Gloucestershire. My grandfather was fairly mad, and spent most of his income trying to breed and promote the perfect terrier – better than a Jack Russell, that is. They were horrible little things, quite deformed really, you don't see many Firegrave terriers around now. Anyway, his son was killed in the Desert and his daughters all had homes of their own to repair and make fit to show the public, so eventually it was demolished and the grounds were made into a golf course.'

'So now the gardener rakes the first green?'

He laughed. 'Oh, you know about that? No, she's not sentimental, Mama isn't. I've offered to send in the builders, but she says it'll upset Father.'

'Won't it upset him more if it falls down!' said Emily, with a little shudder.

'Oh, come now, it's not that bad!' he said with mock reproof. 'Still, we really should do something soon, because it's Grade One, and if English Heritage find out it's in bad nick they're going to be down on us like a ton of bricks. And

138

the sad thing is, I think Father loves it almost more than us.'

'He told me he intends to stay there after he dies.'

'That doesn't surprise me in the slightest. Anyway, we were talking about the present ghost or ghosts — no one's ever decided which it is. It only seems to appear or make itself felt to women, which means the Currans have had rather nervous daughters and a high turnover in housemaids.'

'Lady Curran said she'd seen it.'

'Yes,' he said carelessly, 'I believe she did occasionally. Never turned a hair, of course. But my poor sister was a different matter. She left as soon as she was twenty-one, and has hardly been back since.'

'How sad for your parents.'

'Yes.' He looked away. 'Is that one of your paintings? I like the ones you did of Holly House, Father's been showing them off to us. I suppose I couldn't see Walter Tappett, could I? Or is he still in intensive care?'

The jocund image suddenly jarred when she thought of what had really been done to Walter. It would have taken more than intensive care to put that right.

She took him up to the studio. He was interested, impressed and curious, looking round at the paraphernalia of embroidery and the sketches and paintings propped against the skirtings and pinned to the walls.

'My goodness, you know what you're doing, don't you? I bet the Little Hocking Embroidery Committee are reeling with shock. Margaret W.B.'s never allowed a professional to get in on the act before, and she's been running the shoot since she was the vicar's daughter in the fifties. He let her do what she liked in that direction, and although she was always a good needlewoman I can't say her taste was mine. Like those insipid bunnies around Baby Jesus in the Sunday school corner.'

'Did you go to Sunday school?' asked Emily, laughing.

'Nanny used to march us across, but then Father refused to let us go any more. He had a disagreement with the old vicar, who was absolutely *terrifying*, by the way.'

He glanced up at the open rafters.

'So you took the ceiling out? What a good idea, it makes a much better room. I haven't been in this cottage for years

139

and it looks much bigger altogether, particularly with the hall and the living room thrown in together. What else have you done? I expect you've modernised the kitchen.'

'No, we demodernised it. I wanted a proper dresser.'

'Like next door, eh? They like you, you know,' he said, suddenly serious.

'Well, your father may, but I don't think your mother approves of me at all.'

'Good God, what gave you that idea?' he asked in surprise, leaning against the wall and crossing his arms. Walter's outstretched hand hovered near his jacket as if it were about to feel the quality. 'She told me that you're a poppet.'

'She said the vicar was a poppet.'

'Well, yes, this one is. Have you met him yet?'

'No, in fact I'm not sure he exists at all,' she said with some exasperation.

'We've all wondered that at some time or another, he's not quite of this world. Isn't there anything we can do to persuade you to come back?'

'Look,' said Emily firmly, with a 'positively for the last time' inflection, 'I told them I'd go into the newer parts but not into the sixteenth-century block, yet they hauled me back in in the dark, which I think was really inconsiderate. That time it spoke to me,' she added hesitantly.

'Did it? Goodness, you're honoured. Are you psychic?' he asked in a respectful tone.

'No, I'm extremely ordinary in all particulars,' she said, hurriedly fending off the next blast of possible praise.

'Ordinary people can't draw like that,' he said, turning round to Walter again. 'What's he saying?'

'The committee are still arguing about it. I think he's saying, "Now look, why can't we be reasonable about this?"'

'Yes.' He looked into the mended face. 'And there wasn't a reasonable man in the room, and not too many in the country. Everyone then seems to have been either high on theology or in a state of terror about God, the Church and damnation. What did the ghost say to you?'

She moved uneasily. 'Please. Just please, over and over.'

'Really?' asked Simon, looking fascinated. 'What

did he want? And who was he? We none of us know.'

'I don't know either. I don't much want to,' said Emily, her left hand instantly going to the aid of her right. She turned off the spotlight. Outside, the winter afternoon was being given a lift by the sound of children playing.

Simon followed her down into the living room.

'Won't you come over just for half an hour? Or less?' he added as she betrayed complete lack of enthusiasm and the beginnings of impatience. 'Look, I would like you to meet the rest of us, and I promise you we're all outside. Please?' (Sweet lady.)

'Half an hour in daylight I could probably cope with,' sighed Emily.

The Currans were expending their energies on the garden. Three adults were tidying and weeding, and children whose state of being permanently on the move made them impossible to count were scorching back and forth among the beds, disappearing into the shrubbery and poking their heads out of the cellar waving new discoveries.

Simon introduced her to his wife Deirdre, a plump, comfortable lady with a beautiful complexion and a voice like the very best quality toffee, his sharp-featured brother, who looked more of a Firegrave than a Curran, and his brother's thin, greying wife Isabel, who was sitting on a garden chair with her coat collar up, looking disconsolate, bored, chilly, and altogether not happy. She shook hands with Emily and scanned her with large, near-desperate eyes.

'Hello, I hear you've been a victim of the family ghost. How awful for you.'

'Overstatement, Isabel,' corrected Simon, 'it was very polite to her.'

'Have you ever experienced it?' asked Emily, noting Isabel's air of waiting for the day to be over, and remembering the overheard coversation of a few weeks back.

'Do you think I'd be here if I had?' she said fervently. 'As it is, I think the place is a total nightmare.'

Simon rounded up the children into a polite row and they were introduced to Emily, shaking hands and saying how do

141

you do in the way that it is generally believed children don't do any more. They then dispersed back to their several occupations, and the boys were soon hauling a venerable, full-sized tricycle up the cellar steps at the foot of the red brick walls. Isabel's eyes followed Emily's up to the blind mullions and then the nursery.

'Hair-raising, isn't it? All those generations of kids thundering about in that room with only one bar on the window and a forty-foot drop. I die every second mine are up there.'

A skinny little girl of about eight was picking snails out of a patch of rockery around a birdbath and another, rather better-covered, was lashing out wildly with a golf club. Lady Curran emerged from the shrubbery, holding by the hand a lurching toddler built with the solidity of a garden ornament. He had a big, blond head, big, wide features, ice-blue eyes with an expression of ferocious aggression and all the charm of a South African policeman.

'Wave to Mummy,' Lady Curran instructed him and his stone head turned and stared in their direction.

'Is he yours as well?' asked Emily.

'Yes, he was a bit of a surprise,' said Isabel, looking as haunted as a woman who had given birth to a Midwich Cuckoo. 'Isn't he a thug? Anne is sports mad,' she indicated the plumpish girl, 'and Charles is the mechanic of the family – he's getting his great-grandfather's tricycle out to mend. Jeremy's always been good with his hands, too. He's putting up something hideous in Docklands at the moment. My other two are away at boarding school. Have you any children yet?'

'No.'

'Well, think twice before you start, that's my advice.' She shivered with cold. 'Why on earth I married into a family who love the great outdoors I can't imagine, it's not me at all. Do you think if we tiptoed off to a nice warm kitchen and made a private cup of tea they'd notice?'

'I'd rather not if it's that kitchen.'

'Oh, yes, I see. Do tell me more about this ghost. What did it do?' She leaned close, her big, mournful eyes full of alarm. Her cheeks were ravaged by little dry lines, and her lipstick was all but worn off by her nervous tongue.

'Which time?'

'Oh my godfathers! You mean it's happened more than once? Poor you! And yet you can sit here cool as anything.'

'I am not cool about it at all, and the only reason I continue to come in here is because your mother-in-law won't leave me alone,' said Emily with irritation.

There was a roar from within the cellar, the sort of sound which sends mothers' hearts into their mouths and their feet running in the direction of their invisible children.

Emily joined the adult rush to the rescue, but remained obediently at the top of the steps when Simon and Jeremy disappeared with the curt words, 'Everybody stand back!'

Deirdre pressed her whimpering daughter against her child-bearing hip and said, 'It's all right, Vicky,' while Isabel stood with both hands against her mouth. Still armed with the golf club, Anne hugged her round the waist and said, 'It's all right, Mummy, calm down.'

Lady Curran swept up the stone child and marched across the lawn. 'Simon, are the boys all right?'

'Nobody hurt, Mother,' Jeremy's voice bawled from within the dusty cavern. He appeared with a filthy face and an even filthier son, whom he delivered into his mother's trembling arms. 'Oh, Mum!' he grumbled. Simon came out with his own offspring in similar condition.

Lady Curran handed her grandson over to Emily, as the only adult with free arms, and strode down into the cellar to inspect the damage. The child bellowed with rage.

'What were you doing, you cretins?' asked Simon sternly. 'Vicky, go and tell Grandfather everything's all right.'

'Trying to get something off the top shelf,' said his elder son, rubbing his bruises. 'It came down.'

Emily held on to the screaming toddler, feeling like Alice with the Duchess's baby. The child kicked her, scrambled down and stomped away across the lawn, where Anne cornered him behind the birdbath and hooked a snail out of his mouth. He roared, struck out at her with both hands and both feet, and consequently fell over.

143

'I say!' called Lady Curran's voice. 'Come here!'

The family started to move down into the cellar, leaving Emily and Isabel alone in the chilly garden.

'Would you like a cup of tea in *my* kitchen?' Emily asked, feeling sorry for Isabel's obvious misery.

'Oh, you sweet soul,' she said fervently, 'I thought you'd never ask.'

'I used to smoke,' said Isabel, twisting her teaspoon round and round between her fingers, 'but the doctor said if I didn't stop he'd refuse to treat my bronchitis any more. I knit when I'm at home, but it's difficult to know what to do with your hands when you're out. I like your cottage. Old enough to be charming, but not reminiscent of an Egyptian pyramid. Emily, I just can't *tell* you how much I hate that house. It's not just the ghosts, though that would be bad enough on its own, it's the whole state of it. It's always been a nightmare to keep up, and now Abigail's stopped bothering it's going to bankrupt poor old Simon and Deirdre when they finally get landed with it. Yes, I'd love another cup. And the cellar's full of mice, eating away at the foundations I shouldn't wonder. And as for cleaning it! The dust comes up through cracks between the floorboards and down through cracks in the ceiling, the bathroom is falling apart, the gutters leak –'

'It doesn't look quite that bad,' demurred Emily, 'and the ground floor is really beautiful.'

'Oh, yes, that's still all right,' admitted Isabel reluctantly, 'and so was the rest until a few years ago. Do you know, if George could see what's happening up above his head he'd murder her. It's all her fault.'

She took the cup of tea and the flow was interrupted for a moment while she drank it. Emily sat there sympathetically, very much hoping she'd go soon so that she could get back to work. But it was another half hour before Jeremy came round to fetch her. He had a perpetually watchful, thoughtful air, as if he was sizing up how you worked and whether you were due for a service.

'The kids said you were here. You must come and have a look, Isabel, we've found another priest's hole.'

'Oh, can I stand the excitement!' exclaimed Isabel. 'Jeremy,

144

you know I'm not going to come down and grovel in the rubble with the rest of you, so why didn't you leave me in peace? We were having such a nice civilised time.'

'Did you say *another* priests's hole?' asked Emily, interested despite a twinge of nerves.

'Yes, there's one upstairs, but we didn't know about this one. Interesting piece of construction, actually.' He leant into the fireplace and looked up the chimney, then ran his hand down the brickwork. 'Did you rebuild this?'

'No. Isn't it the original?'

He considered. 'I think it's basically the same stack and opening,' he reported at last, 'but it's been covered over with newer bricks.'

'How old were the others?'

'Well, the original cottage was probably put up about forty years after Holly House, when the Babington Conspiracy brought the wrath of the government down on the Catholics.'

'I don't see the connection,' said Emily, feeling an uncomfortable sensation in her stomach as she looked at her lovely, cosy, reassuring, wood-burning fireplace.

'As an escape route. There was a passage which came out in your fireplace. If you looked up the chimney you used to be able to see where it'd been bricked up. I see you've got a baffle inside the flue now (don't blame you, it used to smoke like a − well, like a chimney), and the opening was about three feet above that.'

'So the Lethabys got persecuted in their turn?' said Emily with a brief recognition of retribution.

'That's right,' he said, turning his attention to an articulated city gentleman of painted wood, who did something reprehensible when you pulled a string. 'That's neat, did you make it?'

'Wedding present from a friend who did.'

'Ah. In fact one of the Lethabys went across to Douai Seminary and trained as a priest. Later, he paid a secret visit to his parents but suddenly died, so there they were with a dead body on their hands, no way of burying it in consecrated ground, and absolutely no chance of giving it the Catholic burial service it ought to have.'

145

'What did they do?'

'Put him in a barrel, filled it up with wine and put it in one of the priest's holes. The next time a priest came to stay they got him to say a requiem mass over the barrel, and the next time they were clearing old ground in the churchyard they loaded it on to a cart, took it across the road and put it in the charnel house under a load of new bones. They found him when it was cleared in the last century.' His attention moved on to the vacuum cleaner which stood in the corner, waiting like a hopeful dog for the morning outing Emily hadn't given it for several days.

'Jeremy,' protested Isabel, 'I just cannot swallow that story, it's full of inconsistencies. How could you possibly get a barrel into a priest hole, when they have entrances no bigger than a drain cover? How come nobody noticed the barrel being unloaded, particularly the gravediggers? And how did the people who found the body in the charnel house know who it was and why he was there?'

'Well, he had a cross and a missal with him, and another man confessed he'd travelled to England with Lethaby, who was never seen again. Anyway, that's what Dad's always told us, and it's such a good story, who cares if it's true?'

'How dreadful for his parents,' said Emily, imagining with heartache the bizarre and macabre ordeal of the Lethabys in arranging the obsequies of their son.

'I think he was damn, lucky to die when he did,' said Jeremy, examining the wall clock and trying the weights, 'he'd almost certainly have been captured.'

'Yes, at least he wasn't tortured and burned,' she agreed sadly.

'Oh, they didn't burn Catholics,' said Jeremy, sending the pendulum swinging. 'Burning was for heresy, and the English Mission priests were executed for treason. It was always hanging, drawing and quartering for them.'

'Oh goody, goody,' said Isabel. 'Just think, if I'd married into a family from a semi-detached on the by-pass my after-lunch coffee would never have been accompanied by appetising anecdotes like that. Jeremy's father was going on about your Walter Tappett today. I was nearly sick.'

Emily could imagine Curran watching Isabel's face screw

up as he recounted the nasty bits. It was the sort of verbal sadism which sometimes developed in those afflicted by physical helplessness, a way of asserting that they still possessed some power over others.

'You'd better come back now, Isabel, Mama's getting tea ready.'

'I've just *had* some tea,' she pouted. 'Goodbye, Emily, it's been lovely meeting you and thanks for the asylum.'

'Would you like to see the priest's hole?' Jeremy offered pleasantly as he opened the front door and ran his hand down a loose piece of draught-proofing.

'Not just now, thank you.'

'Next time, then. Goodbye.'

She heard them going down the path and into the road, Isabel grumbling and moaning, Jeremy answering with vague mmms and yeses. His apparent permanent detachment from the present moment probably owed a lot to living with a not quite suitable wife.

Emily sat down on the settee, between John's corner and the pile of books, needlework and opened letters at the other end. If he'd been home, it would all have been tidied away.

Within the open brick mouth of the fireplace the velvety grey logs settled into their red-sequinned bed. A shining braiding of flame crept along their tops. Scented grey chiffon smoke rose straight, then went into graceful whorls as it encountered the draught of air which entered at the keyhole in the side door, crept across the kitchen and made itself felt in the living room. The convolutions of smoke writhed on and disappeared through the baffleboard across the chimney.

And there, in the darkness above, it passed the bricked-up doorway into the secret passage which she'd never known was there. All around the stack her bright happy life had gone on among the pleasant stimuli of her personal furnishings and belongings. She had run her house, cooked and washed up, painted and sewed, planned her garden, eaten and talked with John, shared experiences and made plans. They had comforted each other in moments of anxiety and made love in the pretty bedroom only feet from where that umbilical cord which connected the cottage to the architectural brute next door gripped secretly on to her home.

147

It was the unused places in buildings which frightened. Nervous children feared attics and cellars, chimneys and cupboards, the enclosed emptiness behind panelling and the dusty caverns under beds. A house might be bright and modern and cheerful and totally above board, but the striking of knuckles on a wall would betray empty space which could not be accounted for, and immediately the imagination peopled it with dirt, rot, insects, mice, secrets and ghouls and ghosts.

She felt her lovely cottage had deceived her, and that the attractive face it had shown her in her few weeks' occupancy had been a lie, because this hidden space lay within it. The door might be bricked up, and bricked up for many, many years, but the passage might not have been filled in. It might still snake from the cellars of Holly House, under the red brick wall, beneath her kitchen and living room floors and rise by a tiny, cramped, crumbling drainpipe of a staircase within the brick stack. And within its emptiness, the terror of men fleeing for their lives might still reverberate.

Please, if you please, sweet lady —

— the fear of men who faced obscene torture and an obscene death, devised by good, upright, Christian men for the purpose of discouraging and punishing wickedness.

Supposing the infection of recorded terror were to seep back down that invisible passage and into her home? Supposing it were like an ancient hidden drain, sending out deadly germs to sicken the house's inmates? She felt as if she'd avoided a sufferer from infectious disease and then recognised the first spot on a member of her own family.

The cottage didn't feel safe any more.

She fixed Walter's head into the frame and prepared to embroider his features.

His face grew beneath her needle. His eyes became gradually three-dimensional and, with the stitching of the white specks within his irises, sprang suddenly into life. His brows thickened and bristled and stood out on the bony ridge of his skull. His nose thrust out under the pressure of the shadows on either side, and his obstinate mouth half opened ready to remonstrate with his accusers. Beneath his firm chin, slanting stitches laid down the shading of his Adam's apple

148

and moulded the muscular column of his neck. Mrs. Lake was most definitely going to fancy him.

She took John's phone call in the bedroom, sitting on the bed and looking at the wall behind which lay the secret passage. He described another difficult day and more pillars of the American establishment.

'When are you coming home? I miss you terribly.'

'Soon, really soon, Em. We've nearly got it tied up, until the court case, anyway. How's things in Little Hocking?'

'Abysmally awful without you.'

'Well, I miss you too. How's Walter?'

'Staring at me full-sized from the embroidery frame.'

'And the next-door neighbours?' She felt the house's presence at her back and shifted on the bed, glancing up in case it was peering in. It was only twenty feet beyond her bedroom wall, and if it fell those pitted red bricks and blinded windows would come upon her through this ceiling.

'All right. Oh, John, come home. Please come home.'

In the kitchen, she sensed the house beyond the closed curtains. In the living room, she sensed the passage above the fireplace. She took her evening meal up to her studio and ate it with Walter.

'No, I don't think it's you, it must be priests,' she told him. 'You'd have thought they'd have gone straight to heaven. Poor men, they were so sure they were doing the right thing, it just wouldn't be fair if it were any of them.'

'Nobody can know for sure what the right thing is,' said Walter. 'I didn't, and I said so.'

On the television news, a lot of people said that they knew exactly what the right thing was, and all agreed that it necessitated killing. Certainly, the alternative of just walking away didn't look right at all at that moment.

She worked on until her eyes were smarting with tiredness and her mouth was yawning into Walter's face.

She couldn't bring herself to turn out the light in the bedroom. It was too quiet in there, and the void where John ought to have been was even worse because she could imagine it being filled by a sensation of pressure and cold and vibrancy, and a plea of, Please, oh please, sweet, sweet lady —

149

She turned on the radio and sat looking at the wall. Who'd have thought that that house of four centuries' secrets might have established a colony within the heart of her home?

She got up, went to the studio and fetched the mended drawing of Tappett. She took down a painting and hung him in its place between the windows, then returned to bed.

'Now look,' he said, 'you don't know what any of this is about, and you don't know whether God's there or not, but you've got nothing to lose if you put yourself in His hands.'

'He didn't look after those poor priests who got carved into living pieces in His service. Nor you.'

'I made the decision,' said Walter, 'so I only had myself to blame. I wasn't expecting to be looked after.'

Yes, if that was how it was, you would surely rest in peace. But if you'd expected help or deliverance ...

Chapter Twelve

After quite a few raucous, old-fashioned rings, the telephone was delivered from its anguish.

'It is just coming up to twenty minutes to four in the morning, and you have interrupted something which was well on the way to becoming a deep and meaningful human relationship. Whoever you are, your reason had better be a bloody good one.'

'Hello, Matt,' said Emily, unmoved.

'Who's that?' said the voice, its aggression subsiding. 'It's not, is it?'

'Yes, it is. Who's the meaningful human relationship this week?'

'Emily Derby! For God's sake, you beautiful piece of womanflesh, how are you?' The voice was of that texture only to be produced by years of dedicated smoking and drinking and a lot of shouting.

'All things considered, I think I'm bearing up rather well.'

'One of the things considered being that neurotic yuppie of yours, I suppose? How is he?'

'In America at the moment.'

'For God's sake, you haven't split already, have you?' Matt demanded with renewed outrage.

'No, he's there on business. Look, Matt, I want to ask you something.'

'Anything, darling, and the answer's yes. I forgive your previous refusal to accept my advances and you can come back any time.'

'Weren't you brought up a Catholic?'

'Nobody's perfect,' the voice grated indignantly, 'why bring that up?'

'I need to know a few things about Catholic doctrine and attitude. It's to help me understand – someone.'

'Ah, another saint, eh? How many sacred Emily Derbys are there around now? I still think it was a crying shame you gave up painting, you were bloody good.'

'I haven't given it up, I just earn more at needlework and I like eating. Look, Matt, correct me if I'm wrong, but the Catholic church believes that once the bread and wine is consecrated it becomes the actual physical flesh and blood of Jesus, the same body that was born to Mary as a baby and lived for thirty odd years on earth and died and rose and eventually floated up into heaven, is that right?'

'Yes, that's it, unless there've been some changes I haven't heard about since I opted out. Why, you on the turn, or something? You always seemed perfectly happy as an agnostic to me.'

'Now doesn't matter, it's the traditional stance I want. And it was considered absolutely necessary to salvation that a Catholic should receive mass regularly?'

'Yes, if you missed you were under penalty of serious sin.'

'So any priest at all, let alone a really devout, dedicated one, would consider the bringing of the Host to his people a sacred and essential duty.'

'Yes. You got to embroider the rules of the club all over something? Be easier to paint them on the wall, wouldn't it?'

'And the priest would believe he'd endanger the souls of his flock if he failed to do so.'

'Yes, yes, yes.' Matt was getting impatient.

'He would therefore be absolutely, morally right to do anything in his power to achieve that, even at the cost of his own life?'

'Oh, it's the Elizabethan persecution, is it?' exclaimed Matt, sucking and coughing as he lit up another coffin nail.

'It is. And therefore, whether he was right or wrong in

152

believing that was nothing to do with it. Even if he and the whole church were completely wrong on that point of doctrine, he would still be morally right to do it.'

'I – suppose – so!'

'In that case,' Emily went on earnestly, frowning with concentration as she worked out her argument, 'supposing he did lose his life doing it, and got to heaven or purgatory or whatever he discovered to be his next port of call, where he was told that actually the mass was not necessary for salvation at all, but that he'd still won his Brownie points for courage, responsibility and all-round good intentions. I'd expect him to have been welcomed with open arms and given eternal rest, wouldn't you?'

'Talking of rest, Em, it is getting on for three forty-five and I have a moderately delectable lady beside me in a semi-recumbent posture, and dragging up all this stuff is reviving my hangups,' he grumbled. 'Can't you come to the bloody point?'

'That *is* the point. If he'd done all that, why shouldn't he be able to rest? What would keep him from the reward he probably had every expectation of receiving?'

'Oh, good God, there's nothing definite about the reward, Em. You've got to be earning it and battling for it to the very last moment, and you're still a miserable sinner who's only hope is a signed chitty from the Mother of God countersigned by her Son and endorsed by as many saints as you can muster. And even when you've snuffed it, that's when your troubles really start; they start praying for you harder then ever. Getting to heaven, I remember, was three steps forward, two back and quite often three or four back. That's how it came through to me, anyway, you daren't relax for a minute. There was no "Hallelujah, I'm saved."'

'That's really how it was?'

'Well, I'm sure there are millions of sincere and happy Catholics who'd tell you I was wrong, but that was how it looked to a miserable little worm in a 1940s Catholic orphanage. I was left feeling permanently dangled over the abyss on a hook, and eventually found the best way to endure it was to take a leaf out of the priests' book and always have a bottle with me on the end of the rope.'

153

'How was the last cure?'

'I am happy to say it failed completely. Last time I was on the wagon I couldn't paint anything worth looking at for the whole eight months. It is now nearly ten to four and my lady has got up. She might just as well. After this trip down Via Dolorosa Lane I'm probably going to be completely unable to do anything for her. May I now go and make a feeble effort?'

'Yes. Sorry, Matt. I couldn't think of anyone else who stayed awake all night.'

'So why aren't you asleep?'

'I've got a problem that's worrying me.'

'You, worried?' he exclaimed incredulously. 'You should give up religious work quick, it's ruining your mission as Little Emily Derby, the light of every home she enters. Go back to painting, you silly cow. Good night.'

'Goodnight, Matt, all the best.'

She went into the studio to commune with Walter's fully-featured but bald head. Her hand moved towards the needles and threads, and within seconds she was fitting his hair, cut in shaggy piled wool, around his face. Immediately he took another bound towards reality.

By sunrise his whole head was tacked on to the cambric, and the blue of his undergown joined to his neck and emphasised with dark, cotton cord. His coarse brown robe was tacked down and his outstretched right hand had been put into the frame, embroidered, removed, pressed and fitted beneath the loose flap of his sleeve.

Through the window she could see the sun streaking the sky with colour behind the hedge. The creative adrenalin was still running and she went downstairs to make a pot of coffee to keep herself going. She sat down on the settee in front of the dying fire to wait for it.

She awoke with the absolute certainty that she was not alone. The electric lights were on, but daylight was coming through the chink between the closed curtains. In the kitchen, the caramel smell of overbrewed coffee filled the air and the red light of the percolator glowed in the curtained room. She knew someone had come in, and looked round quickly for the dumped cases.

'John!' she called, running eagerly up the stairs. In the spot-lit studio Walter lay on the table with one arm and both legs missing. In the darkened bedroom she drew the curtains and looked for another prostrate male figure. The empty bed was like a blow to the heart and yet still she looked round for the sentient being she knew was there, because she could feel him and smell him, and knew that if she listened hard enough she would hear his breathing, quick and shallow, with the sob of panic.

Lady, lady, for the love of Jesu, sweet lady —

Very quickly and very quietly, she tiptoed back downstairs, opened the glass door and went into the garden. The day was well in business, with frost melting from the grass, birds hunting for food and Mrs. Mumford's head just visible over the red brick wall as she pinned out the washing. Her blank face nodded in acknowledgement.

'Did you mend it?' she called, looking with curiosity at Emily's dressing-gown and slippers.

Emily nodded, momentarily unable to speak, though willing to talk to anyone alive. She walked to the side of the lawn and spoke across the barrier of bare shrubs, beneath which the Christmas Roses were pulling themselves round in a truly valiant manner.

'If I pass it across to you, would you give it back to Mr. Curran?' she managed to say in a husky voice.

'Yeah, all right.'

She handled the cottage on the principle of a smoke-filled room, holding her breath, rushing in and not letting her breath go until she was back in the garden. She ploughed through a recumbent conifer she didn't like anyway, and thrust the rolled-up drawing over the territorial boundary.

'Ta,' said Mrs. Mumford, still staring. 'Is that a dress you're wearing?'

'No,' said Emily, clearing her throat and pulling the wine-coloured belt tighter, 'it's a dressing-gown, I was working for a lot of the night.'

'Fancy,' said Mrs. Mumford with envy, 'you can't do that with kids. They want their breakfast prompt in the morning.'

155

Emily picked some jeans and a tee shirt out of the laundry basket in the kitchen, dressed and made herself brunch, since it was nearly one o'clock. She went back into the living room. It felt all right in there but she opened the window, as if the molecules which made up the twentieth century would flow in and clear out any lingering, stale, historic air. She rummaged through the epistolary muddle beside the telephone and found a business card, with a home address and number scribbled on the back.

Mrs. Denise White, former wife of Mr. Tony White, car salesman, was home for lunch in her very new house in Prince Harry Close, Hatfield Peverel. She answered the phone with bright friendliness and retreated quickly into embarrassed reserve when Emily made herself known.

'It's about Holly Cottage,' Emily said, coming straight to the point but trying not to sound as if she was complaining or accusing. 'You said you were here about a year, didn't you?'

'Yes,' said Mrs. White uneasily.

'Well, please don't get the impression we're not happy here, we have been very, but there seems to be a bit of a problem and I wondered if you'd ever encountered it.'

'No,' said Mrs. White distantly, sounding as if she couldn't think what she was talking about. 'We had the roof lined and the central heating completely renewed and it was running perfectly when we left.'

'It's nothing like that, and I'm sure your husband never even noticed anything at all, but I thought perhaps you might have done. A sort of, well, a presence, as if there was someone there you couldn't see who was desperately anxious to talk to you.'

There was a shocked silence at the other end of the line, then, 'Certainly not,' said Mrs. White.

'Oh please, Denise,' begged Emily, reverting to the temporary first-name intimacy of people thrown together by the sale of a house, 'if you ever felt that, please say so. I'm not annoyed you didn't tell me, I want to know it's not just me.'

Denise immediately sounded as if she'd kicked off a pair of tight shoes.

156

'Oh, I *see*. Well, yes, Emily, I did feel that sometimes, and it wasn't nice at all. Eventually I told Tony and he nearly hit the roof after everything he'd done to the place. He went straight out and put a deposit down on something being built, and the minute it was ready he put the cottage on the market. I did wonder about telling you, but Tony said if I did and you backed out of the sale he'd never speak to me again. As it was, we broke up anyway. Honestly, Emily, the trouble I had with that man! Oh, I'm sorry,' she said in a rush, 'you don't want to hear about all that. This presence thing, is it really frightening you?'

'Quite,' admitted Emily, 'but not half as much as when I met it or a near relative in the house next door. Did you ever go in there?'

'Ye-es!' Denise made the word speak volumes. Emily remembered her as a very slight, neat, getting-on-with-it type of person, who probably organised an office impeccably and went jogging with her overweight Tony at weekends. 'Isn't it *horrible*? I called there when I was selling Prize Draw tickets for the Health Centre, and Lady Curran asked me in to meet her husband. I was standing talking to him in that spooky bedroom of his when I felt something touch me, as if it was trying to attract my attention. Well, I was out of there like lightning, I can tell you, but after that I sometimes got the same feeling in the cottage, usually by the fireplace.'

Emily breathed a sigh of relief. 'Oh, my goodness, that does make me feel better. Was it you who cased in the old bricks?'

'Yes, Tony thought they looked slummy. I don't think he likes old houses at all, really, but he bought it to please me. I've always had this dream of an old cottage with roses round the door. Not any more, though,' she said with feeling. 'I think I may throw out everything I own the day it reaches its tenth birthday, just in case. So it's happened to you. What are you going to do about it, move?'

'I don't want to, I really love living here.'

'I wonder who it is,' said Denise intensely. 'One of the Currans who got killed in a duel, do you think? Or perhaps he had a tragic love affair and took poison or something. Or,' she went on enthusiastically, her safe distance from the problem allowing her to wax romantic about it, 'perhaps he murdered someone, and can't rest from remorse.'

'I rather think it's something even sadder than that, to do with ideas, not deeds.'

'Do you know anyone psychic?' Denise suggested, beginning to sound as if she were actually enjoying herself. 'There's a girl in my office who's sort of psychic; she can look into your eyes and read your character and your aura and all sorts of things. She's really good. She told me I was really affectionate, and much more sensitive than people realised, and that someone had hurt me at some time in my life. Shall I ask her to call you?'

'Oh no, don't worry, I'll sort something out. Thanks anyway, Denise. 'Bye.' Emily put the phone down, thinking that the last thing she needed was amateur clairvoyance.

She went to the studio, where Walter welcomed her with open arms to a four-hour stint at the needle. At the end of that nature called, followed by food, and just before five-thirty the phone rang.

'Emily darling, I've had another run-in with your Mrs. Witherley-Bashe. That is right, isn't it, Witherley-Bashe? How absolutely marvellous, does she look like she sounds? Oh, good, I thought she might. Well, she's still being difficult about money. If I were you I'd hold everything until we've got an advance through, because I have a nasty feeling she's going to hang on until the last possible moment and then pay less than we expected, hoping we'll be glad to get anything at all. How far have you got?'

'Quite a long way. I can't stop now, I think I should feel quite ill.'

'Well, I've told her you *will* stop, so don't let her catch you at it. I've asked for a cheque in the post tonight, and I'll let you know if it's forthcoming. How's John?'

'Four thousand miles away,' said Emily in a flat voice.

'That's men for you, never there when you need them,' said the twice-divorced Sophie. Emily's eyes pricked as she put the receiver down, partly with longing for John and partly with anger at Mrs. W.B., the sort of tight-fisted patron who has been the curse of artists since someone first put his palm print on the cave wall. She certainly couldn't stop now; the pain would be almost physical if she were to interrupt the creative process so far along the road to completion.

John's call came within minutes. He was on his way to a lunch meeting in a totally different State, and this place wasn't called the windy city for nothing, believe her him, he was being cut to ribbons. 'Love you, Em. See you soon.' She rose from the Victorian chair, crossed the hearthrug towards the stairs and walked suddenly into cold; icy as a refrigerator, live as electricity, charged with presence.

She drew a breath and found she gasped fear in with it, straight down her throat and into her lungs to grip them with terror, to weaken legs worn out by running, to prickle the scalp which senses pursuers behind, to tremble hands scraped sore by contact with rough, damp bricks.

Lady, for the love of God, sweet lady, please, oh dear God, lady, please –

As she jerked away from his invasion her hand remained caught in the invisible cell of fear and cold and she couldn't deliver it. Instead she was drawn back in, the temperature closing over her and filling her lungs.

'No, I can't,' she called out wildly, 'I can't! Please leave me alone. I can't do anything for you, it's too late!' And this time his response was not just felt in her brain but heard in her ears, like the sigh and the moan in the bed-drawing room of Holly House.

It was a low sound of such despair that she felt as if she had killed.

She found herself out in the garden, her face in her hands, crying hysterically and vocalising her sobs so that they carried like the wailing of the lost all over the garden. Heavy grey clouds were building up all around; above the hedge, above the cottage, above the house. She shivered with the Christmas tree in the sharp wind and looked back through the open glass door which was allowing all the advantages of John's electric central heating to run away with her into the outside world.

She simply didn't know what to do. For half an hour, she hugged herself and walked restlessly up and down in the dark, still sobbing, still shivering, still staring at the open-mouthed cottage, the lit window of the studio, the dark hulk of the

159

house behind the wall with lights burning in its kitchen.

The cold began to bite into her – real, serious, winter cold, arriving at last. She was wearing only indoor clothes, but she endured it as long as she could, until at last her fingers and toes were acutely painful and her teeth were chattering. She approached the open glass door and looked inside. The wind she had allowed to enter was making free with the room, blowing papers and magazines on to the floor, using the billowing curtains to knock over a pot plant, filling the air with powdery grey ash from the edges of the fire.

She went round to the kitchen door, rushing in before the lurking house could get her. It was as bitterly cold in there now as in the garden, and she fetched a thick shawl from the hook behind the kitchen door and wrapped herself up in it. She drew the side curtains to blot out Holly House, reflecting on what a pointless, useless exercise it now was, then stood and looked into the living room, as if she expected the intruder to materialise before her eyes. Presently she backed away towards the sink, crouched down and reached into the cupboard. Now she braved the living room, sliding each foot forwards in case it might stub against something invisible, knelt slowly before the fireplace with sobbing gasps of breath and set the candles upright on the brick hearth. There were six of them, all she had in the house, plain and white and utilitarian, for emergencies only. She lit them with a shaking right hand which had to be steadied by the left before it found the wick.

'They're for you,' she whispered, 'I know they're not the right sort, but they're all I've got. I'll pray for you, but I'm afraid it won't be in the words you want, because I don't know them. Listen, please don't catch hold of me again, because I can't do anything else for you. I don't even know what you want. If it's prayer, you shall have it, and I'll try to get a Catholic to pray for you properly. And I'll keep the candles burning, I'll get more in the morning. I hope they'll last all night, but if they go out, don't come for me again, please. I'll try to help, I really will, but please, please, let me alone!'

She searched the bookshelves for her Bible, scuffed grey from long-ago life in a school desk, and put it by the candles. Perhaps she should open it. Where? She drew the cover back

and revealed the introduction: James by the Grace of God . . .
Oh no, no, no!

In the cupboard in the studio, among old drawings and designs and papers to do with her commissions, she eventually found the paperback life of Edmund Campion she had bought from the Catholic Truth Society.

'It's the best I can do,' she told him as she laid it among the candles. 'There must be words in there which'll comfort you and I'll get a Vulgate tomorrow. Or would you prefer a Latin missal? Don't touch me again, please. I'm trying, I'm trying!'

The wind tore in and the candles guttered. She rushed for the garden door and closed it, then relit them. Finally she left her poor, non-believing, superstitious little offering alone in the room and retreated upstairs to the studio and Walter's sensible, down-to-earth comfort.

'Who is it,' she asked him desperately, 'and for God's sake how can I help him?'

'Don't ask me,' Walter's face said, 'I'm the one who doesn't know the answers, remember?'

Chapter Thirteen

The place was cold and draughty and there was a strong smell of paraffin from the heater by the desk. It was in a town ten miles away from Little Hocking, and yet the nearest secondhand bookshop listed in Yellow Pages.

Emily's hands ran along the shelving, picking books up, opening them, putting them back. She peeped into glass-fronted cases and crawled under tables to investigate dusty agglomerations of outdated literature. 'What are you looking for?' asked the owner, appearing after ten minutes from up a flight of bare wooden stairs. He looked as if he'd been asleep.

'I want a Roman Catholic Prayerbook.'

He faced into the muddle, like a mother sheep who recognises her young in the midst of a vast flock.

'No, that one's in English. I want the old Latin Mass.'

'It's in there as well,' he said, reaching out a long dingy arm and lifting it down. The smell of stale perspiration accompanied the gesture. He held the book open and Emily saw the pages dotted with red rubric, English words on the left, Latin words on the right.

'I don't know whether he'll approve,' she said anxiously, mostly to herself, 'haven't you got a completely Latin one?'

'How much were you thinking of spending?' he asked ironically. He was only about forty-five, but greying, grubby and appearing to have given up on life early.

'Are they expensive?'

He moved across the dusty floor and unlocked a bookcase

162

with torn, sun-faded silk behind its glass doors. The books within were either antique or outré or both. The missal was blackletter-printed, woodcut-illustrated and published a long time ago. By Emily's standards it was extremely expensive.

'This is the completely traditional thing, is it, the same that had been going on since the Middle Ages?'

'Well, I don't recall much liberalisation before Vatican Two, do you?'

'And it's the only one you've got?'

'Yes,' he said, preparing to take it back.

'I'll have it,' she said, swallowing. 'And do you have a Vulgate?'

He turned and moved away in another little cloud of personal unfreshness. He couldn't have washed that sweater in months.

This was a nineteenth century edition with a cover dangling by dry, gluey threads, retrieved from a pile in the next room and dirt cheap.

'Your husband a religious scholar, is he?' he inquired, giving her the benefit of his indigestion.

'Yes,' she said shortly, in order not to prolong the conversation, and took out her chequebook. If Mrs. W.B. didn't cough up today she could find herself having to draw her expenses from the joint account, which would make her feel dishonest. This was very silly of her, as John not only wouldn't mind at all, but would be quite pleased by her temporary old-fashioned dependence.

She left the shop. She was both physically and mentally tired, and not feeling herself at all. Last night she'd shut the door on the rest of the cottage and worked away at Walter until she couldn't keep her eyes open any more. Then she'd wrapped herself up in a huge, gaudy crochet blanket made by her mother, and employed a few hours in shallow and unrefreshing sleep. In the morning she had tested the other rooms and found them empty, to her immense relief. The biography of Campion lay unopened and unmoved, the candles had died into a solid, starred puddle of ashy wax sprawled over the bricks. It seemed probable that the greasy stain would remain there for ever.

163

The car was pestered by small snowflakes bouncing around it like midges, though the few which reached the ground behaved more like white dust than the foundations of a cold, deadening blanket. When she got home the townscape of Little Hocking was still uncovered and Holly House as nakedly threatening as usual.

The central heating had restored the cottage to its normal comfortable temperature and a pile of unopened letters and John's unfolded newspapers remained where she had put them on the settee. She stood just inside the front door and looked at the fireplace and the wall above it, and at the remains of that fearful, primitive obeisance to the unknown which eventually becomes religion. She had never felt the need of such things before. No unmanageable disasters had barged their way into her life, no unforeseen events had left her feeling incapable of coping, no overwhelming grief had ever torn her apart and set her searching for reasons and explanations and panaceas with which to rebuild her peace of mind.

But now she'd experienced the helpless fear in the face of trouble which has caused Man to search for things unseen, and if he couldn't find them, to invent them. She did believe in God but she couldn't have defined him, as others seemed to find it necessary to do in order to make Him more safely theirs. She believed in Him because she believed in goodness, both the necessity for it and the existence of it, because life without it would not be life at all. And because there was enough goodness in her fortunate life, it had been enough. But it really wasn't enough to stand in the presence of this tortured, terrified soul and bring him nothing but the belief in goodness. If he was what she suspected him to be, he had required so much more, from people, from life and from eternity.

He had needed certainty. Rules and rituals, abstinences and prohibitions, everything seen and unseen codified, defined and so safely certain that question and contradiction became blasphemy. He had needed to know that the world beyond death and sight and human comprehension was tidily divided into heaven, purgatory and hell, and to know exactly by which steps human souls were allotted to each. He had needed to have his whole earthly life ordered by others, and to have this renunciation of personal initiative pardoned by the elevation of obedience into sanctity. It had been the most vital thing in his world that the unchanging beliefs and practices of his church should relieve him of the terrors of doubt and the responsibility for thinking things out for himself.

To her, the messy remains on the hearth were silly, trivial, pathetic, and a sign of personal failure. To him, they might well be important enough to calm his spirit, so they had to stay.

Once the little shrine was redressed she glanced through the post, which was all for John, and crept up on the newspaper headlines, trying not to care too much. Equities weren't as steady as John would have liked them to be, the battleship *Missouri* was shelling Baghdad and the Iraqi armies, and Saddam was calling for widespread terrorist support, even from the country he had fought for eight years. And John wasn't home yet.

But at least Sophie's phone call was cheering.

'Darling, you'll never believe it, she's stumped up! Not even a letter with it, just a cheque drawn on St. Mary's account and looking as if she's written it with a Stanley knife.'

'Oh, thank goodness for that,' said Emily with deep relief, looking at the last knockings of her financial capital lying on the dirty bricks of the hearth. She had opened it at the Mass and the black letters flickered in the shivering flames of the slim candles which surrounded it. 'Can you forward it as soon as possible, please?'

'Of course,' said Sophie, sounding extremely jolly and quite relieved herself. Even agency for the fine arts wasn't as flourishing an occupation as it used to be.

In the bedroom all was at peace, though Emily's complete mental comfort could only have been achieved by the demolition of the chimney stack. In the studio, Walter now lay dressed in his gown, with two hands, one grey-stockinged leg, and the other within calling distance on the frame.

She sat down and continued the detail on his leather shoe where she had left the needle stuck in the fabric at two o'clock that morning. Occasionally she stepped out on to the landing and looked into the bedroom, taking the psychic

165

temperature. When she went down to get some food she made sure the candles still burned, then walked, quaking, up to the hearthrug and held out her hand, to seek the frozen reserve of a psychic manifestation and find it not there. After lunch she went into the garden and watched leaden skies coughing puffs of dusty white snow across the grass. She tried not to look at Holly House but did just the same, windows, roofs, walls, stone head, fudged pargetting, silent bell. When the light failed she started to get nervous, and the knock was partly a shock, partly a relief.

Mrs. Witherley-Bashe was not smiling. She stood there in a hooded waxed jacket, breathing rather harder than the walk uphill from her cottage warranted.

'Ah! You are back. You really are quite difficult to get hold of, Mrs. Wakelin. I hadn't realised that the convenience and co-operation we'd expected from our employment of you was not, in fact, to be forthcoming.'

Emily said nothing, because she really couldn't be bothered. She stood waiting for her patron to come to the point, with a non-committal smile upon her face.

'I have come to see the progress of the project,' said Mrs. Witherley-Bashe eventually, with repressed heat. 'As I have had to pay out a very large amount towards it already, I feel I am fully entitled to do so.'

'You most certainly are, Mrs. Witherley-Bashe,' agreed Emily and stood to one side to allow her to enter.

She closed the door and turned to find the woman with her eyes fixed in the direction of the fireplace, staring at the strange little Catholic Mission. 'Never apologise, never explain,' she told herself, a rule she had always found useful, and waited.

Mrs. Witherley-Bashe turned with magnificent slowness. She took in Emily's rich brown hair, her dark blue eyes, her pale skin and the offensively high level of her beauty and charm, and seemed to find that here at last was an excuse for it all. She brought up her big guns and smiled a salvo.

'Are you Irish, Mrs. Wakelin?'

'No,' said Emily pleasantly, and left it at that. 'The studio is upstairs.'

Mrs. Witherley-Bashe followed her up the uncarpeted stairs, her critical eye noting black ankle boots, a flowing, coloured skirt and the black, cotton, lace-edged petticoat which swirled out beneath it.

'Do you make your own clothes?' she asked with the tone of one kindly offering an excuse to a sinner.

'Sometimes,' said Emily, again pleasantly and not adding any rider or plea, and led her into the studio.

Her patron went to the end of the table and craned her neck, endeavouring to add a useful six inches to her eye level. Emily pushed a wooden stool towards her and she mounted it. Walter stared up at her, his hand looking as if it was about to grab her by the skirt and tumble her into bed with him. Emily stifled the thought in case she should burst out laughing.

The smile hardened, mostly for Emily's benefit, but she refused to play the part of nervous employee awaiting approval and turned away to tidy the threads scattered on the table by the frame. As Mrs. Witherley-Bashe's silent, critical pose became prolonged into near-melodrama she sat down and got going again on Walter's left leg.

'He looks so coarse,' said Mrs. Witherley-Bashe at last, becoming aware that her expression was not just producing no reaction, but going unobserved.

'Well, I expect he was, rather,' said Emily, 'it was no job for an aesthete.'

Mrs. Witherley-Bashe breathed hard, abandoning the useless smile for the moment.

'I suppose you'd have preferred to depict him engaged in his working activities.'

'Oh no,' said Emily with apparent careful consideration, 'I just like him to look as if he had some.'

'His hair's so shaggy. I would much prefer it smooth.'

'Curly hair is generally assumed to be more saintly,' Emily suggested.

'Who told you that?' Mrs. Witherley-Bashe protested, unaware she was being gently sent-up. 'Those hands!'

'The committee did vote not to change them.'

She blushed, got down off the stool and came over to stand behind Emily, like the self-appointed critics who pester artists when they paint in the open. Emily's needle dipped in and out

167

of the layers of fabric, moulding Walter's muscular calf with deft, accurate stitching.

'You're a good needlewoman,' her visitor admitted at last.

'Thank you.'

She leant closer and frowned, 'Is that *string* you've used for his shoe laces? It *looks* like string.'

'Yes, it is. Best quality string, of course, or it wouldn't have done the job.'

'But, but – I mean it's so poverty-stricken.'

'He *was* poverty-stricken.'

'Yes, I know that,' she said impatiently, 'but surely we can do better for him now? I mean, he's a martyr and worthy of respect and reverence.'

'Yes, he certainly wasn't then, was he? I suppose one of the advantages of being a martyr is that you acquire an honorary position in the middle class. I wonder if they'd have thought that was a good idea, all those labourers and tailors and fishermen and tentmakers and carpenters ...'

'Mrs. Wakelin! I find that extremely offensive!'

Emily parked her needle in Walter's knee and turned round.

'I'm sorry, Mrs. Witherley-Bashe, it wasn't meant to be offensive at all, I was just remarking on an interesting fact. I remember at the first committee meeting I attended Mrs. Gage said something rather similar, about how dead people are treated with respect that they would never have received when they were alive. I mean, look at the dedication of your parish church, for instance. If you had lived in Palestine in the first century, would you have invited Mary Magdalen to tea, even after her conversion?'

'There are a great many people I would not invite into my home for tea,' burst out Mrs. Witherley-Bashe, 'but the standards of social behaviour are a completely separate thing from spiritual standards. The two have nothing to do with each other. Now, when can you bring this across to the church for the committee to see?'

'I'm afraid I can't yet. They could always come and see it here, as you've done. So can the vicar, of course,' she added, putting out a feeler.

168

'Yes,' said Mrs. Witherley-Bashe, looking distant. 'Yes, we will have to arrange that. Thank you, Mrs. Wakelin.'

She went carefully downstairs, giving the impression that the stairs were not only old and narrow but also a purpose-built deathtrap aimed at her, and opened the front door. She turned to aim a last accusing stare at the flickering candles.

'Extraordinary,' she remarked, and marched out into the night.

Emily laughed as soon as the door was closed and went back to the stairs, itching to get that leg finished and in its right place holding up Walter's short, solid body.

He caught her halfway there, frozen in a block of cold air, paralysed with his terror, gripped by his hand, his desperate message entering her brain as if it came by telepathy.

Lady, lady, lady, I perish, sweet lady —

Her tears started to flow, triggered by the double terror of their two souls. 'Don't, don't, don't,' she repeated over and over again. 'I can't help you if you don't let me go. I'm not ignoring you, I'm really trying to help. Let me go, let me go, for God's sake let me go!' Her last words were a scream which gave her the strength to pull out of his cold presence and fall on her knees before the smoking candles on the hearth. The wind through the opened front door had extinguished them and tipped the front cover of the missal over to shut its comforting words away from him.

She lit them again with tears pouring down her cheeks and opened the missal at a new place, searching for one of the few Latin phrases she knew – *'Requiem aeternam'*. Give them eternal rest, O Lord and let light perpetual shine upon them. But why didn't You? If he's what I think, why in the name of Justice didn't You give him rest?

She passed the long, terraced row which contained Mill View Cottage and turned into the footpath which ran between long cottage gardens to the main street of Little Hocking. The wind was getting stronger and it was now bitterly cold. The snow whirled around in the light from the single lamp-post, and it was thicker and the flakes larger and stuck together. The sound of traffic grew louder and a motor bike ripped the air open just ahead of her as she emerged onto the pavement.

She wasn't quite sure where it was. She had the impression that it was up at the other end of the village, but had never actually noticed it.

The cars of returning commuters ground past her and whirled the snowflakes into greater agitation. New closes of squeaky-clean houses with polychrome brickwork appeared where big, old Victorian mansions had been demolished. A fully-occupied block of 'period' retirement flats now flourished where a dairy had finally fallen down.

At a crossroads, where a small roundabout attempted to deter the commuters from colliding with traffic emerging from the side roads, a black and white notice pointed to the left. 'To Our Lady and St. Edmund Catholic Church.'

It was about two hundred yards down the turning and about thirty years old, like the housing which sat around it. It had no tower, just a little bellcote on the roof. The supports of the porch slanted like lances and its brightly lit windows were mostly clear glass except for long, thin, ascetic saints in their centres. In the east window, its eponymous patrons greeted each other with transcendental joy.

Not sure whether St. Paul's phobia still held sway, she drew her shawl tightly over her hair and went in.

The lobby was white, with full noticeboards, well-stocked book stall and three happy angels on a 1960s high, holding out their arms from the level of the ceiling. The inner swing doors were of the assembly hall variety and admitted her with a screech. Within, a cassocked priest in his thirties was in the act of walking down the side aisle at the other side of the church. He saw her and changed his trajectory to reach the corner where she stood looking like an orphan of the storm.

'Have you come for confession?' he asked, looking at her flushed, windblown, anxious face.

She shook her head.

'No, I just need to talk to someone − I need to know − could you tell me −'

'Sit down,' he said, and ushered her into the back row of metal and leatherette chairs. He sat down two seats away from her with his elbow on the back, and waited. He was balding early, and his face and hands seemed very smooth and white, as if his vocation and perhaps his celibacy had preserved him from normal wear-and-tear blemish.

'Can you tell me . . .' she started. 'Well, yes, of course you can, that's why I've come – sorry. Look, I want a mass said for someone, someone dead, I mean. Do you still do that?'

'We do,' he assured her, 'if they are Catholics, of course. I get the impression you are not. Is it for a relative?'

She shook her head and the shawl slipped down off her shiny hair. She pulled it up again. 'Sorry.'

'That's all right,' he said, his own meagre hairs unturned, 'it's not an absolute requirement these days. Now, can you tell me the name of this person, and when they died?'

'I don't know either, really. It's just someone I met who seemed to be in a lot of trouble, and he died quite a while ago. Is it too late to try and help him?'

'It is never too late,' he said. 'If all this happened so long ago, why are you only asking for a mass now?'

She bit her lip. 'I've only just realised how terribly unhappy he is. Was.'

'Is?'

'Was,' she repeated, dropping her eyes. 'I said "is" because I can't forget him so it feels as if he's still around. Couldn't you help him, please?'

'Of course I will, but I need to know a little more. You can't remember a name at all?'

'I never knew it. I wish I did.'

It was an extremely awkward conversation altogether. She wasn't sure why she didn't want to tell him the truth, but her ignorance and therefore slight suspicion of Catholicism certainly had a lot to do with it. Perhaps she had visions of him rushing round to the cottage in full vestments accompanied by at least one exorcist, and couldn't bear the thought that that poor ghost might be treated like a cockroach infestation.

The final embarrassment came when she found she had no cash with her and had to pay the mass stipend by cheque. It seemed so totally unfitting; it should have been done with silver groats or golden angels.

The wind was howling down the streets and the snow starting to lay as she struggled back home.

171

Chapter Fourteen

She had left the lights on, not to stop burglars entering but to give herself the courage to do so. As she came in, the candle flames swung in the draught and the pages of the missal waved and tried to turn. She fetched two glass paperweights from John's desk and put them one each side to keep the place open. Fire danced within the coloured globes.

She went to the kitchen. The light stared at her across the wall. She drew the curtains and got some food together, took it back into the living room, pushed the settee well back from the hearthrug and sat down. The phone rang.

'Hello, Em! I'm starting home in a few hours! We'll be refuelling at Kennedy and landing at Heathrow early evening tomorrow, your time.'

'What airline are you booked with?' she asked, her emotions swinging between relief, delight and anxiety.

'Aer Lingus, so not even the I.R.A.'ll get me.'

'Please don't joke about it. He's inciting every homicidal nut with an axe to grind to join him in a World Terrorism Festival.'

'Well, what do you want me to do, stay here until it's all over?' he inquired in a disappointed tone.

'No, no, no, I want you home as soon as possible, but *alive*. Oh, John, do take care!'

He burst into surprised laughter, temporarily released of his pilgrim's burden of life-long worry by her bearing it for him.

'Well, to be rational, Em, having chosen a low-target airline, there's not a lot more I can do. Even if I go and stand over the pilot in the cockpit I don't think it would make a lot of difference.'

'I know,' she admitted. 'Oh, John darling, have a safe, safe, paralysingly boring journey, and I'll say a prayer for you.'

'Will you?' he said, startled, as if the gravity with which she viewed his danger was only now revealed.

She put on the television while she ate, mainly because it provided human voices, as it certainly didn't provide much cheer.

The candles were getting low. She replaced them before they could gutter.

The fire was burning up and the central heating was on twenty-four hours, but she wasn't really warm. Later, she fetched another sweater from the bedroom, tiptoeing through it with her ears pricked and her hands held out to feel for any cold spots. The wind was buffeting the windows, and outside she could hear next door's holly trees rattling like shingle on a beach.

She closed the studio door, put a long, comforting tape of Kreisler salon pieces on the deck and withdrew the needle from Walter's divorced knee.

Once he had both legs and the hem of his gown was fastened down over them, she restarted the tape, wrapped herself up in the rug and tried to let sleep anaesthetise her fears before the lilting, worldly music ran out and left her with only the sound of the wind and the creaking of the cottage for company. But when she awoke and saw the green light of the silent tape deck staring at her from the top of a cupboard, the time was only a dark, dispiriting five-fifteen.

Quickly she filled the room with no-nonsense Gilbert and Sullivan, and was carried downstairs on a cheering tide of 'When I first put this uniform on'.

The new candles were on the point of guttering in their turn. She changed them before she did anything else and wiped the wet black specks of dirty snow which had come down the chimney from the pages of the missal. Outside, the wind was still prowling around and it wasn't any warmer. She glued her nose to the front window and saw the world outside like a luminous negative under the street lamps, clarified by a light covering of snow. She moved cautiously round the hearthrug and into the kitchen. The breakfast she collected together on the tray was a mere picnic, her choice being made for convenience and speed, not taste or fancy.

She shut herself up in the studio with Gilbert, Sullivan and Tappett, brewed up tea on the sink draining board in the corner and ate with memories of such meals enjoyed in her childhood tree-house hideaway; solitude, privacy, food and drink, a favourite book or perhaps a new drawing book and a sharp, green, aristocratic Venus pencil, the chief joys of one happy in her own company and full of resources for her own amusement.

But supposing your hiding place was as strait as a coffin and made of cold brick and dusty board; your only air through a hole punctured not to the open but to another enclosed, secret space; your only light a candle which grew sick in the heavy atmosphere and deposited greasy black soot on the walls of your enclosure? Supposing your food was thrust in with haste, and consumed slowly and abstemiously because you had no way of knowing when more could be delivered? Supposing you were the filling in a sandwich of brick walls only two feet wide and fourteen feet long, as at Ingatestone, so you could exercise but barely turn at the end of each pacing; or shut up in a claustrophobic brick sentry box with the exit through a hole in the floor, as at Oxburgh, so you could not exercise at all? Supposing you had to crouch in a yard-square cavity beneath a floor for hours or days, the only thing making your confinement endurable the knowledge that the alternative was slow and agonising death?

She renounced all pleasure in her food in pity for his misery.

By sunrise she was stitching the details of Walter's gown. It was torn in a couple of places and there was a darn on the leg of his tights.

She turned on the radio. They were sending a last ditch embassy to Baghdad, but American bombers had landed in Gloucestershire. There seemed little likelihood of escape for the bombed Middle East, but at least no civilian aircraft had been blown out of the sky as yet.

'He's coming home,' she told herself with carefully controlled excitement, 'he'll be sleeping with me here tonight.'

174

The milk she took in off the step had a stopper of white ice pushing up its top, and the fussy wind was still moving the thin snow around. The papers administered their cwn icy chill to the feeling heart.

She opened the fridge and found she was out of nearly everything – no eggs, no butter, only two crusts of bread and nothing for tonight's dinner, certainly not for two. Her bowl of cereal was made up from the last remnants of packets of cornflakes, muesli, puffed wheat and left-over crumbs from John's wheatflakes.

She took a shopping trolley up to the village and filled it to overflowing. She also paid in the cheque which had arrived with an exultant note from Sophie. 'Is there a Mr. W.B.? Poor man!'

She didn't know. The post must have been filled by someone at some time, but as she had never yet heard him mentioned, it seemed likely that he had long ago relinquished it.

She must get some more tacking thread, she'd been using it as if there were no tomorrow. Unfortunate turn of phrase there, Emily; if things go on as they are there might well *be* no tomorrow for a large portion of the human race. Oh it was absolutely bloody *awful*, and more than that it just wasn't *fair*. Everyone thought the threat of World War Three had all gone, and now here it was cropping up again from another villain with another army and another huge stockpile of weapons of mass destruction. Remember New Year 1990? Only a year for the world's hopes to be dashed. Oh John, John –

'Hello,' cried Mrs. Hubbard. 'Well, so you took the job! Hope you're not regretting it.'

'No-o-oh,' said Emily with a twisted smile which said it all.

'How's it coming on?'

'The figure's nearly finished. I've just got to put his belt on this afternoon.'

'And the wording?' Mrs. Hubbard shrewdly perceived the nub of the whole matter, probably gathered from the remarks of other customers.

'Not decided yet.'

175

'Mm,' she said with a meaningful nod, 'everyone with their own idea, eh?'

'I rather think they'll be fighting it out at the next committee meeting, as I can't go any further till I know.'

'Oh, how I should like to be a fly on the wall. Still, you'll probably be there, won't you?'

'I'd much rather not,' said Emily. 'I'm pretty sure it would mean being pig-in-the-middle. But the final decision must lie with the vicar anyway, so why don't they go and ask him what he wants and take the discussion from there?'

'In case they don't like what he says,' grinned Mrs. Hubbard. 'She's probably going to present him with a fait-accompli. He usually gives in if she does that.'

'Oh dear, how very depressing,' said Emily, quite shocked by the vicar's apparent lack of authority in his own parish. 'What was Mrs. Witherley-Bashe's father like? I was told he was terrifying, which seems all wrong to me for someone in his position.'

Mrs. Hubbard pursed her bright pink lips and widened her big, mascaraed eyes. Her knitwear had broken out in rows of frogs today. 'Well, he was a big man, not in height but in bulk, and he had a very red face and lots of white hair. Used to go in for denouncing sinners by name from the pulpit, which didn't go down at all well. In fact there were complaints to the bishop, and one man threatened to take him to court for slander, only they settled out of court. But he was sincere, no question about that − well, that was the problem, of course,' she said dismissively. 'Personally I find "totally committed" people an absolute pain, they cause so much trouble, particularly to people who aren't. He just couldn't leave *them* alone, seemed to think of them like stamps he had to add to his collection, and if they weren't available to be collected he came down on them like an Old Testament prophet, even if they were chapel or R.C. There wasn't much ecumenism around while he was here, I can tell you. And if they weren't church-goers at all!

'Poor Mrs. Staines happened to mention to him once that she thought there was a lot of good in Buddhism and he went right up in the air, accused her of idolatry and said she was dabbling in the powers of darkness. Yes, he really was frightening when he got like that, as if someone had pressed a destruct button in his head and he couldn't control himself. There was a group of Theosophists started up at Great Hocking and he went over there with some of his five-star holy rollers from the congregation and held a prayer meeting outside while they were having a service. It made all the local papers for miles around.'

'Oh dear, oh dear,' said Emily wryly. 'What on earth would he have said to the Tappett chapel?'

'Well, that would have been all right. I mean, he was a Protestant, wasn't he?'

'Of a kind. Whose idea was it anyway? Did Mrs. Witherley-Bashe think it up?'

'Shouldn't be surprised,' said Mrs. Hubbard. 'When can I see the hanging? Do I have to wait until it's up in the church, or do I get a private view?'

The needlework committee arrived unannounced for their own private view after lunch, in other words just as Emily was remembering the existence of such a meal at ten to three. She had the impression that their chairwoman hoped to catch her in the act of adding a final unforgiveable outrage to the design. The reflection of the dry snow moving restlessly about the back garden added support to the spotlight playing on Walter Tappett, whom Emily now hauled carefully up on to the wall, still mounted on the cambric whose flimsiness seemed to accentuate his solidity. She was surprised herself by the impact of his standing presence, and moved back a few paces in case his vigorous step forward collided with her.

'Oh, you've torn his robe!' Miss Barton remarked.

'No, that's intentional.'

'*Is* it?' she exclaimed, her voice hitting a near-squeak with incredulity.

'And he's got a darn in his tights,' said Mrs. Witherley-Bashe coldly. 'What is this, Mrs. Wakelin, socialist realism, blasphemy or merely extremely poor taste?'

'I think I would define it as truth.'

'Truth! And exactly what sort of truth is that?'

– said jesting Pilate. She's not going to understand and neither is Miss Barton, so I'll have to work on the others.

177

She turned to Mrs. Bolsover, Mrs. Lake and especially Mrs. Gage, who was looking at the figure with incredulous joy on her round, rosy face, as if she couldn't believe her luck.

'This is how I believe Walter Tappett probably looked, and how he would have appeared to you if you had met him in the streets of Little Hocking four hundred and forty years ago. When people walk into that chapel I want them to feel almost as if they are meeting him in the flesh and experiencing his straightforward, sincere, perhaps rather naive character. I want them to understand the sort of man he was and the reason he felt as he did, and to appreciate the enormous personal courage needed for such a lowly person to stand up to the pressures on him to conform, and to hold on to his personal idea of Truth right through an appalling experience of torture, cruelty and death.'

'His *idea* of Truth? My dear Mrs. Wakelin, the truth Walter Tappett was upholding was Protestantism, drawn from the clear, unchanging truths of the New Testament,' stated Mrs. Witherley-Bashe, smiling with icy serenity.

'If they're that clear one wonders what all the centuries of disagreement were about,' said Mrs. Bolsover dryly. 'It quite obviously wasn't crystal-clear or they wouldn't have had anything to argue about, would they?'

'He was standing up for the truth,' repeated Mrs. Witherley-Bashe, going pink. 'Everyone knows what is meant by Truth. It's all in the Bible.'

'Well,' said Mrs. Gage, shrugging, 'there are lots of things in the Bible I don't understand, and I don't just mean set-piece debating points like the identification of the unforgivable sin.'

'If he's not standing up for Bible Truth, how can he possibly be a saint?' Mrs. Witherley-Bashe demanded, her unanswerable question supported by the returning tight smile.

'I don't suppose he thought of himself as a saint,' said Mrs. Gage enthusiastically, 'he just cared about truth. If the truth was that he didn't know the truth, that was *his* truth and he was right to stand up for it. Everyone else wanted to force their truths on to him, but he wouldn't have it. His truth was what *he* knew as the truth.'

'Pardon?' said Miss Barton, looking quite panic-stricken

as the conversation swept her off the safe sandbank of religious orthodoxy and plunged her way out of her depth.

'Yes,' Emily agreed with Mrs. Gage, giving her a grateful smile, 'that's exactly what I meant. What I didn't want to depict was just another pretty, sanitised, bowdlerised saint that no one can identify with, blessing people with a nice, clean hand. I want people to think, Why, he's not on a different plane, he's as ordinary as I am, and what he went through was as difficult and terrifying for him as it would be for me. If he could do it, then maybe so could I.'

'A saint's halo in every Christian soldier's haversack,' said Mrs. Witherley-Bashe.

'Yes,' said Emily with joy, then realised she had been employing sarcasm. 'Now, what about the wording?' she went on quickly before the argument started up again. 'Have you decided, or are you discussing it now you've seen the figure? And what does the Vicar think?'

There was a momentary stiffening visible in the stance of the committee. Mrs. Lake stared on at Walter Tappett and spoke up for the first time, in a meditative, dreamy way.

'That's what we'd all like to know. Really, Mrs. Wakelin, I've never seen anything quite like this. In some ways it's the most revelatory religious experience I've ever had. Sort of "Behold the man".'

'Mrs. Lake!' the chairwoman protested.

John rang at five. Security alert at Kennedy, no one being allowed back on plane for the foreseeable future.

She could have howled or put her foot through something with disappointment. She stood looking out of the front window, watching the wind tossing bigger and bigger snowflakes around, as if it was deciding just where they would cause the greatest inconvenience. Not tonight, then, perhaps tomorrow morning. Which meant another night alone with that importunate presence, another night when she daren't sleep in her own bed because the end of the secret passage was just behind the wall and he might pass through it and come upon her as she slept.

And John's return wasn't going to cure that. He'd be there to hold on to, but she'd have to explain everything which had been happening, and he'd be so anxious to protect her he'd insist that they moved, just like Tony White, and she'd loved the cottage and Little Hocking so much, and what would happen to that poor, lost soul pleading for help? Why, he'd do the same to the next woman who moved in here, or the next strange woman who visited the house next door, seizing them by the hand, sighing into their ear, thrusting his words into their minds and begging, begging for – what?

And anyway, why women? Because he knew only too well the hardness and cruelty of men and was looking for softness and mercy? Because after the unrelenting male discipline of the priesthood he yearned for the merciful kindness of Our Lady? And for how long? After four centuries, for how much longer must he suffer permanent anguish? And was he really there at all, or was it all just a psychic stain left behind like the wax on the hearth?

I won't think about him. I've given him what comfort I can, with the candles and the missal and the Latin Bible, and the priest will have said the first mass for him today.

A group of people appeared on the pavement at the point where the red brick wall separated the cottage from its heavy parent, and they were talking very energetically and very loudly for a genteel, respectable, country-parish needlework committee.

Within minutes they had broken up, still sending last words in each other's direction and turning their heads to add another irrefutable point. Mrs. Witherley-Bashe sailed across the road in the direction of the church and her cottage. Mrs. Bolsover and Mrs. Gage disappeared behind the wall. Miss Barton and Mrs. Lake came past her gate, bearing their opinions on towards Mill View Cottage, where all would be rehearsed and re-argued in the presence of Miss McCarthy.

Mrs. Lake glanced at the cottage, saw Emily's head silhouetted in the light of the window and waved. Miss Barton did likewise, with rather less friendliness. Mrs. Lake stopped and called out something.

Emily went over to the door and opened it.

'No, don't get cold,' Mrs. Lake protested, 'I was just saying that the wording is nearly decided. You should hear the decision tomorrow.'

180

'Oh, good. Thanks.'

Well, that's something. She went back to the window and watched them pass on out of her sight, then saw in its reflection that the candle flames had gone.

The cold came for her in a sudden smothering, suffocating embrace. Lady, sweet lady, I beg of you, help, help, for the love of God –

'Stop it! Stop it! They're praying for you! They're helping you! Be patient, can't you? And for God's sake let me go, let me go, let me go!'

Sweet, sweet lady, I beg of you, by the blood of Christ, by the sweat of Jesus, by the bones of all the saints, lady, lady, lady, help me, in the name of God's precious wounds help me –

She was held helpless against the window, staring into the outside darkness, her back icy with his presence, his words somehow feeding through the back of her head. It was like the sensation she experienced when she was painting and it was going well, as if the artistic flow came not from within her brain, but beyond it.

She stared out at the whirling snow, wanting to scream and scream until some passer-by heard or saw her but robbed of the ability to do so by the frozen immobility of her lungs. She was paralysed, terrified and imprisoned, it seemed for ever.

It was actually about fifteen minutes before he ceased his frantic entreaties and allowed her to move.

181

Chapter Fifteen

'Ah! Mrs. Wakelin.'

'Good morning, Lady Curran.'

'George would like a word with you.'

'Would he?' Emily's voice was flat and blurred with tiredness. She hugged the crochet blanket around her and brushed its corner back and forwards against her cheek, as she had done when very small. She was cold, although hot water hummed through the pipes and into the radiator by her chair, while the wind outside moaned an accompaniment. The full-sized drawing of Walter stared at her down the length of the room, striding foward with hand outstretched to offer his aid. The embroidery itself had been safely replaced on the table. Her eyes closed again as she cradled the portable receiver amongst her hair.

'Coffee time will suit him very well. About fifteen minutes.'

'Well, actually – '

'Goodbye.'

Oh no, no, no, no – Oh for crying out loud – Oh Lady Curran you are completely, utterly, unbearably, the absolute final – I won't go! I'll stay here all curled up and safe, in my dear studio with good old Walter till my darling John comes in through the front door. I'll do something I really want to do as a treat and then I'll feel better. I know, I'll start working out the design for the Victorian chair. I can't do anything more to Walter until the committee stop arguing or the Vicar starts behaving like a real vicar, and I'll feel better and safe, and back to being Little Emily Derby, the light of the home. Ha, ha, very amusing, Matt. Is that how I look to people? Remorseless jollity and good cheer? Pollyanna? And do they find that appealing or merely wearing?

She shuffled across the room and filled the kettle at the tap. The biscuit tin was empty and she was hungry. She opened the studio door.

Across the corridor her bedroom sat silently waiting, bathed in cold white light; not very tidy, clothes lying on the floor by the wall, a couple of dirty mugs on the bedside table, the coverlet dented where she had sat down yesterday to change her shoes for boots.

She went downstairs. In the living room the settee was covered with odds and ends, the hearthrug was crumpled up, the logs were nearly consumed and the candles she had lit at three o'clock that morning were engaged in a last desperate struggle for life. Through the uncurtained front window the blinding whiteness of snow shone as uncompromisingly as truth in a world of lies and deception. She walked across and looked out. The world was blurred with white and more was coming down all the time, not straight down but from all angles, the thick flakes only finding a resting place once the wind had done with knocking them around. The hollies sagged over the red brick wall like a row of Christmas puddings under a burden of white custard. The front path was gone, only shallow dips remained to record the milkman's footsteps of many hours ago.

As she opened the front door a foot-high cliff of snow fell inwards onto the mat and exploded into chunks, while the wind leapt in with the alacrity of a bailiff and put out the candles. Without waiting to dig the milk bottles from their mound, she shut the door, ran into the kitchen and grabbed the next new box, on whose lid a quartet of sophisticates prattled around a dinner table.

She beat the world record for speed candle-lighting and did another mop-up job on the soot-and-ash-spotted missal, reflecting that its value must be going down with the same speed as property.

Supposing Mr. Curran died soon and poor old Simon decided he just couldn't keep the family albatross flying any more — what could he sell it for, and could he, in

183

fact, sell it at all? Who'd like it enough to spend at least a quarter of a million getting it back into order and be prepared to take on ghostly sitting tenants?

She put on her wellingtons, went out of the kitchen door and round to the front garden, shying away from that high, time-battered wall of windows. The detailing of snow on its features made it look dirtier and showed up its dilapidations. Supposing it fell? she thought. Supposing it falls on me? She dug out the milk with a trowel and carried it back into the kitchen.

The phone rang.

'Mrs. Wakelin, it's half-past eleven.'

'Is it?'

'George is getting agitated.'

'Lady Curran, he isn't the only one who gets agitated. Didn't Simon explain to you how I feel about going into your house?'

'It seems so remarkably silly.'

'And I'm busy. I've got lots of work to do.'

'You can't get on until you've seen George. He wants to tell you about the words for the hanging.'

'Oh! How does he know?' asked Emily, the wind taken out of her sails.

'He discussed it with the committee yesterday.'

'I didn't realise it was anything to do with him. Has he spoken to the Vicar too?'

'I told you, he doesn't speak to the Vicar. Margaret will inform him of his wishes.'

And how *will* he take that? What breathtaking arrogance. What sort of a parish is this?

'Is Mr. Curran in his bedroom?'

'The dining room. I moved him in there specially.'

Emily struggled to summon up the assertiveness to demand he should meet her in the kitchen and found she hadn't got it.

'Can't I speak to him on the phone?'

A complicated near-silence followed, textured by rustling movement, footsteps, hand-muffled discussion, then at last painful breathing.

'Are you there, Emily?'

184

'Good morning, Mr. Curran. How are you?'

'I am very well, thank you.' His weak, breathy voice gave the lie to that. 'I hear the embroidery of Walter Tappett is nearly complete. I should like to see it.'

'Well, I'm afraid it wouldn't be a good idea to move it before it's on its permanent backing. Cambric isn't designed to take the figure's full weight, you see, and might tear if it's pulled around too much. It's surprisingly heavy.'

'Is that the usual way it is done?' he sounded quite accusing.

'It's the way I do it,' she said calmly. 'I shall put the backing into the frame and work the wording straight on to it, and only then mount the figure. Is it right that the committee have told you what they've decided? They haven't told me yet.'

'I should like it to read, "Because you say you see you are the more blind".'

'Oh, really?' Emily thought it over. 'That's not quite right, is it? Shouldn't it be "Because you say 'We see' your sin remains with you"?'

'They are Tappett's words, not the Bible's. He was paraphrasing what he'd heard read out loud by others, and that wouldn't have been from the authorised version, anyway.'

'Er, what do the others think about it? Won't it look anti-church?'

'He was anti-church,' said Curran's thin voice, as cutting as steel wire, 'that is the whole point.'

'Then it's hardly the tactful place to make it, is it? In a church, I mean. I don't really think that was what the parish had in mind, and after all, they are the commissioners of the work.'

'I am the commissioner of the work,' said Curran with dry satisfaction. 'The money for the renovation of the chapel and its furnishing comes entirely from me, and if it is not done as I wish it the full amount will not be forthcoming. Have you had any money so far, Emily?'

'Yes.'

'Good, I shall make sure you receive the balance as soon as you have finished. Don't bother to approach Margaret for it, come straight to me. Now remember, I want those words clear, in straightforward black capitals – no gold and sequins, no arty Gothic letters that make them difficult to read, just plain modern lettering so that people see it means *now*, not way back in a time which has nothing to do with them. Don't make any concessions at all to softening the message. When can I see it?'

'As I've just explained, it can't be moved until it's finished or it could be damaged.'

'I will come round.'

'Come round! Well, yes, of course you can. I didn't realise you were able to get out, Mr. Curran. Oh, the studio's upstairs I'm afraid –

A high voice could be heard in the background. He spoke away from the phone. 'Then Simon can take me. Get Simon to come down today –'

The high voice was not having any. It took the phone away.

'Exactly how long are you going to be, Mrs. Wakelin.'

'What, to finish it? I don't know. I told your husband that I must have a word with the Vicar and the committee first, then if they're agreed I'll get started right away –'

'By the weekend.'

'Heavens, no! Lettering takes quite a long time to set out and then it will have to be hand embroidered –'

'Well then, the boys will try and bring him round on Sunday. If we wrap him up —'

'Lady Curran, have you seen the weather? I should think it might well kill him, and you'll never get a wheelchair through that snow. Look, let's leave it for a few days and see if it melts, then we can decide what to do.'

'He's getting so agitated,' she said, the cold, flat timbre almost giving way to an anxious note. 'He must see the figure. Is it just like the drawing?'

'Pretty well.'

'Could you perhaps hold it up at your kitchen window and he can sit in our dining room bay ...'

'What about the wall?' asked Emily, daunted by the thought of trying to display a six-foot embroidery through a two-and-a-half-foot cottage window *and* keep it out of the sink.

186

There was hurried discussion going on. Lady Curran came back.

'Look, we'll see what we can do. I'll ring you back, Mrs. Wakelin.'

The line went dead and she was left feeling she had had a brush with Bedlam, or at least Wonderland. Yes, there were a great many more undercurrents to this commission than she had realised, combining into a positive whirlpool. She felt quite cross. She would have liked to have been warned, officially, that was. But there was no need for her to take sides. If Mr. Curran really had full control of the thing, then that was their problem, not hers, and if the Vicar couldn't be bothered to take charge of the project as it was surely his responsibility to do, that was his.

But she'd had enough of being played off one against the other. Today was going to be Vicar-meeting day.

The wind did its best to drive her back into the house, forcing her off-balance and plastering snow against her all the way down hill to the schismatic cottages.

The lane to the lychgate was ankle-deep, except for a trough trodden up its middle and a few tributaries reaching out from front doors. Snow dripped from picturesquely swooping eaves and sat on empty windowboxes, and the flowering shrubs which glowed against cottage walls in calendar-photographing time were mere white heaps. A warm, complacent ginger cat looked out of a misshapen window at the discomfort of the rest of the world.

The lychgate itself could only be opened halfway before it wedged against a pile of displaced snow. She fought her way on into the churchyard and through the very Victorian-looking iron gate into the vicarage front garden, where the snowdrops had been completely buried.

Within an equally Victorian porch was a picturesque iron bellpull which Emily recognised as being in a state of retirement, and a plastic bellpush with an automatic light beneath it which she rightly decided was in business.

The Vicar opened the door himself and stood looking at her for seconds after he should have exclaimed, 'What a day!

Do come in!' and what he actually said then was, 'Oh, is it still snowing?'

'I'm Emily Wakelin,' she announced.

'Oh. Er, do you want to step inside?'

'I'll ruin your carpet,' said Emily, shivering on the doorstep but incapable of behaving in an inconsiderate manner. He went and rummaged in a rug chest and brought out a ground-sheet, the sort which went with boy scouts' tents, and Emily knocked snow off her coat and boots, shook herself like a dog, and eventually stepped off it in sweater, trousers and stockinged feet.

In the depths of the house an unaccompanied voice like translucent crystal rose and fell, stooping tenderly to low notes, rising up to ecstatic union with high ones. The line of melody had the unpredictability of direction of a dragonfly glittering in the sun.

They joined the voice and a thick fug of cigarette smoke between the timbered walls of a small room with a coal fire. The Vicar hovered, as if uncertain where to settle. The floor was covered with piles of books and there were only two chairs in the room, so Emily made the decision for him by taking the armchair by the fire.

'Oh, yes,' he said, seeing the logic of her choice, and sat down at the desk, which faced out on to the foot of the tower. A second's more thought instructed him to turn the chair round. It was a swing office chair, the sort that went with roll-top desks, but this one was in attendance upon a small rectangular dining table which had endured a lot of hot dishes. The voice twisted and turned in its search for perfection and was joined by others on the same pilgrimage.

The Vicar of St. Mary Magdalen, Little Hocking, was of average height and of average English colouring, with fine, light brown hair beginning to thin at the temples and sprout grey above the ears, nondescript pale grey eyes, light lashes and slightly rabbit-like teeth which kept his lips parted in an expression of apprehension.

He was fiftyish, plumpish, slightly bowed in the shoulders and dressed in an old darkish suit and an old greyish cardigan over his clerical collar and stock. His shoes were checked carpet slippers and his socks were odd. Not outrageously

188

odd, such as one black and one white, but Emily's needle-woman's eye recognised the slight difference of dye and texture which meant that not only were they from different pairs, but that one of them was inside out. His appearance gave an impression of old-fashioned, even inappropriate respectability, like a small boy dressed in his grandfather's clothes.

He reached for the cigarette which extended an inch of grey ash into the centre of a brass ashtray.

'I know I shouldn't,' he said as a sort of Mea Culpa, drew in the smoke and offered the packet.

'No, thank you,' said Emily, already feeling as if her lungs were being eaten away. 'What's that music?'

'Hildegarde of Bingen,' he said, and hurried to turn it off, as if he expected disapproval.

'It's beautiful. Like stained glass would sound if it could sing.'

'Oh. Yes. Er – ?' He looked as if he didn't quite know what to do with approval.

'I thought it was time I met you and talked over the project. I've never had a commission before where the incumbent wasn't in on things from the start, and I've felt rather uncomfortable about it. I have tried to arrange a meeting, but somehow it didn't happen.'

'Yes,' he said politely. 'Er, it's the Lenten suppers, is it?' His eyes looked wary, as if he was fishing for information.

'No,' said Emily, getting a sudden impression that he was in a world of his own, perhaps with Abbess Hildegarde. Changing her mode of delivery to a slow, clear enunciation, she told him, 'I'm Emily Wakelin, from Holly Cottage across the road. Mrs. Witherley-Bashe and the needlework committee asked me some time ago to do some work for the new chapel in the church. An embroidery,' she added, as his expression remained unillumined by understanding and he pulled nervously on the last millimetre of tobacco before the tip.

He stubbed it out, rubbed his square, pale hands together and said, 'You mean the repairs to the north transept? We had a donation from a parishioner, you know, a very generous one. A new dampcourse has been put in and they've replastered several places.'

189

'Yes, so I saw. Well,' she urged gently, 'can you tell me what the wording is to be? I'd like to start on it as soon as possible.'

He seemed nonplussed and reached for another cigarette. 'Margaret's organising all that. Has she shown you the kneelers?'

'Yes.'

'Did you see her embroidery in the baptistery? She was only about twenty when she did that. It's getting rather grubby. I suppose it should be cleaned. Do you know about cleaning embroidery? Or perhaps it would wash. What do you think?'

'You do know about the theme of the chapel?' Emily asked, becoming quite concerned about him. Surely they hadn't kept him that much in the dark? How did you do that to someone who went into the church every single day of his life?

'Yes, Margaret told me − er − it's going to be all blue and yellow isn't it? I did see some of the kneelers and they've taken down the charity board from above the altar.'

'Did they tell you what's going to be in its place?' asked Emily gently, as if she was trying to break something to a sensitive child.

'Er,' he said, and stopped with an expression of helpless distress, as if he hadn't done his homework and expected punishment if he admitted it. He took comfort in the cigarette.

'You've heard of Walter Tappett, of course?' said Emily confidently, trying to test his knowledge without appearing patronising. For all she knew, he might be a brilliant mind with the detachment from everyday things which sometimes went with it.

'Yes,' he said, 'there's a brass tablet in the nave.'

'And the person who's given the money for the renovation, you know who that is?'

'Yes, Mr. Curran of Holly House. I was quite surprised, not what I'd have expected of him at all. Still, it's always a mistake to judge people too quickly and too harshly. You never know what's hidden deep within the soul.'

'That's very true,' said Emily, meaning every word. 'Well, part of the renovation has been to make a better memorial to Walter Tappett, and one of the things they're doing is to put

190

up a wall hanging of him, so that people can see exactly what he was like,' she added, putting in a crafty piece of special pleading on behalf of her concept, to prepare him for what might be bad news.

'Oh, really? Well, Margaret did tell me that something was being done professionally, and was that all right? Of course, I said yes, as long as the expense was covered by the amount of the gift. Now just a minute, did you say that you were doing the work? They're not getting a professional after all?'

'Yes, they are. I *am* a professional. I moved to Little Hocking a couple of months ago and Mrs. Witherley-Bashe asked me to do it then. I get the impression,' she said tentatively, 'that she's quite a force in the parish.'

'Oh, goodness me, yes,' he said, smiling feebly, 'I don't know what we'd do without Margaret. There isn't a curate here, you see, even though the parish has grown quite considerably over the last ten years, and I find I lean on her more and more. And the rest of the Parochial Church Council, of course,' he added hastily, as if he was answering a persistent complaint yet again.

'Well, Vicar, I've finished the actual figure of Walter and I'm about to start embroidering the wording, and I thought I should hear your ideas on the subject. I've already had a suggestion,' she warned him, 'but I should like to make sure you approved.'

'Oh!' he said, looking surprised and pleased at the same time. 'Well, I hadn't thought. I mean, I generally leave everything to – ' He looked uncomfortable. 'Well, not everything, of course. But really, you know, there's such a strong movement towards reconciliation these days, I don't see it as at all helpful to accentuate the divisive elements in church history. Why should we celebrate him more than Father Francis Lethaby? I know he wasn't actually martyred, but he died in the act of practising his religion, and he is buried in the church.'

Emily looked at him with sudden respect, wondering if her attempt to treat him as a holy fool had been obvious enough to be offensive.

'Mr. – I'm sorry, I don't even know your name.'

'Leigh.'

'Mr. Leigh, I must say, I think you're quite right, but would you be allowed to commemorate a Catholic in an Anglican church?'

'I see no good reason why not,' he said, shrugging, 'after all, we have a whole crypt-full of Catholics in our care.'

'I would like you to see my design,' said Emily persuasively. 'I've been so nervous you wouldn't like it, and I just hated to think that you didn't know what was going on,' she added in a confiding rush brought on by relief.

'Yes,' he said thoughtfully, then after a pause in which his mind seemed to wander off at another private tangent, 'would you like to come and see, Mrs. – er –'

'Yes, I think that would be a very good idea,' Emily agreed, getting eagerly to her feet, 'then perhaps you would like to come back with me and see the hanging.'

Chapter Sixteen

The Reverend Leigh plodded across the churchyard through the snow. His black overcoat had worn cuffs, a threadbare collar and a hint of green about the shoulders; his grey muffler whipped behind him in the wind as large, juicy snowflakes settled on his bare head. Following in his footsteps several yards behind, Emily was reminded of some anthropomorphised character from children's literature, such as Mole or the Hobbit.

They arrived in the church porch and stamped their boots on the red Victorian tiles. She glanced up at the timbers and saw old swallow's nests tucked between them. How nice; the sleek blue-black birds must bomb in and out all day during the summer – she would look forward to seeing them.

Within, the church was not a lot warmer than outside, but it was still and the deliverance from the wind gave an additional dimension to the feeling of peace. However, as they walked up the centre aisle they could hear noisy activity of the 'To you, Fred' and 'Watch it, Charlie' variety going on in the chapel; also a discussion about how unhealthy the temperature was for man, beast and brass monkeys. The transept had been curtained off from the rest of the church by large sheets of plastic, and a powdering of white dust spilled out beneath them into the crossing.

The Vicar stopped at the carved screen and bowed his head in the direction of the altar, but instead of turning left to examine the work in hand he walked on through the chancel into the vestry. Here he opened a door of the size which is universally considered to represent the low average height of our ancestors. He switched on a light and began to descend narrow spiral stairs, his coat shoulders brushing against both walls and its hem sweeping along the edges of the worn treads. Emily followed, wondering what on earth he was doing, bracing her fingertips against the icy wall and wrinkling her nose to stop the sneeze threatened by the smell of dust.

There was another arched door at the bottom, but this time with the clean lines and painted planks of comparatively recent restoration. He unlocked the door and invited her in with a wave of the hand. 'Would you mind the step?'

She would, fixing her eyes on her feet in the dimness as the last pale, luminous snow dropped off on to the stone floor, raising them again only as he pressed a light switch and sent the banal illumination of three metal-caged bulbs sliding along the stone lines of the vault, deepening the hollows between time-worn stones and beaming down onto the contents of the chamber.

She felt as if she'd been hit in the chest. She hadn't been expecting this, she hadn't realised that was what he'd meant by: 'Would you like to come and see, Mrs. – er – '

She'd thought he'd meant the chapel, of course she had. Anyone would have thought he'd meant that. Anyone would have assumed that this was now unseeable. Who'd want to see it? It wasn't decent to leave such an experience available so that one might be forced to experience it, it wasn't right to have to look at it, it was dreadful, it was frightening, and oh it was so, so unbearably sad.

'I thought this was sealed up,' she said, choked with emotion which was in part anguished complaint.

'Only the outside door,' he said.

The cold in there was intense and yet dry; even the floor which showed between the stacks was dusty rather than damp. The long bones were piled in criss-cross fashion, layer upon layer, around the pillars supporting the vault. Between them could be seen gatherings of small ones, vertebrae and fingers and knuckles, thrust in to fill the gaps. There were lines of pelvises, the fans of bone arranged to make zigzags around the square blocks, and then more long bones and so on to above the level of her eyes, where the whole carefully erected

194

masses were weighted down by a layer of jawless skulls, crowded together like commuters on a station platform or a crowd on a football terrace, all looking in the same direction with blank, thoughtless eyes and their individuality lost to the crowd.

After the first shock, the dominant emotion aroused in her was pity. All these people, these ex-people, who once looked and functioned like her, and knew life was about speaking and smiling and touching and feeling, about eating and drinking and enjoying and suffering, and who probably felt the earth was, even in some small degree, theirs, were now disinherited, stripped of their beautiful, living flesh, revealed in the minimality of their ugly bones and cast for ever in the cruel role of admonitory lesson to their inheritors.

'He's over there,' said Mr. Leigh, beginning to move down the narrow corridor between the stacks.

'Who?' asked Emily, hanging back, loth to intrude upon people in such ultimate affliction and at such total disadvantage. Oh no, cremation is better than this. Let us be consumed in a clean fire and leave no rotten ugliness to end our journey through the world. Only the rottenness was past now. The bones were picked clean, by nature and by science, and as long as the vault remained dry they would remain unchanged − a kind of eternal punishment for the flesh the mediaeval church had so despised and hated. How terrible not to be allowed to disappear, but to be kept on stage long after your talent to perform had departed.

He had disappeared behind the stacks. Stacks, she thought. It makes this sound like the back room of a library. Supposing one could come in and say, I want to look at John the Smith, who died of plague in 1348, or Joane Browne, who died in childbed in 1503, or Master Faithful Retainer, who lived at Holly Cottage when it was first built and sometimes helped priests down from his chimney; and who perhaps knew in the flesh that presence who now wanders lost in a century not his own. And suppose they went and brought out Faithful Retainer's bones and you could study them and read them likie a book and say to them, Who was it, who is it, tell me who it is and why?

'Here!' the Vicar's voice echoed from the other end of the vault.

'What?' she called quietly, finding herself afraid to raise her voice in case its vibrations dislodged these balanced houses of bones, or even awoke them.

'He's here!'

She steadied herself and walked forward, breathing carefully, drawing in her arms so that there was no danger of touching. At the end of the aisle she turned left and passed down another.

The Reverend Leigh stood looking at a glass case about two foot wide and three feet long, the sort which used to furnish old-fashioned museums, especially the local variety; in fact a label with most of its gilt worn off was still under the impression that it contained fossils, flints and bone spear-throwers. It did not. The lower part of the case held pieces of curved wood and rusty old iron, the centre layer was of much stained and fragmented bone, and sitting on it all like a kettle on a fire was a dark skull which still possessed its jaw and slight traces of hair and skin adhering to its scalp. On one side of it lay a sticky brown wodge of something which looked like burnt puff pastry, and on the other a three inch pewter crucifix on a chain.

'I'm glad they didn't put him in with the others,' said the Vicar. His woolly-gloved hand patted the glass, then stroked gently up and down its length, moving the dust aside so that Emily could see Father Lethaby more clearly.

'So the story about the barrel is true?' she said with the incredulity of one who finds that there are such things as fairies.

'Yes.'

'And it was hidden in a priest's hole?'

'One can only guess about that, but it seems rather unlikely to me. The staves prove that it was quite wide. Perhaps they hid him in a cellar, or an outhouse, or even up a chimney. Who knows?'

'Was he the son of Sir Jervase, who interrogated Walter Tappett?'

'No, the grandson. Are you very cold?' he asked, as he saw her shudder.

'Yes.'

'Fortunately, I don't feel it much, but Margaret's always telling me off for not wrapping up. She made these.' He held up his gloved hands, darkened with dust.

Sounds as if she mothers him, thought Emily, wondering if Mrs. W. B. had her eye on the Vicar as a second husband, even while remaining acutely conscious of the packed mortality all around her. They didn't marry or give in marriage. They didn't feel the cold. They didn't need officious busybodies to knit them gloves and tell them what to wear, they didn't anything. They did nothing, they were nothing, they had no valid role, they shouldn't even exist any more. They should have been allowed to disappear from the earth centuries ago.

'Can we go now?'

'Yes, of course.' He caressed the glass case again, then blessed its contents with what seemed to be affection. The pathway between the bones was too narrow for him to pass her and she went ahead, right down, round the right-angled corner, straight along to the step and the release of the little door. She climbed the winding stair without waiting for him, and once in the vestry, which was equally cold but homified by the modernities of cassocks, papers, books and an electric heater, closed her eyes, hugged herself to feel her own warm flesh and had a sudden fit of trembling. The skyed vicar looked out across her head and catechised a noseless corbel tucked under the ceiling on the other side of the room. The present one emerged into the vestry and closed the ancient little door.

'There,' he said with a smile. 'Well, goodbye then.'

'But what about the chapel? We were going to discuss the furnishings,' she added as he looked blank.

Poor Father Lethaby. Poor all of them. It might be one of them, I suppose, though if they were buried properly shouldn't it mean that —

'Oh, you want to see it?'

'With you. To make sure we agree.'

Perhaps it's another priest, one who didn't die naturally and receive Christian burial, but who was caught, tortured, hanged, torn apart while still alive . . .

197

'Oh, I see.'

He stepped down the chancel steps and drew aside the plastic screen. The men at work appeared suitably sobered by the sight of his collar and bade him good afternoon.

He stood looking at the transept with such intensity that Emily almost felt he had never really seen it before. He looked at the charity board leaning in the corner, at the resited radiator and at the Lethaby tomb, whose owners were being smothered in their state bed by plaster dust. He studied the partly swept floor, where a few later Lethabys lay under grey stone slabs, the newly rendered east wall and the large hook which had been cemented into it.

'What's that for?' he asked Emily, turning with an anxious face which was expecting the worst.

'I expect it's for the hanging,' she explained. 'You remember, the embroidery – '

'Yes, yes,' he said, 'blue and yellow kneelers.'

His attention passed on to the deposed mural tablet. 'Where's that going?' he asked the man who was shovelling rubble into an old cement bag. The shoveller pointed to the west wall.

'Who told you to move it?' he asked, appearing to be surprised, if not disturbed.

'The lady – Mrs. – er, Bashe, isn't it?'

'Ah. Yes. Mm,' he told himself. 'What about that one?' He indicated a recumbent marble cartouche crowned by a skull, on which curly black letters informed that, 'Near this spot lie the mortal remains of Francis Lethaby, *aetatis suae* 38, who was struck down fighting for his Anointed Sovereign in the lamentable battle of Naseby during the late Rebellion. Also his wife, Mary Lethaby, daughter of Sir Peter Spender of Pindon in the County of Bedfordshire, also of three infant children, Francis Peter, Mary Catherine and Francis Charles, who were taken from their sorrowing parents within days of coming into their arms. The Lord giveth and the Lord taketh away. This stone was set up in the year 1661 by one who knew them and their Virtues. *Requiescat in Pace*.'

'The lady said to move that too.'

'What else have you taken down?' he asked with some distress, screwing up his face in an effort to remember how the transept had looked before this transformation had started.

'Well, just one or two more smallish tablets,' the man said, looking as if he was ready to put up the only-obeying-orders defence.

'Where are they?'

The man turned to his mate, who had been painting industriously at the radiator as if it was nothing to do with him. 'In there,' he said, nodding at a pile of tarpaulins.

The vicar pulled it back and disclosed a jumble of marble and stone, some of the pieces broken. 'Oh!' he cried. 'Oh, dear me! I didn't know,' he told himself. 'I mean, she never said. Whatever will they say? Oh, *what* will they say?'

'Who?' asked Emily, feeling genuinely concerned for his mental health.

'The Diocesan Advisory Committee. You have to get permission,' he said, tugging agitatedly at the ends of his scarf and facing her with haunted eyes. 'You have to get a Faculty before you touch a thing. Oh, my goodness, whatever was she thinking of?'

'Didn't you realise what was happening?' Emily asked with incredulity. 'I mean, you must be in here every day, so how come you never noticed?'

'They divided it off last week to keep the dust out of the nave and chancel. Just repairs and decoration and some nice new furnishings, she said. It's really too bad.'

His hands shot out at the workmen, palms emphatically down.

'No more,' he said. 'Stop! No more!'

He rushed down the aisle and opened the church door with an echoing clatter of wooden bolt. Emily followed, to find he was away out into the snow again, hurrying through the blizzard to the lychgate, ploughing down the foot-wide trough which was all that remained of the gravelled lane, squeezing past the builders' lorry parked axle-deep on the road to Great Hocking. Fortunately the weather had now banished all traffic, for he hurried straight across without looking, slithering and stumbling and nearly crawling through the gate of a cottage on the other side, which wore the complete uniform of thatch, timber and pargetting. He banged the knocker and stood in the wind awaiting an answer. There was no porch, merely a small wooden pentise which might have sheltered a thin visitor standing to attention among very polite precipitation in a dead calm.

Emily stayed at the gate like a nursemaid keeping an eye on a vulnerable child. The snow clung to her eyelashes, gathered in the crannies of her face and weighed down the heavy curls of hair so that she was nearly blinded.

Mrs. Witherley-Bashe opened the door and to Emily's amazement, caught the Vicar in the chest with an open hand as he made to stride straight into her immaculate home. Any conversation was to be carried on just inside, where a raft of plastic and *Daily Telegraph* floated on the fitted carpet.

'Margaret,' he cried in an agitated voice, 'did you get a Faculty?'

Mrs. Witherley-Bashe stared past him at Emily with a strong hint of '*Now* what have you done?', bowed her head in a stiff gesture of dismissal and closed the door.

Emily stood abandoned in the road. The snow continued to assail her, riding on the back of wind which came howling down the lane from the direction of the village. She started to trudge uphill, raising her knees high above the drifts and holding out gloved hands to balance herself.

The houses ahead smoked and waited. The hollies now surrounded Holly House with a white rampart, and its gables and turret sat on it like a white, spiked helmet.

At her own cottage she stood and looked through the living-room window, actually afraid to enter, although the log fire glowed enticingly on the hearth and the settee looked infinitely inviting to her tired body.

Although the cottage kept the main blast off her, the wind slid round the side and tore at her clothing. She put her open hands either side of her face and leant them against the glass. The candles still burned, but if she opened the door in this wind they would be blown out instantly. She could go in the kitchen door, but she hadn't got the key – nobody took back door keys around with them unless they never used the front one.

The flames trembled continuously in the draught from the kitchen, then ducked down and away as another belched down the chimney and puffed ash over the missal like a wraith.

I'll have to go in in a moment. If I stay out here I'll die of cold and it's not as if the situation will get any better for waiting. In fact, it will get worse. Do I really want to go in in the dark, see the only bit of light instantly extinguished, and then grope for a switch in a blind emptiness which might contain — him? Of course, the trouble is the way the front door comes straight into the room. It probably seemed such a good idea when the Whites knocked down the internal wall, but they really should have put a porch on. Still, it might have been such an ugly porch — oh I'm cold, cold, cold, but I daren't —

Then she saw the red light winking on the telephone table. John! He'd rung while she was out and left a message.

She blundered into the room, along with snow, wind, cold and more built-up drift from against the shiny, olive green paintwork she had brushed over the Whites' mahogany-coloured stain. She slammed the door, tore off her boots and hurried through the scattering of snow on the carpet to relight the smoking candles. She was on her knees fumbling with matches when the phone rang again. She cried out with frustration, afraid to leave the flames unlit, afraid to hear the fourth ring break off and tell John no one was at home. She scraped the flame into life, saw it take tremulous hold and seized the receiver.

'John?' she cried.

'Er, hello? Is that Mrs. Emily Wakelin?'

She sat down on the floor and leant her head against the brocade cloth which covered the table to the floor.

'Yes,' she said in a subdued voice.

'Oh, sorry, your voice sounded different. Did you run to answer?'

'Yes.' She watched the nervous flame trembling on the very tip of the black wick, crawled across and picked up the matchbox.

'This is Mildred Gage. I just wanted to tell you again how absolutely wonderful I think your embroidery is. It couldn't have been more right if I'd designed it myself. However do you do it? I mean, I can embroider perfectly well so long as

I've got the design ready made for me, but to make it all up from scratch –

'Thank you, I'm so pleased you like it.' She tucked the telephone under her chin and struck a match. There was only phosphorus on one side of the stick. She dropped it and took out another.

'We all went to see Mr. Curran after we'd seen you yesterday, you know, and he really laid down the law about the wording. Margaret suggested, "Blest are ye poor" but he wouldn't have it. He wants, "Because you say you see you are the more blind." Well, even I thought that was a bit tactless, though I can see what he means. I mean, something like, "Hold fast to the truth" would be appropriate without offending anyone. I don't think the Vicar is going to like it.'

The phone slipped from its position, slid down Emily's chest, struck the open box and bounced off the bricks onto the hearthrug among a shower of matches. As she grabbed wildly for all the escaping objects, the impacted snow in the front of her hair fell melting on to the hearth and the reluctant flame went out again.

She abandoned the phone and scrabbled among the matches searching for one which had avoided the melt water. She struck, discarded, wiped and struck again – oh, you *fool*, Em – She picked up the candle and held the wick to the redhot log. Its smoke became gradually heavier and thicker, but just before it finally burst into flame the cold swept up her back. Her hand jerked out and clutched the missal as if it were a straw.

'Don't! Look, there's comfort in here, why can't you accept it? You were so brave and dedicated, why can't you rest?'

I perish, lady, I perish. I am lost, abandoned by God and man – in the name of the Mother of God help me, deliver me – Oh sweet Jesu I perish –

His grip was like iron. She tried to put out her hand and retrieve the telephone but couldn't move. 'Let me go!' she begged, her voice rising.

The phone quacked with alarm.

Oh heavens, she's still there, is that good or bad? Do I want her help, and will it do any good if I get it? Won't it just lead

202

to a whole string of complications which I really don't want to be saddled with, the very least of which would be to make her think I'm completely up the wall? No, better pretend we've been cut off. O dear God, I am so, so frightened, won't you at least help me? Please touch this poor, lost being and stop his terrible pain from spilling into me —

— succour, succour, I beg, oh sweet sweet lady, give me succour. I have sinned grievously, I tremble on the very brink of hell, and there is none who will deliver me. Oh my most sweet Saviour give me succour —

She wept as his mental agony poured through her senses and his abject terror begin to bore into her sanity. Her hands clenched on her thighs and the nails pierced through cloth to wound her flesh. Her voice moaned, then whimpered, then burst out in a cry of the utmost despair, and it was his despair, not hers.

She encountered horror so strong she feared it would never leave her again. 'God help you,' she whispered with all her heart, but she said it to herself because now he was herself. She heard her own blessing but her terror and desolation instantly destroyed it. In the depths of the pit she endured his agony until she could bear it no more.

Chapter Seventeen

The knocking seemed to be going on inside her head. After a few seconds' pause it became a light, hard tapping, then knocking again. Bang, bang, bang, *bang*!

The smell of burning jerked her conscious, with a wracking sneeze and a quick smart of pain. Her hand shot up and held her cheek, then went into a frenzy of beating as it touched fizzing, singeing hair.

The knocking became tapping again. Emily looked up and saw a white-hooded figure at the window, with wide, frightened eyes and a mouth shouting in panic.

For a traumatic moment she thought it was him, then a soprano cry of 'Mrs. Wakelin!' disabused her. She crawled across the hearthrug, staggered to her feet, made the rest of the journey and opened the door. Wind and snow bore Mrs. Gage into the room, in an entrance worthy of King Lear.

'Oh, my dear girl, are you all right? Who was it? Did he hurt you? I got here as quickly as I could, but when I saw you lying there on the hearth with all that lovely hair just about to go up in flames — '

She kicked the door shut behind her and put her arms about Emily. 'Come and sit down.' She steered her to the settee like a solicitous gnome, her bright red face on a level with Emily's shoulder.

'I'm all right,' Emily assured her and at once fell down, fortunately in the right direction. Mrs. Gage lifted her feet and went to tuck an antique brocade box-patchwork cushion under her head. She admired it for a few seconds, put it back on the Victorian chair and employed a plain one. She took off her wet hooded coat, slung it on the back of a kitchen chair and removed her boots, which had already added considerably to the mess on the living-room floor.

Emily lay with her eyes closed, feeling absolutely dreadful. She was sweating, shaking and totally exhausted by the experience of extreme terror. Mrs. Gage squatted down beside her and took her pulse.

'My goodness, just look at you shivering! You're suffering from shock, that's what you are. Stay there.'

I am quite incapable of doing anything else just at the moment, thought Emily. Behind her eyes, the experience came back and back, and the resonance of his reflected emotions battered against hers. Dear God, so that's how it is not to be at rest. I've never felt remotely like that even in my very worst moments, and he is in a state of permanent torment, with no hope of escape. No wonder he latches so desperately on to anyone whose character promises understanding, however minimal. It's never before occurred to me why the most earnest wish made for the dead has always been that they should rest in peace.

Stockinged feet thudded down the wooden stairs and something soft was dropped over her.

'There, I remembered seeing this up in your sewing room. I just stopped for a moment to have another word with Walter. I like the leather belt − and it's properly worn, too, isn't it? Nothing brand new about him, a completely convincing picture of a poor, hard-working man. Wonderful. Now, I expect you'd like me to ring the police, wouldn't you?'

Emily's eyes opened quickly. 'There was nobody here, Mrs. Gage, I just came over ill.'

Mrs. Gage frowned and put her head on one side. 'Mildred. I distinctly heard you say, "Let me go", but if you say so ...' Her expression said it was nothing to do with her, of course, but −

'Yes, I did say that,' Emily admitted, perceiving the awful misunderstanding already being conceived in Mildred's quick mind. Her hands pushed into her hair, and the right one was through while the left was still travelling down damp, silky locks. 'Oh, my hair!'

'Yes, I'm afraid you've really done for that side. What a

wicked shame. Do you know, if a good fairy had asked me at my christening what I should most like, I think I'd have chosen to be tall, graceful and beautiful, just like you. Only she didn't, and I turned out short, fat and plain. Still,' she sighed, 'I've always had a good brain, and that's a lot to be thankful for.'

'What do you do?' asked Emily, knowing she was only putting off the moment of explanation but not yet recovered enough to attempt it. She drew her mother's multi-coloured blanket up around her face and played miserably with the crumbling remains of hair above her right ear.

'I'm a retired librarian. Would you like a cup of tea?'

'I'll do it,' said Emily, pulling herself upright and keeling over towards the floor.

'No you won't. You know, Emily, when I first saw you I thought you were one of the strongest, happiest, healthiest young women I'd ever seen, but now here you are as weak as water, and I'm told you came over funny several times at the Currans', too. I suppose you're not −'

'No, I'm not,' said Emily wearily. 'Oh, Mrs. − Mildred − on your way to the kitchen, would you very kindly press the playback button on the answerphone? I think that message may be from my husband.'

The machine clunked, whirred, peeped, and finally burst into crowded background noise against which John indulged in a seething moan.

'Hello, darling. Well, I got across the pond at last, but absolutely nothing is landing in England because of the snow. We are now, would you believe it, in Madrid. God knows how long it'll be before they deliver us to our final destination. Anyway, I'm alive and well and fed up to here. Look after yourself, Em, I love you. 'Bye.'

Tears of disappointment were trickling down her face when Mrs. Gage brought in two mugs of tea. 'I didn't know whether you normally took sugar, but I put some in anyway for shock. If you don't like it, try and be brave. You still look awfully pale. How about getting a doctor?'

'There's really no need, and anyway, it would be criminal to bring one out on a day like this.'

'I saw Dr. Claridge out this morning, on foot,' said Mrs.

206

Gage, sitting down in the Victorian chair and setting her trousered knees comfortably apart. 'Abigail called him in to look at George, he'd had another bad turn. I'm not surprised – he was getting far too excited about the chapel yesterday. I really don't know why he started it at all, with his opinions. Margaret wasn't the only one who wondered if it was a good idea, but the north transept was in such a mess that we couldn't afford to refuse his money. Of course, we're very grateful to him; any P.C.C. is grateful for help with the fabric, but we never expected him to take a personal interest.'

'Is he the patron of the living?' asked Emily, who had decided that this was probably the reason, if not the excuse, for George Curran's high-handed way with the clergy.

'Oh no,' said Mrs. Gage with a smile of such satisfaction that it approached jollity, 'we don't have problems like that here. The parish is its own patron, and has been for more than three hundred years.'

'Goodness, I don't think I've ever come across that before,' said Emily in surprise. 'How did it happen?'

Mrs. Gage sipped her tea and continued to grin. 'Well, the original patrons were monastic, then it passed to the Crown until the Civil War. Little Hocking was a pretty small place then. There was the church and the cottages around it, Holly House and Holly Cottage in a lot of land, probably the mill, the main village street and a few scattered farms. Great Hocking was quite a bit bigger, as you would expect from the name, and the church was in good condition, whereas St. Mary Magdalen was in dire need of some expensive repairs which no one could afford. What's new, eh? During the Commonwealth there were the usual comings and goings of ministers, accompanied by bad feeling and unseemly rows which gave uncharitableness a whole new meaning, and then the parish bought the advowson. We've been electing our own vicars ever since.'

'You mean you have a proper election?'

She laughed with delight at the thought. 'Afraid not, though they used to; it was a proper shambles, rather like Eatanswill. It's all in the hands of the P.C.C. and the churchwardens now. This was never a quiet parish, you know. In fact, religion in Little Hocking has traditionally been a devoutly uproarious business and some of the vicars have been holy terrors.'

'How did this one get elected, then?' Emily couldn't help asking. She took another mouthful of very sweet tea, trying not to pull a face, although she had to admit she was feeling a bit better.

'Have you finally managed to meet him?' asked Mrs. Gage with interest. 'Margaret guards him like a fire-breathing dragon, you know. It's so ridiculous. If only she'd have left him alone he might have got his confidence back, but as it is he might as well be a glove puppet with her hand up his − er − back.'

Feeling even better, Emily actually giggled.

'Do you think she wants to marry him?' she asked.

Mrs. Gage looked positively stricken. 'Well, no, I don't think things have ever been *that* louche. Goodness me, what a thought. Just like the ancient Egyptians. Inheritance through the female line, eh?'

Emily became aware that her remark had, for some reason, been more risqué than she'd intended, and wondered with a twinge of embarrassment just how she'd put her foot in it. She changed the subject very quickly.

'It sounds as if the old vicar was more in the village tradition. Did you live here then?'

'No, I didn't, and I don't think I could have got on with him, from what I've heard. Not my sort of person at all. Margaret's got his picture over her bed. I can't think what her husband must have felt about that, poor little man.'

'Oh, so he *was* a poor little man? I rather suspected he might have been. When did he die?'

'Must be about six years ago, now. The awful thing was, no one missed him once the funeral was over and Margaret had stopped looking brave. Hardly used to say a word, even at work.'

'Did they have children?'

'No.' Mrs. Gage meditated, smiled, struggled against her thoughts and finally gave in to them. 'I don't suppose she ever let him,' she suddenly burst out, and went into helpless laughter. It helped Emily back to normality more immediately

208

than any amount of sympathy could have done. Her laughter returned and with it her habitual cheerfulness and optimism.

'I expect it was a case of nobody coming up to Father,' she managed to say at last, infinitely relieved to be wiping tears of laughter away again instead of those of grief and pain. Mrs. Gage was mopping up too, with sobs and 'Oh dear mes', and other expressions of ecstatic helplessness.

'Oh dear, aren't we awful? Yes, I think there probably was something of that about it. Mr. Leigh was her idol.'

'No, not Mr. Leigh. I meant the old vicar, her Father.'

'That's right, Mr. Leigh. *Old* Mr. Leigh. He made it very clear in his will that he expected the P.C.C. to elect Desmond as his successor. Well, the whole council was his to a man by that time, as everyone who disagreed with him had been worn down and edged out, so they did. And a very different cup of tea he turned out to be, because he'd been worn down himself, and Margaret, with the best of intentions, has made sure that her little brother stayed that way. All that poor baby does is say the right words and obey the rubric, while she pretty well runs the parish for him.'

'Good heavens!' Emily experienced another, but very different, sensation of being poleaxed. 'But doesn't anyone stand up to her?'

'Some of us still try,' said Mrs. Gage valiantly, 'but she's got her supporters ranked behind her and always has had; they're mostly terrified of her. Those who aren't sooner or later get fed up with all the power politics and get out. Some of the new people have really tried. Mr. Bolsover, for instance, he's still in there with the gloves on, but really it's no way to live. Who wants to waste their energies battling over every footling little proposed change, just because Daddy always did it differently and wouldn't have approved? It's like being haunted.'

Emily went quiet. She looked at the splurging mess of wax which marked where the recumbent candles had been quickly consumed by the fire. Her hand slid over her burnt hair.

Mrs. Gage looked at her hard. 'What's the matter?' she asked.

'You'd laugh,' said Emily, staring into the fire and brushing her palm up and down the reeking stubble. It would smell like that. To start with, it would, then like cooking, then as if you'd burnt the roast, then the foul stink of burning, still-moving entrails ...

'Not at something that makes you this upset. Is it your husband being away?'

'Partly, I suppose.'

'You're not long married, are you? Oh dear, love's a wretched business. You probably won't believe it, but I remember what it's like to eat your heart out for someone, and it wasn't the man I eventually married, either. And what's the other part? You're not *really* ill, are you?' she said anxiously. 'It would be so cruel if someone like you were going to – oh dear, it's none of my business, just tell me to shut up. More tea, or shall I make you a sandwich?'

'I'm not hungry,' said Emily. Mrs. Gage got up and looked out of the window. The snow whirled about blindly in the dark as if it were looking for the way home.

'It must be a foot deep now,' she remarked, 'it was already over the top of my boots when I came.' She looked at her watch. 'Would you mind terribly if I watched the News? I know that's very bad manners of me, but with things as they are at the moment I don't suppose I'm the only one who daren't miss a bulletin.'

'Please do,' said Emily. At least John's on the ground and safe in a bland, boring, international-style hotel. Oh dear, how selfish and personal one's worries are. Hundreds are being bombed to death, thousands are about to die in battle, millions are starving or dying of disease, and I am just full of relief that my husband is in pampered, expensive comfort. Think of the appalling things which happen every second of every day to other people's husbands. Or sons. Priests didn't have wives to grieve for them, but they had parents. I wonder if Walter was married? I can't remember if Foxe said. If he was, he'll have had children, too. Did they watch? Some of the martyrs' families did, according to Foxe. And did they become outcasts afterwards, or did good, brave people care for them? Would I have had the courage to do that? Would good, beautiful Emily have lived up to her unwanted reputation? Being good's easy when they can't touch you for it, but supposing it could cost you your life?

Mrs. Gage sat through the half hour of gloom, then turned

210

to Emily to find her miles away, with her eyes still fixed on the fire. She went over to the window again, looked worried and came back.

'You couldn't lend me some wellingtons, could you?'

'Yes,' said Emily, trying to rise.

'Just tell me where they are.'

Emily stood swaying precariously on the rug.

'By the side door.'

'Do sit down again, you look terrible. Look, I'm going to get you some supper whether you want me to or not. I'll leave it in here and it's entirely up to you whether you eat it. What were you going to have tonight?'

'I don't know,' said Emily. She sat down again on the settee, leant her head against the back and let it slide wearily down on to the cushion on the arm. And did you get anything to eat before you were executed? And could you have swallowed it if you did? And did all those righteous, conscientious, holy men who were going to do the deed and watch the suffering make a hearty breakfast and manage to keep it down afterwards? And did they really, honestly, in their heart of hearts, believe that the Father, the Son and the Holy Ghost, Blessed Trinity, God of Love, approved of what they were doing?

'You've got a piece of cheddar here which is going a bit hard, so I'm making an omelette. Do you want bread with it, or a bit of salad?' called Mrs. Gage.

'I don't mind. Whatever's easiest.' And, greatest and worst conundrum of all, if they did believe it, were they right to act upon that belief? Who says what is good? Who knows better than others what is right? Who can recognise good when they see it? Is the individual conscience always reliable? How do you know if you are right or merely brainwashed and blinkered? So many times you hear of people talking about the power of God telling them to do things, but are they just experiencing the powerful force of conditioning, or the literally irresistible compulsion of a psychological kink they never even know they've got? After all, how many times has 'God' told people to kill?

'Ah, you've got a nice Iceberg lettuce in the chiller, I'll put a bit of dressing on it.'

211

'Thank you.'

So supposing religious belief is nothing more than the institutionalising of our mental habits and the sanctifying of our weaknesses. Supposing goodness is not absolute but changeable, according to different societies and mores. Well, yes, it is, isn't it? That's how society regulates itself. You will do this because it is good. You will not do that because it is bad. Obedience to these rules will obtain you an easy, respected life, disobedience will bring terrible penalties, so get in line and don't rock the boat.

But people still did disobey and rock the boat badly enough to drown themselves, so for them at least goodness was not merely the received wisdom of their society but something independent of it.

'Here you are, Emily. Sit up, dear, I'll put the tray on your lap.'

She did as she was told and looked dully at the golden omelette, glistening and popping with beads of hot oil. Foxe said the fat of burning bodies ... She retched. Mrs. Gage whipped the tray away quickly.

'I'm so sorry,' said Emily, tears coming to her eyes, 'I really can't at the moment. You have it, Mildred. I'd rather just lie down for a bit, I'm suddenly dreadfully tired.'

'Haven't you been sleeping?' asked Mrs. Gage, taking the tray to the Victorian chair with a certain alacrity.

'Not for the last few nights.'

'I suppose you're not used to being alone in the house.'

'Not here. It never used to worry me in London. You won't be going just yet, will you, not until the snow stops?'

'No,' Mrs. Gage assured her and watched with concern and a full mouth as Emily relaxed and fell asleep.

She awoke to find light still shining through her lids and trying to force her awake. For a minute or two she fought against it, then remembered Mrs. Gage waiting patiently to go home. She opened her eyes and found that the lamp by the telephone was still on and that light was streaming in from the kitchen, but strangest of all, that there were two candles burning on the hearth. She didn't remember putting those there. She remembered lying on the sofa and thinking

212

she ought to but couldn't while her visitor was present, and she remembered thinking as she drifted off that it would probably be all right just for half an hour or so, but there they were alight and she had certainly been asleep for much longer than that.

She saw Mrs. Gage still in the Victorian chair, but with a cushion behind her head, a footstool beneath her feet and John's old overcoat from the hooks in the side door lobby covering her from chin to ankle. She wasn't asleep and there was something stiff and expectant about her posture. 'Hello,' said Emily, sitting up, 'however long have I been asleep?'

Mrs. Gage jumped, then tried to look as if she had done no such thing. She divested herself of the coat and put her thick-socked feet to the ground, summoning up a cheering smile with which to greet and encourage the patient.

'Ah, good morning! Well, my watch makes it just after quarter past seven. Goodness, you look better. Could you manage a cup of tea?'

'Yes, and I'm well enough to make it, too.'

'Don't move! Look, I'm on my feet already.'

She walked behind the settee and drew the curtains.

'Oh no, look at it!' she exclaimed in dismay. 'I'm going to have to dig my way home!'

'Why did you light the candles?' Emily asked in a low voice. Mrs. Gage came back, in front of the settee this time but keeping off the hearthrug.

'Isn't that what you've been doing?' she asked conversationally, not looking at her. She put out her hand, pulled the string on the wooden businessman and said, 'Oh dear.'

'Where's the book?' Emily asked, looking around.

'On the mantelpiece, it was getting dreadfully dirty. Do you think it ought to go back, then?' she added casually.

'Yes,' said Emily, 'don't you?'

'I don't know as much about it as you do. I've never spent a night here before.'

'Did you know about it?'

'Not really. I'd heard some rather silly stories, especially when the Whites went so soon. I know about next door, of course, but I've never seen anything.'

213

'So what did he do to you? Did he touch you, or speak to you, or take your hand – '

'Oh, you think it's a him, do you?' said Mrs. Gage, looking very controlled and sensible, and taking a great deal of notice of a small watercolour.

'Yes. In fact, I know it is.'

'I don't think I'd define it as any of those things,' said Mrs. Gage, carefully getting the picture absolutely straight. 'It was just rather like an invisible dog following you around and occasionally making a sad little noise. It wasn't in the kitchen, just near the fireplace in here. Then I started to understand what the candles might be for.' She went over to the window again, ostensibly to study the snow. 'There's a broken branch from one of the hollies hanging over the wall; must be quite a big one because it's left a gap. You can see next door's courtyard. Have you been having a difficult time?'

'Yes,' Emily owned up, staring at the candles. Their flames were streaming straight upwards. Outside the wind had entirely departed and left still white silence behind. 'I have to admit I've been having an absolutely terrifying time. I don't know what to do.'

'Why not ask the Vicar to say a few prayers? He's quite sympathetic about that sort of thing, although he doesn't let Margaret know. His father regarded praying for the dead as rank Popery.'

'I've already asked the Catholic priest to pray for him and say a few masses, but it seems only to have made things worse.'

'What a kind thought,' remarked Mrs. Gage, turning round to send her a glance of approval, 'but suppose he isn't a Catholic? If he was a rabid Protestant that could upset him even more.'

'No, I know he's Catholic because of the expressions he uses. He calls on Our Lady and the saints a lot.'

Mrs. Gage at last lost her mask of composure and appeared shaken rigid. 'You mean he *talks* to you?'

The embarrassed Emily put her head down and caressed her right temple, which was quite sore. Her trousers were creased and rubbed and altogether in a state, and her

214

sweater still felt slightly damp in the folds. She was a total mess.

'You poor thing,' said Mrs. Gage, looking appalled. 'I've got a spare bedroom, you know. Would you like to use it until your husband gets back?'

The telephone rang. Emily got up to answer it, not allowing herself to hope that it might be John, which was very wise of her.

'Ah, Mrs. Wakelin.'

'Hello, Lady Curran.'

Mrs. Gage picked up the missal from the long, cracked beam which acted as a mantelshelf. The first page of the Requiem Mass was now grey, spotted and even specked with spark-burns.

'Mrs. Wakelin, I really must ask you again. Is the embroidery ready to be moved.'

'I'm afraid not.'

The phone went down.

'Oh, goodness,' said Emily uneasily.

Mrs. Gage pulled a bibliophile's face. 'Emily, have you any idea of the value of this book?'

'I certainly have,' she said tersely, 'I had to buy it 'specially.'

'Oh, you are a good, generous girl!' she said with wonder.

'Please!' Emily pleaded with exasperation. 'Don't call me good! I've never been tempted to be anything else. I've never been so desperate that I'd do anything, so whatever is nice or attractive about me is entirely a matter of default. I am not good, or virtuous, or admirable in any way whatsoever, I am merely lucky, and I am beginning to feel thoroughly ashamed of it.'

A crash came from beyond the kitchen, followed by a tumbling sound like coal being delivered.

They stared at each other, looked at the candles, which were still serenely upright, then backed away from the fireplace and into the kitchen. The crash was repeated and they followed the direction of the sound, moving towards the sink and drawing the curtains to reveal a scene of quite astounding surrealism.

Holly House was staring down curiously at the boundary which separated the two buildings. The creepers had been torn away and the snowdrift halfway up it appeared to be blood-stained. A nightmare creature with long, thin limbs loomed over it on some invisible perch, dressed in baggy trousers, old leather riding boots, and a too-big leather overcoat, while a woollen shawl wrapped its head so that only the tips of a sharp nose and chin could be seen. Its arms rose and swung down again, to attack the old brickwork with driven violence.

Wielding a pickaxe that a sane, calm woman in her seventies would not even have been able to lift, Lady Curran was demolishing the red brick wall.

Chapter Eighteen

'I'd never have believed she was capable of such passion,' said Emily, leading the way to the studio. 'She's normally about as animated as a glass of iced water.'

'She's very devoted to him, I believe,' said Mrs. Gage, following her and going into silent raptures as she saw Walter Tappett on the worktable.

'Yes, but even so! At her age! You know, I could have tacked Walter on to the backing temporarily, but I was so frightened of going in there again. Supposing it's too late?' Her hands measured out two and a half feet against the embroidery. 'I don't think this is going to work, you know. That window is very small and he'll still be about twenty feet away.'

'You can only try,' said Mrs. Gage sensibly, 'and if it isn't satisfactory we'll just have to carry it in there together.'

'I wonder if he's really going to die?' said Emily unhappily, stroking the folds out of Walter's rough, worn clothing.

Mrs. Gage shrugged her shoulders. 'No way of knowing; he's been bad a good many times in the past. Shall we roll it or fold it?' Below, the clamour of Lady Curran's battle with the wall culminated in a roar which shook the cottage from underpinned foundations to worm-treated ridge-piece.

'Oh, good heavens, what *has* she done now? Roll it, I think, and wrap some sheeting round it to keep it clean. We'd better spread something over the sink, too.'

They manoeuvred Walter downstairs and laid him on the settee while Emily fished out a new plastic tablecloth which had been a wedding present from a distant aunt, and which still smelt pungently of its chemical constituents. 'Would you do it, Mildred? I don't think I should leave him in here alone.'

'Really? You think someone might take exception?' she asked in a low, curious voice.

'The original drawing got torn,' said Emily shortly.

'Oh!' Mrs. Gage went into the kitchen and stood at the window. 'Do you know what that last bang was? A whole stretch of wall has fallen over into your sideway. Lucky the snow softened it a bit.' There was scuffling and busyness, then she called 'I think that's the best I can do, but he's not going to get much of an impression, is he? Just head and shoulders if he's lucky.'

'Is anything on the kitchen table?' asked Emily, keeping a loving creator's eye on her handiwork and well away from the fireplace. Are you there watching? Do you object to the presence of this heretic? Are you going to attack him again like you did in your usual haunts? Gosh, that's the first time I've encountered that expression with a literal meaning.

There was the sound of china being stacked and moved, then more bustling of the wiping-down and covering-up variety before Mrs. Gage came back and prepared to lift one end of the roll of fabric. 'Mr. Curran's in there,' she said, 'I can see right into the room. My goodness, the poor man's so *thin*!'

Now they carried Walter into the kitchen and laid him on the table. Emily went to the shrouded sink and for the first time ever didn't raise her eyes to the crowd of spying windows which stared down at the cottage, because she no longer needed to. The obstruction of the red brick wall had gone and Holly House stood full length on the other side of the breach, like a triumphant besieger preparing to despatch the poor, cowering little cottage. The leaded bay disappeared into snow; in fact the whole house appeared to be sinking, giving an alarming impression of instability.

Mr. Curran was sitting just behind the snow-flecked, misted panes, framed by an area which had been rubbed clear. He was wrapped up to his chin in blankets, above which his bony face stared out with the impassivity of the inhabitants of the church crypt. He looked even paler and thinner than she remembered,

218

and all life seemed to have withdrawn from the rest of his sick body and become concentrated in his eyes, where expectation glowed with the urgent impatience of one who feels he has very little time left for waiting. Slung around his neck was a large pair of old-fashioned binoculars which would have looked more at home on the deck of a Second World War destroyer. Lady Curran stood behind him in her scarecrow garments, holding the back of his chair and peering out of her turbaned shawl in a way which reminded Emily of E.T. The whole situation and exercise was so ridiculous that she was near to desperate laughter.

This is mad, the whole situation is mad. The world is getting keyed up for Armageddon. The British Isles are up to their knees in snow. My husband flew home to London and finished up in Madrid. Mrs. Gage and I have been tiptoeing round my home trying not to upset someone who has been dead for four hundred years. A crazy old woman has just demolished a wall with a lump of wood and iron she couldn't normally lift. I am standing at a sink which looks as if it has been prepared for a surgical operation and waving and smiling at two old aristocrats who are staring at me and leaning foward as if they can't believe their eyes — oh Lord, it's my hair!

Curran certainly looked stricken as his hand rose up from within the blankets and waved feebly in her direction before patting the side of his head. She smiled ruefully, put on a 'Yes, isn't it sickening?' expression and gave a theatrical shrug which said, 'Still, never mind, eh?' Oh God, this gets sillier and sillier. Come on, let's get it over.

They started to unroll the shrouded Walter, carried him over to rest his unrolled portion on the plastic and crumpled the cambric in their hands in order to present his head and shoulders to the man who had commissioned and paid for his very existence. Mrs. Gage's arms reached only halfway up the window, so Emily took her side from her and bore the whole burden. Gradually they fed him to his audience, right down to his square, determined feet and up again to his head. Her arms started to ache and she dropped them slowly, wondering what she would see.

Lady Curran was still in the same position, staring out of her white woollen swathing and holding her husband's shoulders. Her expression hadn't changed and her stiff upper and lower lips were not moving.

But as he lowered the binoculars it could be seen that Curran was quite obviously in tears. He nodded at Emily, harder and harder, trying to lob his approval and gratitude across to her while the tears dripped down on to the blanket and his yellow-white hair jarred free of its controlling hairdressing and fell across his brow. She nodded back in acknowledgement, smiling with pleasure even while her own eyes were filling.

'He seems to approve,' said Mrs. Gage, 'and so he should.' Emily nodded and smiled once more before they carried the creased-up martyr back to the kitchen table. Lady Curran's phone call followed within seconds.

'I say, he's frightfully pleased. Now he wants it put on to the permanent background immediately, so he suggests you do the lettering on a separate piece of stuff and add it later. Then he can see the whole effect as soon as possible. How soon can you do that.'

'I don't know. All I can say is that it'll be as quickly as I can manage. I'll phone you as soon as it's done.'

'Good. The very minute please, even if it's late at night. We are not sleeping a great deal at the moment.'

I know how you feel. 'I'll start at once, Lady Curran. Goodbye.'

'Shall we take it straight upstairs?' asked Mrs. Gage excitedly. 'Look, Emily, if you want to get down to it I'll knock us up some food and bring it to your room. Or would you rather be alone?'

'No, not at this stage of the work − it's fairly tedious, so I should quite appreciate some company. Haven't you got things you should be doing?'

'Well, I'll ring my next-door neighbour and ask her to see to my cat, but there's nothing else that won't wait. I live alone now.'

Emily's relief at having someone in the house who was in on its secret was so great that it unleashed a flood of relaxation, and after breakfast and a much-needed bath, the moment of sitting down to work was filled with the old joyous anticipation. She heard a lot of bustle and occasional singing

220

going on beneath the floor of the studio, and was reminded of the infinitely comforting presence of her mother around her childhood home. It had seemed that nothing could harm you so long as that good genius was there, and as if she was permanent, ubiquitous and immortal. She had sensed that her father, who rarely opened his mouth except to blow out smoke or say 'Come by' to a sheepdog, felt the same. There had been no ghosts in that house, though parts of it had been old when Holly House was only foundations. The story of the past wasn't always a Newgate Calendar.

She got coffee and biscuits at eleven. After it was consumed, Mrs. Gage sat on in the studio, watching every step she took with earnest, silent interest.

'I hope you don't mind,' she said apologetically, 'but I've never actually watched a professional embroideress at work before, and it's so interesting. The nearest I've ever got to the real thing is Margaret pointing out that our stitches aren't even and that a kneeler worked in the hand is never going to look as good as one put on a frame. What she never says is that she likes what you've done. Poor Miss Barton gets it in the neck most, partly because she can't stand up to her and partly, I must admit, because she's not all that good. I know for a fact that anything she makes is given a very discreet little cotton cross underneath and eventually put in to the darkest pews.'

'Does she know?' asked Emily, stitching fast.

'I don't think it's dawned on her yet. She's only on the committee so that Margaret has one member she can totally rely on.'

Toasted cheese came up at one o'clock, tea and biscuits at four. By seven Walter was stitched down on to the yellow, evenweave background and ready for pressing.

'Do you want dinner in the living room?' asked Mrs. Gage, poking her head in at the studio door with oven gloves at the ready.

'How are the candles?'

'All right, but your next box is the last. I've worked out they take about eight hours to burn, so one of us will have to go straight out tomorrow morning and get some more. You don't mind if I put the television on, do you, dear?'

221

She'd cooked chicken quarters – the ones Emily had intended for John's welcome home meal. Oh, well. Channel Four News reported that the whole country was paralysed by snow and that a mortar bomb had gone off in Whitehall and narrowly missed the Cabinet, who had carried on with true British grit.

Emily left her in front of the box and went back to the studio. To the strains of The Marriage of Figaro, she pressed, lined, stitched, finished, pressed again, and at just after six next morning went stiffly downstairs to find Mrs. Gage asleep on the settee, which had been pushed well back from the fireplace, just in case.

Emily made a mug of tea and sat down at the kitchen table, drinking with her eyes closed. Well, with the exception of those highly contentious words, it was done. Walter Tappett was ready to stand up in public and once more make his challenge to conformity and convention. But this time, thank God, it wouldn't kill him.

I wonder how Mr. Curran is? She did say to ring the minute it was finished, but surely she didn't really mean this early? I could do with a couple of hours' sleep, but supposing when I wake I find that he's just died, how could I ever forgive myself?

She rose and her hand went to the curtains over the sink. The upstairs light shone in the darkness, the fluorescent snow glowed around the base of the house, the tumbled, broken brickwork lay among it like casualties after a battle. There was no light in the dining-room bay, but she could see that the inside door was open and that the foot of the stairs was illuminated.

She dropped the curtain and went into the living room. Mrs. Gage woke at the sound of her footsteps, and after two or three nervous seconds appeared immensely glad to see her.

'It's finished,' said Emily, barely able to talk clearly through fatigue. 'Do you think I should ring Lady Curran at once, like she said? It's only six o'clock, but the hall light's on next door.'

'It's my experience that she generally means exactly what she says,' said Mrs. Gage, lowering her woolly socks to the

222

ground, 'but you look as if you're having a job keeping your eyes open.'

'Supposing he's dying?'

'Look,' she patted Emily's arm, 'you lie down and get some shut-eye and I'll ring her and see what's happening. If he's in no danger I'll tell her you'll bring it in in a few hours.'

Emily flopped down onto the vacated settee and was asleep in minutes.

'She says ten o'clock,' said Mrs. Gage, putting on her coat, 'which means I've just got time to go and get those candles. I've tried the wellingtons, they'll do. You go and get our Walter ready for visiting. Oh, and there's some coffee in the percolator and buttered toast keeping warm in the oven.'

Emily dragged herself off the settee and availed herself of the breakfast in the kitchen. The immediacy of the house seen through the sink window was quite shocking, and she closed the curtains quickly. It was nine-thirty already and she had to clean herself up. It was no weather for long skirts and flowing hair; she put on trousers and sweater and pushed her tresses, both long and ridiculously short, into a Rasta-type woolly hat she had bought in the wilds of south London.

Mrs. Gage returned with a whole plastic bag full of candles. 'Weren't all that easy to find, I can tell you, Christmas has run the stocks down. "My word", the man said, "having a birthday party?"' She laughed and knelt down to replace the wavering flames bobbing within hollows of melted wax. 'There you are, my poor dear, and God bless you,' she said as she rose to her feet. 'Right, here we go.'

It wasn't going to be easy to get Walter to Holly House. The snow was thick, Emily would have to wear John's boots stuffed with socks, and it was quite a walk round to the lean-to while carrying a long, awkward, heavy parcel. Mrs. Gage pointed out the obvious answer.

It wasn't easy to clamber over the mess of snow and broken brickwork, either, but having once achieved it, the kitchen door was a mere step round the corner.

Holly House was warm, except for the draught from the letterbox and the pressing cold front which descended the stairs from the unheated floors above. Lady Curran was wearing exactly what she had worn the day before and had almost certainly not been to bed at all as her eyes had dark circles and puffy lids. She showed them into the dining room and helped them to hang the embroidery up from the same bolt as a picture. It was a portrait of a nineteenth-century Curran wife, a preoccupied young woman with immense striped sleeves and lace dripping from every contour of her bosom. The gilt frame made a ridge near the top of the fabric, but then Walter hung clear and smooth, his shoes about two feet from the floor.

'Oh!' said Lady Curran. She went over to the fireplace, where the electric fire was already on, looked at Walter again and said, 'Well!' One could have got the impression that she approved, but she wasn't saying so. It was his opinion that mattered, not hers.

The other committee members arrived and met the centre-piece of the Tappett chapel with various shades of reaction, not one of which was indifference. They stood before him in the house where he had once faced the first of his many ordeals, dressed like bundled-up plastic revellers on a Christmas cake. Even when they removed their gloves, scarves and hats, there was something so unceremonious, so everyday and so simply utilitarian about them, that Walter might just have been one more of their number. This wasn't a saint and his devotees, it was a party of ordinary, down-to earth human beings, one of whom had done something very out of the ordinary indeed. Yes, thought Emily with delight. *Yes*! *Right*!

Just after ten, Lady Curran pushed open the panelled oak door and wheeled George Curran into the room. Emily had never seen him in a wheelchair before, though she had caught a glimpse of it folded and stowed in the dark lobby between the stone hall and the inner one. He had probably resented it bitterly and kept it hidden, but now he was no longer able to pretend that he didn't need it. He was pathetically thin. His emaciated hands stuck out of the sleeves of his beautiful dressing gown like hermit crabs in too-large shells, and his neck was like a white, wrung rag. The very sockets of his skull showed through the thin flesh around his staring eyes and on each temple a zigzagging blue vein seemed to be pulsing actually outside his body.

There was a shocked and embarrassed silence as the committee saw him. Even the chairwoman was taken aback, though the smile twisted itself into a sympathetic smirk. Emily saw Mrs. Gage wipe an eye and then whistle a silent tune to the wavy surface of the polished dining table. As they seated themselves around it, with Curran in the centre of the fireplace side, communication consisted only of whispered requests as to the comfort of other members and smiles at the Currans which were meant to affirm that of course things weren't that bad really.

'I am dying,' said Curran, knocking that silly idea on the head for a start. 'I have been dying slowly for many years and I am now very impatient to complete the process.'

'Oh, no, George,' said Mrs. Witherley-Bashe, leaning forward and smiling for all she was worth, 'I'm quite sure God will give you a little longer, if only so that you can see your generosity to the church in its finished form. There are still many things to discuss, and I can't help thinking that the hanging before us, beautifully made as it may be, is probably not quite what you had in mind when you planned the chapel. You just cannot be spared, and we wish you a quick and full recovery, don't we, ladies?'

The noises round the table were inconclusive. Curran studied her with formidable intensity.

'I thought Christians were supposed to tell the truth and be unafraid of death,' he said, then turned his scrutiny upon the rest of the committee. They all looked exceedingly uncomfortable except for Mrs. Gage, who nodded hard.

'Now, I can't talk for long, so I'll be grateful if you don't interrupt me. Firstly, I wish to offer my deepest thanks and admiration to Emily Wakelin, who has made this most beautiful and inspiring work of art. Had I possessed the skill, which I most certainly do not, I should have created just such a portrait myself. It is Walter Tappett as I have always imagined him, with no pretentions, no self-importance, and above all, no sanctimony. He was an ordinary man who didn't aspire towards saintliness, but I believe he was a good man. He didn't waste time and energy on things which can't be proved this

225

side of death, and he put no faith in superstitions like holy rituals and holy images and holy buildings. He treated the whole of life as of equal importance and thought goodness was a matter of living the life of the world. There are not enough such men and far too many of the other sort.'

Mrs. Witherley-Bashe was very pink, the committee were startled, and even Emily felt that he was reading far more into the very little known about Walter Tappett than was permissible.

'You are all aware, of course,' continued Curran, his voice already slowing and becoming tired, 'that I have no liking for religions and churches, and no doubt some of you will assume this means atheism. I am not an atheist, I am an agnostic. Atheism requires the same arrogant assumption of knowledge as blind religious belief, whereas I merely accept that I possess no knowledge of anything I cannot experience with my five senses, and no trustworthy way of acquiring it. Now there are many people, particularly churchmen,' he added with another cold-blooded stare at Margaret Witherley-Bashe's stressed smile, 'who will insist that all has been revealed, either by a pen held in the hand of God or by his dictating verbatim to a long succession of secretaries. And they will say that refusal to believe in this divine authorship means rejection of the very idea of God, or of any dimension beyond this one in which we live and struggle and often suffer scandalously. That is not so either. I do not say there is no God, and I certainly do not say there is no life after death. Anyone who has lived in this house knows that there is.'

A shudder rippled round the table like a kind of Mexican wave, and at least some of the committee looked uneasily into suspicious corners. Emily's scalp crawled under her gaudy crocheted headgear and her head tilted up towards the first floor beyond the chimney stack.

'What I say,' Curran pressed on, beginning to pant slightly, 'along with Walter Tappett and thousands of other brave, free-thinking, independent and rational men and woman, is that I *do not know*. And I have chosen the wording on that hanging to warn of the great danger of thinking you do. "Because you say 'We see' your sin remains with you", or

226

as Walter had it in the final moment of his trial, "Because you say you see, you are the more blind". It seems to me that his version is more apt and easier to understand. I must also quote to you, "He is less remote from truth who believes nothing, than he who believes what is wrong." That is not holy scripture, of course, it is Thomas Jefferson, and though I considered having it on the hanging even I realised that the clergy wouldn't accept it. So I will make one final point for the benefit of those who think religion means chanting biblical texts and waving their big black book.'

There was an involuntary gasp of shock from Miss Barton. He turned to face her, not aggressively but with deep earnestness, and kept his eyes on her as he continued.

'Let me give you a quotation from the prophet Micah, the simplest and wisest answer to all those tortuous questions which for thousands of years have torn mankind apart in the name of religion. "What doth the Lord require of thee, but to do justly, and to love mercy, and to walk humbly with thy God?" And that,' he said, leaning back in exhaustion, 'is *all*'.

For at least a minute, the St. Mary Magdalen Church Needlework Committee was struck dumb.

Chapter Nineteen

'I – er – have to report a slight difficulty,' said Mrs. Witherley-Bashe at last.

She was having another of her seeming-seizures, with hands, nose, lungs working away, only this time her eyes were not seeking support from a clergyman who died in 1902 but from a shifty-looking Lethaby who had kept remarkably unwise company in 1605 and spent the rest of his life in Rome.

'Yes?' said Curran, breathing laboriously with his eyes closed. His wife was gripping his shoulders as if to prevent his soul from getting away.

'Your request that the monuments should be moved round ... The men had started on this, and all would have been rearranged within a few days, but unfortunately' (her eyes flicked accusingly at Emily) 'that process was noticed halfway through, with the result that the Diocesan Advisory Committee has been informed and instructions given that everything must be replaced as before.'

Mr. Curran went on struggling with his tiring body, then wearily opened his eyes and regarded her with dislike. 'You said the matter had been approved.'

'Yes, indeed. The committee and the churchwardens and most of the P.C.C. were quite amenable, once its importance had been explained to them, but – '

'You hadn't actually told Desmond?'

'It would not have been necessary,' she stated irritably, 'had he only seen the chapel when finished, because he wouldn't have remembered where they'd been before. I mean to say,' she appealed to them all, 'the whole parish knows what a sweet, saintly character the Vicar has, and how unaware he is of the everyday world and its problems.'

'He hasn't been allowed to be,' said Mrs. Bolsover.

Mrs. Witherley-Bashe's chin rose with her temper. 'As one who has only been in the parish for five minutes, I don't consider your rather slanderous observation as of any value whatsoever, Amanda. I know my brother's character better than anyone and I have always considered it my sacred duty to protect him from whatever interferes with his spiritual mission.'

'Such as the responsibility for his parish?' said Mrs. Gage. 'Anyway, what is all this about monuments? *I* don't remember it being mentioned to the churchwardens or the P.C.C. I know there was some talk about dealing with damp, and replastering, and a certain amount of temporary disturbance, but I most certainly didn't vote to shuffle everything around like a pack of cards, did you, Jean?'

Mrs. Lake looked worried. 'Well, no. What is it you want done, then, Mr. Curran?'

His eyes were closed again. He shook his head and made a weak, almost petulant gesture in the direction of the Vicar's keeper. Lady Curran's hands slid down to his forearms and appeared to be giving him injections of her own energy by way of the laying on of hands.

Mrs. Witherley-Bashe's hands were rubbing over the polished surface of the table, seeking out irregularities and attempting to eliminate them with fanatical fingertips.

'The idea is to have the east wall of the transept cleared, so that the hanging and the altar will have the greatest impact, and that all Lethaby memorials should be resited on the west side. With the exception of the table tomb in the corner, of course,' she added hurriedly, 'there was never any question of disturbing that.'

'No, you'd need a crane,' remarked Mandy Bolsover, 'and I think even Mr. Leigh would have noticed that.'

Miss Barton suddenly leant over the table and pointed a knobbly finger at Mrs. Bolsover. Everybody jumped, as if they had forgotten she was capable of movement.

'You're always digging at her, aren't you? No matter what

she says or what Jean or I say, come to that, you have to make some smart, sarcastic comment! I'd like to see you run things the way Margaret does, organising and planning and keeping everything running smoothly. I don't see what's wrong with moving a few old pieces of stone around if it'll make the church look nicer, and I like the idea of all those Catholic Lethabys having to sit looking at an altar in memory of the martyr they helped to burn. You outsiders are forever poking your noses in. I expect it was you who made sure the Vicar stopped it, wasn't it?'

'No,' said Emily meekly, 'it was me.' The committee's faces swung towards her. 'I'm sorry if I've caused trouble, but all I wanted was to make sure he approved of what I was doing, and if you'd brought him to a meeting I could have done. Now I think I ought to go. Mr. Curran has accepted the hanging and once the decision on the wording is unanimous I will carry it out, but the rest of the things you are discussing are nothing at all to do with me.'

She rose from the table and went to offer a farewell hand to Lady Curran. She stayed rigidly attached to her husband with her eyes fixed on his head, which now leant back against her hard, skinny body. 'Emily,' he said.

'Yes, Mr. Curran?'

'It has been a privilege to know you.'

'Thank you. I'm glad you feel I've carried out your wishes.'

'My wish,' he said, barely moving his lips, 'was to right a wrong and prevent other such wrongs. When people are sure they're right they very often do terrible things, but when they believe God is on their side they are capable of any evil under the sun. They persecute anyone who tries to approach Him without their permission as if they'd bought Him like a franchise, and make harmless people feel unworthy of His love and barred from His presence.' His voice was infinitely bitter. 'They say ''we see'' and blind the eyes of others so that they have to rely on them to show them the way, and claim to love and worship God when they really love religion and worship the Bible. They cram people's heads with fairy stories so that they won't have room for reason. They brainwash them into believing that goodness means repetitive rituals instead of doing justly and loving mercy – '

'It's not fairy tales, it's all true!' cried Miss Barton, twisting her hands together. 'The star, and the manger, and the miracles, and all those prophecies coming true, like the donkey and being born in Bethlehem and His mother being a virgin, of course it's true! And He did save us all and rise from the dead! You clever modern people want to take all those wonderful things away and leave nothing to comfort us and make us happy. You shan't do it! It's cruel and it's wicked! Every word of the Bible is *absolutely true!*'

Mrs. Lake got up quickly. 'Come on, Miss Barton, I'll take you home. Goodbye, Lady Curran, goodbye Mr. Curran, I hope you'll be better soon.' She drew Miss Barton out into the hall and thrust her tweed coat and woollen pixie hood into her arms, while she continued to protest in the unstoppable flow of one who normally dares say nothing.

'So where are the monuments now?' whispered Curran, with no precious breath to spare on trivia like Miss Barton.

'In the transept, waiting to be put back,' said Mrs. Witherley-Bashe. 'I'm afraid – er – one slipped, they're very heavy things and – '

'Whose?'

'The one to Sir Jervase Lethaby and his family. The men tell me they got it down in one piece but then knocked it over. I mean, it's particularly annoying because if anyone ought to be paying their respects to Walter Tappett, it's him. And it isn't even large for one of that period, it's very discreet indeed.' Another glance at Emily seemed to indicate that it was she who had broken it.

'Seeing that he lived to 1570 and died in his bed, his discretion seems to have paid off,' said Mrs. Gage. 'Well, there's no point in worrying about it now, we'll just have to see what the church authorities say. The main thing is that the chapel is repaired and clean.'

Curran seemed to be enduring the meeting now, not taking part in it, but his eyes opened again and his pale lips opened with a gasp which carried words through his mouth. 'One more thing. The carpet before the altar.'

Mrs. Witherley-Bashe struggled out of her slough of

231

umbrage and pinned her smile into a shape of grateful surprise. 'But I had no idea you were intending to pay for that as well. How very generous. May I suggest that a plain blue would look extremely tasteful?'

He tried to speak again but had to wait until he could spare surplus energy from the small reserve which was keeping him alive. His head pressed into Lady Curran's body.

'It is upstairs,' she said.

'Oh! You've already bought it?'

Lady Curran's eyes fastened on the only two other people in the room. 'On the bed in the little bedroom off the landing. Bring it down, please.'

Emily and Mrs. Gage stood at the bottom of the red-carpeted stairs, looking up at the window. Its casements and fastenings were black iron, its tired leading pushed the thin, glittering diamonds hither and thither so that their surfaces reflected in all directions. The cold fell continuously and remorselessly down the wide treads to chill their bodies as well as their spirits.

'It would have to be upstairs,' said Emily tensely. 'Do you think she did it on purpose?'

'She's not spiteful,' said Mrs. Gage with reproach, 'she just doesn't think. Her rheumatism seems bad today, doesn't it? I suppose it's lifting George.'

'I'm surprised she can move at all, after yesterday's performance.'

'Oh, yes, of course, that would be the reason. Well, Emily,' she said gently, 'we've got to do it, dear. The last thing the poor Currans want today is another person making a scene. After all, it's broad daylight and there's all that lovely bright snow shining in at us.'

'It was daylight last time,' said Emily.

Mrs. Gage put her arm about her, gave her a little shake and urged her up the stairs, chattering about the pictures as they passed them.

'That's George's great-grandfather who rebuilt the kitchen wing. Rather a handsome man, isn't he? This one's a Lethaby, Sir Jervase's father. He's in the big table tomb in the church, so's his wife. He wasn't well off and he didn't live in this

232

village, but once Jervase had built his fine new house he wanted as many ancestors around here as possible to keep him company.'

'Don't,' Emily requested shortly.

They looked down into the snow-drowned garden and across to the spangled shrubbery.

'Pretty, isn't it?' said Mrs. Gage encouragingly.

'Yes,' said Emily.

They turned up the second flight and approached the square landing.

'Now this one,' said Mrs. Gage conversationally, as if she could talk down any imminent psychic disturbance, 'is a Witherick – that was the family who owned the house after the Civil War.'

'Oh,' said Emily, fixing her eyes across the landing and trying to pretend that the intervening topography, especially the cupboard door, wasn't there.

The small bedroom door was a misshapen one, cut and patched to fit a doorframe which was no longer a rectangle but a parallelogram. Mrs. Gage turned the Victorian brass handle which had succeeded at least two previous ones, to judge by the filled-up holes in the wood, and pushed it open with womanful decisiveness.

Emily remembered the room above the dining room from Lady Curran's guided tour; small by the standards of Holly House, but larger than her bedroom at home; low-ceilinged and seventeenth-century, without the sixteenth-century new man's striving for impressive proportions. It contained lots of old oak and a fair amount of old rubbish. Outside was the blank side wall of her studio, and when she went nearer the window, the cottage kitchen below. This was where she saw the light through every night, probably hanging out on the landing. The fallen red brick wall, in various-sized chunks, scattered the snowy space between the two buildings.

'Here it is,' said Mrs. Gage jovially, endeavouring to pull a ten-foot sausage packed in a dusty hessian bag off the bed. 'At least, I suppose it is. It's the only one in here.'

'I've got the other end,' said Emily, 'let's hurry, please.' They hauled, staggered and tiptoed across the dulled red carpet in their stockinged feet, though the boards beneath let them know that the house had observed them.

There's no corridor there. There's no cupboard there. It's cold up here because it's a bright, white winter's day and there's no heating on.

'Careful!' Mrs. Gage warned, going ahead. 'Don't push me, dear.'

We're very nearly down again. Thank God for that. All I've got to do now is dump this on the dining room table, put on my coat and boots and go. No, I'll wait until Mrs. Gage leaves too, I can't face the cottage alone at the moment. Oh John, when are you going to get home?

Mrs. Gage was now on the bottom step and Emily glanced up through the half-dozen carved banisters along the landing in a gesture of involuntary thanksgiving.

'Made it!' Mrs. Gage announced triumphantly.

It passed four of them but not the rest. It made no sound at all and existed for no more than two or three seconds. It was tall and black with a paleness at the top, and moved with apparent haste through the cupboard door and in three swift strides across the landing. It didn't come down the step from the sixteenth-century block, but continued straight on like a cartoon character which didn't realise it had walked over a cliff, only it never did come to realise it, but passed on through the invisible boundary erected by time and change and vanished.

Emily pushed the carpet down the last few steps with her entrails filled with ice, and with gall rising to burn her gullet. Her unshod feet snatched themselves away from the ground before it could snap at them, and shuffled her sideways into the dining room so that nothing could get at her back.

She heaved her end of the carpet up on to the long, oaken table, slid down into a chair still warm with the passionate protests of Miss Barton and hid her vulnerable hands in her armpits as Mrs. Gage shut out the cold of the stairs.

You need never come in here again after this. It is positively the last time you have to experience this horrible, creepy house, so grit your teeth, Emily, and hang on. Don't think about it, don't even remember it, not at this moment, anyway. Perhaps later in the open air. After all, it's a pretty interesting experience; thousands of people devote their lives to trying to see things like that and never manage it. You ought to feel privileged ... But unfortunately she just felt sick.

The hessian bag was pulled off in a cloud of harsh, throat-catching dust and discarded on the side of the hearth. Mrs. Witherley-Bashe had risen eagerly to her feet and now helped Mrs. Gage to unroll the unwieldy, fringed carpet, which was certainly not a new one. Emily stood up again and drew it away from them across the table, hardly able to believe what she was seeing. It hung over all four sides as if it had been made for it, worn but in one piece, pile ground down by the feet of furniture but carrying the pattern in its knots. A rusty, reaching-out ink stain was stamped on one place like a handprint. The colours still spoke, though in a quieter voice than its vegetable dyes had originally given it; faded madder and weld were braced by fast indigo, in a geometric dance of strappings and lozenges and palmettes.

Emily had seen many such carpets, under inkpots and quill pens and papers, beneath the clean, clear shapes of lutes and viols, pressed by the square fists of men of affairs and with the white, boneless hands of great ladies resting upon them. In all wealthy homes of the sixteenth century and therefore in all portraits painted within them, these table carpets from Asia Minor held their sumptuous, glowing, central place.

Curran breathed harder, the pollution of dust in the air tormenting his air passages.

'This was in the house when Tappett was here. It saw his degradation, it must lie before him in his new dignity.'

'But it must be worth a fortune!' Emily exclaimed. 'If you have that permanently on show you're asking for break-in and theft. Unfortunately, you just can't leave valuable antiques in churches any more, there are too many organised gangs going around robbing them.'

'It's the decline of religion,' said Mrs. Witherley-Bashe, making a quick point. 'No one's afraid of being blasphemous any more. It wasn't like that in my father's time, I can tell you. He could leave the offertory boxes unemptied for a week.'

'There was certainly fear in your father's time,' remarked Curran, his pale eyes hard. 'I require you to put this before the altar in the Tappett chapel and how you look after it is your problem. I have put all my wishes about the project down in writing and any departure from them will result in the withholding of all further monies. With the exception of the embroidery,' he added, turning to Emily who stood with her hands once more under her arms, imagining the dark thing upstairs seated behind this carpet and knocking over the ink well with its dead hands. 'How much do we owe you, Emily?'

She fled through the house to the telephone, had a few brief words with an amazed Sophie and returned, her head turned away from the dreadful presence of the stairs.

Lady Curran wrote out the cheque, steadied her husband's weary fingers as he signed it and handed it over.

'From now on, all matters to do with the chapel will be in the hands of my wife,' said Curran and closed his eyes.

His wife had returned to her previous pose behind him, with both arms holding him hard against her body.

'You will all please go now,' she said.

They went quietly and obediently away, to put on coats, scarves, hats and boots, to depart from the banal back entrance of Holly House and to leave its master and mistress alone together. Outside, Mrs. Witherley-Bashe left them with barely a goodbye.

They picked their way over the broken brickwork, very aware that the eyes of both Currans were probably fixed upon them through the dining-room bay window.

'My goodness me,' whispered Mrs. Gage, 'that was nearly my ankle broken. You'll have to get this cleared up soon, Emily, or it could be yours next. Would you like me to help you with it this afternoon? I'm a mean hand with a spade.'

'Well, it's very kind of you, Mildred, but I'm hoping John will be home soon. Anyway, now the hanging is finished I can get on with things like that myself. I can't keep taking advantage of your kindness.' She unlocked the kitchen door and stepped into the lobby.

'Well,' said Mrs. Gage, beating Emily's boots against the outside wall to get rid of the snow, 'I don't see it as taking advantage at all. To be quite honest with you, I've enjoyed the last day or two. I know it's been dreadful for you, and

236

I won't pretend that I haven't been pretty on edge, but it's been so nice to be useful to someone again. Of course, there's all the parish work, and the Brownies,' Emily found herself smiling, 'but it isn't the same as doing a favour to a personal friend who really needs it. I'm a widow, you know.'

'Yes,' said Emily sympathetically, discarding John's boots, shutting the door behind them and going to put the percolator on for coffee. 'Have you any family living round here?'

'No,' said Mrs. Gage, donning the ankle boots which had been awaiting her patiently under the table. 'I only had the one girl, and she married an engineer who lives up in Shropshire. I've got a grand-daughter who's training to be a teacher and a grandson in the army. He's out in the Gulf,' she added in a matter-of-fact tone as she stripped the sink of its plastic veil and prepared to wash the few dishes left over from breakfast.

'Oh, I *see*,' said Emily, looked at her watch and turned on the radio for the eleven o'clock summary.

'Thank you, dear,' said Mrs. Gage, scrubbing the draining board hard.

She went home just before lunch, but offered to return again for the night if Emily needed her company. Emily said that she was hoping John was going to make it, but in the event that he did not ...

'Look, Mildred, let me cook dinner for you tonight. Please come — unless you'd rather get back home for good, of course.'

She put on an apron, tied her head up in a scarf and gave the house a thorough clean, with the exception of the areas near the chimney stack. The candles burned on fairly steadily, though the breeze was stirring again and carrying more snow-flakes down from the leaden sky. As she dusted the front windowsill she looked left at the red brick wall, where its first twenty feet still supported the burdened holly trees. Through the gap left by the broken branch she saw a bundled-up man with a black case forcing open the iron gates and picking his way through the snow with high, careful steps. Dr. Claridge, she presumed.

She started to wash the well-trodden kitchen floor. As

237

she emptied and refilled the bucket her glance went straight through into the dining room of Holly House, whether she meant it to or not. One of the table lamps was on, and she caught a glimpse of Mr. Curran in his wheelchair beside the fireplace, his face turned towards where the embroidery had been hung. Lady Curran came and went. Once, when Emily looked up, she was sitting beside her husband with her arms about his neck.

Emily abandoned the half-filled bucket and left them in privacy. She went up to her studio and tidied that. The light was going and the snow lit the deep blue like white fairy lights. She tested the atmosphere in her bedroom, moving slowly across the floor towards the old stack.

It seemed all right until she was a bare foot away, but when she stretched out her hand there was a vibrant coldness coming off the wall which might well have been caused only be freezing air coming down the chimney, but on the other hand might not, so she left the room and went downstairs.

Mrs. Gage had said she would come as soon as it got dark. Emily lit new candles and stood them beside the guttering remnants of the last ones. As the new-born flames undulated towards the chimney, the dying ones alternately stretched and decreased, fluttered as if gulping for oxygen and shrank down into glowing stars as the wick began to drown. The last quarter-inch of pink wall disintegrated and the wax spilt out in a smoking film to solidify over the previous drippings.

She heard the groaning of a car ploughing through snow, then the sound of voices and the clanging of metal. From the window and through the gap in the trees she could see a vehicle parked in the courtyard and dark figures getting out. When she went to put the dinner on, the dining-room window was fully lit and people were moving about within. She drew the curtains, for their sake this time, not for hers.

Mrs. Gage arrived bearing Emily's wellingtons in a plastic carrier bag, and also produced a pot of white lilies which she set down on the hearth. 'There you are, you poor dear,' she said. When Emily carried the cloth and cutlery into the living room half an hour later, her guest was standing with the curtain lifted in her hand, staring out.

'There's the doctor again,' she said shortly, 'and there

seem to be a lot of family there. I think this could be it.'

She watched the television news, and this time Emily noticed the tension of her head and shoulders as our brave boys were shown trying on science fiction clothing ready for chemical warfare. God, what a way to go.

They prefaced their meal with raised glasses and self-conscious toasts, Emily thanking Mrs. Gage for her moral support, her guest thanking Emily for an excellent meal and her very pleasant company. She then turned round to the fireplace and said, 'God bless him and give him peace,' before draining her glass.

Much later, when the dishes were cleared and washed up and Mrs. Gage was drinking the hot chocolate she had brought with her, the sound of internal combustion in pain stopped next door again and she went to the window, nightcap in hand.

'More cars arriving. Ah, and unless I'm very much mistaken, that appears to be an undertaker's van. He's gone. Oh, poor Abigail. And poor George, too. But he must be so glad to have got out of that poor, sick body.'

'Do you think he knows he's out of it?' asked Emily, joining her at the window and seeing lights and movement filling the snowy front courtyard of Holly House. 'With his attitude, perhaps he's just gone to sleep and hasn't even noticed he's dead.'

'Goodness, what a sad thought. No, I'm sure he knows, because he was aware of his ignorance and therefore ready to learn.'

'We'll never know, will we?'

'No. Not till our own turn comes.'

Not long after they'd dropped the curtains, there was a thudding and clattering at the front door. It opened and the chill breeze swept across the room and jarred the candle flames. Three went out immediately. Two dipped and recovered before being struck down again. One held on for a little longer as Emily cried out with sheer joy and flung her arms around the man in a black overcoat who threw his suitcase in ahead of him and slammed the door.

Even Mrs. Gage, touched and charmed by the reunion going

239

on before her eyes, didn't notice the slam whip the flame off the last candle and leave a surrendering plume of smoke.

In the next few joyful minutes, as explanations, introductions, exclamations about the weather and a pot of hot coffee were made, nothing was further from all their minds than candles. They went into the kitchen and Emily made John a meal, while Mrs. Gage thought he was charming but not what she would have expected, and John thought she was a bit odd but a nice old biddy.

'Well,' said Mrs. Gage at last in a jovial voice, 'you won't be wanting me here tonight after all, will you, Emily? I'll hop off now and leave you two alone. I'll go out of this door as my things are in the lobby. Would you mind drawing the curtains so I can see where I'm going?'

Despite their polite demurs she quite rightly refused to stay another minute and disappeared down the sideway into the night while John gazed blankly at the demolished wall.

'Don't tell me, it was an air raid,' he said at last.

In the bay window before them, people were talking and moving around with strained, straight faces. Emily saw Simon sitting in thought at the head of the table with his hand over his mouth, and turned away.

'I've got an awful lot of things to tell you about, John, and that wall is the least of them. Come in by the fire and have your dinner.'

He was settled down on the settee with a glass of wine on the table beside him and his plate on his knees, before she turned to throw another log on the fire and noticed that the candles were dead. She stepped back with an intake of breath, and was about to run for the box in the kitchen when the cold slid over her and wiped out the loving warmth of John's embrace. Her hands went up to push it away and her fingers caught the scarf and whipped it from her head.

'Em!' John exclaimed with dismay. 'Your hair!'

Please, please, please, I beg of you, deliver me, help me, succour for the love of Christ, sweet lady, oh sweet Jesu, help me, help me, help me!

She stood imprisoned in the embrace John could not see and sent the plea on to him augmented by her own.

Help me, help me, for the love of God, *help me*!

240

He dumped his plate with such haste that gravy slid off on to the settee, and came towards her with arms outstretched. His hands hit the cold and he stopped, open-mouthed, while she reached towards him with infinite pain.

Help me, help me!

He pressed on against the barrier until at last their fingers touched. The contact released her frozen voice.

'The candles,' she whispered, 'light the candles.'

Dear God, sweet lady, don't abandon me! Don't send me away! On my soul's salvation, lady, deliver me from this hell!

The candles were lit.

Explanations lasted long into the night, and put all thought of making love out of their minds.

Chapter Twenty

The events of those days caused Emily to look back on them later with a feeling of unreality, as if she was not sure they had happened at all. Her young mind was not used to being forgetful. Up to then life had been interesting and enjoyable enough for her to remember every minute with pleasure, and to smudge none of the record with the wasteful, wishing-time-away of the bored or disappointed.

But during that time the days were stained with distress, not the least being John's near-disorientation at the blight on his home and his dread at the threat which it posed to Emily, in whom he had invested the whole of his emotional security. He fussed over her with continual anxious solicitude, lit candles in every room in the house as if he was fumigating it against dangerous disease, and did the most amazing and touching thing of all: he took a week off work.

It wasn't as difficult as he would once have believed, his American job having been completed apart from paper work he could do at home, and the continuing snow making the use of Network South-East and the road system increasingly impossible, anyway. Marooned in their snowy isolation, even the increasing awfulness of the Gulf War seemed less of a personal threat and more the concern of other people.

He asked her over and over again exactly what had happened and how she had coped, and tormented his mind over what else he could do. He went up to the Catholic church and paid for more masses, he rang up his friend who had seen the ghost in Poultry, he tramped across to the snow-bound St. Mary Magdalen's, dragged the Reverend Desmond

Leigh out of his smoke-filled cell and brought him back to the cottage to do his stuff.

Emily took the Vicar's outdoor wrappings and hung them by the door, noting that there was a button off his overcoat. Black mark, sister Margaret. John steered him to the fireplace, where roaring log fire and battery of candles put the by-now filthy missal in permanent danger of going up in flames. The heat had wafted the perfume of lilies all over the house.

'It's here,' he said urgently, 'roughly the area covered by the hearthrug, and sometimes the same upstairs. There's a secret passage walled up in the chimney stack, and it seems to be something to do with that. What can you do about it?' He sat down and waited confidently for the consultant expert to weigh up the possibilities, make his judgement and put in his report.

The Reverend Leigh looked with wonder at the blaze of light, then held out his hands, bowed his head and was silent for some time. 'It's been here for so long,' he said at last in his mild, detached voice.

'You know about it?'

'Oh, yes. There's been so much human trouble in this corner of the village over the centuries, it's bound to leave its mark.'

'What did you do last time?'

'Oh, well, Mr. Wakelin,' he said, smiling wryly, 'I've never before been invited on to this ground, and neither was my father after he had a disagreement with the Currans. He did know about the ghosts, but his mental bent was to attribute everything he didn't understand to Satan. Had he been asked, his method of dealing with it would have been aggressive onslaughts of commination and demands that the evil one should depart to whence he came.'

'And what would your suggested method be?' asked Emily quietly. She was sitting on the arm of the settee, dressed in layers of skirts, shirts and sweaters, her hair drawn over to one side of her head in a long, loose plait which nearly hid her scar. The Indian silver and turquoise necklace which John had brought her from America hung around her neck.

The Vicar shook his head. 'The only answer has to be

243

prayer. I believe implicitly in its power to influence all things for good, whether physical, mental or spiritual. By that, of course, I don't mean that we can just do nothing ourselves and expect God to put everything right. We may be His children, but even children are expected to grow up and take their own decisions. Yes,' he reflected thoughtfully, 'it is fatally easy to forget that and enjoy a prolonged babyhood.' He sighed and rubbed his brow with an endearing reminiscence of Stan Laurel. 'We must also try to fill our thoughts and lives with goodness to counteract any evil left by former days. Do you feel that it is evil you have here?'

'Yes,' said John, terrified for Emily.

'No,' Emily countered quickly, 'not at all. He's just in the most terrible distress. I've felt it, and it's like being in the very depths of a dark pit. He's trapped. It's dreadful,' she said, her voice starting to tremble. 'I'd always thought that dying meant leaving your troubles behind and getting the answers to all your questions. It's terrifying to realise that it mightn't at all.'

'I suppose,' said the Vicar seriously, 'it very much depends on how you got into trouble, and what your questions were.'

Trouble multiplied in the Middle East and continued to raise unanswerable questions. *The Times* reported that a fed-up Iraqi soldier was seeking a martyr's death as a quick way to Paradise and the attentions of at least seventy beautiful girls. Emily wondered if the report were true; it had the smack of Western Christian prejudice about it. If it was, it exposed martyrdom as a way of running away, and illustrated that it was a lot easier to die for something than to live for it — it was quicker, for a start.

The comings and goings next door were extraordinary. It was as if with the death of its ailing owner the house had acquired new life, and was surging forward with renewed power into the next chapter of its long history. Some relatives remained there, among them Simon and Jeremy, and numerous strangers of the artisan class arrived with vans and made loud noises within.

On Tuesday the Man could be seen shovelling snow from

244

the pavement, the courtyard and the garden paths. He then produced a wheelbarrow and proceeded to move the remains of the wall into the kitchen courtyard.

Emily watched from her station at the sink. The snow had all been cleared from the Currans' side of the boundary, and as the brickwork was moved Mr. Selby did the same on theirs, so that the house appeared to be coming nearer. She almost felt like rushing out and stopping him, as if a rampart of snow was at least some protection against it.

Within the dining room, Lady Curran could be seen conferring with a group of women which included Mrs. Mumford, the only one of them not dressed in an overall or an apron. Mr. Selby hurled a final massive lump of burnt red clay and mortar at the loaded barrow, misjudged and knocked the whole thing over, making a grab as it tipped and following it in its thunderous collapse.

Emily and the alerted ladies watched from their windows as he sank slowly into the ground.

'I knew it,' she said, holding on to John as they watched the shenanigans. His portable computer sat winking impatiently on the kitchen table, halfway through his report. 'I just knew it was still there. His body must be down in that passage, walled up because it was too dangerous to get rid of any other way.'

'They wouldn't have done that,' John disagreed, his eyes fixed on the hole outside the kitchen window. Jeremy had produced a hard hat and a torch from the boot of his car and descended with the air of a cobbler returning to his last. 'You know how conscientious they were about Father Lethaby, he got a mass and at least a burial of sorts. Why should a devoutly Catholic family treat another priest like that? It would have been unforgiveable.'

'Perhaps this one wasn't their son,' said Emily with a touch of bitterness.

He looked at her with concern. 'That's not my sweet Em speaking.'

'I think I've caught some of Mr. Curran's cynicism. Oh, John, I don't want anyone to be unhappy, especially after they're dead. It's bad enough having an unhappy life, but to go on being unhappy afterwards — the way I feel I'd give anything to make sure that poor man could be forgiven and at peace, even blotted out, so long as he felt no more pain.'

'And it would mean peace for you, too.'

'Never mind me,' said Emily with passion, 'it's him that matters.'

But it turned out that there was nothing down that hole but a yard of mouldy brick passage and a couple of feet of black, stinking water. Beyond that it had been blocked, on the cottage side on purpose, on the house side with what appeared to be desperate haste, hence its instability.

Jeremy returned to the surface.

'It's partly rubble and bricks, but mostly earth, lumps of wood, bits of broken earthenware. You might get the impression that on the house side at least, they've just grabbed everything they could find to fill the hole.'

'And on our side?' asked Emily anxiously.'

'A slightly more leisurely job, perhaps done later when they'd got more time.'

'Do you think it really is blocked for the rest of the way, or could it still be there under our kitchen floor?'

Jeremy gave Holly Cottage a quick up-and-down appraisal. 'Didn't the Whites have the foundations seen to?'

'Yes.'

'Well, I'd have thought they'd have found it, then. And you haven't got a cellar now, have you?'

'Now?' she said with alarm.

'Well, there was once, of course. Only small, just the place to store food in the cool.'

'Please,' said Emily, shivering, and not just because of the snow, 'I know you're busy with the preparations for your father's funeral, but if you could possibly spare us a few minutes ...'

The heel of Jeremy's boot struck on the kitchen vinyl, making new dirty marks on the floor.

'I'd have thought it would have run to about here.'

'What about the living room?' asked John, striding in there and examining it as if he expected sixteenth-century brickwork to erupt out of the floor.

Jeremy tramped up and down, soiling the hearthrug. 'Difficult to tell with this thickness of carpet, but I should have expected –'

'Em, get the hammers.'

He was down on his knees before she came back, and within seconds the three of them were at it, pulling out tacks and unhooking carpet holders, dragging back rug and carpet and underfelt until bare boards blinked at the ceiling with amazement and bounced slightly beneath their feet.

'They're all new,' said Jeremy with surprise. 'Used to be old ones hand-cut in a sawpit. The Whites, I suppose. They fell on the place like a development corporation.' He tramped up and down, listening for difference in tone. 'Could be here, it sounds a bit less resonant, doesn't it?'

'Rip 'em up,' said John without hesitation.

They went at it again. Emily tucked her long skirt into her belt and knelt to her task, her eyes glancing up at the flickering shrine and telling it, 'We're coming.' The hammerclaws bit under planks and prised the new wood up from what turned out to be old joists, brown, bent with age and bedded on what appeared to be centuries of dust and cobweb.

'Well, they didn't do much down here, did they?' said Jeremy with interest. 'Look, there's a cigarette packet. Something old, perhaps? Oh no, just Embassy. Got a brush?'

Emily ran for it as if what they were digging for was still alive. Jeremy brushed away at the gaps between the joists while John gathered the mess between his hands and flung it into the fire, where the burning particles spat and leapt for the chimney. Emily joined them, thrusting her hands down into the dirt and shrouding her gleaming necklace with grey.

'There it is,' said Jeremy suddenly.

It was a very slight raising of the hard ground beneath the dust which, when scraped, showed scratches the colour of brick. It continued beneath adjacent joists, moving away towards the kitchen and Holly House.

'By jiminy, this is exciting!' exclaimed Jeremy with glee. 'I wonder why Grandfather or Father never did this?'

'Perhaps they didn't dare,' said John, suddenly realising what they were doing and turning pale under the dust. 'I

247

suppose this is a good idea, is it? I mean, we've got trouble enough already.'

'What do you mean — settlement?' For the first time, Jeremy seemed to notice the strange state of the hearth. His head leant on one side and examined the dust-laden book. 'Oh,' he said. 'It's come in again, has it?'

'Yes,' said Emily, 'it has.'

'Ah. Dear me. Well. Do you want to go on, or would you rather leave well alone?' He dusted his hands absorbedly as if he cared about their filthy state, and John and Emily looked at each other with anguish.

'Yes,' they said, almost in unison.

'You mean stop?'

'No,' said Emily, near to tears. 'Go on.'

About fifteen minutes later their chisels broke through the bricks, not with a sudden release into space, but with a crunch which bit into loose rubble. They knocked along the roof of the passage until it passed under the wall into the kitchen, but elicited only the thud of solidity, not the hollow ring of emptiness.

'Well, sorry, that's it,' said Jeremy, 'it really is blocked. Of course, that doesn't mean there isn't something down there under the rubble, but it would take days to dig it all out, and you might have to rebuild your entire floor afterwards. What are you going to do?'

'Leave it,' said John in a dull voice, the adrenalin suddenly running out.

'Right. Well,' he said, his own face losing its animation and clouding over with the return to real life, 'better get back. Only a couple more days to get everything ready. Mother's being splendid, of course, and all her friends are in helping to clean the house from — well, I was going to say from top to bottom, but we all know that's not practicable. Let's just say it's going to look a lot better. There's going to be an awful lot of people coming. You'll be there, of course,' he added with confidence.

'Only if your mother wants us,' said Emily, thinking that the house might be almost bearable cleaned up and with crowds of people in it.

'Of course she does. So do we. So we'll see

you at the house at eleven o'clock on Thursday morning.'

'But we're not family or even close friends,' said Emily. 'Surely it would be better if we went straight across to the church?'

'No,' he said, his eyes suddenly becoming withdrawn as he appeared to be working out how to patch up the scar which the plait failed to hide completely, 'at the house. Oh, and it's no flowers.'

Only when he'd gone did it hit them what they'd done to their beloved home.

Emily's wardrobe contained plenty of black, including a fairly new long black coat. Practically every youngish woman in the country must own one now, worn with black tights and black shoes or boots. The fashion had swept across the female population as if in preparation for universal mourning, and even the fact that it was generally worn with brilliantly coloured scarves and shawls only emphasised the temporary nature of the celebratory colour. She was getting morbid. Once upon a time, such superstitious thoughts would never have crossed her mind.

On the Thursday morning they exchanged Valentine cards, and a huge bunch of red roses arrived for Emily shortly afterwards. She arranged them in a blue earthenware pitcher and set them on the hearth with the lilies.

The morning papers bludgeoned them with the grief of men searching for wives and children in a bombed Baghdad air-raid shelter, and those legendary warriors, the Afghans, had arrived to join the assembled world armies on the sands of the killing ground. Oh, yes, it was a time for black.

She pushed her hair into a huge grey velvet beret, fastened it to the side of her hair with a silver and garnet brooch which matched her earrings, and softened the coat's neckline with a silk scarf in many shades of grey. John, who had had no difficulty in finding clothes suitable for what was certainly going to be a pretty classy funeral, held her at arm's length and marvelled.

'Em, darling, you are quite breathtakingly beautiful. No one would imagine you spent yesterday sweeping up dust, nailing down floorboards and relaying carpet.'

'I wish it had all been worth it,' she said sadly. 'Did you light the new candles? We don't know how long we're going to be.'

'Yes, I did.'

They went downstairs. On the hearth the gathering of lights was like the corner of a high church, the lilies had opened all their buds and the perfume of roses now joined them to fill the room with floral incense. John put the answerphone on and ushered her out of the door with his hand under her elbow, for all the world like one of the formal Establishment figures who had been arriving at Holly House for the last ten or so minutes. They walked silently down their front path and along the pavement which Mr. Selby had so thoroughly laid bare.

There were cars parked everywhere, with the exception of the area outside the open gates of Holly House, where roadspace clear even of snow awaited the arrival of the funeral procession.

Within the courtyard, men with black coats, hats and umbrellas and women in dark hats which pulled no punches talked and nodded and moved towards the house. The dullness of snowclouds hung above them again, and all windows on the ground and first floors were blazing with light. In the centre a wide brilliance drew the guests in like a mouth.

The blank hardboard shuttering had been removed and the pair of front doors stood open. Through the porch which had probably not seen the light of day for a decade, the mourners stepped into the stone hall and shared condolatory handshakes with the Curran family.

John drew in his breath.

'My God, what a place.'

The armour and portraits looked down on them and reflected the fire burning within the great chimney-piece. The stone floor had been scrubbed white, so that the hollows of usage undulated under the light of the many-branched brass chandelier. To the right a heavy panelled door stood open into what Emily realised was the bed-drawing room.

They shook hands with the family, who stood before the hall fireplace as correctly dressed as if it were a royal funeral. The boarding school contingent were there and the only child missing was the stone one. The grandsons wore grey suits and black ties, and Victoria and Anne wore black tights and shoes and dark woollen dresses with a lot of lace about the neck. They shook shands solemnly, like well-schooled princes and princesses. Deirdre and Isabel were not in the reception party; it was Curran blood only.

Lady Curran's face was even more haggard and even more painted. The streaky hair was uncovered, which surprised Emily among so many correct hats, and her dress was a black silk velvet which did not seem weighty enough to withstand the cold draught sweeping in from the open front door. But she showed no sign of shivering, greeted them without expression in either sharp eyes or flat voice and passed them on.

'Do you want sherry?' A glum-faced Mrs. Mumford offered the silver tray, in dark clothes and probably the first apron she'd worn for years. It was white, frilled organdie, and could have dated from whenever the Currans gave up housemaids.

They took the delicate, engraved glasses and moved out of the way of the continuing influx of guests, through the drawing-room entrance which had previously been blocked by the beds. There were about a dozen people in there, including Deirdre making restrained conversation with a very distinguished-looking couple by the window.

The drawing room now looked more as it must have done when the first Curran forced Georgian taste on to the Tudor house — pale grey panelling, gleaming gold frames around portraits and paintings, priceless china and superb furniture. All the bedroom furniture had been removed so that the room appeared much bigger, and an expansive fire glittered on the steel dogs within the four-centred arch of the chimneypiece. Beyond the mullioned window, St. Mary Magdalen's church awaited George Curran in the hollow.

'Is that *all* Meissen?' John asked incredulously, looking across at the cupboard.

'Except for the Bow and Chelsea. No, don't let's go over there, please.'

251

'Is that where it happened?'

'Mm. Look, my pictures,' she said, drawing his attention to this side of the room.

'They're lovely, Em,' he said with admiration. 'So that's how the house looks on the other side? Beautiful door.'

'They never use it. Well, perhaps they do now. Do you know, John, this is the first time in years the front door has been opened?'

'Sounds like my Aunty Agnes's house.' He pointed at the other painting. 'What's that halfway up the wall?'

'It's a head,' said Deirdre, passing them with the couple's empty sherry glasses. 'It's from the image of St. Mary Magdalen in the church,' she informed them in her beautiful voice. 'It was knocked off, in both senses of the expression, during the Reformation and Jervase Lethaby must have salvaged it. The Withericks found it when they were rebuilding about 1668, and stuck it up on the wall.' She passed on in a flurry of grey woollen suit and antique cameos.

'How many priest's holes are there?' John asked.

'I don't know. One's in the cellar,' she said nervously.

'What's that big oil?'

'Go and look if you like.'

He advanced cautiously on the opposite wall, keeping well away from the china cabinet.

Deirdre came back, recharged glasses in hand, closely followed by Jeremy in search of a quick, urgent word.

'Where is she?'

'In the kitchen with Isabel.'

'Well, can't you get her to come in? She ought to be with the rest of us.'

'I'll try again in a minute.'

He darted out again as she delivered the sherry with a smile.

Emily stood back against the wall between her pictures, watching John examining the painting which had previously been half-hidden behind a chest of drawers. The place where the drawing of Walter Tappett had hung had been restored to its usual occupant; a florid Curran in a tie-wig accompanied by the insignia of the country gentleman — books, dogs and guns.

John came back. 'That painting's dated 1554 and it was called Holy Name House then, did you know that? I'd always presumed Holly meant the trees, but it must be a corruption.'

'Hello!' Mandy Bolsover appeared through the door from the hall. It was the first time Emily had seen her in anything but red, and black didn't suit her; it made her look as if she was at death's door herself.

'I'm glad you're here,' she said confidentially, 'this is all so high-powered. I should think every local worthy in North Essex must have come, and that's the Lord Lieutenant over there.'

'I was pretty surprised to be asked myself,' said Emily in a low voice. 'Have you met John?'

'Hello, John. Terry's told me all about you. The whole needlework committee has been given what's practically a royal command. Poor Miss Barton is sitting petrified in the corner of the hall, looking as if she's in the house of the Antichrist. Funny to have everyone gathering here first, though. I suppose they're having a good, old-fashioned, feudal procession across to the church on foot through the snow. I hope they've got a policeman on hand to hold up the traffic, or they might need a few more hearses.'

There was a feeling of something about to happen out in the hall. Jeremy appeared in the doorway again, looking solemn and preoccupied, this time with things his clever hands and brain couldn't possibly put right.

'Ladies and gentlemen, the hearse has just arrived. May I ask you to assemble in the hall?'

The talk was immediately hushed, and historic glasses were set down on historic furniture. A tide of black and grey quickly washed up against the walls of the stone hall, and left room for black-overcoated men to walk in the front door and set up polished wooden trestles on the flags. Puzzled, Emily looked over at the family group waiting with expressionless faces by the fireplace. Simon and Jeremy stood either side of Lady Curran. Simon's hand was cupped gently under one of her elbows, though she gave no impression of needing any support. Her sharp chin was raised and her bright eyes were undimmed by tears.

253

Through the carved door which led to the dining room and stairs, Deirdre and Isabel quietly came to join the party, another woman between them. She was tall, thin and middle-aged, with thick, greying fair hair and a lined, anxious face. Her mourning garments seemed acquired and worn with little thought and her stringy silk neck-scarf was held by a brooch so lacking in design that she might as well have used a safety pin. Her face seemed on the point of distress, and her escort aware of it and ready to minister or even subdue.

All heads were now turned towards the door, as the shuffling of feet approached Holly House.

Through the carved stone doorcase and past the oaken inner door fastened back against the wall, the polished coffin bore George Curran into his ancestral home for the very last time.

Chapter Twenty-One

Simon stepped foward and took up his position at the foot of the coffin.

'My lords, ladies and gentlemen, relatives, friends. On behalf of my mother and the rest of my family, may I thank you for coming here today to give us your support in our loss, and to say goodbye to my father, our very dear George Simon Hayton Curran. You will all know how much he suffered and how valiantly he endured his suffering. You will have observed with admiration, as we did, the tireless loving care expended on him over the years by his wife, Abigail, and been moved by the great strength of the bond between them. It would be impertinent and insulting to thank her for all that she did for him, as it would never have occurred to her to do anything else, but I hope she will not be offended that I remark upon it.'

There was a low murmur of discreet assent around the hall. Lady Curran's face remained blank.

'Those of you who knew George before his illness will remember him as an active, lively, likeable man with an immense appetite for life and enthusiasm for a hundred different interests. My grandfather, as you know, followed the tradition of his ancestors and took up no particular profession, although his time was spent on countless enterprises and organisations for the benefit of the village and the county during the whole of his life. But George went to Oxford, to the college to which I was privileged to follow him, and obtained a degree in law. He was on the point of entering chambers when the outbreak of the Second World

War caused him to volunteer for the army. He fought in France, North Africa, Italy and finally Germany, always with distinction and courage, and always earning the admiration and affection of the men who served under him. But the suffering he witnessed during those years affected him deeply, and I feel caused him mental pain to the end of his life. It was during the North African campaign that he met Viscount Seagry, and had the melancholy duty of writing to his father, Lord Firegrave, concerning his death in action. After the war he visited Firegrave House to tell the family more about Jeremy's death, and it was there that he met Abigail. They were married in 1946 at St. George's, Hanover Square and their devotion never faltered from that day to their parting.

'George had now received his discharge from the army and started his career as a barrister. He and Abigail moved into a small house in Kensington, and it was there that my sister, my brother and I were born. We all have dim but happy memories of those days, the vitality of George and the immense strength and determination of Abigail.'

He cleared his throat, took a sip from the glass handed him by his brother and folded his hands together again.

'George's father died much too young in 1955, and he brought his family here, to Holly House. I can remember to this day the wonder with which we explored it, though I must say that my parents' feelings on seeing it must have included a certain amount of dismay. It had been requisitioned soon after the beginning of the war and was only handed back shortly before my grandfather's death. It needed repair and decoration from top to bottom, and although much of the furnishings had been put in store, what remained was in poor condition. The vigour with which George and Abigail set about that task was an example to us all, and even we joined in as best we could, under the guidance and discipline of our admirable Nanny, Evadne Morris. George used to say that if ever a woman was ill-named, it was Nanny, and it is true that "well-tamed" was a completely inappropriate description for her. Nobody ever tamed Nanny, not even Abigail.'

There was a ripple of amusement, seized upon with

256

gratitude by those feeling oppressed by the heavy atmosphere. Emily looked at the shiny coffin before her and thought of Mr. Curran rushing around Holly House and making jokes. I hope he's like that again now. I'd really like to believe that, but I've no intellectual right to do so. From my own experience I've no right to believe anything except that the dead, or at least one of the dead, still suffer.

'I will never forget the passion with which Father set about transforming his family home. Our school holidays were much looked forward to so that we could return to that greatest game of all, Holly House. We children explored it from top to bottom and found places that no one had seen for centuries. Some of them disappeared again under Father's repairs and alterations, but I am certain that when my children take up residence here they will rediscover them. We Currans are a curious, inquisitive race, and nothing remains hidden from us for long.'

Another gentle titter. Emily's eyes moved over the massed group of Currans, trying to read their faces. Lady Curran had no expression to read. Jeremy was thoughtful, the older children stood at near-attention, the younger fidgeted and looked around nervously. Vicky was biting her lip and holding Deirdre's hand. Isabel was staring at the scene before her with appalled depression and the tall thin woman now became the first, and in fact only, one of them to exhibit tears. Her eyes were fixed on the coffin, and Emily had the impression that she might at any moment do a Laertes and throw herself at it. Her escort seemed aware of that from the instant she produced her handkerchief and moved in closer.

'I hope I thanked my father enough for those happy and adventurous days, and for his immense support and encouragement in everything we children wanted to do. We took our happiness for granted then, so it is possible I did not. Be that as it may, it was in the sixties that George's health first started to fail. I will not weary you with the history of his decline into invalidity. This not a time for speaking of the suffering which he so resented, but for remembering him in his full health and to trust in God that he is so again now. Despite all that, the house remained a much-loved home and we have always returned to it with

257

pleasure, first alone, and since then with our own wives and children.'

Isabel's face was a study.

Simon now seemed to relax slightly, as if the formal eulogy were over and his next words could be more personal.

'Now, you will know that George had a remarkable and clear brain, trained to its highest capacity by his career at the bar. He was organised in whatever he did and punctilious in every task he set out to do. You will not be surprised, therefore, to hear that in addition to his Will, he had set down exact instructions as to his funeral and everything to do with it. You will also know, as he never hid them, that his religious beliefs were largely agnostic. He believed that this world was probably not the only one, and that much existed that we could neither see nor understand, but never found himself able to accept any of the explanations put forward, and would not go through the motions of a religion he could not believe. All arrangements for today are therefore exactly as he laid them down. It would not have occurred to any of us to go against his wishes, we respected him too much, and I ask you therefore to accept them for his sake and ours. Those who would have liked to send flowers are asked to give donations to charities which relieve physical and mental suffering. If you please, Mrs. Mumford.'

The family group parted, and Mrs. Mumford, Mrs. Witherley-Bashe and two of the ladies Emily had seen engaged with Lady Curran on the clean-up of Holly House, entered the hall with large silver trays bearing glasses of champagne. Most guests betrayed slight shock in their eyes, but took them. When all were served, Simon raised his glass.

'May I ask you all to join me in saying farewell to George. We rejoice with him that he is at last out of pain, we thank him for the privilege and pleasure of knowing him, and we hope, in whichever way our individual religious beliefs tell us, that we shall meet him again one day, in a better, happier place. To George Curran. Bon Voyage.'

'Bon Voyage.' The words echoed round the hall. Lady Curran's glass was still raised while the rest were drinking and her eyes were fixed on the coffin. 'George,' she said, and drained the glass in one swallow.

258

Simon stood in silence for a moment, then nodded towards the door where the undertaker stood waiting in morning suit, with his top hat in his hands. He opened the door and the bearers emerged from the porch where they had been waiting, a very faint whiff of cigarette smoke coming in with them. The double doors were flung wide and a blast of bitter cold air surged into the hall. Outside, the open iron gates and over-throw made a black lace frame to the snow-covered church and cottages in the hollow beyond, and in the foreground, immediately outside the front door, the hearse was parked with its hatch-back raised.

The silent guests stood watching awkwardly as the coffin was carried out. Glasses of champagne remained undrunk in embarrassed hands, throats were cleared and noses discreetly wiped. Emily watched with a lump in her own throat as the door was lowered and the family walked across the expanse of stone floor to stand in the porch. There was the sound of a quiet, expensive engine purring into life. She wondered when they were going to put on their coats.

After a few minutes' talk and mutual comforting in the near-privacy of the porch, they came back into the room, where the champagne was now being sipped amid slightly scandalised whisperings.

The outer and inner doors were closed.

'Ladies and gentlemen, will you please now enjoy the hospitality of this house as George has requested? A buffet luncheon is served in the dining room and he asks that you should drink as much champagne as you like and leave his house happy. You may leave your coats in the bedroom upstairs.'

Emily, John and Mandy were not the only people to look into each other's eyes with profound shock.

'Aren't they going to the graveside?' whispered Mandy out of the corner of her bright red mouth. 'Not even Abigail?'

'It is at St. Mary's, isn't it?' murmured Emily. 'There's a south transept full of Currans over there, and probably more in the churchyard.'

'No, I don't think it is,' whispered Mandy.

'Goodness, so it's a final snub to poor Mr. Leigh!'

Mrs. Gage, in checked grey suit and black felt hat, wriggled her way through the crowd making for the dining room and drew close enough to speak discreetly.

'Well, you've got to respect a man who keeps his nerve in the face of death, and I bet God does too. I've never been very impressed by death-bed conversions, and it's surely more mature to find your own way rather than take the package tour. Have you heard the latest about the Tappett chapel? Apparently poor Desmond has had an uncomfortable brush with the archdeacon, and now he's decided that that quotation will be too offensive.'

'I think Mr Curran wanted it to be.'

'Yes. So it rather looks as if the money stops from now on; Abigail will never go against his wishes. And the rural dean is insisting that he starts turning up at the Deanery Chapter. What with one thing and another, Margaret's smiling so hard in an attempt to look as if she doesn't mind, it's practically meeting round the back of her head. Oh, dearie, dearie me!'

She and Mandy moved away to rescue Miss Barton who really did look quite panic-stricken.

Emily and John drained their glasses and moved in the direction of the dining room, which proved to be already well-packed, so they stood just outside its door by the staircase. There was no descending cold today. The heating was on throughout the entire, spring-cleaned house.

Emily looked up it, unafraid because she was hemmed in on all sides by living human beings, most of whom wouldn't deign to acknowledge a ghost if they saw it. John wandered around and discovered the Queen Anne glass door. 'My goodness, you could get a few K for that!'

'You should see the side door. Here, come and have a look now, I'm sure they won't mind.'

In the lobby they found that the letterbox now fitted snugly, the bolts were shot back and the chain hung straight down the doorframe.

Deirdre came through the kitchen door with more champagne, and met Isabel coming through the Queen Anne one.

'Where is she?'

'In the cloakroom. I think she's all right.'

'Well, keep your eyes skinned.'

Isabel held the door open for her, then came up close to Emily and John.

'Well, I don't know which family Simon was talking about, but it wasn't one that I recognised. My *God*, what a grisly business. I'm surprised they didn't have the lid open so everyone could give him a farewell kiss. No, I suppose it's not the Currans' style, really, kisses. Not good form, chaps.'

'Isabel,' Emily whispered, trying not to be overheard by the lady helpers continually coming and going, 'where's he being buried? And why didn't the family go? Is it all happening later when the party's over?'

'The wake, dear, he said he wanted a wake.' Isabel's eyes widened and she pulled a face which said, By Golly, have I got a story. 'No burial, no cremation, no service, no nothing. He's being taken straight off to Bart's medical school to be dunked in formalin.'

'What?'

'He's given his body to science. And being George, he's sent a complete medical history of all his illnesses along with it, so they've got a guidebook to the mechanism and can get the best possible value out of slicing him up.'

'What was wrong with him?' John asked, looking fairly gob-smacked and getting out of the way of Jean Lake and another basket of hot rolls.

'Lungs, heart, bowels; liver, kidneys; neck, back, legs; everything in turn. Every time they thought they'd found what it was, he developed more symptoms somewhere else.'

'You mean it was all psychosomatic?'

'Gosh, no, it was real all right. It was as if all that anger and worry and bitterness was wandering around his body and occasionally settling down for a real gnaw. His heart gave out eventually, it was just worn out.'

'How did it start?'

'Well,' confided Isabel, her eyes opening wider, 'according to Jeremy, it was after he had that row with the old vicar. He was so angry that it seemed to burn him up from the inside. He couldn't even work — he'd get emotionally involved with his cases and kept going over the top in court and getting slapped down by cold-blooded old judges.'

261

'What was the row about?'

The Queen Anne door opened and Deirdre escorted the tall woman through, still in tears.

'Come on, Gwendoline, it's nice and cosy in the kitchen. Isabel, would you please get Gwendoline a cup of tea and some aspirins?'

'He's damned,' said Gwendoline, in distress, 'he's utterly lost!'

'Come on, dear,' said Isabel, scooping her up with a thin arm. 'See you later,' she mouthed to Emily and John.

'Who's that?' John asked with awe as the kitchen door closed.

'I'm almost certain that must be the Currans' daughter. Simon told me she'd hardly ever been back here since she was twenty-one. No wonder she's upset.'

'She's not just upset, she's bats,' said John. 'Did you hear what she said?'

'Yes. Looks as if she doesn't share her father's religious opinions, or rather lack of them.'

Another lady came through the Queen Anne door with a tray of empty glasses. She had crisp white hair and a monolithic bosom draped in black and grey pin-striped silk. 'There's more room in the dining room now, if you're waiting to eat. Are you the lady who made the embroidery?' she added, taking in the length of Emily's skirt.

'Yes.'

'I thought so. George was very pleased with it.'

'But you weren't?' Emily murmured as she disappeared into the kitchen. There were going to be a lot more comments like that in the future.

Towards the end of the afternoon, the remaining guests started to leave. The Lord Lieutenant and his lady had gone much earlier, having another function to attend that evening, and those who had come from some distance away had preferred to tackle the snowy roads with the aid of as much daylight as possible. Miss Barton had waited until all family members and Mrs. Witherley-Bashe were safely in the dining room and then scuttled out of the kitchen door and down the road to Miss McCarthy, who was dying to hear

262

what had gone on and who was in no way disappointed. Together they chewed over their shock until the last bit of flavour had been got out of it.

Emily had rather wanted to do the same, but had been encouraged to stay longer by Simon and Jeremy. Once the helpers bowed out and only relatives were left she retrieved their coats from the Georgian lobby (she had drawn the line at taking them up to the bedrooms) and insisted that they must go. They shook hands all round, looking briefly at grey-blonde Curran hair and into sharp Firegrave eyes, mostly transmogrified by age into vivid individuality or daunting eccentricity. Lady Curran said goodbye in her usual high, flat tones.

'Mrs. Wakelin, you will come in for coffee again.'

'Yes, Lady Curran, of course.'

Isabel came and whispered to Simon. He made his excuses and handed over the task of showing them out to his sister-in-law, who accompanied them into the empty hall. From the drawing room conversation could be heard taking flight on wings of champagne, and the subject off the ground seemed to be the House of Lords.

'She's off again,' Isabel informed them with gloomy relish. 'Poor old Simon, he'll never persuade her to stay the night, it'll mean driving all the way to Frinton and back.'

'It's his sister, is it?' said Emily, catching on that Gwendoline was throwing another wobbly in the kitchen. 'Is she ill, or just very upset about her father? I couldn't help hearing — she's very religious, is she?'

'Well, if that's being religious you can keep it,' said Isabel with distaste. 'I've only met her a few times, but from what I've heard and seen she's right round the bend and halfway back. Nobody actually says so, of course. Things like that don't happen in happy families like the Currans. She lives with a nurse who keeps her eye on her, and if things get too bad she sometimes goes inside for treatment.'

'Poor thing,' said Emily, remembering the panic on Gwendoline's face, and the hint of terror ready to burst out of her tormented mind. 'How long's she been like that?'

'My dear,' exclaimed Isabel, 'haven't you heard the

story? The Big Row? The local schism between Church and State?'

'You mean the disagreement between Mr. Curran and the old vicar?'

'Yes. *Well*,' she said with glee, steering them farther away from the drawing room door into the corner by the hall fireplace, 'it seems that she was always quiet and a bit nervous, but no one took a lot of notice of it, they were all too busy getting on with being jolly good chaps with their feet firmly on the ground. Then one day when she's about twelve or thirteen her father finds her in her room beating herself with a belt. She bursts into tears and says she knows she's damned and she's got to try and get God to forgive her her sins and save her from hell.'

'Whatever did she think she'd done?'

'You may well ask. "My dear girl",' her parents tell her, "you are a Curran, a nice, decent girl of good family and you go to church and Sunday school. God would never *dare* to send you to hell".'

'It was the Vicar's sermons?' asked Emily, remembering Mrs. Hubbard's account of the Vicar's highly anti-social zeal for denouncing sin.

'Right,' said Isabel. 'One of his favourite subjects was that stuff about the Elect; you know, some people are born to be saved, others to be damned, and there's nothing you can do about it because it's God's arrangement. She'd decided that she'd drawn one of the short straws in the holy lottery, and nothing could make her change her mind. I don't think she ever has. In a way, she's spending her whole life waiting for hell. No wonder she can't enjoy it.'

'As a stick to beat sinners with, that seems to me about the stupidist ever thought up,' said John with some heat. 'The only sensible way to respond to it is to sin as much as you like for as long as you like, because you've got nothing to lose. I sometimes think people should have their brains tested before they're allowed to preach, it's like a licence to kill.'

I am damned. I am abandoned by God and Man. I am in torment. Oh poor, poor Gwendoline, you as well.

'So the three of them were whipped out of church and never allowed back again. Jeremy said he and Simon couldn't see

what all the fuss was about – they'd never taken it seriously anyway. The idea that any of it was true had never
even occurred to them. I really think some parsons are like
that, you know. If you pin them down they'll often admit
they don't literally believe the things they spout at the congregation every week. Look at Adam and Eve, there can't
be many left who can still swallow that. "It's allegory", they
say, "and in that sense absolutely true". Wriggle, wriggle,
wriggle. Still you've got to have them.'

'Have you?' said John.

'Yes. Well, it holds the country together, doesn't it? That's
what it's for, really. Westminster Abbey and St Paul's and
all that – hello, Simon, how is she now?'

'Oh, I expect she'll be all right,' he said, with normal
Curran sanguineness. 'But we can't get her to come out of
the kitchen again, so someone will have to drive her home.
I don't suppose you or Jeremy –'

'Well, not me, I've got to pick up Hugh by eight o'clock.
My mother said she didn't think she could cope for any longer
than that. Last time he broke the television. Anyway, didn't
Uncle Robert bring her? Why can't he drive her back?'

'He was expecting to stay the night and he's gone rather
heavy on the champagne,' said Simon, grimacing towards
the drawing room.

Emily suddenly felt John's hand squeeze her arm with an
intensity which said: 'Don't!' The thought had only drifted
across her mind, and she was surprised and then pleased that
he had sensed it. Perhaps they were growing closer, as she had
hoped, and he was quite right: Gwendoline Curran sleeping in
the cottage would not be good news, for her or for them.

'Well, goodbye,' said John firmly, making quite sure. 'It's
been very nice meeting you, Simon, and we look forward
to being your neighbours. Will your mother be moving
out soon?'

'No, not for some time. Father left the house to her, to
avoid death duties, and she'll move into rooms upstairs until
she can start transferring ownership to me. He had it all
worked out, as you might expect.'

Simon and Isabel departed for the kitchen and Emily and
John walked across the stone hall towards the porch. She

wasn't feeling all that well. She'd spent most of the last few hours on her feet, she'd had rather more champagne pressed on her than she was used to, and there was no denying that Holly House, even when showing its most welcoming face to the world as today, had never entirely lost the oppressive atmosphere which disturbed her so much. Even now, in the firelit hall with the chandelier blazing above their heads and the sound of conviviality coming from the drawing room, the approaching dusk outside the mullioned window seemed to squeeze the house in on itself, to intensify its essence and press it down upon her head.

John put out his hand and opened the inner door. It was a lot heavier than he'd expected and he staggered slightly as it swung against him. 'Drunk again,' he said, grinning. He waved her before him into the porch.

She moved forward with sudden reluctance which quickly became a feeling of inevitability. She felt the vibration around her and put out her hands to protect herself even before the iron latch on the double doors clicked up before her eyes and allowed them to fly open. The cold blast knocked her back into John's arms and fled past her into the house, searing its warning message into her brain.

They come, they come, fly for your lives! Dear Jesu, we are utterly lost!

Chapter Twenty-Two

Emily turned and marched across the hall, past the foot of the stairs and through the glass door into the lobby. She hurried into the kitchen, with John asking, 'What's the matter, Em, it was only the wind?'

Gwendoline Curran was on her knees by the table in floods of tears, her hands pressed tightly together in prayer.

'Oh dear God,' she was sobbing, 'dear God, forgive me. Deliver me not into the bitter pangs of eternal death.'

'I suppose dear old Mr. Leigh would have said, "bad luck, my dear, he's already made the booking",' said John with barely repressed rage.

'All right, Gwenny,' said Simon, patting her on the shoulder. 'Hello, Emily, did you forget something? Sorry about this, she'll be all right in a minute.'

'She will not,' said Isabel scathingly, pouring tea. 'She hasn't been all right for forty years. Why pretend otherwise?'

'Your front doors,' said Emily, white-faced but determined not to back off, 'they just opened all on their own. Is that why Lady Curran had them boarded up?'

'Oh,' said Simon, trying to get Gwendoline into a position in which he could ply her with tea. 'Come on, old girl, upsadaisy. It didn't hurt you, did it, Emily?'

'It didn't leave any marks, no. What's it all about?'

'Well,' said Simon, giving up and handing the tea back to Isabel, who sighed and drank it herself, 'we don't really know. Look, go out the back door if you prefer, you can get through the gap in the wall.'

Gwendoline pulled herself out of his hands and fell face-downwards, howling with despair.

'Have you filled in the hole?'

'Er, not sure, actually. Isabel, could you go and ask Jeremy? I think he said he was going to have another look down there first.'

'My sins cry out,' Gwendoline cried, hitting her head on the floor, 'the secrets of all hearts shall be known, and the Lord shall say, "depart from me, ye accursed, into ever-lasting darkness!"'

'Oh God, the poor woman,' muttered John. 'Come on, Em, they don't want us here, this is private.'

'She's not always like this,' Simon explained, 'it's just the funeral upsetting her.'

'The voice cries out, "Dear Jesu, they are come, they are come, we are utterly lost!"'

Emily fell to her knees beside Gwendoline and flung her arms about her. 'Did you feel that as well? Does he speak to you? Who is he?'

'He is lost,' groaned Gwendoline, 'he is abandoned of God and Man. He wouldn't let me go. He must suffer forever. The Unchosen cannot be forgiven of God.'

Emily drew Gwendoline's shaggy, greying head on to her shoulder with a rush of pity, though reflecting that an inter-esting psychological study might be made of the influence of fervent belief upon syntax.

Simon bent over her apologetically. 'Look, Emily, there's no need, really. She'll be all right in a minute. She's just talking nonsense.'

'She's not,' Emily contradicted earnestly, 'I recognise what she's saying. I don't think there's any doubt that when she was a child she experienced what I've done the last few weeks, and it must have been absolutely terrifying for her. It's just possible she got the impression, as children often do, that she'd done something terrible and was being punished for it. Then she was regularly exposed to that self-righteous, uncharitable old windbag over at the church and started thinking that her punishment was going to be

268

eternal. If there's anything in this reincarnation business, I hope he comes back next time as a nervous, over-sensitive little girl!'

'God was against them, you see,' said Gwendoline, turning and looking into Emily's face. She was a tear-stained cross between George and Simon Curran with Abigail's wrinkles. 'They were in error to start with, but once they did that there was no hope for them at all. They weren't Chosen, and they tried to kill those who were.'

Simon gave up and turned away. He looked at John with an apologetic shrug. 'Would you like another drink?'

'Not now, thanks,' he said, looking utterly wretched.

'So who is he, Gwendoline?' Emily prompted gently, stroking her hair.

'They left him there. They ran away and left him.'

'Did he tell you that?'

She cried harder.

'He couldn't move, he was ill. They'd cut off his hand. I could see – they'd cut his hand right off.'

'Oh Gwendoline, how awful! You must have been so frightened. Where did he appear to you?'

She sobbed louder, putting her head in her hands.

'Was it through the door on the landing? Or in the bedroom? Or the corridor? Did he speak to you near the fireplace in the drawing room? You see, it's happened to me, too. Where did you see this poor ghost with one hand?'

'I was so afraid he'd come and get me,' whispered Gwendoline, 'so I covered him up again.'

There was an intake of breath from everyone in the kitchen, even Simon.

'Where?' asked Emily, hardly believing what she'd heard. 'In the secret passage or one of the priest's holes?'

'Come on, old girl,' said Simon, getting down on his haunches and taking Gwendoline's hand. 'Tell us. We'll take him away, then he won't bother you any more. I know it's not the hole under the clock room, because I got into that, and we found the one in the cellar only the other day. Nothing in it. Is there another we don't know about?'

Gwendoline closed her eyes and put her hands over her

ears. 'One shall say "it is here", and another "it is there"', she cried.

'She's not going to tell you,' said John, wincing. 'Please leave her alone. And anyway, if she did, are you going looking for it now?'

'Lord, no,' said Simon hastily. 'We'll have to wait until all the guests and the children have gone. Now find Gwendoline a hanky, Isabel, and I'll go and tell Jeremy he's got a return trip to Frinton.'

By the next day the powers confronting each other in the Middle East had paced a ritual dance around the conditions of withdrawal and returned to their original positions. The land war moved a step nearer.

In Britain, the temperature rose a little and started to soften the snow.

At Holly House, more relatives and all children departed, and about mid-morning the Curran brothers came through the broken wall and knocked at the side door.

The fire crackled and lapped at the logs, the lilies dropped more petals and the already full-blown roses exposed their orange stamens like staring eyes.

Jeremy looked at his notes.

'Let's take it in what seems to be the right order. Someone rushes in the front door and says all's lost so get the hell out of it. Right, Emily?'

'Yes.'

'In the drawing room, something in the corner by the fire-place sighs and gives an impression of misery and longing.'

'Yes.'

'In the guest bedroom above, something takes hold of women's hands and tries to stop them leaving the sixteenth-century block. Also, a figure that can actually be seen leaves the room through the cupboard at a hell of a lick and very possibly goes down the staircase which isn't there any more. He could be obeying the warning to leave the house.'

'Seems logical,' Simon agreed. They were enjoying this, these two; the Curran bent towards adventure was alive and well.

270

'Did anyone sleep in that room after the funeral?' asked John with concern.

'Yes, Mama's two older sisters.'

'Two women!'

'Dorothea and Thyrza don't really count as women,' said Jeremy. Simon burst out laughing. 'This end of the secret passage,' Jeremy continued, waving at the fireplace before him, 'Emily senses someone in great distress and terror. He feels he's abandoned and in spiritual danger, and seems to be looking for some kind woman to help him.'

Emily clenched her fists. It all sounded so banal put like this, almost like soap opera or pulp fiction, but it wasn't. No, it wasn't banal at all. Put the strongest, most passionate of feelings into words and they instantly started to shrink.

'Now, poor old Gwenny. She appears to believe that she once found someone with a hand cut off and that she covered him up again because she was afraid he'd come after her. If that were true it could explain practically everything. No, not Old Beaver on the landing. Presumably he got away.'

'Why do you call him Old Beaver?' asked Emily, her hands now held tightly by John's.

'Mother said when she was a girl you always shouted "beaver" after people with beards.'

'Oh,' said Emily, not quite seeing the joke. 'This business of having his hand cut off, could it have been a punishment?'

'You're thinking of Islamic law, for stealing.'

'No, I'm sure there was something like that in the sixteenth century. They loved chopping bits off people then. Simon, what did you children think of that awful execution picture up in the guest bedroom? Didn't it frighten you?'

'Well,' said Simon, stretching out his legs to the blaze, 'I suppose it did give us a bit of a jolt when we first noticed it, but after that it didn't seem anything to do with life as we knew it. Kids build their own worlds, don't they?'

'Gwendoline seems to have built her own private hell,' said John, looking increasingly upset. It took a worrier to understand another obsessive worrier's pain.

'She was too sensitive to shut things out and she was female. Look, the hand.' Emily experienced a slight shudder, despite her calm voice. 'It was definitely pulling

271

me somewhere. Where does the passage come out on your side?'

'We've always assumed it was in the cellar, but the floor's been relaid so many times there's no sign of it.'

'Supposing it's in the chimney stack, like in the cottage? It might go right up beside the flue, through the drawing room, into the guest bedroom, perhaps even right up to the top within easy reach of the clock room hole.'

'I think you've got something there,' said Jeremy, thoughtfully doodling a tight spiral staircase up the side of the paper. 'We'll have to have a tactful word with Mama about investigating. Emily, would you come back with us and help? We'll keep round you like a bodyguard. Please?'

Please, please, please, for the love of God —

They went down into the cellar from outside, as the inside stair had long been removed to make room for the cloakroom. It was dirty, rubbishy, ill-lit, vaulted in red brick and bitterly cold, and it reminded Emily a great deal more than she liked of the charnel house. At the far end a jagged wound in the wall allowed them a peep-hole into the claustrophobic world of the hunted missionary priest — a wooden ledge to sit on, a brick niche to hold food, drink, books and candles, a space under the ledge for a chamber pot. A floor just long enough to sleep on, though not to stretch out.

'How did they get in?' asked Emily, thinking that it was every bit as bad as her imagination had pictured it. The discomfort, the loneliness, the fear, the cold — and eventually the cramp, the airlessness and the stench.

'Probably through the top,' said Jeremy, running his hands over the brickwork. 'Can you see that rough bit up there? We're right under the service lift. Originally there'd have been separate cupboards all the way up, and a loose flag in the hall, one with a wooden trap underneath.'

'How many of these hell-holes have you got?' asked John, measuring its dimensions against his own with shocked disbelief.

'Well, two we know about, and a few corners which might have been used as hiding places for a very short time, but certainly not specially built. There's a possibility that Nicholas

272

Owen worked here, he was the expert. Now there was a horrible fate, if you like. Makes this existence look like a bijou residence in Purley.'

Throughout the cellar they measured, consulted, knocked and scraped, but the brickwork was so battered and so much altered that anything could have been anywhere.

In the drawing room Jeremy pulled out his steel tape again and Simon poked his head up the chimney above the dead remains of yesterday's fire. On the half landing Jeremy hit the wall with a long stick. On the main landing Emily put both arms around John and closed her eyes as the Curran brothers led the way along the corridor and into the guest bedroom. A bent, white-haired caricature of Lady Curran was strapping up a leather suitcase on the bed.

'Oh, sorry, Thyrza, thought you were finished here.'

'I am,' she declaimed on a high, ringing note, 'the carriage is coming at twelve. Who's that gel? She's only got half a hair-do. I've been ringing and ringing for coffee, but the maids are all deaf.'

'It's down in the dining room, Aunt, that bell doesn't work. Now,' said Simon eagerly as she hobbled off down the corridor, 'here, do you think?'

The chisels went in under the painted panelling and the hammers struck. Wood splintered and was pulled away and discarded. Plaster behind was scraped and hit and broken off in chunks. They were like irresponsible, hooligan teenagers, indulging in the joys of licensed vandalism. John looked as if he'd rather like to join in, but his arms never left Emily.

More and more of the brickwork was uncovered, but there was no sign of a door; the courses ran uninterrupted to where the edge of the old open hearth abutted the eighteenth century's in-fill. They argued about where and why and how and should we anyway? They went up into the nursery above and attacked that. They went down into the cloakroom and laid predatory eyes on the tiled wall.

Lady Curran appeared in the door, back in tweeds and woollens. Emily was painfully aware that this was where she had tended George over the years, and that her sons were probably on the point of tearing down her memories.

273

'George's father told me there was a door behind there,' she said.

The hammers and chisels were laid down.

'Mama,' said Simon gently, 'why didn't you say so before? We haven't done upstairs any good at all.'

'I forgot,' she said. 'Anyway, you can do what you like, it's your house now. Oh, by the way, I'll have that shower up in my bathroom.' She left them to it, all interest lost in surroundings which no longer had George in them.

It was like following a ready laid trail for a treasure hunt – very nearly Enid Blyton stuff. There was varnished floral wallpaper and plaster behind the tiles. The blocked door was behind the plaster. A narrow brick stair was behind that. At its top, somewhere in a mysterious no man's land between the guest bedroom and the staircase, was a tiny, filthy wooden door, clothed with brick-dust, cobwebs and dead spiders, which showed no sign of having been touched for centuries. It was locked.

Simon squeezed down the horrible tube of brickwork and popped out into the cloakroom. As Jeremy took his turn to look, he made his report to Emily and John. 'We'll have to make a hole in it and see what's on the other side. If he's there, I don't see how Gwenny could possibly have seen him, the wall was plastered before we moved in.'

They measured again and discussed and went back to the first floor, then came down and got out the power drill. The weather outside was darkening now, and a cold rain had started to soil the snow and punch little black holes in its perfection. On the stairs, the landing light seemed ready to greet Old Beaver, and Emily only wanted to see it from her own cottage.

'Do you mind if we go now?' she asked.

They went out of the kitchen door and through the broken wall, past the board-covered hole in the ground. Behind the dining-room bay, Lady Curran sat with the last rump of the funeral party, looking much as she had done when Emily first saw her from her studio window. From inside came the scream of the drill.

'They don't muck about, do they?' remarked John.

She sat on the settee in front of the fire.

Fire, candles and flowers. Words. Blessings. Good intentions. Terrible mistakes. Being right. Not knowing you're wrong. Death by fire. Death by hacking apart. Death by suffocation? Abandoned by God and men.

But it was all her own thoughts, there was no intrusion of another's. Her own distress. Her own pity. Even her own love. And yet she was not alone. Something was waiting. She had only to rise and step forward –

'You don't mind if I do some work now, do you?' asked John apologetically.

'Of course not. Would you like something to eat as we missed lunch?'

'You're a star, Em.'

She made sandwiches and stood at the sink waiting for the coffee to percolate. The landing light shone through the bedroom window like a very small good deed in a positively dreadful world. The rain drizzled on and the bare paving swam in melt water running to hide itself under the boards covering the hole. He must have fled along there, but not in this direction. Whatever he was running from, he would have come to the cottage first so that no suspicion would fall on the house, then gone through the passage. He still does. It's not really there now, but he's living in then.

She poured a cup of coffee and set it ready for when John took his eyes off the computer. She didn't want anything herself – who could eat during an exhumation? Well, no doubt the Currans could.

At the hearthrug she held out both hands. 'Not long now,' she said very quietly. The candle flames waved and the logs hissed under the attack of rain coming down the chimney. Another lily petal fell. She reached forward and found him. Just his hand. Only one hand. She felt the sweat break out on her face but didn't pull back.

Lady, sweet lady, they come for me, sweet lady –

'They won't hurt you,' she whispered, so John wouldn't hear her. 'It'll soon be over, then you'll be at peace.'

I'm lying to him. I have no idea at all whether this is going to help, or whether his impression on the fabric of these two old houses can ever be removed.

But she no longer reacted to him with horror; perhaps that was why he allowed her hand to slip so easily out of his.

By the time the phone rang it had been dark for an hour.

'Emily?' Simon's voice was serious, with no boyish excitement in it. 'We've found him. Are you coming back?'

'Tomorrow,' she said. 'I'll come and see him tomorrow.' She started to cry.

Once or twice during the night she sensed him over by the chimney stack wall. She tried to send comfort across the dark feet of separation, but didn't let go of John. In the morning she could no longer feel him, and they left the cottage hand in hand to spend the strangest Saturday morning of their lives.

He wasn't where she'd expected. The Currans passed the cloakroom and led them up the broad stairs to the landing.

'Did you open the door?' asked Emily, who had been deeply dreading the torch-lit, confined climb and the close confrontation at its end.

'No. We drilled a hole and shone a light in, but there was just brick behind. It was probably just a service stair no longer needed once the new stairs were built, though that doesn't mean he didn't use it to get up here; it was probably discreet enough.'

Through the door on the landing and up the present servants' stair. They threaded through the maze of passages and rooms and entered the nursery.

'Not here,' she almost pleaded, thinking of all those generations of children only feet away from such horror.

'Not quite,' said Simon. His face was very straight and even Jeremy's thoughts were on nothing but the matter in hand. They walked up a step and through a door beside the fireplace, out of the sixteenth century and into the seventeenth. The upper part of the room was in the roof, and the ceiling sloped in.

'This was Nanny's room,' said Jeremy.

The flooring had been pulled up along the fireplace wall, and below the joists lay a deep shelf of old brick and stone.

276

'It's the wall up to the top of the guest bedroom. This one's thinner, and belongs to the rebuilding,' explained Jeremy.

She didn't grasp his explanation, and was in no condition to try. There were a lot of removed bricks and rubble on the unlifted boards, and towards the corner, a long piece of plywood from an old tea-chest lay across two bare joists. Jeremy picked up a very large torch. 'Ready?' he said. She nodded.

She didn't stand close while they removed the wood and shone in the beam, and she approached very slowly, to try and reduce the shock. The skull was about four feet down, and the face was looking upwards. There was long hair clinging to its scalp and a dry nest of beard falling away from its bare teeth. The body was covered by the unmistakeable shape of a doublet with a crumbling collar and the sleeves stretched out before it, resting on what appeared to be a small table. The bones of the left hand seemed to be scrabbling in a pewter dish. The right sleeve was terminated by a large black blob. The upper part of the body had slewed over, revealing a stool beneath, and down beside the full breeches and stick legs a tall-crowned hat leaned against the wall.

Quite apart from the scattered mortar, there was an enormous amount of dust in there; it was on the table, on the clothes, on the floor, and it was almost certainly the remains of his flesh. It was the charnel house all over again – humanity reduced and derided and turned into a hideous travesty like a guy. It shocked, it horrified, it outraged the sensibilities and lacerated the emotions.

Oh sweet, sweet lady, have pity on me in my extremity.

I have, I pity you with all my heart. She turned away, her face screwing up. Simon put his arm about her as John took his turn to stare down into the hollow.

'It's in the wall above the cupboard,' said Jeremy, the mechanics of building engaging him even now, 'just above where people walked in and out of the first floor great chamber. There must be an entrance down there behind the panelling we can get him out from. We were looking the wrong side of the fireplace.'

John turned back pretty quickly, looking pale. 'He's got a sword. I wouldn't have expected a priest to wear a sword. So how come poor Gwendoline stumbled on that?'

'We all had a good poke around when we first came here — you should have seen the mess after the army and the refugees. All kids think that a loose floorboard means hidden treasure and secret papers, and she must have heaved it up and removed the rubble. She'd put it all back on top of this piece of ply. Did you see the label on it?' He picked it up and held it out. Messrs. Pickford. Curran, Holly House, Little Hocking, Essex.

'Do you think your nanny knew?' asked John.

'No! She'd *never* have looked under floorboards, it would've been like reading her employer's letters. Historic houses all have secrets in them somewhere and good servants keep their noses out. It's part of the job.'

There are too many secrets. They corrode the soul. I needed confession.

'Do you know the story of Lord Lovell?' said Emily, tensing as she realised his messages were again nagging into her brain. 'They found him two hundred years after he disappeared, and he still looked alive. Then the air got to him and he fell to dust. If Gwendoline really was the first person to find him, it's just possible that when she looked in she saw for a second or two a real face looking up at her, perhaps even with its eyes open. And if you ask me, that's enough to send you off your trolley for life, even without the help of religious melancholia.'

If she had told, sweet lady, if only she had told.

'Why did no one find him before, 'specially when they rebuilt?' asked John, leaning against the wall with his hands in his pockets, apparently trying the difficult experiment of pretending that It wasn't there.

'It's part of that massive chimney stack, and the builders seem to have scrubbed round that. You have to admit this seventeenth-century block isn't great architecture. If the Withericks had done a thorough job it could've been a different story.'

I tried then, I kept trying. Oh solemn, diligent lady in satin and lace, come and find me, come and release me.

'Goodness knows who he is, though he's obviously Elizabethan,' said Simon, stealing another look.

'More Jacobean,' said Emily, standing very still as she felt him move closer to her, 'those very full breeches are early-seventeenth-century, and so are those high-crowned hats we associate with witches and Welsh ladies and Guy Fawkes. Simon, what were the Lethabys doing around the fifth of November, 1605?'

'Funny you should mention that,' said Simon. 'One of them was rather given to visiting White Webbs at Enfield, and just happened to turn up at that hunting party at Dunwich. As soon as things started to look unhealthy he disappeared.'

'Could it be him?'

'No, he died in Rome some years afterwards, but perhaps he's Old Beaver, being told the bad news and flying for his life. There's actually a portrait of him in the dining room, but done when he was young and beaverless.'

'What was his name?'

His name is Judas. And Cain. Where is thy brother, Cain?

'Henry. Perhaps his sense of guilt brought him back here after he died.'

'So who's that in there?' said John, giving up his vain attempt and strolling around restlessly with hands under armpits.

'A friend, a servant, a fellow hanger-on of the Gunpowder Plot who came here looking for shelter? We're not likely to find out now,' said Jeremy.

'Not a priest?'

'No,' said Emily with sudden certainty, feeling she was speaking for him, 'he was a sinner, not a saint, and he knew it.'

'And what about his hand?'

'He may have been involved in fighting while they were rounding up the conspirators,' suggested Jeremy. 'Perhaps a wound which went gangrenous.'

'So they cut it off and shoved the stump into hot tar,' said Simon. 'He'd have been pretty ill, running a temperature and barely able to walk, and when Lethaby decided to run for it he'd have been a liability.'

I was abandoned by God and Man. Take pity on me, sweet lady, and help me to rest. Give me your prayers. Give me the

279

infinite joy of masses. Give me eternal rest and let light perpetual shine upon me.

His hand touched and enclosed hers. Jeremy, who was near her, shivered and looked accusingly at the blameless window.

How unbelievably strange for him to be here in their company, observing with them the ghastly wreckage of his own body and perhaps now realising that he had clung to that brittle raft for centuries while he had been within reach of dry land. Whatever had it been like? So many questions, so many possibilities; that he hadn't known he was dead, that he had thought he was his body, that he had been imprisoned by rage at betrayal and driven by compulsion to expose near or actual murder, whichever it was.

The hand drew her forward and she obeyed. She couldn't possibly have denied him.

Jeremy handed her the torch as she passed.

It was still terrible. She felt that it was terrible for him, too. Do ghosts weep? Are these my tears or his?

Dear, sweet lady, the blessings of all the saints rain upon thee. The angels of God keep thee from all harm. They come for me and their faces are forgiving. Live well and sin not, sweet lady. *Nunc dimittis, Domine* ...

His hand was drawn out of hers and led away on the journey to freedom.

'You've heard that Mother won't release any more money for the chapel?' Simon said, not looking at her as they walked downstairs. 'The Vicar refuses to go along with Father's wishes about the wording.'

'Yes,' said Emily, wiping her eyes, 'and to be honest, I'm not really surprised. He wouldn't want anything which would cause rows, or should I say more rows? Is there much more to be paid for?'

'Oh, dear me, yes. All that taking down and putting back of monuments doesn't come cheap, you know. However,' he suddenly looked embarrassed, which wasn't the Simon Emily had come to know, and addressed his thumbnail, 'I am prepared to take on that debt myself, and I've come to an arrangement with Desmond Leigh. I hope it'll be agreeable to you.'

'It's hardly my business now.'

'Mm. I think it will be. Oh, I didn't tell you — Mama saw Old Beaver again last night, and he looked positively beside himself, poor old devil. Same routine, though. Through the door, across the landing, and hey presto, gone.'

'So *he* hasn't found peace yet.'

'I wish I could see him,' said Jeremy enthusiastically.

'As a matter of fact, I got a glimpse of him just before your father died and it was pretty upsetting,' said Emily in a subdued voice, reaching the bottom of the stairs and moving quickly away towards the kitchen. John's arm went round her. Oh, how good it was to have John's arm about her.

'Simon,' she said as they passed through the Georgian lobby, 'why didn't your mother use this door?'

'It used to stick,' he said, looking vaguely surprised at the question.

'Oh, of course, why else?' she said, and very nearly laughed.

On the morning of Friday the first of March, Emily drove into Braintree, imagining, despite herself, the commercial activities of the market place being inconvenienced by Walter Tappett and two others — burning alive in the centre of the road.

She sat on the train, staring at the wet, bare fields and working out the figure of Father Francis Lethaby. He, also, would be holding out his hand to the observer. Between the two men, a third hanging of gold, silver and blue lettering would demand: 'He that loveth not his brother whom he hath seen, how can he love God whom he hath not seen?'

It had been the Vicar's decision, and one taken with unexpected determination and conviction. 'I cannot believe,' he had told Emily, 'in a God Who loves the whole human race but gives exclusive contracts.'

Between one and two o'clock, Emily sat in St. Cyneburga's, Nunnery Court, EC4, seeing her handiwork bathed in light among carved pearwood and panelled mahogany, and listening to song and prayers in praise of God and the noble army of martyrs. Afterwards she was favoured by congratulations from the rows and rows of suits, and honoured by the courteous praise of the Lord Mayor.

She went out into the muggy, noisy City and walked past the rabid triumph of the newspaper posters. Thousands of young martyrs lay incinerated in vehicles on the road out of Kuwait. Baghdad was wrecked. The oil wells were on fire and a poisonous black blanket was choking the Gulf to death. The Allied casualties were so few that they might have included Davy Gam, Esquire, yet one would have been too many. But Israel had held back and the fight had not surged forward to Megiddo. Armageddon had not come yet.

She walked to Smithfield and stood looking at the road opposite the gate of the Priory, while vehicles passed continually over the ash-stained earth beneath.

She went on to St. Etheldreda's, Ely Place, and stared with respect at the eight Catholic martyrs in their everyday Elizabethan dress.

She went back across the square mile of the City to sit among tourists on Tower Hill and try to think herself through those stone walls, bland with their self-assurance of duty done. That was the most terrible thing about it all – that it had seemed the right thing to do at the time. Catholics, Protestants, priests, laymen; sovereign, church, state and gunpowder plotters – every one of them believed they were in the right, and did what they did with a clear conscience. Even the torturers and executioners.

She tried to imagine herself into the mind of a terrorist, prepared to blow up all the estates of the realm in one 'terrible blowe' for the sake of his cause, for the benefit of his religion and even for the health of his soul. She nearly managed it. The fifty years of persecution, the denial of personal religious conscience, the crippling fines, the refusal to believe in the loyalty of people who regarded Elizabeth and then James as their lawful sovereigns, must have worn down patience and sharpened despair until violence seemed the only remedy.

It was probably only when he had time to think about what he had so nearly done that remorse hit him. Shut away in that dreadful little room, with pain, sickness and fear for companions, he must at last have said to himself, 'I have sinned.'

282

And before the end came, whether by nature or by murder, he had decided he was abandoned by God and man.

A conscience trained to seek out sin could be a cruel, unforgiving thing.

The candle in his pewter candlestick had burnt right to the bottom; death had probably come in the darkness. His pockets had held a tinder-box, a few coins and a missal with no name written in it to betray him. He remained anonymous; they would never know his story.

His sword hung on the stairs at Holly House for a short while (God, *what* an iron-nerved lot the Currans were!) then it was put on the coffin at his funeral. She wondered if he had watched himself being buried in that big, modern Catholic cemetery among the well-scrubbed madonnas and angels. If he did, he didn't make himself known.

Now the sword had gone to join his clothes on permanent loan to a museum, and the exhibit promised to be a crowd-puller. What on *earth* would the poor man have made of that? Emily hoped he was far, far away from bothering about it, or anything earthly, and that he would never need to look back to this world again.

At sunset she rose from her vigil and went to meet John. They sat hand-in-hand on the five twenty-two out of Liverpool Street together, going home, watching the lighted City merging into the beginnings of Essex and the tower of Canary Wharf twinkling like a Christmas tree.

Soon after Stratford, John turned to her with a worried frown and broke his silence.

'Supposing Old Beaver comes in?' he said.

You have been reading a novel published by Piatkus Books. We hope you have enjoyed it and that you would like to read more of our titles. Please ask for them in your local library or bookshop.

If you would like to be put on our mailing list to receive details of new publications, please send a large stamped addressed envelope (UK only) to:

Piatkus Books: 5 Windmill Street
London W1P 1HF

PIATKUS

The sign of a good book